FREE FORM
JAZZ

FREE FORM JAZZ

A Ray Tate and
Djuna Brown Mystery

Lee Lamothe

A Castle Street Mystery

DUNDURN PRESS
TORONTO

Copy Editor: Cheryl Hawley
Design: Jennifer Scott
Printer: Webcom

Library and Archives Canada Cataloguing in Publication

Lamothe, Lee, 1948-
    Free form jazz : a Ray Tate and Djuna Brown mystery / by Lee Lamothe.

(A Castle Street mystery)
ISBN 978-1-55488-696-8

    I. Title. II. Series: Castle Street mystery

PS8573.A42478F74 2010   C813'.6   C2009-907484-2

1   2   3   4   5   14   13   12   11   10

Conseil des Arts du Canada   Canada Council for the Arts   Canada   ONTARIO ARTS COUNCIL CONSEIL DES ARTS DE L'ONTARIO

We acknowledge the support of the **Canada Council for the Arts** and the **Ontario Arts Council** for our publishing program. We also acknowledge the financial support of the **Government of Canada** through the **Canada Book Fund** and **The Association for the Export of Canadian Books**, and the Government of Ontario through the **Ontario Book Publishers Tax Credit** program, and the **Ontario Media Development Corporation**.

Care has been taken to trace the ownership of copyright material used in this book. The author and the publisher welcome any information enabling them to rectify any references or credits in subsequent editions.

J. Kirk Howard, President

Printed and bound in Canada.
www.dundurn.com

Dundurn Press
3 Church Street, Suite 500
Toronto, Ontario, Canada
M5E 1M2

Gazelle Book Services Limited
White Cross Mills
High Town, Lancaster, England
LA1 4XS

Dundurn Press
2250 Military Road
Tonawanda, NY
U.S.A. 14150

For Lucy White, Katy, and Michelle Lamothe.

What kind of times are they
When a talk about trees is almost a crime
Because it implies silence about so many
horrors?

— Bertolt Brecht

Prelude

The day Pious Man Chan was anointed police chief he looked for a grave for Ray Tate.

Pious Chan's head was lumpy and pure bald and he had an angry mole under his right eye. A long, straight, black hair poked from the red mole. Chan thought of himself as a godfather Buddha who blended wisdom with ruthlessness in his dealings with his *capos* and *consiglieres*. As a young Chinese copper, Pious Chan had tried to assimilate, slowly working his way invisibly up the ranks, speaking softly and forgetting no slight or dig. He knew the name and rank of every Anglo fucker who'd ever called him a chink and sent him out for laundry and egg rolls.

When the fat doughboy mayor was elected for a second term, the powerful Chinese Menu, who delivered up Chinatown votes like dim sum specials, urged him to look around for one of their puppets to shove his hand up into. He found Pious Chan toiling in obscurity far down in the ranks. Chan was the kind of cop the mayor liked: he carried his gun locked in his briefcase and left the briefcase locked in the trunk of his car. His bullets were rusted but his pencil was sharp. The doughboy pulled Chan up by his figurative pigtail, skipping several ranks, slapped a handful of fruit salad onto his shoulders, and arranged him behind the burled walnut desk.

To the smiling nods of the benevolent Menu the doughboy began affixing strings to his dancing puppet right away. Pious Man Chan was prohibited from raiding anything in east Chinatown: no gambling clubs, no whorehouses, no boiler rooms, no sweatshops. Chinatown was packed with three things: cheap vice, cheap labour, and cheap votes. The doughboy also forbade arrests at left-wing demonstrations, wiretaps on city politicians, and investigations into unionized companies doing business with the city.

With an eager grin that hid what Pi Chan thought was oriental deviousness, he let the mayor jerk him around like a spastic little Pinocchio. "That's all, sir?"

"Other than that, Pi," the mayor told Chan in an anteroom after the police commission blessed him, "knock yourself out."

"What about the ... ah ... blacks?" Chan said timidly, navigating his way through the mayor's funny tastes. "The box is up for refunding."

"The box? Box of what? The fuck?"

"Black Organized Crime Squad. BOCS. They're getting swamped by the Bik-Big shootings up in the projects."

"Fuck sakes, Pi. Give them some money but change the fucking name." He frowned down on the chief. "Did I make a mistake, here? I could've got a broad or a Paki. Should I've 'a got a Paki broad in a sari up there, behind the desk, that understands how democracy works? I thought you Chinamen invented democracy."

"We invented gunpowder," Pious Man Chan said softly, mentally chalking one up against the mayor.

"Same thing."

"Umm." Chan stared off for a moment, fingering the fine black strand growing from his mole. "Safe Neighborhoods Initiative Program. SNIP."

The doughboy nodded and flipped at his silver blond locks. "SNIP. Perfect." He took a piece of paper from his inside suit pocket. "Let's go down this, fast." He glanced up. "Hey, Bik-Bigs, you said? Bik-Bigs? What's that? A gang?"

"B-K B-Gs. Black kids. Big guns." Chan shrugged. "Bik-Bigs."

The mayor laughed. "The little cocksuckers. Clean them out, Pi. We don't want another season of gunsmoke. Grab up some white guys too, while you're at it, make it fair. I don't want to see an ethnic chain gang tap dancing across the front page. You got any white guys committing crime?"

"We got a joint task force on the go with the Feds and the Staties. They're after speed cookers, labs. Couple of kids were killed by bad ecstasy so they go after the X-men too. Mostly white biker types, white trash down from the badlands."

"Perfect. Roll 'em all into one." The mayor consulted his list. "You got anything on Dickie Price down at Works? He said he came out the other day and saw a couple of cars around his house, guys in them talking to the sun visors. Recognized one of the drivers from a bodyguard detail when that fucking cowboy president was in town."

Pious Man Chan nodded. "Price was scoped coming out of a mob gambling club over at Stateline two weeks ago, up in Prior. They didn't know he was a ward heeler when they went after him."

The mayor chewed his mean pout. "Okay, I'll choke Dickie off. You taking anyone down? You can drop the wops but you lose Price in all this, Pious. I mean it. Anything written down, unwrite it, but get me a copy, first. The guy who wrote it down, give him a soft landing. Dickie is one of the good guys. He likes unions, bums, and bicycle lanes." He looked at his list. "Rest of this is shit. Except this guy, Tate."

"Ray Tate. The gunner."

"Him. I'm getting static from the black constituents. Lawsuits. Riots, if another black guy gets aced by a white cop."

"Ray Tate's in the weeds. Intelligence. He's buried, looking for the Dog Man on the east side."

"How deep is he buried, though, Pi? Those alleys lead to streets, and people, including black voters, walk those streets. If he digs himself out and walks the earth, we're probably going to hear about it, and it's going to sound an awful lot like rapid-fire and spades hitting the ground."

"He's hanging by his thumbs. No uniform, no company car, no partner. Sits in the trees, growing his hair, scratches himself raw, and watches for the guy feeding rat poison to dogs."

"Not deep enough. He's shot two guys — black guys — dead, for Christ's sakes. I want you to put a stake through his heart."

Pious Chan wagged his head. "Both his shootings were clean. Witnesses are strong. He's a hero, especially after that last one. He went hand-to-hand with the guy. We dump him out and it looks like we're admitting guilt for something. We'll pay. He won't go, anyway, without a fight. If we put him out we're going to have trouble."

Pious Man Chan stepped away when a police commissioner approached the mayor and shook his hand. She held it a long time. The mayor used his other hand to flip his locks. He made his boyish face blush a shy red and smoothed his school tie while sucking in his gut.

"And you, Mr. Chief." She grabbed Pious Chan's hand. "An *ethnic* police chief. We're setting a *new agenda*, an agenda of *inclusiveness*." She gave them both smiles and walked away, calling, "I hope to see some *progressive females* moving up there in the ranks, Pious."

Pious Man Chan waited until she was out of earshot. "The joint chemical task force, sir. The Feds run it. We've dumped some dead meat in there. The Staties put in one of their loose cannons. Dykes, fags, losers. We could jam Ray Tate in there. There's lots of loose cash floating around, lots of temptation, bikers, and white trash. Best case is we catch him taking some dough. Worst case is we get a bunch of white ecstasy cookers in handcuffs, sir, and if Tate shoots someone, hopefully it'll be one of them."

PART ONE

Chapter 1

Just before dawn cracked, a ghost car rounded the block. Then, a few minutes later, rounded again from the other direction, this time with the bright cone of a spotlight running like quicksilver through the margin of the park. The wheelman rolled to a stop, backed up, then ran his front wheels over the sidewalk and nudged the back of a park bench. The rack lights were activated. Two young chargers disembarked the ghoster, leaving the engine running and the doors open. The wheelman muttered to the shotgun and they sparked their flashlights, pushing jerky funnels of light to a man bundled in a smudge of an overcoat, sitting in the overgrown bushes rimming a flower garden.

The shotgun called, "Yo, you, man."

The man recognized the casual authority of the voice and could hear a night-desk dispatcher's honey voice reciting a hotshot: woman with a gun in Stonetown, sergeant on the way, tacticals rolling, duty lieutenant notified. He climbed to his feet painfully, his joints making audible popping sounds. It was soft autumn but cold had revealed itself with a hard vengeance in the night. Lake Michigan was miles away but its cooked scent hung over the city. The hot early afternoon had boiled up some simmering stew. He groaned a painful cloud of breath. He was careful to keep his hands away from his body, to brave the searing light and keep his paws away from his eyes; he kept them out from his torso in crucifixion. An urge came to say the hell with it and scratch ferociously at the tiny bites on his legs and a fresh group on the back of his neck. His left ribs throbbed from a week-old spider bite, the same kind of broad, angry bruise left on the flesh when a bullet was stopped by a Kevlar vest.

He looked at the heavens as he awaited instruction. The sky before him was in a reluctant black of the end of the night. He studied the new purples of pre-dawn as if in delirium. He wondered why art canvases were muslin off-white. He had several tubes of yellow paint but hadn't opened them yet. They were still in the art shop bag in his barren apartment, but he'd gone through an awful lot of black and purple and the thickest blues. There was a faint rim of dawn on the very tips of the trees far to the east. He didn't know what to do with bright colours, where they fit into anything. Silver stars winked and faded, imperceptibly dead. The dying moon was glittering somewhere out of his sight. The Maglites, now separated, gave him two shadows growing apart from each other and he wondered if this might mean something profound. Duality of man, maybe.

"I'm an armed detective, on duty," he said, his voice hoarse. "Ankle holster, right leg. Intelligence. Four-niner-four-sixer. Tate, Ray."

"Right, you're on dog patrol," the shotgun said, "and we've come to get you."

"Sir," the wheelman said, "we've come to get you, sir."

The shotgun said, "No, Brian. You don't sir a sergeant." He called to the man, "Right? Am I right or am I right?"

Ray Tate said, "Yes, sir."

The shotgun laughed easily. "You can pull in your wings. We know you won't fly away from us."

The wheelman said, "If you did, we wanted, we could take you down on the wing anyway."

Ray Tate lowered his arms slowly and turned. They weren't wearing their caps and they held their flashlights away from their torsos. Both had shaven heads in the strobing ghoster lights, an annual police rite to raise money for cancer kids in the state hospital. Ray Tate had been shaven six times in six years, but not lately. His hair hid his ears, curled at the nape of his neck.

The shotgun stepped into the cone of the wheelman's light. "We've come to get you, sarge. Bring you home." He looked around. "You got anything here you want to take?"

Ray Tate looked at his blanket and bindle bundle. He bent and sorted through the rubble and picked up his rover. The battery was long dead. Nobody ever had to reach out for an alley rat. There were two used tubes of After Bite and a small sketchpad he carried for moments of inspiration, of which there'd been none. He hefted the rover in his hand and put it into his billowing, filthy German surplus greatcoat. He kicked the sketchpad, the blanket, and the bindle down the hill into the ravine.

"Nothing, just the radio." He fired mucus from his nose. He was suddenly cold and he wrapped himself deeply in the coat. His guts twisted audibly in hunger. "The rest is shit."

Brian the wheelman took the car to the car wash and the shotgun delivered Ray Tate to the central desk sergeant. There were crossed flags behind the desk sergeant's table and a list of officers' family members who'd died in combat from the Civil War to Iraq. The police force had given a lot of sons and daughters to war and there were signed photographs of a half dozen former presidents. Obama was framed but still on the floor, leaning against the wall.

The desk sergeant welcomed Ray Tate and shook his hand: "You done good, Ray. Fuck what they say." The shotgun went to get fresh coffee. The desk sergeant looked after him as he headed to the day room. "Good guys, those guys. About the only two I got. One gets a toothache and the other has to go to the dentist. Partners."

"What's it about, Bob? That they came out to the wilderness?"

The desk sergeant shrugged. "Fucked if. A beam from Planet Chan. You hear? They crossed the holy water on his forehead the other day. He's blessed." He twisted his mouth. "Cocksucker. Now there's a real plague on the kingdom."

The shotgun brought out coffees and gave one to Tate. He told the sergeant he was going to walk over to the car wash. "Brian fucks it up, sarge. Lets them get inside and they see all the blood on the backseat." He shuffled and turned to Ray Tate. "I just wanna say you something, I'm not outta line." But he didn't say anything.

After a moment the desk sergeant said, "He knows, Larry."

The shotgun shook Ray Tate's hand. "Fuck 'em, right?" He didn't mind the grime and refused to wipe his palm afterwards on his trousers.

"Without doubt."

Larry nodded solemnly. "If it gets real bad for you, remember you always got a home in Central '04. Brian don't drive too good, I can always use a wheelman, even a drooling old fuck that falls asleep a lot."

Ray Tate laughed. The desk sergeant told Larry, "Get back out there, you dumb fuck."

"So, how's things up there, Ray? Intelligence?"

Ray Tate shook his head in wonder and sipped his coffee. "Fucking paradise, Bob. Overtime out the ass, clerks with big tits. Cappuccino machine in the day room."

"Ah, fuck off."

"No shit. Would I stand in front of your table and lie right to your fucking face?"

"Lots of overtime? Like, how much?"

"Well, I got an accountant now, head off any problems later with the IRS."

"Jesus, Ray. If I had your money, I'd burn mine."

Ray Tate was safe at home. Drinking coffee and bullshitting over the table, a stream of uniforms hustling handcuffed prisoners behind him, the rumble of voices. He heard a couple of voices murmur his name and some of the chargers found pretext to cross by the table for a look at the double gunner.

Someone said, "That poor fucker. That's what they do to you, you go the distance for them. You go there twice and then they really fucking hate you."

Someone else said, "Fuckin' bum, looking for the guy poisoning dogs in the ravine, that's all he's good for."

Someone else, a woman, said, "Fuck you, Foley, you dumb dildo."

There was a sudden burst of struggle and Bob the desk sergeant launched himself around the desk. "Shirley. For fuck sakes."

Ray Tate showered in the locker room. He waited in the steam until the day crew finished banging their lockers and bullshitting about Shirley taking out Foley with a hoof to the nuts. He loved the echo of the rooms in the stations, the jocking and jilling of the troops as they prepared for work. The thumping boots and songs and whistles. The camaraderie of the ultimate outsiders: not white or black or yellow or brown. Just blue. Not liberal or conservative or unionist. Just blue. That famous blue fog that was really a world of grey.

When the last charger had slammed out of the room Tate turned off the shower and in the steaming silence worked a towel into his hair and beard. Bob, the desk sergeant, came in with a pile of neatly folded clothes: two thick blue union sweatshirts, a worn khaki windbreaker, baggy grey track pants, and a pair of woollen socks.

"Jesus, Ray." He was looking at the mass of insect bites up and down Tate's legs, crossed with red gouges where his fingernails had involuntarily ripped at the stinging itch. "Ah, man. Fuck. We got some shit in the kit. Stand by."

When he came back he had a handful of tubes and sprays and an Iraq vet's mug with a chipped gold insignia on the side. Tate sipped coffee and worked on his wounds.

"I just got the call. They want you to go to a satellite in midtown, see the skipper over there. I got a car going to take you over. You want to stop first, at home?"

"Naw. What's the satellite?"

"Task force. Us, the Feds, Staties. They're after crank shufflers, X-men." Bob shrugged. "Run by Gordie Weeks. You know Gordie?"

"Nope. Good guy?"

"Well, one time I was shopping down the Tower Mall. Gordie got into the revolving door behind me but he came out ahead of me." Bob laughed. "Gordie's very ... quick. They say he plays table tennis with himself."

"Ah," Ray Tate shook his head. "Ah fuck."

Chapter 2

The skipper loved the early morning hours. They were productive and he prowled the desks and closets of the midtown satellite office. The long, dim drive in from the northern suburbs helped clear his head on the mornings when he battled a hangover and couldn't face the sun. There were plenty of strip plazas with dough-nut joints studded into them and, if he needed to, on really bad days he could find a washroom to puke in.

But it had been a good week. He'd found a match-book from an Indian casino and a tube of bright red lip-stick under the seat of a car signed out to one of the city slobs. The slob had booked off sick the previous week. The skipper had calculated the mileage to the casino, checked it against the slob's daily expense sheets and the odometer, and called the security office down there. Now there was an empty desk in the tactical office.

He'd picked the lock on Djuna Brown the Statie's

desk and found it empty except for a stained tampon and note reading, "Fuck You, You Fat Irish Fuck."

"Nice job, Gordie," the Big Chan's new deputy had told him when the city slob had been written out. "This is what we want to see. We call it personnel disenhancement."

"Yeah, but now I'm short-handed." The skipper was aware that how high he went depended on how many there were stacked below him. "I'm down a guy."

The dep laughed. He sounded like he hadn't laughed in a long time and was out of practice but was getting the hang of it. "Short-handed for what? You guys aren't actually doing anything, right?"

"Well, the bosses want us to take down this mutt, Captain Cook."

"Just kidding, Gordo," the newly minted dep said. Then he called back: "We got a guy we're sending you tomorrow, beef up the roster." He paused. "The guy we're sending you, he's your top target. Orders from Beijing."

The skipper felt a sinking feeling but he kept his voice casual. "What is he? What's his degeneracy? Booze? Little chickies? Goats?"

"Don't knock goats, Gordo. Goats is ... If you haven't tried it, don't knock it, right?"

"What is he, then?"

"Well, he's a gunner." The dep hung up quickly and the skipper could tell he was smiling.

The next morning the interoffice line buzzed. "Skip? There's ... ah ..." the receptionist faltered. "Ah, a party here? To see you?"

"Buzz him through."

"If you say so."

Through the glass window of his office the skipper recognized Ray Tate behind the straggly, grey-shot hair and the beard dripping down his face. Even in the lumpy sweatshirts and the windbreaker the skipper could see where stress had burrowed into Tate's body and chewed its way out. In the media photos he'd looked buff and robust, a perfect poster cop. Now he looked like a fucked-out degenerate in sweatpants and a ratty sweatshirt hanging down under his windbreaker.

Tate stood in the doorway of the satellite office and looked around at the half dozen vacant desks, at the criminal organization charts tacked to the wall, at piles of mug shots and fuzzy surveillance photos of mutts. There were posters of various pills, warning that "Speed Kills," and observing that "Ecstasy. Isn't." A close-up of a woman's ravaged face was blown up and framed above the base radio: she had no teeth, corroded pits in her face, and straggling hair balding from the front. Block handwriting read: "Don't Forget Your Mom on Mother's Day." There was a blown up photograph of a pile of pink pills with interlocking Cs stamped into them and under the pills a question mark.

Off to the side were photographs with "Captain Cook Crew" printed above them. The top box showed a question mark over a happy face. Beneath it was a surveillance photograph of a long-haired, middle-aged man with a badly burned face. The man, identified as Philip Harvey, wore a long, black leather trench coat and sunglasses hooked into his sweater neck. He glared directly into the camera as he walked out of a strip club. A handwritten note read M/I/XV followed by a series of exclamation marks and the 24/7 phone number for the SWAT teams. The M/I stood for Mentally Incompetent, the XV stood for Extreme Violence. Branched off from the burned man were assorted men and women, most of them young, all of them in groups with their faces circled in black ink and numbered.

With a rat's toothy *bon homie* the skipper bounded out of his office and across the room, his hand out. "Fuck me. Ray Tate. They told me I was getting a first-rate guy, but ... well, holy fuck. A real cop, for a change." He shook his head as he pumped Ray Tate's hand with one hand and hustled his holstered sidearm with the other. "Gordie Weeks. Welcome to the Crank Squad. Let's get coffee."

The Chemical Squad was housed on the ninth floor in a commercial building. The upper floors had a long, clear view to Lake Michigan. Visitors who stumbled onto the ninth floor were greeted with a bland, long corridor with light green doors down either side. Each door had a number pad. Each door, if someone knocked on it, was found to be steel instead of the flimsy hollow cores of the other doors in the building. Video surveillance cameras peeked out of the ceiling tiles. When someone stepped off the elevator a red-headed receptionist instantly appeared, as though coincidentally, from the first door on the right-hand side. She wore a small automatic pistol under her secretarial garb and a panic button disguised as a funky bracelet on her left wrist.

When the skipper and Ray Tate came out of the tactical room the redhead was whispering into a headset and keeping an eye on the hall monitors.

"Gloria, we're going for some caffeine. Half hour, okay? I'm on the cell."

She nodded and made a note. She stared at Tate.

"This is Ray Tate. The last real cop. He's going to be with us so don't get all tactical when he comes in, okay? He's one of the good guys." He winked at her and said to Tate, "Watch out for Gloria. She's got two forty-fives. She's also got a gun."

The red-headed woman stared at the skipper without expression. The skipper was shrugging into his suit coat at the elevator when the doors opened. A tiny black woman in a smudged, stained pantsuit was leaning bonelessly against the back wall, looking as though she'd just jolted awake from nine floors of deep sleep. She had almost white bleached hair that exploded from her head. The butt of a holstered compact automatic pistol hiked her ghastly jacket above her hip. Her face was thin and the colour of scummy, forgotten coffee. Her eyes had an Asian, catlike slant. She'd made herself up by stabbing a tube of lipstick at her face, giving her mouth an arterial aspect. With effort she detached herself from the wall and stared dully at the skipper until he moved out of her way. She passed them and shuffled ghostly past the receptionist. She wore tiny embroidered slippers.

When the elevator doors closed the skipper hit the ground floor button and shook his head. "Dyke. A Statie."

Tate noticed he was gnawing his lip and blinking rapidly at the crack of elevator door.

Across the street they made their way through the breakfast crowd and sat at the farthest booth. The skipper held two fingers up to the counterman. When coffee was delivered the skipper poured an inch of sugar into his cup. "You know anything about us? About our satellite? That's okay. Nobody does. The Feds put in the infrastructure, the radios, the prosecutors, and the brainiacs who do the chemistry work. The Staties put in a few bodies and some cars. We put in the workers. Essentially, we handcuff pills. The Feds pick the target, we chase down the pills. We grab mutts if we have to, some labs, sometimes some dough. But what we want is pills, great fucking mounds of them. There's not much overtime and mostly, I got to say, we're Sleepy Hollow. We mostly work on ecstasy since some club kids croaked on it, but I haven't sweated in months. We've been getting a lot of crank lately."

"But sometimes we get to beat people up, right, lieutenant? Real police work?"

The skipper held up his palm. "Fuck that lieutenant stuff. Skipper's okay in front of the troops, Gordie if we're off campus. We get a lot of white trash guys. Some Chinamen come down from Canada with barrels of precursor chemicals or shipments. A few bikers. The main guy we're looking for is Captain Cook, if he even exists."

He held his cup up and the cook came down with a carafe and refilled it. The skipper poured in another inch of sugar. "I got to tell you also, there's some dead meat in the squad. Feds use us for training their young guys. They're okay, just stupid. Our guys dumped some slobs in. The Staties managed to dump one of their zombies in. That's the black broad in the elevator. You heard of her? Brown?"

"Don't think so. But I've been with the dogs in the weeds for a while."

"Dyke. Psycho. Nobody'll work with her. Djuna Fucking Brown. She's sleepwalking but we can't get rid of her. She's a triple threat: black, a dyke, and a broad. The commissioners can't sleep at night, the thought of her filing a suit. The mayor's fucked now that she's with us and if she goes off, having a black dyke broad screaming he's a sexist, racist fuckpig to the media won't look good. She's his entire constituency, for Christ sakes. Even got some Chinaman in the eyes, you notice?"

"Yeah." Tate made a nasty laugh. "Yeah, sure, I heard of her. She's the one from up in the boondocks, took out her partner, right? Beat his gums in with a baton."

"Yeah. Her. Fucking horror story, that mess was. He said some redskins off the Reserve grabbed him on the roadside and tuned him up. But word got out and nobody'd partner with her after. They shifted her around but guys took sick days, wives complained she was hitting on their hubbies. Fuck, as if. Anyway, when the Feds set up the Chemical Squad they asked out for bodies and the Staties must've thought they were in heaven. Two days later she's seconded down here."

"Tough chick, if she took out her partner."

The skipper looked into the distance over Tate's shoulder. His face took on a fearful fascination and in its nakedness Ray Tate saw the marks of the mean, feral boozer, of the paranoid, the frightened guy who could tell you how many minutes were left until he could hit happy hour. Two inches of sugar in ten minutes told the tale. The skipper blinked a couple of times. "How the fuck? I mean, you saw her. Weighs about fifty pounds. Beats a big strong cop so bad he cringes whenever a bird flies over his head?" He shook his head. "Fucked if I know. I'd 'a aced the bitch. Put her in the ground."

Ray Tate warmed up the bullshit. "So, except for us, you and me, skip, how many real cops on board?"

"Not a lot, Ray. Not a lot. Mostly I got slobs waiting to die or get their papers."

"But we're doing real work, here, right? Chain up the bodies?"

"Oh, yeah, once in a while. Bodies and pills. Pills make a great press conference. Everybody's happy. Somehow we manage to meet our projections. We're doing okay. We haven't got anything into our main target, this Captain Cook guy yet, if he even exists, but we're doing okay." He looked around. "Look, I gotta be straight with you, Ray, they want me to get the stuff on the dyke, put her to sleep once and for all. I know you've got troubles. That's okay. You came by them honest, doing the job. No real cop's gonna fuck you up for carrying the water. You're safe here with us. I stand by my guys, especially my city guys."

Ray Tate nodded and drained his coffee cup. He kept his face neutral. "I 'preciate that, skip. All I want is to get back in my blue suit and stripes and drive around the town, harassing citizens."

They stood up. The skipper bounced some quarters on the table. "If that's what you want, Ray, you're on your way. First step, though, is we spike the dootch-bag in the ground. I'm gonna partner you guys. You up for it?"

"Sure. That'll let me see a close-up, see what I'm after here."

"Good. I'll memo her. I gotta keep an eye on her. She's here then she's gone. Working a source she says, but I think she's got some real bad habits. Be nice to find them."

Ray Tate was assigned a desk in the empty tactical room. He looked around for Djuna Brown but she was absent. He was staring at the duty roster on the wall, memorizing the names and emergency contact numbers, when the skipper came out of his office and said he had three guys off with on-duty injuries, two were out someplace doing something, and the others were sitting on a chemistry set in the east end. "The dyke said she's out working, but she's probably just licking something." Tate saw he was gnawing his lip again.

"Who's this Captain Cook guy?"

"Don't know. That's his product, the interlocking Cs. We grabbed up a bunch of them on some dealers, but no one's copped where they came from." The skipper pointed to the photograph of the pile of pink pills. "That's the logo. One of the mutts said it stood for Captain Cook."

"Could be Cook County, over Chicago way."

"Naw, the Captain Cook thing has come up a couple of times since we first heard about it."

"We got any intell on the guy?"

The skipper shook his head. "We don't got dick. People are talking about him, though. The hydroponics guys took down a farm out in the badlands and somebody said it was Captain Cook's. A crank lab in the hills, same thing: Captain Cook's. Could just be a nickname, you know? Like he's a cooker, so they call him Cook." The skipper stared at the photograph of the pile of pink pills. "Fuck it, Ray. Take the day. Come in in the morning, at eight or nine, unless we give you a call out."

"No problem, skip. But sign my notebook out, okay? I know you're not going to put the hat on me, but if they come looking to rub admin shit on my head, I don't want you caught in the middle, things go for a shit at the Swamp."

"Good thinking, I appreciate that. We got to look out for each other," the skipper said. "Leave your coordinates with Gloria at the desk."

Chapter 3

Agatha Burns thought the people at Chanel might be a problem. "They already got the interlocked C's," she told Cornelius Cook, frowning with officious concern. "You use that stamp, Connie, they're gonna come after you."

Cornelius Cook used a flat razor to make a little nick in the flesh on her wrist. The skin was thin and pale. Her blond hair was dying by shades. Not a grey, exactly, but a leaching absence of colour. He licked the droplet of blood and put his finger tightly over the hole, feeling her pulse. It was slowing: she was coming down.

Agatha Burns said, "Six, that's six, Connie. You filled your daily diet."

Her wrist was a red blizzard of tiny nicks in various stages of repair. He thought her blood was starting to taste a little different, sour, less sweet. "I think if there's a knock at the door, Ag, it won't be the guys from trademark infringement. It'll be a whole bunch of cops with dogs and shotguns, wearing white bunny suits and gas masks."

"Still ..." Agatha Burns took her wrist back. "Enough, Connie."

He made his face sad. "I'll worry about the finer things of commerce, you worry about those chicklets, okay? Harv's coming by later and I want them bagged and counted. Harv's making me a snowbank."

Agatha Burns looked at the hundreds of bottles of cold pills scattered around the living room of her apartment. She hated dumping them out and separating and counting the chicklets. There were bottles of all sizes, all brought to the stairwell at the end of the hall and left by thieves and scammers who scoured the county's drugstores. After dropping the bottles in the stairwell, the bandits walked down the hallway and tapped three times on Agatha Burns's door. Agatha Burns hit speed-dial on her cellphone, let it ring once at the other end, then clicked off. A man sitting with a shotgun at the top of the stairwell walked down the stairs and checked the drop. He hit speed-dial on his cellphone and told the guy at the other end, who was sitting on a patio on the ground floor apartment with a big, unleashed Rottweiler, what the drop was. The man on the patio used a clothes peg to attach a couple of bills to the patio rail and waited for the delivery folks to pick it up. Sometimes he was feeling bored and he pegged the money to the Rot's collar. Agatha Burns, watching the scene from her balcony, went down the hall to the stairwell and retrieved the bottles.

Connie Cook didn't like being in the apartment. He didn't like being in the building. He was a ghost, a status he carefully crafted. He saw himself as the elusive Mr. Big, the unseen hand. But he had urges to visit Agatha Burns, to eat a bit of her flesh and bleed her. He'd loved her and he'd hated her and would ultimately consume her for one reason or the other.

Like an artist, he signed his work: each ecstasy pill had two Cs, the first one backwards, interlocking with a C printed correctly. He had pressing machines with other logos. Apples, death's head, RIP, hearts, stars, tombstones, USA. But he gave his interlocking Cs pride of place, monitoring its chemistry and production closely.

He glanced at his watch. "I gotta go, Aggie. Deal with a problem." Another bunch of Chinatown cookers, Willy Wong's boys, were jealous of his success and superb product and had taken to stamping the double C logo on their X. Complaints had been instant: the X pills crumbled and turned to paste the moment they hit saliva. There'd been overdoses, some deaths, because the Chinamen didn't have his precision. Connie Cook's henchmen had traced the stream of product back to some high school chemistry whizzes in east Chinatown.

Agatha Burns offered him another hit of her blood. "Stay a while, Connie. I don't like being here alone all the time. I'm gonna miss you. I got to work late, getting the stuff done. Give me a tap, eh, get me through?"

Naked, she was all long limbs and deteriorating muscle tone. Her habit was voracious. He slid himself around and ran his finger up the tracks behind her knee. "You're running out of vacancies, here, Ag.

You're getting all full up." He felt a huge satisfaction but an unaccountable sadness, too. The loss of love.

"C'mon, Connie. I got work to do, I need a boost. Huh, huh?"

He sat up. She put her hand into his scant crotch, disappearing it under his flowing stomach. She didn't notice any longer that he was a victim of almost morbid obesity — when he lay on her she was drowning in a fleshy sea of grunts and grinds. But he had the product and she had the need.

"You take a pack for it?"

"I don't like that, Connie. It hurts." She leaned forward to suck, hoping to allay his desires. He was a thruster and a biter and she feared both.

"I get to pack you or nothing," he said, pushing her away, the ruthless businessman replacing the sad romantic. "You let me know before I leave." He ran his hand over her ass, humming. He was just about done with her and, with a little regret he admitted, he started putting her lights out. "You hearing anything? About the Chinaman and the X? Maybe Harv or somebody's helping them out?"

"I don't get out. You know I don't hear nothing about nobody. Will you be careful? If I do? If I let you?"

He stared at her ass. "You think Harv's got funny?"

She tried to read him. If Harv was on the way out, maybe she could be on the way in. If she could get a job outside the apartment, it would make it more difficult for Captain Cook to pirate her ass. She could avoid him and stay high.

She kind of liked Harv. He was sad and tragic but

she had her own need to think about. "Well, I dunno. Maybe. I guess. He's in the rub and tugs lots. The girls make him put a towel over his face while they do him. Maybe, maybe he's with the Chinamen. If I take the pack, can I move up? Move out of here, maybe go to the country?"

He fiddled with his class ring, rotating it around his fat pinky finger. "You want to do that? Play with the chemistry set? Become a professional woman?"

"Well," she purred and ran her hand down his distended, pure white belly until it was nestled back at his crotch. "I should get a shot. I got good hands. I did good in chemistry at school. If Harv's got funny and goes over to them, who'll you get? I can be like one of those guys at baseball, in the pig pen."

"The bullpen." He felt a sudden brief fondness for her. "It's the bullpen."

"Right, that."

"You want a shot. I want to give you the packer. How you with that? Quid pro quo."

"C'mon, Connie. I don't like that." She looked at him staring at her. "Look, okay, but take it easy, okay? Last time I had to wear a scarf and a turtleneck. It hurt."

"You look good in a turtleneck. But no problem, Ag. I'll be good."

When she went to the washroom for lotion and preparation he stretched his jaws and jowls wide and cracked the joints. He'd always hated being fat but found it was delicious to see her slim figure vanish under him.

She came out with a bath towel, a box of condoms, and a tube of gel. He watched her hands quickly

make him hard and skin the rubber on. She stayed
down there massaging the gel onto the condom and
stared at him. He made her wait a few moments then
took a tube of crank from beside the bed. He positioned her, then tapped a mound onto the sticky tip of
the condom. Her ass was his favourite delivery system.

While Agatha Burns was in the washroom, cleaning
up and crying, Connie Cook called Harvey on a cellphone. "Hey, where you?"

"Cookie? What's up, man?"

"Well, I was, a few minutes ago." He laughed.

"You at Ag's? She got the stuff ready to go?"

"Yeah, soon. Give her a couple of hours. She's got
to work standing up for a while."

"Hoo."

"You been dealing with those Chinese guys, Willy
Wong's kids, out in the east end? Aggie says you got
yellow fever, trolling the massage parlours. Meeting
bad people and pressing and cooking for strangers.
Anything to that, Harv?"

"Fuck, no. C'mon, Cookie. She said that, eh? She
wouldn't say that."

"Yup. And she wants to cook. I said you'd give
her a tryout."

"Ah, well, okay, I guess," Harv said. He waited a
few seconds. "But it isn't the kind of thing you can just
teach someone, like baking brownies, you know. You
make a little mistake they turn out, taste a little bitter,

sprinkle on some sugar and eat 'em anyway. This is different. There are tricks. You know I got tricks and you can't ask me to just give 'em to some scrag you're banging. That ain't right, Cookie."

"Harv, don't worry about it. She's just trying to get ahead. When you come by to pick up the chicklets for your snowbank, you arrange to take her out for a drive. See if she's got the chops."

"Well, if you're sure, Cookie. I got lots of people want me to give 'em night school lessons in avoiding crank combustion."

"Well, look, Harv, I'm not asking you to make her a wizard like you. Just take her to the first step, okay? Let her make suds. She'll feel useful, like she's going ahead. You do the real work."

"Yeah, okay." Harv clicked his teeth. "She said that, eh? That I'm with the Chinamen?"

"Don't worry about it, Harv. She probably meant some fucking fucker."

Agatha Burns stayed in the washroom while he dressed. It took a long time and he was breathing heavily when he finished. He slipped his feet into loafers: it was impossible for him to contort himself to secure shoe-laces. He could hear the shower blasting. He cracked the door called into the steam, "Hey, you okay, Ag?"

She sobbed. "Go away. You said you wouldn't bite."

"C'mon, Ag. A little fun. You gonna be okay to work? Do some stuff with Harv later, become a jour-neyman cooker?" He stepped in and twitched back the shower curtain. "I decided to move you up. Harv's okay on the X but he needs an apprentice for the crank."

Agatha Burns was crouched on the floor under the hard, hot water, holding a soapy face cloth to the back of her neck. The face cloth was stained pink with watery blood. "Really?" For a second her face had a residual cheerleader's glow that hadn't quite been burned away by chemistry.

"Yep. The Harv's a master maker. Don't mention to him that I know about the Chinamen, though, okay? That you told me. I want to move you up quick. I don't think Harv's gonna make it and I want you to have all his secrets."

"Okay, wow." She stood up, beaming. Of all of her, only her eyes remained gorgeous. "Okay."

He could count her ribs. There were bruises on her hips and knees where she'd fallen while high. She suddenly had sagging breasts and he regretted that. She smiled and her teeth looked wobbly and grey, off-kilter. He again felt a bit of sadness. "Finish up the chicklets, and when Harv comes to pick them up he'll take you with him, get you started."

"We going to the super lab?" She laughed gaily, his excesses forgotten, forgiven. "Okay, okay, Connie, I'll do good."

He felt a chill at the echo of her words. The super lab. What was that all about?

He left the building whistling, knowing he'd never need to come back again, and he was sad he'd never see her again. Harv was primed and would make his move, giving Agatha Burns a lesson in crank combustion. Harv, he knew, didn't fuck around.

Chapter 4

When his wife threw him out after he'd shot the second black guy, Ray Tate had poked at the rental section of the newspaper, then went to the nearest police station and leaned on the duty sergeant's table. The duty sergeant, an old Irish squarehead with rockers on his stripes, knew everything about his kingdom: the smokehouses, the homes with domestic violence, what was a rental and what was owned. He knew every neighbour dispute, every squat, every house infested with mental patients who only came out after dark, shy of the light, fearful of eyes.

The duty sergeant shook Tate's hand across the table. "Fuck 'em, Ray. You go forth and smite thine enemies and, well, fuck what they're trying to do to you." He took the slip with the apartment building's address, turned to a civilian operator, and said with polite command, "Run it." To Ray Tate he said: "I know it. Old man Lilly's place. It's okay. Parking kinda sucks. Where they got you working? You got a company car?"

Ray Tate had told the squarehead he was relaxing on paid leave until they sorted out the latest shooting. No gun, no badge, no car.

"No problem, then." The CO handed the duty a printout. "Okay. We got a domestic, we got a domestic, we got a B&E, we got another domestic, another B&E, noise, noise, noise. A suicide by blade. What the fuck?" He read through the page. "Oh, hang on. Okay. You're going into three-o-five, right? That's the domestics and the noise complaints, and the suicide. That's why it went vacant, the guy killed himself. Cutting. A mess." He'd dropped the sheet on the desk. "Make sure old man Lilly gives you a new carpet."

The apartment was one big room with a partial partitioned-off kitchenette with a fragrant gas stove, a half-fridge, and a table that snapped down off the wall, landing on a folding leg. The bathroom was compact but had a tub. Ray Tate had spent many after-shifts sitting on the edge of a bathtub, soaking his feet in salts and soaps after walking his many posts. Calluses on his feet were buttery and rife and as familiar as his thumbs. There was no furniture and no carpet. The floor was scuffed but solid and an attempt had been made to sand it. There was no seepage onto the wood from the suicide. Ray Tate wasn't worried about being haunted by a suicide: he had two black guys who sometimes came around late at night and stirred up his sleep.

The windows faced glorious, indirect north and Ray Tate had instinctively thought about painting.

He'd used a butter knife to chip the encrusted paint on the windowsills until he was able to force the windows open all the way.

Old man Lilly liked having a cop in the building and gave Ray Tate a key to the storage area in the basement. "Go on down, take what you like. When you move out, just leave it."

There was no bed in the basement but a serviceable wooden table and chair were stacked in a corner, upside down on a sprung-out couch. There were two mismatched lamps, a set of cups, saucers, dishes, and some odd pots. He'd never lived alone in his life. Every place he'd ever lived was already someone else's home: first the State homes, then the foster homes, the rooming house with two other recruits near the academy, and finally with his wife. He went to an art store and bought bags of paints and brushes and an easel and set it up at a forty-five degree angle to the window.

While he was on paid off he'd stood at his easel and looked at the canvas. He squeezed paint and stared at it, his thumb poked through the hole in the pallet. His paycheques were automatically deposited and he had little reason to go outside. Until his beard and hair grew out, and he became unrecognizable from the media photos, he crept to the supermarket in a baseball hat and sunglasses. He started smoking again. He drank, each day starting in earlier until he found himself leaning asleep on his easel in the middle of the day. When he awoke his hands shook as he poured his breakfast.

One night he'd borrowed Mr. Lilly's old Chevrolet and drove out to the western suburbs to see his ex and his daughter. His wife had been perfunctory and went to the basement to do laundry and watch television. His daughter, graduating high school, sat with him on the deck he'd built with the firefighter next door, and they talked about her photography and her plan to spend a year in Asia. She looked at him funny and then went inside, returning with a handful of photographs and a sleek Nikon. She stuttered it at him a few times and previewed the pictures on the LCD screen.

"Look, Dad," she'd said. She handed him a photo taken of him before the first of the shootings. The difference was stunning: his face had become lined, his eyes were sunken into his head, his mouth was grim and clamped as though protecting himself from a confession.

"You look afraid," his daughter said with alarm. "Are you afraid, Dad?"

He'd gone home and poured the half bottles of alcohol into the sink. He took to four sugars in his coffee to keep his blood in balance. The squareheaded duty sergeant from the local station came by one after-shift, looked around and said, "Jesus fuck, Ray. C'mon, man."

The following day, three off-dutys and a uniformed female officer appeared carrying a folded futon, pillows, some banal framed pictures of Japanese mountaintops, a set of silverware, a television set, and a stack of bedding meant for a queen-sized bed. Each left a police business card with their cell numbers scrawled on the back. The last one, preparing to leave, a trim blond policewoman with a hurricane of freckles and a wide sad smile, said: "You need, you call, sergeant. You got it?"

Ray Tate nodded.

"You want, I'll stay, sergeant."

Numbly, he'd nodded and she helped him assemble and make up the futon. She stripped off her uniform. She wore men's underwear and socks that sagged to her ankles.

Afterwards, as she slept, he turned on a lamp and tilted the shade away from her. He mixed blues and purples and blacks and painted her sleeping, her muscular arm hanging off the side of the futon, her gun belt curled on the floor, her boots neatly aligned beside the futon. He looked at the long tubes of yellows and oranges and bright reds and could think of nothing to do with them.

Then the sun was coming up and spilling thin, perfect north light into the apartment. He lay down beside her. He felt loved for what seemed the first time in his life, although he couldn't recall her name.

After leaving the satellite and the skipper's greasy brotherhood, Ray Tate stopped at a coffee shop and wrote from memory the names and phone numbers from the duty roster in the Chemical Squad's office into his notebook. Aside from the notorious Djuna Brown he recognized none of them, except for one: Walter Brodski, a stumblebum ex-hero who let the pressures grind him into a bottle.

In his jacket and union sweatshirt, Tate hiked up the hill outside the satellite, past the swank midtown shops and sushi bars, and strode into the gully at the cemetery. At the north end he stopped again for a coffee to warm up, sitting in a window and looking at the streets as though he'd been away a long time. Back on the sidewalk he legged it energetically north, veering off to walk slowly by the local station, keeping half an eye out for the freckled, blond policewoman.

There were framed photographs of his daughter's work on the walls of his apartment and some faced-in canvases he'd played with, to little result, leaning near his easel. With his lack of enthusiasm or real talent it was getting expensive to buy the stretched canvas so he'd bought a case of thick paper pads. There was a teak, elephant-footed coffee table his daughter had found at an antique shop. Little else had changed in the apartment in the months since the charity run by the local division guys and the mercy of the freckled policewoman. She'd never come back. He'd seen her once, doing up her notebook behind an office building when he cut through one afternoon in his shabby alley rat attire. He passed, he thought, unnoticed. In the days since she'd stayed the night he'd thought about her a lot.

There was no mail. He'd been away in the weeds for days and the apartment smelled of cooped up linseed oil, dirty laundry, and the faint scent of gas from the stove. He reefed open the windows. Old Mr. Lilly had mown the lawn and the earthy fragrance stirred something in him. He reached for his brushes and tubes, hooked his thumb through his pallet, and flipped open a spiral pad of thick paper. He squeezed green.

Ray Tate was no fan of Zen but his daughter's photographs of calm gardens and forests made him shut his eyes. He slashed vertical; he swooped in curves. Resisting the urge to open his eyes to examine the result, he instead moistened the tip of the brush with his tongue to thin out the colour and slashed and swooped and let his mind flow like water over unfamiliar stones.

The psychiatrist had told him one of her clients, a small-town policeman from a burg across the state line, had cut off his gun hand with a table saw after shooting a teenager dead during an off-duty traffic stop on the Interstate. Another, she said, quit the job and became a bricklayer, even on his off-days building walls around walls at his cottage on the river. All of it, she said, to protect the world from himself. They all suffered, she said, sooner or later. They became quickly grey and their faces lined, their mouths turned into upside down Us. They became impotent and violent in direct proportion to their libido level prior to their killings. They beat themselves. They beat their wives. They beat their children. Some, she said, just vanished, either dead or gone into a void world where they could become something else, usually with the fragrance of alcohol or smoke.

"What did you do, Ray, after the first incident?"

He didn't like her. She was beautiful and had big brunette hair and perfect legs beneath a business suit with a sexy cut. She looked at him as though he was a specimen. He said: "I answered all the questions, then I went home and ..." He looked down at his hands.

She leaned forward. Her breasts were creamy. She was predatory. "And? And then ... What?"

"I ate a bacon sandwich." His face was bland enough that he knew she could tell he was lying. He didn't tell her his wife, the daughter of a cop, looked at him differently after the second shoot. "Canadian bacon."

"My dad," his wife had said, "was thirty years on and he never shot anyone. Ray, how come you shot two people?"

He didn't answer.

"Ray?"

"Your dad was a crime scene geek, Karen. He shot pictures, not people. When he got there the bad guys were dead on the floor. When I get there, they're not so co-operative."

They'd sat in stiff silence and ate their dinner off TV trays. When the news came on and showed the riots starting up downtown she picked up her plate and went into the kitchen.

He'd become a cop because her dad had talked him into it. Being a doorstep baby of the State he'd had no dad of his own, but had been raised in a series of good but indifferent foster homes where one man taught him to shave, another to defend himself and to how to swing on an inside curve ball, another to play chess, another to fashion a half-Windsor knot in his tie. All good men, he believed. A bit of the duty sergeant in each of them.

Karen's dad, Harry, had extolled the job for the wrong reasons. Good pay, good benefits, a great pension. You can keep my daughter in a good life on that stuff, old Harry had said. Retire early enough to start another career, bank the pension. There was no talk of duty, of public service, of justice or protection. It was to please her dad that he'd applied. The old man's connections had got him in and moved him along, not in rank but in assignments. After the first shooting the old man and his cronies had come to the house and drank him into the floor. It was as though they'd never seen a real cop before, a working cop, a cop who'd done the job. They thought he was the spawn of some old eastside ground pounder who'd bumped up against a loose lady while patrolling an alley. When he got his stripes they'd come by and exuberantly pounded his biceps, to engrave them into his flesh.

After the second shooting, there was only a brief phone call and a message to hang in there. He sat at home and grew his hair and beard in the silence.

One night his daughter, Alexis, had come down to the basement where he'd taken to sleeping. She cuddled up to him on the sofa. "We're okay, dad." Her hair was blond like Karen's. She had his thin features and he wondered often if he was looking at the features of the mother he'd never met.

He sat with his arm around her. "Anything you want to ask me, Ax?"

"Nope." She wouldn't say anything else except, "We're cool."

The next day, in the middle of a fight, Karen flat out asked if it was true, if he was a racist. He packed what possessions would fit into the backseat of a taxi.

At the Swamp his second shooting was cleared reluctantly and they sent him marching orders. He found himself in the alleys, feasted upon by insect life, festooned with bleeding bites and blemishes.

Forgotten, someone joked, but not gone.

Somehow he'd made a painting of the slashing looping greens. A forest, maybe, or a view of a jungle from a long distance away. There was a suggestion of things hidden, verdant things ready to pounce or reveal themselves. Ray Tate carefully detached the page from the spiral book and put it to dry on the kitchen counter.

His first telephone call was to an inspector at the Swamp. Ray Tate didn't really trust anyone above duty sergeant. Duty sergeant was the ultimate, he believed, a mentor to the troops, a guy who never heard a joke he hadn't already heard before. A duty sergeant was the master of his domain, a leader of his tribe. Only good dutys could create good cops. Get above duty sergeant and people feared your career arc instead of respecting your words and deeds. But the inspector he called was a good, young guy whose old man had died early on the job and he'd been raised by a legion of blue uncles who never left him abandoned or confused, who crammed his summer evenings with ball games and winter dawns with hockey practise.

The inspector listened to the list of names from the Chemical Squad roster. Most of the city guys were slobs, he said, duffed-out guys with habits. He warned Ray Tate to beware of the skipper up there. "Gordo s very ... sharp," he said. "Fifteen to the dozen."

"This Statie they got me with. Brown? The dyke? What about her?"

"Not a lot of back story," the inspector said. "She went straight from the State Police training college to the Spout. You know the Spout? Up in Indian country, where they put you when they want you to volunteer to quit, cheap. 'Up to the Spout, where they pour you out.' She's up there, oh, six, seven months with a detachment full of farm boys who never saw a black chick, never mind a dyke. There's something happens and her partner shows up at the local hospital with his face all beat in. He says some Indians jumped him but it gets around that she went after him with her stick. He quits and she hangs in for a month or so but the farm boys and their wives complain. She's down to the Capitol, shuffling paperwork. Then the Feds start up Gordo's task force and next thing, she's seconded down here, driving him nuts."

Ray Tate thought a moment. "I'm partnering with her. They want me to put her down. Could be that she's out to get me? Get out from under her own stuff?"

The inspector hummed. "The word down here, Ray, is that the mayor wants you out. You and all the other city guys working chemicals. You want to be careful, in word and deed. You know? There's a lot of opportunity to fuck up, a lot of loose cash floating around you can stub your toe on."

"Thanks."

"Ah, Ray? Is it interesting that they're partnering you up with a black without breaking your trigger finger first?"

Ray Tate called a half dozen sergeants and duty sergeants. The Chemical Squad, they all agreed, was a shooting gallery where cracked city guys were always in season and you could take your limit. There were warnings about Gordo the skipper and commiseration about being partnered with a psycho Statie dyke.

He called a sniper on the Statie tactical shooters he'd done some training with and listened to a lot of funny stories about Indian country.

Djuna Brown took a photocopy of the skipper's memo home with her. She filed it in a folder stuffed with other sheets of paper. A dated and signed trail of slights, of conflicting orders, of her mileage and hours worked down to the minute. There were the scrawled notes she'd found on her desk, many of them calling her a dyke, a rug muncher, and an all around generic bitch. There were racist cartoons. There were flyers advertising gay revues in the Rainbow Valley. There was a computer-enhanced picture of her face printed over a girl going down on a grossly fat black woman, her tongue a foot long. There were digital pictures she'd taken of used condoms left on her office chair, glued to her desk drawer. There were licence numbers of cars she'd found suspiciously parked near her apartment.

Another folder, much slimmer, contained commendations, atta boy memos, and newspaper clippings: high profile arrests up in Indian country, saving a Native baby from a burning trailer, running a self-defence class for at-risk children, a sex-ed class for teenage girls.

Her duplex was within walking distance of the satellite. She kept her head down as her slippers trudged the same hills Ray Tate had gone up and down a few hours earlier, past the same cemetery. She didn't stop for a cup of leisurely coffee, she didn't look at the streets as though she were meeting old friends. She bought some yogurt at a convenience store, allowed herself to buy a pack of Marlies.

In her living room she ate the yogurt without interest and waited until six o'clock to pour a gin and tonic. By seven o'clock she was smoking continuously and weaving a little through the duplex, straightening up, avoiding looking at herself in the mirror.

The Gay-Glo association after-hours hotline was picked up on the first ring. "Dee-joon," the woman, a perpetually bitter former patroller, sang, "you gonna join up with the folks who love you? Make your voice heard?"

"Soon, I think, Haze. I'm okay," she said softly, making her voice wistful. "So far."

The Glo wanted Djuna Brown with a vengeance. She hit all the right notes: female, dyke, black, some Chinese, and a Statie. It was widely known that she'd been harassed, both physically and sexually, and had fought back. There were no Staties in the Glo, they were barracked across the rural portions of the state.

"So, what can I do for you, sister?"

"You know this city guy, Ray Tate?"

"The gunner? Sure, he shot a black guy back, oh,

before you came down here. He got away with it. So then he shot another one about a year ago. Got away with that one, too. They're protecting him, keeping him out of sight until they can bring him back." Hazel was tapping into her computer. The Gay-Glo had its own little intelligence network. It collected slights and troop movements, helped its members avoid traps, to step around the machinations of the homophobic thugs at the Swamp. "What's up with Ray Tate? You hear something on him?"

"They put me with him today. Any chance he's a rat? Or should I just be worried that he'll put one in my queer black ass?"

"Whew. That guy, anything's possible. You want to write everything down, like you write the other stuff. Tape what you can. It would be nice to be the ones that put the hat on him, drag him before the governor's review board. But be careful, okay?" She paused, revealing the tap of typing. "Look, I'm going to put this stuff into a file, okay? If something happens to you, we want it documented that they put you with a racist killer, in an at-risk situation."

"Sure."

"Perfect. You, ah, seeing anybody? We're having a meeting tomorrow night, why don't we have dinner first? Go out after, have a drink. Strategize. Girl talk."

"Let me see how tomorrow goes, Haze. I might just take you up on it." Djuna Brown hung up and shuddered. Before she could take her hand off the receiver the phone rang.

A man's voice asked if she was Trooper Brown.

She said she was and reached to flick on the tape recorder.

"Did you ever, like, want to be a cop?"

She didn't ask who it was. "I am a cop."

"You're a problem. You're a target. If you want out, just get them to cut you a deal, take the package and move to San Francisco or something. Open a rainbow bookstore. Quit fucking around."

She didn't recognize the voice. There was no attempt to deepen it or disguise it. She played light. "I don't run."

"Do you drink?"

"Who is this? What do you want?"

"Well," the voice said, "I'm Ray Tate. I'm the guy hired to spike you into the ground."

Chapter 5

Phil Harvey wouldn't go into Agatha Burns's apartment building. He called her on the cell and told her to come out the back entrance, to bring the stuff down herself, not to use the muscleman in the stairwell or to let him know she was going out. He said he'd keep an eye on the packages as she made as many trips as it took. He told her not to use the phone, not to call out, not to answer it. From here on, he said, her training began.

He waited in his black Camaro, bubbling the engine while he watched traffic move through the winding streets of the South Project. He was parked where he could see the rear entrance but couldn't be seen by the moneyman on the ground floor patio or be captured by the security cameras in the lobby.

He looked at his hands clutching the steering wheel. Grey, glistening waves of burns disappeared under the sleeves of his beige cotton jacket. He wouldn't wear nylon: nylon, when it burned, stuck to you like napalm. You couldn't get it off. If you pulled it off, your flesh came with it, like pulling off a glove inside out. Sometimes the fingernails came off. Phil Harvey had four fingernails left and he kept them immaculate, although nobody noticed.

His face hadn't suffered as much as his hands, but it was pretty bad on the right side. Tissue had been eaten away. His left ear was a gnarled nub. He wore his grey-streaked, black hair very long, below his shoulders, to hide the angry nub, tying it back in a ponytail when he had to work, loosening it into a curtain he could hide behind when he was in public. Hair burned too but didn't smell half as bad as the pig roast cloud of fire that rose when your flesh melted in a flash fire. When he'd been a young speeder he never thought he'd be a middle-aged man with an Ozzy Osbourne hairdo. He knew the bikers out in the badlands called him Pork Chop behind his back.

It was about dues. Paying 'em, playing 'em, he believed.

When Agatha Burns appeared at the rear door of the apartment building, dragging a cardboard box, Harv punched in Captain Cook's number and started laying track. "Hey, so I'm here. Where's she at?"

"She'll be there. Probably having a bubble bath. Relax, Harv."

"I been here a half hour." He watched her look around, kick at the box, then go back inside, dressed for a party in platform heels, pale, long legs that vanished into a minimal black miniskirt, and a tight, short, red, shiny jacket. A red scarf was looped around her neck a couple of times. "She's not answering the phone."

"Just wait. She's hungry for it. Probably doing herself up, getting ready for her first day of school, impress the teacher."

Harv clicked off. Over the next twenty minutes Agatha Burns made four trips with cardboard boxes. It took her a long time. After each trip she wobbled on the heels then leaned, exhausted, against the side of the building, looking around. Her muscles had clearly deteriorated from chemical excess and she spent bursts of energy at a rapid rate. At a distance her hair looked grey.

A boneless black guy with a baseball hat sideways over a do-rag, a knee-length basketball tank top, and a heavy gold chain approached her.

"Oh, fuck." Harv reached under the seat and dragged out a heavy silver revolver.

Agatha Burns shook her head at the black guy and he touched her shoulder. He jittered. Harv wrapped the magnum in a sweater with four inches of wicked ribbed barrel poking out. He shut off the turbo and climbed out. When he was ten feet away he heard the man whispering, "Where yo tote where yo tote?" and trying to look behind her, to see what was in the cartons, to see if she had a purse.

Harv glanced around and held the revolver in his hand with the barrel sticking out, straight down his leg. "Yo. Hey, Yo."

The black man whirled. "Who the fuck you be fucking yo-ing, Yo?"

Harv felt like laughing. He said, "I be fucking yo-ing you, Yo. Yo?" He'd have to tell Connie about this, later, leaving out the Agatha Burns part. He started laughing and pointed the gun at the black guy. "Don't yo my ho'."

The man saw the size of the gun. "Fuuuuuck." He began backing away, his palms out. "S'cool, s'cool." He spoke rapid-fire in a childish voice: "I'm a player I'm a player I'm a player."

Harv realized the dude was a dummy and hung his arm straight down and wiggled the gun. "Hold on there, player. You want to make ten bucks? Load that shit in the black Camaro over there." He aimed a device at the car and the trunk lid raised. "Neatness counts, right?"

The black guy looked at the boxes, then at the Camaro, then at the silver barrel. "Yeah, yeah I can do that. Twenty bucks, though."

"Twenty, sure," Harv said, still smiling, "if I can shoot you one time, after."

"Naw. Naw, ten's cool." He hoisted the boxes two at a time and fitted them into the trunk. He put some boxes into the back seat. Harv gave him a ten and slammed the trunk shut.

"What happened to you there, mister?" the man said with childish curiosity. "Under your hair. Can I ask?"

"I was going down on your momma and she came in my face. You should fuck off right about now, okay?"

The black man backed away.

Harv held up his hand and Agatha Burns stayed by the rear door. He dialed Cornelius Cook and told him, "Fuck it, she didn't show and I'm outta here."

Cornelius Cook said, "Whatever." Harv heard him stifle a laugh.

He waved Agatha Burns over. He opened the passenger door for her, told her to belt up, and rounded the car. He put the gun, wrapped in the sweater, under the seat. The black guy was standing across the parking lot, watching, shuffling. He had his riff-and-rap persona back. Harv waved and the guy grabbed his baggy crotch and yelled, "Yo this, you bacon faced motherfucker."

Cruising out of the projects, Harv kept his eyes in the mirrors. "Fucking place. Our people must be the only whites in the whole fucking colony."

"Connie wants it like that. Connie likes it here. He's got —" She ran on and Harv didn't listen. A blue Pontiac was behind him and he watched it until it turned off. Then there was a black van but as it got closer he saw it was two Yos bouncing in their seats. It wheeled off into another housing project. When the mirror was clear he headed for the Interstate. He slipped off and on at random, running neighbourhoods, counting cars behind him.

Agatha Burns was still going a mile a minute about Connie and his wants, his needs, his plans. She spoke to the windshield and didn't look at Harv's face. "— so he comes by and says, hey I want you to go to school with Harv. I didn't wanna but he said I hadda. That okay? With you? Harv? That I hadda? I said, no, Harv is the man, he's the wizard, but Connie just said if I don't it's my ass, you know? I don't like that but you know how Connie is. So I gotta, right? If I don't —"

"It's your ass."

"Right. Right, Harv. You got it. So I got, like, no choice." She listened to the silence and didn't like it. Silence was a no man's land where anything could be said by anybody and all kinds of evil things could come out of that. "You know you can trust me, if there's any really secret stuff you teach me. I keep my mouth shut, it's just between you and me. I told him I'd rather work on the farm hoeing weed or something, bailing or something, but Connie just said, no you go with Harv, keep him away from the Chinamen. He said —"

"What Chinamen?"

"What?" She skidded to a stop. "Chinamen?"

"You said, keep me away from the Chinamen."

"Chinamen? No, no I didn't. I don't even know no Chinamen."

"Ag, you said, fuck, Chinamen."

"When?"

"Just fucking now. You said, to keep Harv away from the Chinamen."

"No. Wasn't me. You musta heard that on the radio."

"Ag," he said, swerving into the hot lane and passing the off-ramps at the city limits, heading for the rising open country north of the city, rounding the lake, "you fucking said it. The radio's off."

"I didn't turn it off. I didn't even know it was on. You got any CDs?"

Harv shook his head, dazed. He'd love, he thought, to tell Connie about this piece of classic babble. This and the Yo with his yos. But this part of the coming evening wasn't happening. This part of the evening was a Harv moment.

In one of the soliloquies she asked eagerly if they were going to the super lab. Was she going to see that legendary place?

Harv felt very sad.

She was quiet the rest of the way to the farm. She squirmed a little in her seat, the miniskirt hiking up, adjusting her scarf. Harv thought Cornelius Cook had probably got a little out of hand. He had the weak man's urge to thrust when he could, the weak man's lack of control. And she didn't know it but she'd been lucky. The Captain was a biter and he had a position he liked where the face was available.

He reflected on the crazy Captain: money up the ass, private schools, a Mercedes when he was still in high school, big motherfucking cottage up in the Lakes. At first, Harv thought it was just street bullshit but he had a pal troll the Internet and there was the Cook couple. At gallery openings in the state capital, in Chicago, even in New York City at the ballet. Donating to causes. Announcing huge mergers in the business pages. The Captain was in several of the photos looking fat and prosperous, often in company with a slim wife with a brittle smile. What the fuck was he doing in this fucking life?

A fat, kinky item was old Connie, but not without a certain diabolical flair. When Harv first met him, the

Captain was just a hugely fat fuck among the fat fucks sitting in the dim stage lights of Jiggles, a mob-run club at Stateline where Harv picked up a hundred bucks a night doing the door. One night the bartender pointed Cook out to Harv, saying the fat guy had been in every night but never hit on the peelers, just sat watching. The fat fuck carried a roll of hundreds and never wanted change for his drinks. Harv, who still had bandages on his face from the lab explosion and was on his ass, keeping the door, waited for the Captain outside, near a sleek Mercedes painted a deep shade of grey he'd never seen before that sparkled under the lights, parked furthest from the side entry to the club. The bartender did his thing and after Cookie came out, weaving and collapsing, Harv was amazed. He'd never kicked anything like it. His motorcycle boot seemed to just disappear into the globe of flesh under the bright arc lights. Harv's foot seemed to go into the fat fuck's torso and hit nothing of substance. Like kicking a big pillow. Harv didn't kick him in the head: he'd seen a guy take a light boot, a kiss to the temple, on the ranges in the state pen and the guy had died. Between Harv's boot and the stuff the bartender had dropped on him, the Captain wasn't doing much anyway. Groaning a little. He vomited once, probably more from the fission of the drugs mixed into his cognac than anything Harv was doing.

Two weeks later, Harv was leaning on his door when the fat fuck came in. He nodded pleasantly and Harv nodded back. The fat fuck walked a little off-kilter but he had a big smile for the waitress and dealt out his hundreds.

The Captain waved him over when the peelers changed shifts. "How you doing? You making any money?"

"Fuck off." Harv thought the fat fuck looked pretty pleased, seeing how he'd been given the special vitamin and stomped up a bit. "You don't know me."

"You're Harv, right? Harv. Phil Harvey. Philip One-L Harvey. November six, nineteen fifty. Been up in Craddock, what? Three times? Now you live upstairs, park your bike out back most of the time because most of the time it doesn't run. You drive an old rattletrap bubble van the owner of this place lends you, weekends, so you can go and cook up some stuff for some other guys who make all the dough while you make gas mileage and walking around money. Were you born stupid, or was it the fire or what?"

Harv started to reach across the table and the fat fuck skidded his chair back a bit and put his hand under the tabletop.

"The fuck do you want? Get out of here." Harv had taken twenty-eight hundred dollar bills off the guy, the bartender got five hundred. Harv had seventeen hundred left. He'd take a bullet, if that's what the fat fuck was doing under the table, before he'd give back a nickel.

"You're getting on in years, Harv. You've got too much hair and not enough face. Soon you'll be a pensioner." The Captain saw Harv glancing at the tabletop. "Yeah, I got something down there. But what's more important, I've got three guys with me. Ex-cops, city guys. They're not ex-cops because they got to retire with the pension, you know? They're the ones who told me about you. The other day they visited the bartender and he's been off work, since, right?" Captain Cook closed his eyes. "I'm having a vision, Harv. I predict that the next time you see him he'll be in a motorized wheelchair. And he said he only got five hundred from you, which means: from me."

Harv looked around and instantly spotted the three guys with the fat fuck. They sat like middle-aged bikers, sprawled at a round table between Harv and the side door. One of them, a short-haired guy with a glittering earring and a gold chain around his neck, smiled and nodded encouragingly.

Harv had taken beatings and he'd never run from one in his life. "How you want to do it, you fat cocksucker?"

"Lunch. How's that, Harv? We have lunch tomorrow and you tell me how you're going to give me back my twenty-eight hundred. Or we can do something else, and you can make twenty-eight."

It was probably, Harv thought, because they were two freaks that they got along.

At the lunch Connie Cook had explained about boredom and the emptiness of his life.

"If I was this fat and broke at the same time," he said over hamburgers and fries at a Kelso's in the swanky Stonetown, "I'd 'a killed myself. No shit, Harv. But I'm fat, I know it and there's nothing I can do about it, but also I've got dough. My wife and I go to the art gallery, nobody turns away, nobody goes wow look at that guy, is he one fat number or what. Nope. They all come over. Mr. Cook, you like another canapé? You're losing weight, Mr. Cook. Mr. Cook, you want to fund an exhibit next season? Hundred and sixty thousand, we'll put your name in the program. Gee, thanks. Then the fucker signals another sleek fucker and boom, I got a fundraising guy from the museum over in Chicago on me: Gee, Mr. Cook, we could use some dough to bring an exhibit of Inuit art down from Canada. Your dad used to kick some dough our way, how about it, family tradition? Say, two hundred thousand and we'll put your name in the program." Connie Cook laughed bitterly. "So, my wife's on me to pony up all this dough so she can be in the *Post* on the parties page, looking good with a ballerina or a fucking opera singer. A real good day, she winds up in the *Chicago Trib*."

"Huh." Harv was only mildly interested. "What's this you said, about making twenty-eight?"

"Those guys, those three ex-cops last night, with me at the club? They're security guys from one of my companies. They —" Connie Cook stopped for a moment, chewing the last of his burger, staring at Harv's face. "That hurt? I mean, it probably hurt when it happened, but what about now?"

"No. I know it's there, sure, it feels tight. But you get used to it." He shrugged. "Like anything else."

Connie Cook reached into his suit jacket and put a small tube on the table. "Vitamin E. I told my doctor, I knew a guy with some burns and he said smear this on, twice a day. Tone things down a bit, maybe."

Harv let the tube sit on the table. "So, these guys, your ex-cops?"

"Right. Sometimes I have to spend some time with them, you know? I do a deal and somebody gets pissed off, they lost their equity or their company's been taken out from under them. Or union guys who lost their jobs come skulking around my house. So I get security for a while, move into a hotel. Anyway, those ex-cops love to tell stories. Busting this crook, chasing that guy. Being a cop, they say, except for the shitty pay and the rules, best job in the world. Makes my life look more boring than it is."

Harv casually picked up the tube of vitamin E. "So? You want to be a cop?"

Connie Cook laughed and choked on a fry. "The fuck? Fuck, no. Harv, you're a funny fucking guy. I want to be a crook."

The vitamin E cream didn't work out well, even though Phil Harvey used it religiously. But fuelled by Harv's expertise and connections, and suitcases of the fat fuck's cash, Cornelius Cook's dark enterprises quickly became multi-faceted. He had water farms all over the state, partnered up with Vietnamese body smugglers who staffed the operations with slave labour smuggled down from Canada, who chopped the weed and baled it. He had the X business, he had the crank labs, he had a network of pan cookers throughout the projects where baby mammas stood over non-stick pans on coil burners, baking rocks of crack. It always surprised Harv that the black folk liked the fat Cornelius, but he figured it was because he was so pasty and translucent that he wasn't white at all but a whole other non-colour, a whole other species. It didn't hurt that everybody made out well off the Captain's operations.

But at root, Harv knew, it was the evil that emanated off the porky bastard that curled his toes. Harv himself was a hard man. He'd done hard things and he'd done hard Craddock time. He was getting old and had done almost a quarter of his life in custody. He'd done the hardest thing four times, leaving little trace of the activity, no trace of the victim except once, when a message had to be sent. But he still thought of himself as having a chip left of his soul.

Cornelius Cook, though, was evil because he didn't need to be. He didn't need to reach down into the netherworld for profit, didn't need to do what he did. He could have it by exercising his family's portfolio, by crushing adversaries with financial clout and then picking up the lucrative pieces, sentencing enemies to the poorhouse gulag. Connie had once bombed out a Stonetown bistro because of rude service when he could have bought the place and fired the staff.

People moved into Connie's orbit for a while then they were gone suddenly, without rhyme or reason, like shooting stars that burned themselves out and just vanished as if they'd never existed. Some of them were young women, Harv realized, young women who rotated through the clubs, vacant women who he'd brought around for the Captain's perusal. They came in gorgeous and witty and thought themselves lucky, and wound up hollow and stuttering and chewed and ultimately gone. Not Agatha though. She didn't come from the ranks of peelers. Agatha had been the test: Captain Cook had given Harv the address where she lived and said go get her for me. Take her on a crank holiday and when you come back make sure she needs us — needs me, anyway.

Agatha Burns droned. CD prices were supposed to come down after the technology was paid for. But they were higher than they were at the beginning. What was up with that? She could download music off the Internet to save money but the Internet, Connie had told her, was an evil plot by the government. Who knew what subliminal messages were hidden in there, like, flashing into your brain before your eyes even registered it? Hey, look, she said, there's a sequential licence number on that van. You think the guy asked for it or it was random? Random was weird. There was no ... well, random to it. Well, there was, she thought, in a random way, if Harv got her meaning.

She was deathly afraid, Harv suddenly realized. She'd figured it out. He made sure her seatbelt stayed fastened. The chatter was beyond crank patter. She probably hadn't been out of the apartment in months, waiting for pills to be dropped in the stairwell, waiting for the Captain to come by and pirate her ass, piping himself aboard.

At the hook north of Stateline he stayed on the Interstate, easing into the slow lane to catch the ramp off to the badlands while he thought. He'd done stupid things but he wasn't stupid. He'd acted without heart, but he had heart. The Captain was a manipulator, but that didn't matter: Harv had more money than he'd ever earned either legitimately or in the life. That was the name of the game: to make out, to collect your end. But the Captain didn't seem to care. The family money had been there for generations before he was born, the golden road was paved for him. All he had to do was follow his ancestor's footprints. It was impossible for the Captain to be so stupid he'd ever be broke. There was just too much money.

"You know," Agatha Burns said, "when you look at a tree like that tree over there, that there's actually more of the tree underground, roots and stuff, than we see. Harv, you ever think about that? What we see and what we don't see. I mean, sure, if we don't see it, it probably isn't actually real for us, but there's a lot more to the tree than the ... well, the tree. Weird, eh?"

One night, when Harv and the Captain got drunk and high, the real Cookie got loose. "You should've seen her when she was in high school," he'd said as they sat in their underwear in a hotel room overlooking Michigan, watching Agatha Burns go through jerky cheerleader moves, trying to please them, her eyes on the little baggie of crank on the coffee table. "Perfect. Absolute fucking perfection.

Perfect boobs. An ass that was on ball bearings. Legs up to here. She'd have her pals over and they'd go in the backyard of her house and do their routines. Fucking amazing, Harv. I watched from my house, the six of them, little skirts, pretending they didn't know their boyfriends were watching over the fence. All perfect." He called over the music. "Right, Ag? You and the team?"

She nodded, breathless, a plastic smile on her face, not missing a beat. "Yes, Connie. We were hot."

"Did you know I was watching? From my window, Ag?"

She nodded again. "Yes, Connie. It turned us on."

"Looks don't mean for shit, though, right, Ag?"

Her breath was short. "Right, Connie. I was superficial then, but I'm okay now."

"Take off the top, show Harv how they bounce." He'd turned to Harv. "Watch this. Elastic."

Harv had been uncomfortable. There was a sick aspect to the Captain's jowly, pinched face, a hatred he couldn't imagine, even on his own face when he had to do the hard things. He felt a stirring of feeling for her, for her open face and her fading beauty. "It's okay, Cookie. I seen boobs before."

"Yeah, but not like this. C'mon, Ag, give us the old one-two-three-four. Swing 'em."

The night had ground on. At one point Agatha Burns blew them both, but Harv had been too far gone to remember it afterwards, if it was good or not.

He did remember the Captain, twirling a little baggie of crank, had enticed her to lick away at the scar tissue on the side of Harv's face and suck at his destroyed fingers, tell him she loved him, his scars were beautiful.

Harv did remember that.

And he remembered walking into the bedroom of the suite at dawn, looking for his jacket, and she was almost invisible under the pounding blubber of the howling Captain, her face stuffed into a pillow, her screams muffled, the Captain looking up with blood running down his chin under his huge wreath of smiling jowls.

Phil Harvey checked the odometer and slowed, looking for the sideroad that would take him away from the feeder highway to one of the mom-and-pop labs scattered in the area. Beside him, Agatha Burns's knees were white and knocking. She was talking to the passenger window. The scarf had looped away and he glanced at her, could see she was still leaking blood from the punctures at the nape of her neck. She was essaying a soliloquy on alternative cultures, telling how she'd got an A-plus in high school for paralleling 1960s America with 1930s Berlin.

He found the sideroad and sped the Camaro absolutely straight for several miles, into the heart of the badlands, passing only scattered farms, a few shacks, and remote houses with yellow geometric windows lit in the distance. A cloud of Riders on noisy bikes flashed past him. In his rear-view he could see on their backs the smudged oval colours of the club. He slowed until they'd vanished, then turned onto a rough track, mindful of the washboards and dips, worrying for the undercarriage of the car.

In the middle of a speed revelation about the temperature at the core of the Earth, she turned to him. "Harv? Harv?"

"Nearly there, Ag. Relax."

"You know, I was beautiful, once. I was perfect. It wasn't my fault, how I was. Tell Connie, okay? It wasn't my fault."

"Just a little further." He didn't look at her. "Few minutes."

He felt sad that she knew. Unless someone had fucked you up wickedly, this wasn't the way to do it. If they were wicked rats you had to make them go hard. But if it was just housekeeping, you were jocular and a pal, lolling them off to sleep until you dropped them as though you flicked off a light switch. There was enough old pain in life without making new stuff.

Her knees were knocking audibly, a mile a minute. Her fingers twisted into one tight fist between the tops of her thighs. "Is it gonna hurt, Harv? Can you do it, fast, without hurting me?"

"Don't get paranoid, Ag. It's just the stuff making you think crazy."

He flashed his headlights three times, then once, eased off the rough track and stopped. A rangy woman in an oilskin with a shotgun under her arm appeared in front of the Camaro, squinting through the windshield. The woman was in her sixties, her dead hair balding back from the front. She flashed a half-a-smile of broken, gapped teeth. She had angry sores around her mouth. Behind her was the lab, a sagging pickup truck with a weathered, peeling camper mounted in the back, the windows cranked open.

From the corner of his eye he saw Agatha Burns's hands unlock from each other. Ghostly, one of her palms moved in the air between them. He glanced. Her knees had stopped jittering. She was looking directly at him. He felt his curtain of hair being gently moved back from his face, then the freezing of the palm of her flesh against his face, against his scars, stroking.

"I'm sorry, Harv. What he made me do, here —" her fingers traced the mass of ridges and angry boiled skin, "— that night at the hotel was the worst thing I ever did. To anybody. I'm sorry." She inhaled with a sob, then calmed down and composed herself. "I don't want to die without you knowing I'm ashamed."

Chapter 6

She recognized him from that morning at the elevator, standing with the red-faced mug. He sat hunched at the elbow of the bar of an Irish pub on the furthest possible edge of Stonetown, with a half of stout in front of him. As he'd told her on the phone, he wore a striped rugby shirt. The place was packed with groups and couples but he'd saved her a stool by draping a scuffed leather jacket over it. A widescreen showed a satellite soccer game no one was watching. The sound was off and the players seemed to be dancing to the fiddle music blaring from speakers.

People stared at her bleached head and chocolate skin as she moved through the crowd with her hands jammed in the pockets of a blue warm-up jacket with drawstrings and a hood. Under it she wore a dark blue sweatshirt with faded writing on it, shapeless blue jeans, and battered, dirty sneakers.

Ray Tate stood when she reached him and greeted her with a hug. His hands roamed the back of her waistband, up the middle of her back, and he held her close against him.

"Hey, long time," he said, smiling as though they were old friends. "You made it." His hands lingered at her hips and fluttered at her shoulders. "You're losing weight. You look great. You been working out or what?"

He took his jacket from the stool and she sat. The bartender came down the boards. Ray Tate looked at Djuna Brown and raised an eyebrow. She said gin and tonic. He nodded to the bartender. "And another half for me, Jimmy."

She saw he was younger than he looked with the grey hair on his collar and hanging off his face. Mid-forties, maybe. He looked glad to see her. In spite of having the head of a bum, his body was thin and solid and his eyes were clear. Except for skipping off her face to check out who came in after her, he seemed to sparkle. She was wary. She didn't like cops. She wished she'd called Gay-Glo and had someone come to monitor the meeting.

Jimmy put down the drinks and Ray Tate made a motion with his hand as though signing something. After the bartender went away he leaned in close and put his face by her ear as though romancing her. "Look, we're going to sit here and have one. We're gonna see who comes through the door for the next while, then we'll go up on the patio for another round, smoke some smokes, and talk, okay? If you want, you can pat me down. That's fair, because I'm going to have to pat you down again, for real. I want to talk to you. You can talk to me too, if you want. Or you can fuck off at any time. The drinks're on me. Right now, we're old pals on a date. Anything you want to talk about? Good movies? New bestsellers?"

In spite of his alley rat appearance, she could smell soap and shampoo off him. His breath was soft against her face, a mixture of toothpaste and stout. There were some fading blemishes on his neck that looked like the after-boil of insect pincers.

"What do you want?"

He shook his head. "Later. You reading the Harry Potter series? Good wizard action. Magic potions, flying stuff. My kid says she seen all the movies and the first one was the best. You think?" His eyes scanned the room behind her. "You got kids?"

She twisted her mouth at him and didn't say anything.

"Hey, there's test tubes and stuff. You don't want to miss out. How'd you feel about stem cell research? Now, there's an ethical issue. Science bumps up against morality. I've listened to Bush and the other guys, but myself, I haven't sorted out all the —"

"Look, let's just get this done, okay? I don't know why you set this up. I don't know who sent you, or why. I'm not comfortable. I don't give a fuck about stem cells. I don't give a fuck about Harry fucking Potter. I don't like being felt up in a bar and, mostly, I don't like racists."

He wasn't listening to her words. The sound of her voice was lilting, a bit of the Islands in there, perfect pronunciation. He could tell she was apprehensive but curious. "Okay," he said, shrugging into his jacket, "let's drain 'em and get 'er done. See where we're at."

They paused on the stairway to the rooftop patio and he gave her a more thorough pat-down. He ran his fingers around the base of her ruined bleached hair. There were loose valiums in her handcuff case and she wore her gun, a nifty little automatic, over her right hip. He offered to let her do him. She poked indifferently and he could tell she didn't know what she was doing or didn't care. The patio was vacant except for four smokers huddled at the far end against the cool night breezes. A waitress, hugging herself by a serving station, looked unhappy to see them arrive. Ray Tate ordered another G&T and half a dark.

Djuna Brown sat opposite him at the empty side of the patio. He saw her shiver and took his jacket off. Without consultation he draped it over her shoulders like it was the most natural thing in the world. She didn't know what to say so she gave him a simmering look. The umbrellas shimmered in the breezes. Above them the ambient light of the city sky was silvery. Traffic noises rose from the bum side of Stonetown. The waitress brought their drinks and left and the four smokers clattered down the steps.

He held his hand out. "I'm Ray Tate."

"The guy that's gonna spike me, right?" She looked at his hand out over the table and finally took it. "Or shoot me."

"I'm not going to talk about shooting people. I'm not going to talk about racism. You're not going to talk about beating cops with sticks. We're not going to talk about you being a dyke. I don't care about any of that, and you shouldn't either. We're going to talk about being partners."

"Bonus." She looked at his bland face. "Not much left, then, to talk about."

"Well," he said, "we could talk about fucking up the skipper."

She was interested but cautious. "And how'd we do that?"

"By doing our job." He looked at her raised eyebrow and studied her face. She was actually quite attractive under the white frizz. She had long catlike eyes, high cheekbones, and a pointed little chin. Her teeth were small and even. Stress and maybe hatred had worked into her face, giving it a mean repose, making her lips halfway to a twist. Her hand, when it had been in his, was small but strong and firm, and he knew someone had taught her how to shake hands. Her body, when he'd given her the pat-down, had some long muscle.

He got up and went around the table. She shrank back from his hand. "I just want my smokes." He dug in the jacket, found a pack of Marlboros and a lighter, and went back to his seat. He formally offered her one then lit them both.

She suddenly looked afraid. Politeness was antique to her. "I called Gay-Glo. Just so you know. People know I'm with you right now. If anything happens to me, it's documented."

"Gay-Glo." He shook his head. "Whatever. Relax. I'm going to talk for a while, then if you want to talk you can, okay?"

She stared at him, silent.

"Okay. We're both fucked. You're never going to be a working cop again, I'm never going to be a working cop again. Our lives as we know them are over. The skipper wants me to bury your ass. Probably, he's told you the same thing: bury my ass. I don't know. If I sink you, he says, I'm on my way back to the streets, riding around, doing the job. I don't know what, if he promised you anything, and I got to say I doubt it, I don't know what he promised you."

"Nothing. I don't talk to the fucker."

"Sure. It doesn't matter, anyway. As long as we're partners working in the office, there's no real problem. We can both be careful around each other. That's cool. But if we go outside and do stuff, well, there's a lot of things that can happen and the only two people who'll know what happened is the guy that did it and the guy that saw it. You want to think about that."

She stared at his friendly, expectant eyes. "You think that's why he partnered us? One of us is a rat, going to eat up the other?"

"Most people, they look at something and they say to themselves, what would I do in that situation? The skipper, being what he is, assumes he's normal, so he looks at what he'd do and expects anyone else to do the same normal thing. I'd rat, he figures, so they will too."

"So, he partnered us up because he thinks we're going to spike each other?"

"I guess. I said if I work close with you that when you step on your dick or whatever, I'll be there to tap two behind your ear, get you written out."

"But you won't, right?" Her lips went into full twist. "All this, all this could just be technique."

"Could be, I guess." He chain lit another cigarette. "Look, I don't know you. I know your story, or some of your story, anyway. I talked to a State guy I know about what happened and he said there were weird doings in Indian country. The guy I talked to is a good guy. He said you beat the face off your partner, but he said you did some good work up there. He said he's the first to say he doesn't know it all, but you were a good cop."

"For a black dyke."

"He mentioned that, I gotta admit." He drank some dark and looked at her. She had a smile, not a full smile, but an almost friendly twist to the edges of her lips. He could see chicks going for her, could see a meatheaded partner making a move after dark on a dirt road. He saw her shiver under his coat from the growing wind off Michigan. "But I don't think he gives a shit. Mostly he was curious why they put a black dyke up there in Indian country, what you call it? The Spout?"

"The Spout. Where they drop you in and pour you out."

"He said they must really fucking hate you when they do that. He said that tells him a lot."

"Why?"

"Well, he said it means your problem wasn't beating your partner. The problem was long before that, before you got there, that you fucked up someplace before, and they sent you up there because you were already fucked."

"Smart guy, your pal." She stared at him. "What did you mean, on the phone, when you asked if I ever wanted to be a cop?"

That was what he was waiting for. It was time. Up to now he'd just been bullshitting on the teeter-totter, finding equilibrium. He could chat all night. He'd learned from a Chicago Homicide detective that you solve more cases with the art of conversation than with a nightstick. There was a point in any interview when it was time to make a move. "Reveal who you are, then, when you get a feeling," the Chicago dick had said, "if you're an asshole that's the time to say something, reveal yourself as an honest asshole. If you're a good guy just doing a job, no personal offence, then you say something then. Don't think about it. You'll never be a detective, Ray, but you'll be a hell of a duty sergeant some day. You like cops and you probably, for all I know, like people, you dumb bastard. So, that's what you show. Find that point, where the balance between what you are and what your subject is, then ride it like a little kid standing in the middle of a teeter-totter."

Ray Tate said: "Did you?"

"I did. I wanted to be a cop. I am a cop." She was biting at her lip, trying to prevent herself from saying much of anything.

Her defences were her coat, not her skin. He saw that. He had an urge to put his hand on hers, on the table. But it wasn't a pure enough urge, and his

Homicide buddy had told him: "It's got to be total. When you make the human — the physical — connection, you have to be dead certain sure. You have to be able to separate the certainty from the impulse. If you fuck that up, you'll never unfuck it."

"Okay." Ray Tate put his elbows on the table and said her name for the first time. "Djuna, you can play the rest of this out anyway you want. We can drink another drink and talk about Harry fucking Potter, the little fag, or whatever. Tomorrow morning we're going to be doing stuff. I don't know what you're going to be doing, but I'm going to be making a case, with you or without you. If I'm flying solo, that's okay. It just means I have to keep an eye on my back with you around. I've been doing it for a long time, anyway. This," he waved his hand over the table, "this is just me laying out the land for you."

"What case are you going to make? There are no cases. It's fill time."

"I dunno. There's that guy on the board, Commander Coke."

"Captain Cook."

"Him. If he exists."

She stared at him for a few minutes. He felt he was being evaluated and took it, looking back with calm. She said: "He exists. Captain Cook is a master fucking bandit and an all round fuckhead."

"You've seen him? You're working him?"

"Working him, but I haven't seen him. But I got someone who has. She's seen him a lot and doesn't want to, much, anymore."

Chapter 7

Phil Harvey chewed slowly on a sinker, dipping it into his coffee, and watched the block through the window while the crazy Captain waited for service at the counter. There was a convention in town. He saw cars with Illinois plates, Minnesota plates, some Michigans, and some Ontario, Canada. Drones on their morning coffee break filled the Donut Hole and although there were seats at Harv's table, no one availed themselves of his company. Three office girls carrying blue, rolled up yoga mats stood nearby, raving about the flavour of the chai and sneaking glances at him. Phil Harvey knew he was a thing of the night, not of the morning. The oversized aviator sunglass and the curtain of hair didn't quite hide the scars and his long, black leather pimp coat was tucked around him as though he was suffering a perpetual winter. There was no hiding his twisted claw clutching the sinker. His facial burns glistened with the vitamin E cream he uselessly and constantly massaged into them.

Connie Cook carried his cup through the yoga girls and dropped heavily opposite Phil. He put a leather briefcase on the seat beside him. "You look like you didn't sleep. You up all night, Harv, wreaking havoc?" Connie Cook's rippled jowls were smooth with knowing kindness.

"Ah, you know, Connie. Running, running, running. Either chasing or fleeing. Spent half the night looking for Agatha but she wasn't around, so I fucked off to do something else. I guess she didn't want to become a cook after all."

"You didn't see her, eh?"

"Nope. Not a sign."

"Can't figure that," Connie Cook said, shaking his head. "She was hungry to move up, become a cooker." He had a sudden thought. "What about the chicklets?"

Harv gave him a frown. "Dunno about that, Connie. She didn't come down. I hung around then I went up and knocked. No answer. I wasn't about to go in there. I guess where she went the chicklets went. Unless she left them up there."

"Well, you're gonna have to go in there, now, Harv. Shut the thing down. Get the guy in the stairwell out of there, tell the money guy on the ground to stand by. Then you go clean out her apartment in case she left the chicklets or something dirty behind. We'll need a new place, maybe in Hauser North." Connie Cook pondered creases into his fat forehead. "What else? What else? Fuck, I think I've been ripped off. You really never saw her, eh?"

"I told you, Connie: no. I planned to take her and the chicklets up to the truck lab but she didn't show and she didn't show and I took off. You sure she understood? To wait for me?"

"It'll sort itself out. Anyway, Chinamen."

Harv nodded and finished his doughnut. "I got guys ready. Some real wreckers. You give me the place and the when and we'll go and put an end to their bullshit."

"Well, today, I think, at noon, not too late. You want to catch them sleeping. I got a thing I want to get for you first then you go. You go in there, you guys, and you lay waste. I mean it, Harv. Everybody that comes out of there that aren't our guys, they're walking funny. Take the pressing machines, any chicklets or powder they got, everything. There's going to be some money laying around, I'm sure. You guys split it up."

"You want to come?"

"No." Connie Cook reflected a moment. "Yeah, you know what? I do. Yeah, I'm gonna. I got to pick something up, though, something I was going to give you, but if I'm going I'll need it." He gave Harv a knowing look. "You think something happened to her? To Ag? Boy, I'd like to know the details of that horror story, sometime."

Harv sat back and disappeared himself into the folds of his leather coat. "What do I know? You were the last guy I know of to see her alive. And she was okay when you left her, right?"

"Absolutely."

"Well then, nothing for us to worry about."

Phil Harvey drove the Camaro close behind Connie Cook's Mercedes. They wound through the city, the Captain trying to lose him at stale lights. Harv could see the Captain on his phone, hands-free, head bobbing as he yelled at the windshield as though deranged. At one point the Mercedes went into a skid, bumped the curb, and straightened itself out on the roadway.

On the edge of east Chinatown the Captain slowed, lowered his window, and waved Harv up beside his driver's door. "Turn on the all news, Harv. Strange events up in the badlands." He laughed and sped away. Harv fiddled his way awkwardly to an AM station and heard a roundup of headlines. One of them was about a truck explosion and fire far northeast of the city. Smoking remains had been found; unknown gender, unknown cause of death.

The Mercedes went through east Chinatown and just over the city line it pulled into a metalwork shop. The Captain waved Harv to wait and held up his hand: five minutes. He disappeared inside in a swaggering waddle and came out two minutes later with a long thin item wrapped in a green garbage bag. He popped his trunk, put the package in, and slammed it.

He waved Harv over. "You hear? That truck fire, there, up north? What's that all about, I wonder."

"Fuck if I." Harv shrugged. "I got a rock solid alibi, anyway."

"Yeah? You do?"

"Yep, I was with you." Harv waited a beat. "Back me up or I'll kill you too."

The Captain laughed. "Nice one, Harv. Okay, I'll follow you. You get your thugs over to east Chinatown and we'll meet them there. They cool, these guys?"

"Princes, these guys are, Connie." He punched numbers into his cellphone.

They wended their way down through the city. In east Chinatown Harv pulled the Camaro onto a side street. Connie Cook parked on the opposite side of the street, ahead. He popped the trunk, took out the long package, and held it like a golf club, putting aimlessly.

A few minutes later a black Tundra pulled up further down the block and three beefy men got out. They all had pigtails, thick faces, and wore leather jackets. One carried a long sports bag. They bounced on their toes on the sidewalk as they looked around for Harvey.

Harv climbed out and greeted them with handshakes that changed into biker brotherhood hugs. He waved Connie Cook over. The pigtailed men looked at him curiously as he crossed the road, taking in his perfect suit, the puddle of jowls, the short painful steps.

"That the guy we're doing, Harv? He's one fat fuck."

Harv laughed. "No, that's the guy we're doing it for. We're doing a home renovation. He's okay. He's weird, but we're earning."

One of the men took a coupon from his jacket pocket. "Give him this. He signs up for a year, he gets a lifetime membership at my new gym."

"Wait," Harv said. "Hold on to that and if you want him to have it, after, well, you tell him he's a fat fuck when you give it to him. He likes it when people call him names."

The Captain came up beside them and Harv introduced him all around. The Captain seemed pleased at meeting some real badlands thugs.

The Chinese chemistry students lived in a tall, narrow rooming house sandwiched between a massage parlour and a beauty salon. There were half a dozen mailboxes studded beside the entry door and a Room for Rent sign in the window.

The gym owner looked the building over. "What's the plan, Harv? We know what floor they're on?"

"They got the whole first floor and the basement. First floor is a long hallway, all the rooms on the left. There's a kitchen at the back with stairs down. They cook in the basement."

Connie Cook smiled. "Good that you know that, Harv. I didn't know that."

Harv smiled back. "Ag told me."

The three pigtailed men pulled on leather lifting gloves. One zipped open the sports bag and handed around a sawn-off baseball bat, a hammer, and a lug wrench. Harv looked around at the passing traffic. He took off his leather coat, rolled it inside out, and handed it to Connie Cook.

The pigtailed gym owner asked Harv, "What's the

play? We wrecking the place or just doing the people in there?"

"We get them then we take the place apart. There's any dough, we split it. Powder, we split."

The gym owner huddled with his companions for a moment then they all trooped up the steps. The biggest of the wreckers examined the lock, then stepped back and bulled his shoulder into it. It gave easily and they ran down the hallway, whooping. A Chinese teenager wearing Snoopy undershorts came out of the kitchen with a steaming bowl in his hands. He went down under the stampede. A pigtailed man swung a hammer. A plump girl, naked, flashed out of a bedroom off to the side. The gym owner whacked her legs out as he passed.

A long-haired Asian wearing a suit and an untucked, white shirt popped out of a doorway. He saw Harv and said his name. Harv was on him with the guy with the lug wrench. Harv took the wrench and began bashing at the man's long hair. "I told you," he said, swinging. "I fucking told you, cocksucker." He stood and began stomping.

Connie Cook stayed in the doorway listening to the place being busted up. When the house was secure he told Harv to get everyone to the basement.

The pigtailed guys threw everyone down the steps. The basement was unfinished and had a strong chemical odour. A blackened stove sat in one corner and buckets, tubing, and bottles of chemicals were littered over a sagging chesterfield. There were cheap Dutch pill-pressing machines with different heads scattered among them. The windows were covered with taped on, ripped up green garbage bags.

There were five prisoners. One of them remained unconscious. The girl was crying and huddling herself off to the side, sobbing and examining her knees.

Harv didn't like the scene. The chemical smell made his scars ripple and sing, the crying girl reminded him of Agatha. He decided the thing should be over. That's the way it was done. They'd take the powder and the dough, bust everything in sight, and give everyone a farewell tune-up.

But Cornelius Cook stood at the bottom of the steps looking at his fracas with satisfaction. "Cold in here, Harv. Turn on the stove." He began stripping the green garbage bag from his package.

Chapter 8

When the skipper arrived at the Chem Squad to do his morning prowl he found Ray Tate behind a desk, most of his hair back in a ponytail. Right away the skipper noticed the Captain Cook chart had been untacked from the corkboard. There was a steaming cup of coffee at Ray Tate's elbow and across from it, on Djuna Brown's desk, were a bottle of water and a yogurt container with a plastic spoon sticking out of it.

"The fuck you doing, Ray? It's the crack of dawn. Where's the twat?"

Ray Tate glanced around and shook his head, then nodded at the skipper's glass office. The skipper led the way. They sat opposite each other.

"Okay, spill."

"I was thinking, last night. I'm not going to get her watching her sit at her desk filing paper, right? So, I figure we'll get a little project going, get her out where there's mistakes to be made, and trip her into a hole."

The skipper nodded. "And? What you come up with?"

"This Captain Cook guy. I figure that's the way. We start up a little project, start moving around where there's money and dope, see if she trips. It's perfect."

"If there is a Captain Cook."

"Well, even if there isn't, we get her out there in the land of the bad habits. We're never going to get her sitting here watching her head glow." He shrugged. "I don't know. You got a better plan? She can wait out all of us."

The skipper stared at the beaming eyes behind the grey beard. Taking down Captain Cook and the dyke and Ray Tate would be a hat trick. While the douche-bag was out splashing in shit, Tate would be right there beside her, getting a little on his shoes. A hat trick would get the skipper noticed down at the Swamp where all the goodies were being dealt out in the Big Chan's fan tan game. Not being noticed was worse than not sticking your head up, even if you were fucking things up. If you fucked up under the Chan regime you hung in there anyway, maybe be a hero in the next dynasty.

"Done. Very nice, Ray. We're gonna work out just fine. If you get her for me, what do you want?" He looked troubled. "A bump? To duty sergeant, when all this stuff passes? I got to be honest with you: I can try but I can't promise."

"Nothing, skip. The blue suit, the round hat, and the red lights over my head. You'll never fucking see me again."

"Okay. How you want to do it?"

"Soft. Just memo us both to set up on this Captain guy, give us some room and some time, and we'll have her zipped in a body bag in no time. Maybe get Captain Cook too, if he's real."

"I can't give you paper on this thing, Ray, what we're doing to take her down. If it gets to the fags at Gay-Glo we're all in the shit. I'll make verbals to the brass about what I've got you doing, but that's it. You okay with that?"

Ray Tate sipped his coffee and stood up. "Hey, skip, fuck, come on. If I can't trust another copper, who can I trust?"

They were meticulous in their notebooks. Time in and time out, the memo number when they received the skipper's memo to set up on Captain Cook, the serial numbers of their cellphones were written in each other's books, the assignment number of their rovers. They signed out a company car, noting who gave them the keys and at what time. They noted the mileage on the leased Intrepid and that she was driving and he was the shotgun.

The red Intrepid was a Federal lease with a radio hidden in the dash behind a false-front CD player, a red gumball on the dash, and a sign that thanked you for not smoking. Djuna Brown tossed the gumball on the floor and the non-smoking ticket out the window. She lit a cigarette, pulled out onto Huron Street, and headed for the Hauser South Projects. "What'd he say? We're working, right?"

"We be. I'm supposed to tempt you into malfeasance, make you fall in with evil company." He dropped the false front of the CD player and dialed in channels to the city divisions. He had dried paint crusted around his fingernails and worked at them with a penknife, glancing up every few seconds to read the street.

"But you won't, right?"

"Nope. Like I told the skipper, if you can't trust a copper, who can you trust?"

"What's with the paint, there, on your hands? You redecorating?"

"Yeah. Change of scene, change of pace."

She gave him a catlike grin. "Right. Purple. It's the new black."

"Tell me about this chick we're seeing. That knows this Cook guy."

"She said she works for a guy running some labs. I just started working on her, so when we get up there I'll go it alone, see how it shakes out. Anyway, it was one of those things. I was getting a prescription filled and the pharmacist caught her down behind the counter, jamming cold pill bottles into her pockets. I pinched her and while we were waiting for prisoner transport I give her a pat-down. She's got two of these little pills, double Cs on them. She freaks a little and she says she can give me somebody's stash if I let her go." She shrugged. "I waved off the pick-up cruiser and spoke to the pharmacist. He was cool, so I took her to a Seattle's for coffee."

Unwillingly, Ray Tate took a glance at her.

"Get your mind out of the gutter. We just had coffee and out of the blue I asked her about this Captain Cook guy whose pills she got. She just about shit. How you know about him, she said. She said she didn't know him and if she had said she did know him, she didn't really say it. See, she was flying low when she was boosting, forgot what she'd already told me. So I said, Look, you just told me you knew him, he was your pal. She said, I said that? I said, Yup. She said, Okay, so you know. Then she clammed about him but said if I wanted a pinch there was a guy bringing a bag of pills to an apartment building up in Hauser South that evening. So I kick her and went up there and there was a jittery guy with a bag going in the fire door. He comes out later with nothing. He goes to a ground floor patio and a guy sitting there with a big fucking pooch hands him some coin. My guy leaves and I take him out there, lose him in the projects. I go back to sit and bingo, another guy goes in. Same thing. White guy with a bag. A mutt. He's in and he's out. Sees the guy with the dog, gets some dough, and he's away. I'm going, whoa."

Ray Tate laughed and shook his head. "Holy fuck. I can't believe you just said all that. There's a guy and a bag and a guy with a dog and fucked if I know what all else you said."

She smiled. "I know. They had me at the capital listening to wiretaps before they kicked me down here. I picked up the rhythm." She made an Italian accent softened by Caribbean breezes. "Hey, you know that fuh-kin guy, hangs around with the guy with the red fuh-kin hair, you fuh-kin know, with the guy that's always fuh-kin moochin'? Well, go see that guy, not the redhead guy or the mooch, but the other fuck, the first fuck, you know?" She steered the Intrepid into an illegal left under the Interstate, ignoring a cloud of horns. "It's a wonder how those mutts get anything done, how they understand each other."

"So," Ray Tate was laughing, "this chick."

"Right. I'm back at the Hauser South building a couple days later and she comes creeping out the fire door. I bag her. She's really afraid, Ray, she pissed herself. Turns out the guy she works for won't let her go outside, keeps her in a stash house on the fifth floor. That's why she rolled so quick for me when I grabbed her up at the pharmacy. She doesn't mind going in the bucket for a few nights, waiting for a bail hearing, but if the guy she works for finds out she went out, well, not pretty, she said."

"You think she's up there, now?"

"Dunno. Anyways, we're talking and I see she's jittering, so I say, out of the blue, So where's this super lab you were talking about the other day, that punches out of the double Cs? Fuck, she said, I told you about that? He's gonna kill me. She started crying and shaking. Oh, God, he's gonna pack me to death."

"Pack?"

"She didn't want to talk about it. This is three days ago. I tell her that each day, right about now, she should come down to the fire door, we'll talk if I can make it, if she can make it. I missed the past couple of days, but I think now's the time."

Ray Tate was impressed. "So she copped to Captain Cook and she copped to a super lab." When she drove behind a grimy high-rise building he asked, "So, why'd you do it at all? We're both walking dead, anyway. You could bring in the Big Chan with his moon face glued to a Boy Scout's ass cheeks and it wouldn't make any difference."

"I told you, I'm a cop. I didn't need you to come along and rag me out." But she had a slightly wider feline curve to her lips. She expertly parked the Intrepid with a view to the fire door. "But the gin and tonics were nice."

A happy man, Ray Tate eased back his seat, electronically adjusted his side mirror, and listened to a litany of calls streaming over the city frequency.

The Big Chan's new dep called the skipper.

"Hey, Gordo, you awake over there? I catch you snoozing? You drop my body for me, yet?"

"Naw. But I got something going. I partnered Ray Tate up with that Statie dyke, turned 'em loose in the land of temptation. Just a matter of time now."

"The black dyke? You fucking partnered an armed Ray Tate up with a spook that beats her partners half to death? You're a diabolical man, Gordo. I better start watching my back over here. You're gonna have my job and I'll be out farting my whistle at parades." The dep laughed without mirth. "Anyway, there's a call over in east Chinatown you might be interested in. Mailman finds a door busted, smells something foul, and he goes in and finds a bunch of Chinese kids all beat to shit in the basement."

"I didn't know it was Chinese New Year."

"Huh. But there's a stove, buckets down there, stuff taped over the windows, and a strong chemical smell."

"Sounds like another lab."

"But here's the good part: you're looking for the interlocking Cs, right? On the pills? Well, you go down to St. Francis's Heart and you're gonna find those Cs all over the place. But mostly on the victims. Someone took looks like a branding iron to them."

"Ooops."

"These are guest students down from Canada via Hong Kong, Gordo. Brought in by Willy Wong, a friend of the mayor's, one of his donors. We can't be seen fucking around on this."

"I'm already on it."

"Well, be on it, but be on it better, okay? Let me tell the Big Chan something."

"Tell him we already have a task force targeting the double Cs. We're up and running, my guys are already out there working it."

"Bullshit. If I'm bullshitting him you can't be bullshitting me. You have to tell me, Gordo."

"No, dep. No shit. We've got a task force just set-up on the double Cs. The twat and the gunner are out there, riding around like they're a dozen."

The skipper hung up and voiced out to Ray Tate and Djuna Brown on the Federal radio. "Where you guys at, Ray?"

Ray Tate came back: "Sitting on a place, might be a lead to the Captain. What's up, skip?"

"Head down to St. Frankie's Heart. They got some Chinamen in the Emergency, been branded like fucking cowboys. Double Cs."

"Ten-four."

Gloria came into the office and waved at him. The skipper told Ray Tate to stand by.

"The Staties got a truck fire up in the badlands," she said. "One fatality."

"So?"

"It was a camper van, dead body inside," she said. She held her nose. "Strong smell of chems."

"Let the Staties handle it."

"Around the truck, when they put it out? Double C tablets all over the ground. They heard we were asking about them."

The skipper went on the air. "Okay. Ray, you guys do the hospital then get in here. We're having a task force meeting."

There was silence. Then Ray Tate said, "What task force?"

The skipper laughed bitterly. "You, you lucky fuck."

The Chinese kids weren't talking. Every time Ray Tate or Djuna Brown asked a question, the older of them, with interlocking Cs burned into his cheeks and forehead, murmured in Mandarin and the others clammed. The older guy spoke robotically to Ray Tate in flat

English: "Contact please my uncle Willard Wong." He sounded like he'd memorized his line.

"We should get ICE down here," Djuna Brown said, "see what kind of immigration status these guys got."

"If they're with Willy Wong, they're all papered up clean. Willy runs the Chinese Menu for the mayor."

Djuna Brown wheeled the girl with the casts on her legs down the hall to an empty examination room. The girl's face had been spared but her breasts and been badly burned. Djuna Brown held the girl's hand and made sympathetic *tsks*. "Oh, baby, what they did to you."

When she stroked the girl's hair, the girl began talking.

Ray Tate asked the Chinese mutts a litany of questions. The mutts were sullen and looked at the floor. Only the murmuring guy made any sound. "Contact please my uncle Willard Wong."

Djuna Brown wheeled the girl back into the room and told Ray Tate she got nothing.

"Fuck 'em," he said. "Mutts."

"Mutts be right," she said. She looked at them. "You fucking goofs."

They went out to the Intrepid, noted the time in their books, that Ray Tate was driving, and they headed to the satellite.

As she wrote in her book, Djuna Brown said: "Five white guys. They went into the place and just went ape."

"She talked?"

"Yep. Sisterhood is powerful. Anyway, three guys in leather jackets. They were the wreckers. One other guy had long, black hair and burns all over his face. The last guy, the one with the branding iron, was a big fat fuck in a suit. He was in charge. He had 'ghosty skin,' she said. He kept screaming, 'Tell it to Coco Chanel.' He laughed a lot, she said. He really liked her tits, gave them a lot of attention."

"The guy with the scars? That's probably the guy on the wall, in the Captain Cook chart. Three wreckers? Who knows? The fat guy. The fat guy, he could be our Captain Cook. Sounds like a boss, anyway."

They saw the skipper had big eyes. He sat in his office with a *Federale* detached from the Feds' Hazardous Unit who wore his jacket like a matador. The *Federale* was deputized so he got to carry a gun and he didn't mind shifting it every few minutes as he squirmed about in his chair. A third man wearing a buttoned three-piece suit leaned with his ass on the windowsill, his arms folded. Ray Tate recognized the be-suited man as one of the Big Chan's new dynasty of cunning deps.

The skipper saw them across the room and held his palm up and out. Ray Tate and Djuna Brown went to their desks and pawed through a stack of photos and reports. When the *Federale* and the dep left the skipper's office neither looked at them.

The skipper waved them in. "We've got to do everything right, Ray. This is real work and they're wanting continuation reports daily." He completely ignored Djuna Brown. "They wanted to take you guys off it, bring in their own tactical crew from Washington, but I stood 'em down. I got us a week, max. Can we do it in a week, Ray?"

Ray Tate put a mug shot and a surveillance photograph of Phil Harvey on the desk. "This is the mutt did the havoc in east Chinatown today. I'm pretty sure."

"The cowboy branding the herd?"

"Nope. This guy Harvey was just there, leading the charge. The guy with the branding iron is a big fat fuck that laughs a lot." He hooked his thumb out the door. "Brass and the Feds? For some guys got tuned up in east Chinatown?"

"The Staties had a fatal truck explosion sometime overnight. A lab on wheels went up in the badlands. One dead and a bunch of double Cs scattered around."

"Strange doings."

"The deal is: we're doing the guys that rustled the Chinamen, the Staties'll work the lab explosion. They figure we'll meet someplace in the middle. So, bring me up to speed. What were you guys on, when I called?"

"Djuna's play." Ray Tate looked at her and waited. This was partner territory and he kept to the rules.

She didn't look at the skip. Her voice was desultory and resentful, unlike her upbeat lilt in the car. "There's a girl I've been working, guy keeps her in a stash house up in the north end. Mutts that loot pharmacies here and over the state line, bring their swag in, get paid off. The chick copped to two things: one is she works for Captain Cook. Other is that there's a super lab around. We went up there to her pad and before we could visit you called us down to the hospital, then over here."

"Super lab. What's up with that, Ray?"

Ray Tate looked at Djuna Brown and waited.

"We didn't get into it," she muttered. "I hadda let her go so she wouldn't be missed. We arranged a series of meets, but she hasn't showed up yet."

"You get her name? You run her?"

"I ran the name she had on the library card in her purse. Ginny Wallace. Not on file. Once I called her Ginny and she looked at me, like, who? Then she said, oh yeah, that's me, right. Duh."

"But she said super lab?" The skipper looked at Ray Tate. "You know about this? Before?"

"Hey, skip, we were working it. You told us to get out and work and we did. You thought, what? We'd come back with nothing? C'mon, keep some faith."

Djuna Brown said, "I said super lab to her. I was just fucking with her. She went for it and said this Captain guy's got a super lab on the go someplace."

"She tell you about this guy, the Captain?" The skipper didn't like talking to Djuna Brown; his nose wrinkled as if he could smell the bleach in her hair. "Anything?"

"Nope. She was throwing stuff my way to steer me off, let me get her free. She gave up a pill drop, she copped to the super lab. She's shitless of him, I can tell you that. He's gonna pack me to death, she said."

The skipper mulled. He looked at the photos on

his desk. "What have we got on the Phantom of the Opera here?"

Ray Tate had gone through intell reports and leaned forward. "Phil Harvey. Whacko. Cooker, seems like. Looks like he had a pot of stinky red soup bubble up on his face. Either that, or last Halloween he was the dunce bobbing for onion rings. One of the Chinese victims today said the guy that led the guys laying waste in the house looked like this."

"Ideally, we take the super lab and the Captain, solve the fatal fire along the way. Leave the Staties with their dicks in their hands." The skipper didn't know where to go next. "Ugly fuck."

Ray Tate waited then said, "So, I guess you want us to go back up there, sit on the chick's place and scoop her up?"

"Exactly."

"Take Harvey away if he rolls up? In case he takes us to the Captain?"

"You read my mind, Ray."

"We getting more bodies? We got deps and Feds around and who knows what all else. This thing could grow pretty fast."

The skipper chewed on his lips. "Let me see. You think we can take down this lab. The super lab? Get the guy behind it? Ray?"

"Well, the way to find out is we get out of here and out there. Start grabbing folks up, lay some torture on them." He shrugged. "Basic police work."

"Okay, okay. Go. Keep me in the loop. Continuations at the end of shift."

Tate stood up.

"Stay a sec, Ray. Some personnel stuff we got to go over."

When Djuna Brown was out of the room he shut the door. "Nice, pretty good, that. I almost thought you guys were real partners for a minute. If this thing begins to go on its own, we'll shove her over the side and bring in someone new for you, someone reliable."

"Naw, skip. Leave her in. She's got the only lead so far. She's shaky, anyway." He made a smirk. "I think she's gonna drop before this thing is over."

"No shit?"

"Well, it's just the first day but I have to tell you: she's on the edge."

"Beautiful, beautiful. If we drop her and get the lab, and get this Captain Cook guy, I think, Ray, with this interest from the Swamp, you just might get your own kingdom of cops to terrorize. No promises but I'll go the distance for you."

"Can't ask for more than that, skip."

Djuna Brown worked the phones, filling pages of a legal pad with notes. Ray Tate sat across from her at his desk and watched her. Her fingernails were bitten back to the quick and she dug them into her bleached head, scratching. He'd done nothing except let her drive him around and keep the branded Chinamen busy while she cleaned out the girl in the wheelchair. She looked up and caught him looking. She was using a soft voice with a guy in Records, was distracted, and she had a beautiful smile until she looked over his shoulder towards the skipper's office. Then her face changed, closed, and she looked down.

Chapter 9

The basement smelled of fresh burning flesh and old chemicals, and Phil Harvey had wanted to punch out the covered windows to get away from the smell of seared meat that wasn't so different from his own pork when it sizzled. The stove was rocking, the electric burners glowing red in the corner. The room was sweltering. Cornelius Cook sweated.

The wreckers had found wads of money stashed throughout the first floor of the rooming house. Cornelius Cook told them to take it. The men had been whooping plunderers earning a square day's pay until the Captain heated up the branding iron on the red coils and went to work on the Chinamen and the girl. One, the gym owner, had turned away and stared at Phil Harvey when the Captain had taken the double C brand to the girl's breasts.

Phil Harvey said nothing when the Captain told

him to round up the bottles of chicklets. He kept his teeth pressed together against the taste of the air. The Captain took baggies of double C tablets, meticulously ground them up, and washed the powder down the sink. Satisfied, he'd then gone to the stove, muttering. The double C branding iron was red. He spit saliva on the Cs and smiled when it danced off, was steam before it could hit the floor. He pretended to putt.

"We're outta here, Harv," the gym owner said, taking Harvey aside. "You need something else, just call. But this guy? No." He couldn't take his eyes off the Captain who, with a slow, fat dance, made his way to the Chinese guys and the girl. When the brand hit the girl's breast and she screamed the gym owner had looked at Harv for a few seconds, absolutely neutral, which to Harv was the most diminishing of raw looks. The three men clattered up the stairs and didn't look back.

Harv went out and sat on the porch, wrapped in his black sunglasses and leather coat. The chicklets were in garbage bags beside him on the top step. For a long time faint screams came from the leaks around the cellar windows. Once, Harv thought he heard laughing and loud conversation.

Harv had found his limit. When Captain Cook had manipulated him into taking Agatha for a ride to the badlands he'd felt his first spark of change. He had somewhere to go now. There was a possibility of change, of a different life. He'd already made a couple of moves in anticipation, but this, in the basement, was an afterburner that torqued him. On every level this, what was going on in the basement, was wrong.

Phil Harvey had once had to take a hammer and begin breaking a guy's bones from the toes up, but that was to find a stash. Once he had the location he stopped swinging the hammer, even bundling the guy into a car and dumping him a block from St. Francis Heart. That was the game. Even when you had to take someone out, you just did it as a piece of business. Spending an hour terrorizing and tuning a guy who was going to be dead before the day was out didn't make sense in any way to a normal person.

He knew to the nickel how much he had stashed. He knew how much money he had out on the street with degenerate gamblers and inept small business-men who tried to keep bistros and boutiques afloat in swanky Stonetown. He had almost enough money and he had the vaguest of dreams, of direction. He'd planned to spend another year, max, with the Captain, then strike out. But the keening thin noises from the basement window got him thinking that a year was a long time.

It was that first step that eluded him, he thought, but a shower wouldn't hurt.

At Agatha Burns's apartment building Phil Harvey scouted out the area and spotted the red Intrepid right away. A beatnik looking guy and a black woman with a wild frizz of blond hair that was almost white. He parked the Camaro with a view and waited for the woman's head to disappear and drop down to the man's lap. The man would give her money and she'd exit the car and totter away, her job done, instantly looking into passing vehicles. But she didn't. And she was behind the wheel. No dealer plate. Cops.

Harv laid back and waited for them to leave. He looked around for other cops.

The Captain had been sweating when he'd come out of the rooming house with his suit coat neatly over his arm. There were moons of wet under his armpits and he carried the branding iron on his shoulder like an ax.

"Where's the guys?"

Harv said they'd taken off, they had other work.

"Cool. I guess they made out okay? They found some money around, right? Good guys, those guys. Didn't say much but, wow, they could do the job. Place looks like a train wreck." Cornelius Cook's face was red and petulant. His translucent hair was damp and his pale flesh was filled with a blush. "Fuck, Harv, I don't know how you guys do this shit, day after day. Me, I couldn't. Once a week, maybe, but this? Too much weirdness." He rubbed his crotch and babbled. "Fuck, I'm hard. I'd really like to go back down there and pack the chick. You sure you don't know where Ag is? I could sure use her ass right now."

"She run off on us, Cookie. Joined the circus."

"I guess. Anyway, you'll take care of the stuff at her place? Shut it down, clean it out?"

"I'll head over now."

The cops in the Intrepid seemed to laugh a lot. When a white girl in tight skirt and leather jacket stumbled from the fire door, the black woman behind the wheel made is if to get out, opening her door before sitting back and easing it shut. The girl in the skirt lit a joint beside the door and leaned back, her face to the sun. The same black player who'd loaded the Camaro hustled slowly up beside her and circled her, a beer bottle in his hand. The two shared a joint and the man ran his hand up the woman's ass. She shoved him away and scooted back into the building.

Shut down, the black guy looked around to see who'd witnessed his humiliation and he spotted the black Camaro throbbing off the corner of the building.

"Yo, you, Yo fuck." He grabbed his crotch with his free hand and drained the beer with the other. Winding up, he pitched the bottle at the Camaro. It landed short, but the two cops in the Intrepid looked to see where it went. The beatnik in the passenger seat stared at Harv and he peeled out of there.

Chapter 10

Djuna Brown sat the car off the fire door of Agatha Burns's building. "She's pretty fucked up, old Ginny Wallace or whatever her name is, you can't miss her. Stringy thing, dresses like a slut in a music video. She comes out the door I'll take her, chat her up a little, and get her in here. We make her sit here in plain sight until she talks and invites us in, she won't want to get spotted by the guy. No warrant. We're guests."

Ray Tate didn't care. It was cop work. He didn't care what the actual work was, it was cop work, even if he had to look like some degenerate with his hair tickling his ears. He had a gun on his ankle, a badge in his pocket, and a partner beside him. The sweet voices of the dispatchers took him back to long, slow nights cruising the streets. Once his daughter, in a rare pique of curiosity, had asked him what his favourite recent memory was and he'd said sitting on the hood of his cruiser the previous night, out on the edge of the river, watching two bums hugging after fighting over a bottle of hooch. Two guys who loved each other, once they got the tough stuff out of the way. They'd cried and consoled each other when the bottle shattered, each of them taking fault: "I'm sorry buddy." "No, buddy, I'm sorry."

"People, Ax," he said. "People will surprise you if you let them. You know what I do, right? I control people."

"Granddad calls them dogs."

"Mutts. Yeah, I do, too. Sometimes. But that's just bad habits you let yourself pick up, make you feel like you're better than them." He'd had a moment of insight. "The danger is that you don't be who you are or who you're meant to be. Instead, you become part of the people around you, separate from everybody else. For better or worse."

They'd been sitting on the freshly cut steps of his new deck. He let her sip at one of the beers he'd brought over from Canada. He inhaled the hot new wood smell of the deck.

With daring curiosity, she asked, "Do you ever worry about shooting someone?"

Djuna Brown started to get out of the car. "That might be her."

Ray Tate saw a scrawny girl slip out the fire door.

"Nope." Djuna Brown sat back. "Wrong one."

"She's got admirers though. Look at this dude. Mr. Smooth."

They watched a tall, thin man glide in on the girl, weaving with a beer in his hand. The pair shared a joint. The man put a move on the girl and she shut him down, sliding back through the fire door. The man looked around, his mouth moving, and looked out past the Intrepid. He grabbed his crotch, wound up, and heaved the bottle.

Ray Tate followed the arc of the bottle and beyond it saw Phil Harvey jackrabbiting a black Camaro backwards out of the parking lot, sliding into the street in a Chicago bootleg. He went on the air and voiced out for Chem Squad workers. There was no response. He went over again and the radio burst static.

"Yeah, Chem Six." The voice yawned. "Whaddayawant? Whofuckzat, anyway?"

"Chem Four. Tate and Brown. What's your Twenty?"

"Me? What do you want to know that for? Tate? Ray Tate?"

"I be. I got a black Camaro spinning out of the Hauser projects. Male, white, long hair, burned-up face. He's alone in the vehicle. You nearby?"

"Naw, no. Fuck, Ray Tate. This is Wally Brodski. I knew your father-in-law. How's he doing?"

"Look, Wally, where you at?"

"Uh, south of you."

"Can you haul over to River Street, count the traffic in case he comes through?"

"Sure. I guess. I dunno, I got to get gas."

The skipper came over from the base station. "Brodski, this is Chem One. Get the fuck over there."

"Fuck." Ray Tate rolled his eyes at Djuna Brown. "Here we go."

Brodski came back instantly. "Hey, whoa." There was a pause. "This is Chem Six, I'm booking out, medical. My ulcer's flaring. I'll be off at Mercy, getting checked out."

The skipper called out for him several times but there was no answer. "Ray, you're on your own."

"It was Phil Harvey. He's gone, skip. We're going to take the apartment."

"You got no warrant. Don't go in there."

"Djuna's concerned for Ginny Wallace's well-being." He put the microphone back behind the false CD player.

The black guy watched them approach for a moment then began sliding away from the fire door. Djuna Brown put her right hand out, patting the air. "Hey, hold up, brother, c'mon. I don't shoot too good, but my partner, well, he's a deadeye. Just hold up a sec."

Ray Tate saw some little cellophane wraps on the ground near the black guy's feet. "Hey, you drop something? Those yours?"

"Those what? What those?" The man seemed entranced by Djuna Brown's hair. "Hey, cool 'do, sister. That's good. I like that."

Ray Tate stood a few feet away. Djuna Brown moved up close beside the guy. She was tiny next to him. Ray Tate watched his hands.

"What's that about?" she asked him. "With the

flying bottle? You know him, that guy?"

"What guy?"

"Scarface there, in the Camaro." She waited. "You want a job? Cleaning up? There's these baggies on the ground, there. We can call a city crew to sweep them up, or you can be a citizen, do your part and keep the 'hood clean of litter."

"The guy? Yeah, in the Camaro, I seen him. Riddle me: how's he get prime stuff like that, all that devil marks burned up on his face?"

"He had a girl in the car?"

"No, not now. The last night. He had a girl and he had a piece. Big silver thing with cuts down the barrel. Was gonna shoot me but I stood him down, ran his old hippy ass right off my place. White, fucked-up-face motherfucker."

"He took a girl out of here? What she look like? White girl?"

The lock on the fire door was jammed with a bent Coca Cola can with scorch marks on it. They crept up the stairs to the fourth floor. Far up, a cellphone chirped and a man's voice rumbled softly. Ray Tate craned his neck to look up the stairwell and saw a bushy head ducking over to look down at him, what looked like a piece of pipe in one hand, the cell in the other.

He dodged back and took his gun from his ankle. He whispered: "Mutt. I think with a gun, a scattergun. Up at about, oh, twelve."

Djuna Brown took her pistol from the clamshell on her waist. She didn't know where to point it and clutched it like she'd never held it before. To calm her down, Ray Tate put his into the pocket of his leather jacket. He ducked his head out again but saw nothing. Below them a door creaked open and a dog growled.

"Hey, you fuckers." A man's voice echoed up the stairwell. "You don't want to be here. Get the fuck down here or I'm sending the dog up."

Ray Tate took his gun out. "We're the cops. You send that fucking pooch up here, you'll be wearing its ass for a hat."

"Fuck that. I saw you guys go in. You're not cops." The dog started barking. "Paulie, Paulie, they're a couple of goofs. Spook chick and a fucked-up looking white dude. You work down, we'll work up."

The man, Paulie, called down, his voice booming in echo. "Hey, they might be real cops. Harv just called, said they're all over out there. In a red car."

"Oh, fuck." The man below was quiet for a few seconds. "Okay, you got a badge, right? Hold it out over the edge so I can see it."

Ray Tate took out his folder and held it out at arm's length.

The man at the top of the stairwell yelled, "Cops. Scram."

Downstairs the door slammed. At the top of the stairwell another door slammed. The well was silent.

Djuna Brown was pale. "Fuck, Ray. Fuck." She still had her gun in her hand.

"We're okay. They fucked off. Let's not get tense. We're okay, Djun'. Put it away."

She giggled. "Fucker's going to wear the dog's ass for a hat."

The apartment door had bar marks chipped around the edges. Ray Tate leaned heavily on the door and slid a plastic Bank of America card between the frame and the lock and rattled it open. Inside, the room had a thick, chemical smell. There were empty cold-tablet bottles scattered around, an unmade bed, and brown streaks and bloodstains on the sheets. Dirty clothes were stacked in the corners of the room and in the refrigerator freezer were stacks of chocolate bars. Bent and broken syringes were in the trash and Djuna Brown, prowling, found some double C tablets in a dresser.

"This is the place. Double Chucks."

"Check this." Ray Tate used the end of a pencil to unfold a square of white paper fastened to the fridge door with a cockroach magnet. "To who it may concern, My name is Agatha Burns. I was beautiful. If I don't come back soon ask Connie where he told Phil Harvey to take me to. I think Connie wants me to die. Please call my mother ..." The rest was a jerky scrawl.

Djuna Brown leaned in and looked at the note. "Who the fuck's Agatha Burns?"

Ray Tate stepped back. "Djun', put your hands in your pockets. Walk out the way we came in. Don't touch the door, don't touch nothing."

In the hallway he called the skipper on the cellphone while Djuna Brown wrote into her notebook every item she remembered touching in the apartment.

* * *

Connie Cook lay under his wife and thought about the breasts of the Chinese girl in the basement in east Chinatown. He didn't wonder what his wife was thinking about. She probably wanted something expensive and was riding her way to it. Her mouth had a barbed wire smile and a couple of times he caught her looking out the window overlooking the lake, at a house identical to the Cook house but with larger grounds. The people living over there had suffered some grief a year or so earlier and were finally selling to a developer. The orange bulldozers were lined up down the block and there was a bigger house going in and she was bugging him about buying up a couple of lots further along the street so she could create a pink ice cream house of her own.

Connie Cook didn't pack his wife. They had a relationship that extended to cars and furs and vacations and the ballet and the opera, and occasionally this. But packing was out of the question. Packing was of his other world, a free world with no boundaries or restraints. Besides, Connie Cook loved his wife in a strange way. He'd been gross all his life, as had his father and uncles, and all of them found women who saw beyond the blubber and excess. There was something inside him that Cora recognized, and in his late evenings, when he was alone and she was out, he felt grateful.

The Chinese girl, crouched on the floor, staring at the approaching glow of the branding iron. Now there was an image to make him squirt. Her eyes became impossibly large in disbelief that this could be happening to her. Connie Cookie had imagined she'd been staring not at the branding iron but at his hard dick. Her mouth became round and she shrank back from the sheer horror of being viciously penetrated by that purple piece of oak.

To prolong things, he let his mind wander. Harv had changed. He didn't have the funster thug about him, like he did back at the beginning when he went out and snaffled up the desirable Agatha Burns, brought her up to Indian country so the Captain could lay a bad habit on her. Agatha had clearly been looking for some edge to her life and she took to the crank and Connie Cook's loving attentions quickly. Harv had been into the game then, but lately he seemed to be a little off. The Captain thought about Harv taking Aggie for a drive in the country. Maybe something happened up there, something so horrific it rattled Harv's sense of life's direction. Whatever, that must have been a scary movie, a betrayed Harv and a duplicitous Aggie. Harv wasn't into packing. His years in the joint had turned him off doing it. But there were a lot of games he could've played with Aggie that made that old camper van rock, Harv in his big leather bat coat and insect glasses, before the place turned into a fireball.

The super lab, she'd said. Maybe, he thought, I sent Aggie and Harv off on a picnic just in time.

He'd love to hear the story of that horror, someday. But one participant wasn't talking and the other was playing coy.

Under his trim wife, her hands vanished in the thick soft flesh of his shoulders and her bored mind computing real estate, Connie Cook bucked.

Connie the colonizer, diluting the yellow horde.

Chapter 11

The skipper told Ray Tate to cool his jets a sec, he wasn't about to roll out a murder team because some chick had left some notes stuck to some fridge in some housing project. "We'll just lay back a minute here, Ray. We're riding a pretty rich horse with this task force. We call in the Homicide hammers and next thing you know they pull in the Intelligence guys and the narcos and who else knows what?"

"We come in here, skip, after a guy outside tells us he saw the chick get into a car with Phil Harvey. He saw 'em drive off. He says she's shitless. He doesn't see her again. He says Harvey's got a piece. We go into her crib and there's a note that she's going to be whacked by Phil Harvey. Somebody should come secure this place at least, just in case."

"Yeah, I see that. Let me call the dep, see how he wants to do it. You guys stay there until I get back to you. Any stuff in there? Any seizure for us?"

"Cleaned out. A couple of double Cs but just spillage."

"So I can say we're on the right track, right? This is part of our mandate?"

"No question." Ray Tate watched Djuna Brown close her notebook and look at him with a raised eyebrow. He shrugged. "One of us'll stay on the door, skip. The other's going to get the witness, take a statement from him."

"What project you in?"

"Hauser South."

"This witness, I guess, then, he's a black guy?"

"Yep."

The skipper was silent a moment. "Okay, I'll put out a silent hit on Harvey's car. You send the douchebag to scoop up the witness. Keep him on ice until I get some more bodies out there then take his statement. You stay by the door, Ray, okay? Just in case."

Ray Tate clicked off. "He wants one of us on the door, one of us to go get the witness."

"That's be me, right?"

"He thinks I might get twitchy. You want to wait until some troops get here, take someone with you?"

"Naw. No, Ray, I'll sweet talk him." She made a weak smile. "He'll talk, or he'll wear his ass for a hat."

He laughed and watched her silhouette walk down the long hallway to the fire door. Her slippers whispered on the cheap tile floor. He hadn't spent much time with dykes but he got the feeling she knew he was watching her sway.

* * *

The Big Chan's new dep tasted fruit salad. Another scoop on his shoulder boards would look good. He'd be in line — if he was careful and did it all right — for the big oak desk. He could sit and study the dents made in the surface by the Chinaman's lumpy skull. He could count the dents and send minions out to wreak all kinds of havoc in the squads and stations. There were fuckers who needed fucking and he was just the fucker to fuck them.

"Gordie, Gordie, Gordie. That pouty-faced motherfuck at City Hall is all over us. The Chinese Menu is ragging him. Those kids, fried up in Chinatown, they were Willy Wong's. It's all about chemicals, so gimme something, anything. The Chan wants this speeder, Captain Corn, behind the pipes."

"Captain Cook. His name's Captain Cook."

The dep began yelling into the telephone. "Captain Corn, Colonel Klink, Corporal Cornhole, or Commander Fucking Cocksucker, I don't give a fuck. Where we at? Am I going to have to send someone down there, take over the fucking thing?"

"Okay, okay, yeah, we're on it. We found a stash house, we ID'd one of the Captain's goons. We're doing interviews at the stash, we got a silent hit out on the goon and his car. We got a missing person, maybe, probably a witness we can turn around. We're looking for the super lab."

"Super lab? What the fuck?"

"Those double C pills, like the ones in east Chinatown and the ones at the lab fire, we have intell they come from a super lab this Captain guy's running. Churning out, like a million a day or some fucking bullshit."

There was a pause on the line. "Okay, Gordie. I'm all stupid, okay? First, who found the stash house? Where is it?"

"The Statie dyke and the gunner. I had an idea and I sent them out to the projects and they tracked it like I told them to. Like I thought, it was in the Hauser projects. There was only a couple of pills around, but they had double Chucks pressed in them."

"Right, okay. The goon, this henchman of Captain whatever. Who be he?"

"Phil Harvey. Speed cooker. The Captain's number one henchman. We think he was the guy at the branding out east Chinatown. When I sent the guys up to the Hauser they spotted him lurking around. He got free, but they found a witness who saw him with the girl last night."

"Whoa. Hold it. What girl?"

"The missing witness. Agatha Burnett or Barnett or something. She lived in the stash house, left a note saying if she didn't come back, Phil Harvey had offed her."

"Ah fuck. We got maybe a homicide, here?"

"Dunno. I told the guys to debrief the witness, seal off the apartment. And now I need someone to go in there and take some evidence away, if there is any."

Big Chan's new dep laughed. "And you don't want the hammers from the Homicide Squad involved, right?"

"We lose control of this thing, we get nothing, dep. The pills are real. The Captain's real. Phil Harvey's real. But a dead body? Based on a note? I don't know. You want to take this down to the guy next door that runs the Homicide Squad, we're going to lose it."

"Yeah, yeah. Okay. Good thinking." The dep was silent on the line for a few moments. "Yeah, I get it. Okay. Now, the witness, this missing broad. If there's a strong chance she's in the ground we gotta slide this under the door down the hall."

"Slight chance. Real slight. I think Ray Tate's over-reacting."

"Anything, ah, on that front?"

"Not yet. Tate says he's gonna be able to put the hat on the dyke. Then we'll put the hat on him."

"What did you promise him, if he spikes her down?"

"I hinted at maybe duty sergeant with his own meat puppets to worship him."

"A duty? Right, Gordo," the dep laughed. "Fat fucking chance."

Djuna Brown contacted the Statie headquarters and was told that the coroner said the smoking remains in the burned-out truck lab up north appeared to be that of a woman. DNA was going to be harvested from the bone marrow but it would take a while, then they'd do some comparisons, if they found anything to compare it to. The Statie major-crime investigator said there were tire tracks near the scene from a Firestone set, the wide kind of rubber GM slapped on several performance cars, including Camaros. Djuna Brown tapped out a memo suggesting the remains might be the missing Agatha Burns and the tires maybe indicated the Camaro driven by Phil Harvey. She printed it, gave Ray Tate a copy, and said he could deliver it to the skipper. She'd had her life's limit of Irish dickhead bullshit.

In the glass office, Ray Tate handed the skipper the memo. "We should get the hammers in on this, skipper. This is going to be her, I know it."

"No, no. Ray, slow down. If it's a homicide then it ain't our homicide. The case lies where the body lies. If that's her up in the burned truck then it's a Statie case. So fuck it for now. We'll wait for the DNA. The dep's on it, he's coordinating with the homicide guys and they're working with the Staties, they're on standby. They want something more substantial. The stuff from the apartment, maybe that'll give them something. Right now, we just concentrate on this super lab and the guys running it, okay? The Chinese Menu is leaning on the mayor and the mayor's leaning on us. You guys getting anywhere?"

"We got an address for Phil Harvey. We're going to set up on it later. You okaying the overtime?"

"Sure. For now just note it in your book. I'll try to get you some guys, you give me the location."

"Okay. Send me the memo, skip, okay? You and me've got to protect our asses until we take her out. She's in with the Gay-Glo and when we put her down

they're going be grabbing up paperwork for her law-
suit. We want to be covered."

"Good thinking, Ray."

The skipper was hovering, bugging, questioning.
Ray Tate and Djuna Brown put up with it for a half
hour, then grabbed two rovers from the charger, their
files and jackets, and headed out while he was on the
phone. They took the Intrepid for a spin.

"Interesting things happen when you're around,
Ray. This is turning into, like, work." She turned out
of the driveway and headed north on Huron Street.
"You think we can grab this super lab, put the chains
on Captain Cook?"

"Connie Cook, maybe Conrad Cook, I think.
Maybe Connie the Cooker. She put it in the note on
the fridge. Connie wants to kill me. At least we know
he exists, right?" He saw the entrance to the cemetery
up ahead. "Turn in here, this place is quiet. We can get
some work done."

She shook her head. "No way. You heard of the
ju-ju man? Spirits. Mojo. I'll wind up with steel teeth
and your nuts'll shrivel to raisins. Pass." She had a
wide cat grin on her face but he saw something of hesi-
tation in her eyes.

The rover squawked and Ray Tate grabbed it up.

Gloria, the receptionist, came over. "Skipper says
there's a silent hit on the Camaro you're looking for.
The Staties stopped it for lane change on Interstate

northbound, south of Stateline, where it swings west
to the badlands. Statie guy said it was a white male,
long hair over his face, burns, long leather coat. Solo.
An hour ago."

The Statie doing the traffic stop wouldn't know
about the silent hit. He'd have made a stop, run the
driver and plate, laid down his ticket, and taken off,
none the wiser. The hit would pop up almost instantly
on the main computer and the Chemical Squad notified.

Ray Tate asked Gloria to contact the Staties and
have other highway cruisers look out for the Camaro.
"Take it off that silent hit shit. We have intell he's got
a gun in the car, the guy doing the stop has to know
that. If they see him, grab him for something, call us.
They oughta take the Camaro for ident, especially the
tires. They should seize the tires off it." He clicked
off. "Phil Harvey's running around in the woods. We
can set up on him later." He gave her directions to his
apartment.

"Your place? What the fuck's that about? I'm not
going there, fuck that."

"Okay, Djun', you pick a place. But my place is
okay, unless you go all hetero on me."

She shook her head. "You wish." But she was
smiling. "You just wish them wishes, buddy."

The files were scant and while Ray Tate mixed gin and
waters Djuna Brown laid them out over the rickety
kitchen table that sat in the living room. Feeling home

proud for some reason, Ray Tate folded paper towels to use as coasters.

Her nose wrinkled. "Gin and taps? That's it? Not even fizzy water? No lime?"

"The drink of the people," he said. "Gin and taps. Lake water and juniper. The beverage of nature."

She sipped at her drink. "Jeez, I thought I lived like a rat. But you live like a barricaded suspect, Ray." She looked around, sniffing loudly. "Paint. I thought you said you were painting the place? Why's it smell like paint? This place is a dump." She spied, by the sink, a jar with brushes poking up out of it. "Aha. I detect art." Before he could stop her she went into the kitchen and saw his pallet in the sink. She espied his canvases, face in, under the window. She didn't turn them. "You really are a beatnik, Ray." She seemed pleased at this knowledge. "Officer Bongo." She moved along the wall where he'd hung his daughter's photographs so they wouldn't be in the sunlight. She sipped. "You take these?"

"My kid." He felt a pride. "My daughter's a photographer."

"She really likes green, eh? She should come down to my island. The whole thing's ganja green." She made a smile. "Except the people of course." Confidentially she whispered, "They're black."

"Well," he said, feeling his way in the face of this friendliness, "except for that part, it definitely sounds like my kind of place." He suddenly felt a dread, imagining how the comment would look, typed up on a piece of paper in front of a discipline command.

* * *

There wasn't much in the files. They were just wasting time until they headed over to Phil Harvey's place. Mostly they batted ideas back and forth and sipped their gin and taps. Twice she caught him looking at her. The third time she said, "What?"

"I'd like to ..." his throat clogged "... ah, paint you."

She whooped and drained her glass. "Nice. Nice one, Bongo. You do okay with that line?"

He hung his head. "Not really. Not lately anyway."

Later she said, "There's an elephant in the room."

He nodded.

"We should, sometime, talk about the elephant." She thought for a moment. "No, maybe not." They were tiptoeing in partner territory but not deep enough to get all confidential.

They went through the statement she'd taken from the black guy who saw Agatha Burns get into Phil Harvey's Camaro. Ray Tate stood behind her chair, watching her long brown finger trace the lines of handwriting. She had perfect penmanship. Her fingernails were chipped and worried. He thought he smelled a faint spice off her skin then it was burned away by her bleached hair.

She looked up at him. "You reading this? You read dyke?"

"Sure." He was a little drunk. "Sure. I read all the romance languages."

She laughed and briefly there was something open and unguarded in her look.

On the way to Phil Harvey's place in the east end she drove away from the river into an industrial area and they stopped for dinner at a chicken-and-biscuits joint.

"Maybe we're going at it wrong, Ray. Maybe we should work from Agatha Burns and go backwards. She left a phone number. Maybe we talk to the family and find out how she got from cradle to grave."

He shrugged. An anti-gang ghost car, all black with fat blackwalls and whip antennae, pulled up in the lot beside the Intrepid and two chargers got out. They stood huge in their vests and utility belts in the parking lot, like they owned the kingdom. Their side-arms were tied to their thighs by straps, gunslinger-style. Two lanky guys in gold chains sitting across the restaurant headed for the back door. The clerk yelled into the back to make two with extra hot wings, Petey and Gary are here. The chargers came in and looked at everyone. One kept his eyes on Ray Tate, then on Djuna Brown, then back. They were being added up and divided by suspicion. Ray Tate had done it himself a thousand times, reaching conclusions based on what was visible, reading tea leaves. If you asked the cops next week who was in the chicken joint when they went in that night, they'd get it right, right down to Djuna Brown's slippers and Ray Tate's scuffed cowboy boots. He thought: a competent cop is the best of creatures if they were caught young and mentored out of their hubris and stupidity. These two, he decided, had benefited from a crusty old duty sergeant, not from some crafty self-guided missile heading for a white shirt at the Swamp.

"We got to shake something up, Djun'," he said. "Let's do Harvey's place and if it washes, we'll put the chick through."

"Okay." She reached over to help herself to his coleslaw. While he watched her concentrate on balancing a wad of 'slaw on her fork he saw her lashes were long, her eyes had a Chinese slant, her skin, even in the fluorescent light, was smooth with tiny pores. There was muscle in her neck, long cords that stood out when she jutted her pointed chin out to let falling coleslaw fall on the plate instead of her horrible jacket. The hair was crazy and he wondered about a cop who wore embroidered slippers. But he did want to paint her. There was a hint of the exotic about her. He felt like he was on a teenage date with absolutely no shot.

She dabbed her lips with a paper napkin and caught him staring. She made a wide smile. "Imagine, Ray, if you were a chick. Where'd you have me right now? In the back seat, that's where."

He felt his heart race.

Djuna Brown drove lightly with the tips of her fingers. Periodically she glanced at them and regretted the worried nails. She drove with one eye on licence plates and the other on the traffic flow. The Staties were taught to drive inside a created bubble, to outfit themselves with a zone of protection as they swooped and whipped up and down highways. Beside her, Ray Tate was quiet, listening to the city dispatchers sing their songs. As they drove across invisible sector lines, he leaned forward to change frequencies, each time picking up a new dispatcher. He laughed when a bland charger came on looking for a "female-speaking officer" to search a shoplifter.

Being a dyke had served her well during her time up in Indian country, where the farm boys stayed away as though she had a disease they might pass on to their wives. The one guy who'd tried to jump her had been drunk. He smelled of manure and hay and announced he'd never had black ass, especially queer black ass. She'd surprised herself when she went for her stick and started in on him. She had just one partner after that and he never said a word to her. When he wanted a meal break, he burped. When he needed a bathroom break, he tilted and farted.

There was an ease in the Intrepid. She'd heard about cops like Ray Tate. Not the racist gunner stuff, although there was a lot of that, especially inside the Gay-Glo. She'd heard of coppers who were coppers to their core, who passed on lore and knowledge like old alchemists. You felt safe and never alone and always in company with a keeper of secrets. She'd never met one before; they were increasingly rare. The bitter dykes at Gay-Glo said that was all technique. They wanted to be daddies and get into your pants.

Suddenly, Ray Tate asked: "Hey, Djun', where we at?"

She looked around. "Uh, eastbound … uh …"

"See," he said, laughing. "When I was first in the suit I was out with an old sergeant. Turn here, he said. Turn there. All the while he's talking baseball, he's talking gossip. Then he says, Hey, boy, where we at? I go, Fucked if I know, and I start looking around. He reaches over and grabs me by the ear and twists. Fuck it hurt. He says, If you need help and you go on the radio, what are you going to say when they ask where you at? You're gonna say, Uh … uh. And you're going to bleed out. I guaran-fucking-tee it. Always, always know where you're at."

She looked at him. He was smiling at the windshield. "You going to twist my ear, Ray? Make me a cop?"

"Ah …" He looked at her ear and seemed about to say something but instead flipped through his note-book. "Anyway, Phil Harvey. State Motor puts two vehicles under him. The black Camaro, registered two months ago, and an old knucklehead Harley. The Harley lapsed out and the address was on a commercial strip over in Stateline. The Camaro's registered to an apartment in the Beach. Old Harv had a change of status for the better, it seems."

Ray Tate felt like a working cop. As Djuna Brown drove he watched both sides of the street, counting pedestrians. "The Stateline address is a strip club. The Beach is a condominium. Lake view, tennis courts."

She steered through a jam-up in Little India, four short blocks decorated with strings of Christmas lights that burned year round. A turbaned man was selling grilled corn on the corner, rubbing the cobs down with a lemon, waving a can of salt over them. A woman in a headscarf modelled a sari in a doorway for another woman, both of them giggling behind shy hands. Ray Tate was in love with every colour and smell and weird sitar note blaring from a speaker. Past the street crowd, Djuna Brown cut south and picked up speed, timing the lights.

Phil Harvey's condominium was just across a wooden boardwalk from the lake. Djuna Brown cruised the parking lots in case the Camaro had made its way back from the north country. She drove to a Donut Hole and Ray Tate, following the tradition that the shotgun buys, bought two coffees. At Harv's building she backed into a handicapped slot with a view to the front door of the building and the entrance to the parking lot and they racked their seats back.

"So," Ray Tate said, "let me ask you one. What's with the hair?"

"What's with the painting?"

They were silent. He said, "There's always Harry Potter. That's a safe subject."

"That little fag?"

They sat companionably and didn't say anything for a long time.

Chapter 12

Connie Cook felt at loose ends. Harv had called and given him a heads-up about the surveillance on Agatha Burns's stash house. Agatha was gone, someplace, probably not a very nice place, he imagined. He missed yakking with Harv, he missed packing Ag, he missed the slow trails of blood soaking in the fine hairs at the back of her neck.

"There's heat on Ag's, Connie," Harv had said. "Red Intrepid, a black chick with white hair, a white guy with a beard. They might be there for the local spades, but I'm gonna go under for a while. You okay for now?"

Captain Cook went to a gallery opening in the capital with his erect, frozen wife. The artist scented dough on the fat donor with the champagne glass in his hand and made a point of leaning into him as he did the rounds of the walls. She was a tall woman with explosive red hair and a loose-lipped red mouth. "My vision," she said, "is of angst. But of love, too. That's why all the red and black." She read his vibrations and gave him a sad smile. "Love is pain, pain is love. I have to accept that in order to grow. Accept the sacrifices." She began nattering about the artist's life, of being born too late, of having missed the golden age of artists and their generous patrons.

The Captain bought three hugely depressing oils. The artist put the red dots under the paintings and stood back pleased. She gave him her card and said she had canvases at her studio on the river, or she would anyway, until the landlord locked her out. She looked mournful at the land sharks who were driving property values through the roof. If ever, she said, the art world needed true patrons, now was it. She actually batted her eyelashes.

Captain Cook felt the hustle and appreciated it. It was his money she was in love with, not somebody else's. He scoped her ass and looked at the nape of her neck. He felt a rumbling. He was amazed at what people would let him do to them for his money.

When they got off the Interstate, his wife directed him past their house to two adjoining lots. "We can get them both, a million three they're asking."

Connie Cook said he'd get his secretary to look into it and she wrote down the developer's phone number. Connie Cook stopped at the curb in front of his house and walked his wife in, turned on the lights, and said he had to go out for a while.

It was dark. He drove a couple of blocks then rounded on himself and shut off the lights. The lake was off to his right. On his left he could see his own house, the far side overlooking the backyard of the house where Agatha Burns had lived, had done her high kicks, had been a golden girl beyond his reach. The rich young, he thought sadly, didn't care about money. He wondered if life was satisfying without it. He could have offered her a million dollars to flash him a boob but she'd've turned him down and gone to laugh with her little friends. His life had been like that. Cornie the Horny, a girl at school had called him. Fatty Unbuckle. Jabba the Gut. If a man couldn't get it with money or his looks, then what was left to him? Pillage, that's what. Pillage was the most successful foreplay.

He watched his house until his wife turned out all the lights upstairs and left the light in the portico lit for him. The door glowed with the hall lamps. To a passerby, he knew, the house was welcoming and homey, clearly a place of expensive textiles and furnishings, fireplaces, chandeliers, staircases. He dreaded going inside. There was nothing for him there.

He didn't know what to do with himself. Harv was off someplace, gone under. Ag wasn't around anymore. He thought for a moment that maybe he'd been too quick to sic Harv on her. He should have waited until he had someone else in the bullpen, warming up. The pigpen, Ag had called it, and he recalled with some sadness how that had lifted his heart.

Connie Cook started the Mercedes and rounded the block. He took a long, last look at the old Burns house, almost hidden by new construction hoarding, then continued on and eased through the gates onto his interlocked driveway. He'd been surprised that the Burns couple stayed there so long, after their Agatha had run off or been taken. Old Jerry Burns had been a rich playmaker in the political halls of the state legislature and he'd sat, Connie Cook imagined, for a long time waiting for the call for ransom, waiting to negotiate in his resonant voice, waiting for the call that never came. Or for Agatha to call, regretful, from some roadside phone booth, wanting to come home.

In the foyer of his own house, Connie Cook stood, wondering what to do. Harv was out riding around, doing who knows what, swooping through the underworld in his leather bat coat, pouncing on the weak. Ag wasn't Ag any more. He headed for the kitchen where the food was but even that didn't interest him much.

Who'd've thought, he thought, crooks ever got bored?

Phil Harvey left the Camaro under a tarp in the barn. The farm was abandoned. Two outbuildings had been cleaned up a little and both were fully functioning water farms with trays of hydroponic plants set in neat rows under halide fixtures. The keeper, a toothless old farmer with a double-barrelled shotgun and bib overalls, wandered the buildings. The farm was in Indian country and when the Natives came prowling for their burial grounds or whatever, the old toothless guy gave them a blast of the Old West, complete with cackling and whoops. Set in the furthest reach of the property, not quite on it but in a wedge of government land, was the super lab. In the evenings the fumes drifted towards the farm, away from the highway. A backhoe had dug a huge hole in the ground a hundred metres beyond the lab. It was jammed with the leavings of the crank and X trade. When Harv had had the lab up and running, the Captain had come up and was disappointed. He'd expected a gleaming laboratory with white tile walls and floor, fluorescent lighting bathing pristine equipment, little, thoughtful gnome-like technicians in white coats scampering from stainless steel vats, consulting clipboards. He hadn't been impressed with the reuse electric stoves, the rat's nest of exposed wiring, the patchy dirt floor, the open rafters with rustling bird life, the white plastic jugs rolling around, and the disarray of tangled tubing heaping on old wooden tables.

"What the fuck, Harv? This place is a fucking … barn. I expected something a little more, I dunno, German? Like the place where the Nazis did their experiments. This place is a pigsty." His pride of ownership had evaporated.

"It'll do the job, Connie. Check this." Harv felt sorry for him and took him over to a pill-pressing machine with Chinese characters stamped into it. "This is the best. Taiwanese. This'll turn out more pills than we can handle. We can use a hundred imprints. Peace doves, number ones, death's heads, you name it."

"You can make anything? Any symbol?"

"Yep."

Captain Cook had stared at the machine. It was impressive. It looked industrial and solid. "You ever see that symbol for women's stuff? Chanel?"

Harv put the speeding ticket he'd attracted on the way north into his jeans pocket and wrapped the fluted revolver in a sweater he found in the main house.

Snapping his stringy saliva like it was bubble gum, the grumpy old keeper drove him in a busted-up pickup truck down the long rutted laneway to the sideroad and out to the highway. They went south to Widow's Corners where Harv got out at an all-night diner on the edge of town. The old man spat out the side window as he drove off but the window was cranked up and Harv had a bit of a laugh as he crossed the parking lot to a pay phone booth and called one of his guys to come up and get him.

Harv went into the diner, ordered a meal, and went into the washroom. He stashed the bundled pistol behind the toilet cistern then sat in a booth with a view of the washroom doors and the entrance. Wrapped in his black leather coat he ate a jailhouse meal: meat loaf with instant mashed potatoes and limp vegetables, and several cups of coffee. Truckers came into the place with regularity and barely glanced at him. Long-distance truckers with patches of the flag on their jackets and the words, These Colors Don't Run, hunched over plates, eyes down, yawning. Those guys, Harv knew, had seen shit and he wasn't much different from the rest of it, a white man swathed in leather, wearing sunglasses at night, in a town notorious for Indian ribaldry and criminal doings in the bush.

Waiting, Harv reflected on a life away from the city, a life with a woman and maybe a kid, although that was a long shot, in a place where he could finally stop. He hadn't worked a day in his life, except in custody when he did some cooking and scrubbing in the industrial prison kitchens, or shovelling coal in powerhouses, or hoeing on work farms. On the streets he'd never been more than a couple of thousand bucks from being broke, always with an eye for a decent score. Hooking up with the fat fucker had taken care of that problem: Harv had enough money to last for years. He wouldn't have to work in a chemical fog, wouldn't have to day-dream while watching a Brinks truck rolling up to a bank. Life should've been golden, but associating with Connie Cook had, he believed, diminished him, made him as much a lunatic as a crook. Harv knew he could steal or deal all the livelong day. He could collect loans, hustle huge quantities of dope, even do the odd armed robbery to keep the wolf from the door. That all made sense: no one could fault a man for what he did to keep food on the table, especially if he was willing to pay the grim bill when the cops came knock-ing. But since he'd been with the Captain he found himself thinking of himself as ... something other. Depraved came to mind. Psycho, maybe. Snaffling up a girl and locking her down until she had a bad habit was strange. Turning her over to a gross pervert for months of playtime, that was degenerate. There was no end in it for anyone. Harv made a good end with the Captain's criminal schemes but the weird perversion bothered him. Agatha Burns had cried for him, apologized for sucking and licking his scars. No sorrow for maybe being a rat, no whining about having maybe betrayed him, no remorse for facilitating the drug trade. She just wanted forgiveness for what she did to him. As if that was her biggest crime, the headliner in a theatre of confession.

The Captain had wanted to become a kingpin.

"Where's the money, Harv, where can we make out best?"

Dope, Harv had advised. Water farms, labs.

"Yeah, Harv? How about broads. Any dough in running hookers?"

"Naw, chicks are trouble, they're work, they shoot their mouths off. I don't feature myself as a pimp."

"Oh, okay, Harv. Tell you what: you figure out what you need to get a business going, tell me how much, and we go partners. If you think dope's the way to go then we go that way. I'm just a tourist here. Hey, what'd'you think's a better car, the Camaro or the Corvette?"

"Camaro. Corvette's for homos."

"Homos. Got it. And, hey, Harv, there's something I want you to get for me. This young broad up on the lake, I want her, I want you to get her for me. Can you do that?"

Harv thought the Captain was doing a kidnapping, maybe something to do with one of his Chicago business deals, muscling a commodities broker. He clocked Agatha Burns, snaffled her up, and a few months later Harv had a black Camaro with the rims.

They were in a restaurant one night and the waiter made a comment about desserts and calories. The Captain took umbrage.

"Hey, Harv, you know any construction guys? That can get dynamite or something?"

"Sure, Connie. How much, what for?"

"That place we had dinner at, with the lippy waiter? You think two sticks'll do it?"

Two sticks did it. Two sticks did the restaurant, took the arms off the cook who'd stayed back to braise lamb shanks for the next day's special, and shut down Stonetown for a week.

The windows of the diner vibrated from the heavy trucks left rumbling in the parking lot. Harv thought of Agatha Burns and her knocking knees. She'd been a perfect little thing, the kind of unattainable item Harv instinctively hated, the kind of thing that had the perfect life in the perfect neighbourhood with the perfect mum and dad. It took him weeks of keeping a clock on her movements. One night she came out of her boyfriend's house and Harv was waiting with a panel van and a sleeping bag and she was in the back and on the way to a drop house in the badlands. The waiting, impatient Captain took over from there, squiring her up to the farm in Indian country.

Hey Harv, how much of this stuff do you have to take, like, how long, before you're a zombie, a scuzzy little slave who'll do anything to anybody for more?

Harv had seen insanity in the streets and in the joints. He always backed away from it silently, never judged. Judgment was a smirk in those places and there were guys who would just slice the smirk right off your lips. You nodded and slowly backed away from them, but you never backed down.

But what the Captain did to Agatha Burns in that farmhouse put him into the mood of watching gang pile-ons in the joint: Whoa, that's weird. Not for me, but you pull your time however you have to. No judgment.

Her knees knocked and when the old speeder lady with the shotgun peered in through the window and cackled a smile, Harv felt he was in someone else's strange landscape.

Agatha Burns told him of her shame.

She touched his scars.

She apologized.

The gap-toothed, balding old speeder lady was in her fifties or sixties. Agatha Burns was twenty. How did one get such a long life of misery, and the other a short life that had been mostly okay?

The pickup truck with the camper van in the back had squeaked on rusted springs as he helped her into it, telling her, Don't worry, Ag, you just took too much stuff.

She turned and looked at him and her eyes were clear.

She'd said, "I know, Harv. It's okay, okay?" Her mouth trembled a little when she said, "Can you let my mom and dad know? Somehow? Where to find me? Harv?"

Harv's minion lived halfway between Widow's Corners and the city. He arrived almost two hours after Harv summoned him. He came into the diner, spotted Harv and nodded, got a coffee to go, and went out to a black chromed F-250 pickup. Harv paid his tab and went into the washroom to retrieve his gun. Boiling down the Interstate in the F-250, the minion talked about what happened to the Chinamen in the city who'd fucked with the brand. He rattled about the cooker who went up in the truck explosion. "They say it was a broad, maybe."

Harv told the driver to slow down. "We're heavy."

"Oh, fuck, okay." The driver changed to the centre lane and kept inside a handful of traffic. "That fat guy we're working for. What's he about?"

Harv liked the minion, a failed striker for the Riders. The kid had done some time but he'd done no heavy lifting. Things like that put you in your position on the scale of things. Going the hard distance wasn't something just anyone could do, although everybody thought they could until they were face to face with it. You had to be a certain way. Harv had known he was that way since he was a teenager. It wasn't until he met the Captain and his weird ways that he thought maybe there was nothing lower than himself in the cold swamp.

"The Captain's cool. The Captain's okay. Just a little different."

The driver laughed. "You got that right."

They rode in silence for a while. Harv saw trees and thought of Agatha Burns and her riff about more tree being underground than above it. Not something he would have thought of, taking a ride you didn't expect to come back from. He thought about the conversation about the Chinamen she said she didn't know, and the radio that had been off and she swore she hadn't turned it off and how about those fucking CD prices. He chuckled.

The driver said, "What?"

"Nothing." Harv looked at him. "Let me ask you one. If I asked you to do something, could you do it?"

The driver knew right away. "You need something, Harv? Fuckin' A."

"No question, no problem? You're that way?"

"Gotta be." The driver nodded at his windshield. He had long, feminine blond hair held back by his ears. "You gotta be, in this life. You do or you're done. You're dog or you're dog food."

They passed an open pickup with a half-dozen Indians sprawled in the back. Ahead of it was a sway-backed, rusted, bone white Reliant station wagon in the slow lane with a long-haired guy driving. Harv could see a woman's legs in a long skirt and a kid in the back seat sleeping against a window smeared with drool. "That guy. Him, in the Reliant."

The driver was puzzled and craned to look. "Sure. Who is he, what'd he do?"

"Nothing. I don't know. I don't care. I ask you and you say ... what?"

The driver squirmed a little. "I guess, yeah. But it ain't right. You don't just ... No, that's fucked. You'd have to be nuts." He passed the Reliant and kept an eye on it in the side mirror. "You okay?" He laughed nervously. "You're a funny fucker, Harv."

Harv, his face hidden in the cheesy curtain of rock star hair, was thinking about monsters.

PART TWO

Chapter 13

Nothing happened at Harv's condominium. They chatted and played the tag game. Ray Tate had evens and Djuna Brown had odds. Personalized licence plates didn't count, neither did taxis or commercial vehicles. Of the first twelve cars to roll through the parking lot eight had even numbers at the end and Djuna Brown was going to buy the drinks after.

They took turns dozing and doing feel-outs.

She started speaking in soft patois. "Hey, Ray, mon, what's wit' de painting? Be you some kind of closet artist?"

"Naw," he said, a little embarrassed. "No. Just fooling around."

"You like the dark colours, eh?"

He didn't answer that. "You always lived alone, Djun'?"

"I lived with someone, for a while, before I got recruited."

"How'd that go?"

"Well, I'm sitting in a shitty car with a beatnik. You tell me."

After a while he asked, "Why'd you sign up?"

"My dad wanted me to be a nurse, like my mom. When I got accepted at the Staties he was pretty mad. He said I was too small." She glanced at him. "He was mad as a Chinaman with no thumbs."

"Chinaman. What the fuck? Why not, say, a Macedonian with no thumbs. Or, say, a pygmy?"

"Ray, Ray, get a grip, mon. What's a Macedonian or a pygmy want thumbs for?"

He smiled. "Nice one, Djun'."

She looked pleased with herself. "What about you, Ray? You a single dude on the make?"

"Well, I'm married, I guess. We're not together right now."

"How old's your kid? The photographer?"

"Seventeen."

"You a cool dad, Ray?"

"Not lately."

At nine o'clock Ray Tate tried to raise the skipper on the rover. Walter Brodski came back. There were party noises in the background and someone yelled, "Seven, you cocksucker."

"He's gone hours, Ray. Where you at?"

"We're sitting on a place in the Beach. We're looking for the guy that boiled out of the projects this afternoon. Anybody on the air, can spell us off?"

The radio was silent. Brodski came back. "I would, Ray, but my ulcer's acting up again." The background noise was gone.

A black F-250 pickup dripping with chrome rolled in off the street and did a turn through the parking lot. It slowed passing in front of the Intrepid. Ray Tate saw a young guy with blond hair behind the wheel, scooping them. It rolled off, cut a wide U, and dribbled out of the parking lot. When it was out of sight there was a peel of rubber.

"A mutt." Ray Tate noted down the plate. "I think this is a wash, Djun'. We should pack it in. Even if Harvey and the Captain came and went, we've only got this one vehicle and that got burned off this afternoon. We're going to need more bodies, more cars."

She started the engine. "Who gets this one for the night? Let's go someplace and have a few drinks and wrestle for it." She gave him a bland look. "No, don't answer that. I'll drop you and take it home."

"Just as well," he said loftily, a little disappointed. Wrestling sounded interesting. "I'm not into black chicks."

"Not even black dykes?"

"Well, black dykes. That's a different thing. Black dykes I can dig."

"Cool-ee-oh."

There were three messages on her phone from Hazel, the needy former cop at Gay-Glo, and she listened and deleted. Sober, in daylight, Hazel was a professional organizer and just a little aggressive in a flirtatious, hinting way. Late nights, Hazel was a different matter: she wailed and cried and declared undying love. She cursed and swung between wishes of suicide and dreams of violence. She promised a velvety tongue and threatened with the vengeance of the betrayed and abandoned.

Djuna Brown stirred together a rum and coke and felt creepy until she smiled, thinking of Ray Tate's bohemian artist's pad and the foul gin and taps and the paintings. She'd've never, she thought, figured him for having a creative side. She wished she'd turned around the canvases lining the baseboards and seen what lived inside Ray Tate. She laughed at herself and reflected on her flirt. Wrestling, how artless was that clanger? Aloud she said: "What a fucking clunker, you fucking lesbo."

She sat with her drink at the window overlooking the Intrepid illegally parked in front of her duplex. A very faint dusting of early snow had accumulated on the roof. It wasn't officially a police car, but it had the red dash light in there, a radio, and probably a switch somewhere to activate the siren. She had a gun and handcuffs and if she wanted she could go out and chain someone up, take away their liberty, put a hinge in their life.

Almost a cop, and somehow because of Ray Tate, artistic gunner of blacks.

In his apartment the gin and taps glasses were in the sink. He washed them then put on a Miles Davis CD and went on a binge into the night, wiping down surfaces, cleaning dying food from the fridge, scrubbing the bathtub. He thought about painting and realized he almost had a sense for the bright colours but he didn't trust it and stayed away from the oils and the canvases.

There was a cop lurking in that trim lesbian body, he thought. She had some fear, which was good: awkwardly juggling her gun in the stairwell at the stash house, just nervous enough that she wasn't a cowboy about it. Or maybe a cowgirl. Or something in between. What did you call a dyke wrangler? And she could generate fear. Watching the skipper's reaction when she was in firing range was amusing and instructive, both. As Ray Tate dug a wire brush into the toilet and worked it he wondered where she was at that moment. Had she gone down to Erie Road and made a new friend, met up with an old one? Were they already at her place, tangled in sheets and confusion, sorting out who'd do what to who? He felt a bit of envy but also a bit of stirring.

At two o'clock he was still at it, energetically working in an endless cycle of Miles Davis when the phone rang.

"Cocksucker, Ray, they woke me up, I'm waking you up."

"What's up, skip?"

"Everyfuckingbody, seems like." He sounded drunk and sleepy. "Two kids, white kids, OD'd on X. DOA at St. Frankie's. What's that shit in the background? You got cats on the stove? You drop my dyke for me?"

"Some jazz shit, skip. My daughter left it on." He didn't want to play drop-the-dyke bullshit.

"Sounds like fucking mad cats. Anyway, these kids are white and their families live in the mayor's ward. We had a game, Ray, but I think we're gonna lose it." A glass or bottle clinked against the receiver at the skipper's end. "Little assholes had double Chucks in their pockets. We're so fucking fucked."

Chapter 14

A month after Pious Man Chan's dep shut down the Captain Cook task force and the Feds set up a bureaucracy operating from the Swamp, Chan told the rumpled mayor it was out of his hands. Pious Chan noticed with satisfaction the smudgy thumbprints of exhaustion pressed under the mayor's rat's eyes. Subtle makeup didn't help. The mayor was in the tubes and losing sleep over it. His hair was dull pewter and the word was he was back to bingeing on fast food and midnight takeout.

"We were making progress, sir," Chan told him sadly over lunch at City Hall. They sat at a table in the window of the mayor's den, overlooking the city square where the drab homeless were carrying signs and trudging in a circle. "Our guys were on the edge of penetrating the whole thing, but then." He shrugged. "Anyway, now we've got to move on the Bik-Bigs soon. Winter's coming on and they're all going to fly south, back to the Carolinas or Florida, scheme up another season of discontent. Which means a whole new generation of Black Kids Big Guns and dead bodies come springtime."

"Fuck, Pi." The mayor shook his dead locks and fired a weak probe. "How'd you let it all get away from you, the Chemical Squad?"

Chan too had aged visibly behind the mahogany desk but he'd grown some hard bark. The long, black, single hair had been plucked and the mole looked like a red small-calibre bullet hole verging on leakage. Somehow, the mayor thought, he'd become even more Asian looking. His eyes were sleepy but ready and predatory. He'd taken on the mantra of an old, disgraced police chief from another dynasty. Politicians come and go but cops will fuck you forever. Pious Man Chan let the mayor wait and affected deep thought and commiseration.

The mayor's serfs were getting restless. There were growing rumors of corruption among the wardmen. The community groups were wearying of broken campaign promises, of blame being kicked up to other governments, of the mayor and his soaked crying towel. Led by the inscrutable Willy Wong, the Chinese Menu lobbied for a crackdown on the white thugs coming into Chinatown and disrupting the community, torturing the children. Promised bicycle lanes weren't painted on the downtown streets. The lakefront was a mess of indifferent reconstruction. Building contracts were falling apart because the mayor hadn't found a way to free up state or federal funding. The unions were howling for the jobs. The homeless were a whole other matter. The sleeping bags the city was handing out to the bums weren't of Arctic quality and the social groups were calling the mayor a fascist killer who left the needy to freeze in the streets. The sleeping bags, they said, were body bags. You couldn't, a cheerful dep told Chan, take a shit in Memorial Park without dumping on some shivering bum.

Pious Chan shrugged. "It was those kids, sir. Those kids in your ward who went south on the ecstasy. A little restraint, a little more time, sir, and we could've got the cooker, the labs, and wrapped the Bik-Bigs into it all." He jabbed an asparagus spear and rolled it in a little pot of melted butter.

"Well, what are you guys doing?"

"Us? We're policing, sir. We're not arresting home-less people. We're not arresting those guys down the hall, who, by the way, are getting pretty brazen. Price is back at it, losing tons of money in the Italian gambling clubs over in Stateline. Don't know how he does it, the salaries the city gives those guys. The wife's sailing around in a new Lexus. Me, I'd've gone broke, killed the wife, and sold the car by now to pay for a lawyer. Ten grand Mr. Price dropped this weekend, but he's driving a new car too. Some of my guys are wondering why we haven't started up a project on him, see if there's a con-nection between his dough and the building tenders."

"Pious. Those tenders are for jobs. Union jobs. Union jobs that vote."

"I know, sir. I'm just letting you know. In case the media gets a hold of it. You might want to send me some backdated paper, asking me to start drilling into corruption. I'll sit on it and if the newspapers start their shit, we can say we're on it but can't talk because it's active."

The mayor had no appetite. He looked at the bums stamping a circle in the dirty snow outside his castle, the lights from the camera crews bright in the dim noontime. It was well-organized and destined for the front page, for the tricks at six. They used to love him, the media and the bums and the bum organizers, because he could weep on cue over his heartbreak at their plight. "I need something big, Pi. What've you got?"

"Bik-Bigs. We can take them down anytime. Seven homicides, statewide trafficking, smuggling shit down from Canada."

"No. Not yet. Unless you got some white guys we can put with them?"

Pious Chan nodded at the mayor's asparagus and raised his eyebrows. The mayor nodded and Chan started spearing with gusto. "Only white guys I can think of are Mr. Price and his guys down the hall at Planning. Don't think we want that. Not yet anyway. There's some Chinese guys gambling in the caverns under east Chinatown."

The mayor knew what was going on. Pious Chan had already revealed his oriental hand at the Swamp: cops who'd pissed him off over the past twenty years were riding marked scout cars in the dark, piloting the prisoner wagons, adding up paper clips in obscure offices. The mayor had ten years of superior private schooling in Boston and Paris. Chan had two patient decades of accumulated personal slights and centuries of bloody revenge. A hundred generations of time were to the Chinamen as they were to a rock: imperceptible.

"I can't see a chain gang of young black kids and old Chinese gamblers doing it for us, Pious."

"Well, sir, we can go back after the cookers. The Feds haven't got this Captain Cook guy, whose pills killed the kids. Or the cowboy who went nuts with the branding iron last month, on the exchange students. Or the super lab everybody's talking about. Our special unit is still up, although it isn't running too well."

"That where Ray Tate is still? The Chemical Squad? What's going on with him? I'm still paying his salary?"

Pious Chan nodded. "The gunner's still with Gordie Weeks's bunch. They're doing nothing, sir. Some raids, little stuff. Nothing heavy that Tate can trip over, lose his way. At least he hasn't killed anyone of the black persuasion. We've given the new Fed task force some space and some manpower, but if they ever somehow take down this Cook guy and get his lab the headlines are going to be Federal, out of Washington, how they saved the children because we couldn't."

The mayor shook his head, frustrated. "Take it back, Pious. Can you find a way to work around the Feds? Nail this Captain cocksucker, make him ours?"

"No problem, sir. Just send me the paper and I'll kick Gordie and his gang into gear." Chan was sick of the buttery asparagus but he asked, "You going to finish that, sir?" He wanted to eat the mayor's lunch for him, literally and figuratively.

* * *

Gordie Weeks spent the month trying to figure out what was going on with Ray Tate's scheme to spike Djuna Brown. The pair showed up separately each morning, drudged their way through paperwork, and seemed to get along all right. When the brainiacs down the hall had a fix on a lab they called the skipper and he put together a raiding party. The most likely time for reactive violence on lab raid was the go-in. The skipper mandated that Wally Brodski and the dyed dyke hit the door first, followed by whatever slobs were working. Ray Tate was the keeper of the keys, a fancy clerk who took down the names and numbers of the detectives, technicians, State Haz-Mat, and fire officials who went through the place. Ray Tate was swimming in boredom and seemed to be going downhill quickly under his matted hair and behind his thickening beard. He smelled sharply of paint and linseed oil, his fingertips were crusted with shades from the unhappy end of the rainbow. The raids yielded little mom-and-poppers, chemistry sets in basements, bathrooms, attics. None of the bust-ins had yielded a single double Charlie.

The dep had stopped calling. Gordie Weeks's calls to Intelligence for intell coming out of the raids were unreturned.

Almost daily, the skipper cornered Ray Tate. "Hey, Ray, what's going on with the dyke? She dropping today?"

"My partner, skip. She's my partner."

The skipper wasn't sure if Ray Tate was being devious and arch. "You're not gonna get her for me, are you, Ray? You were fucking me all along."

Ray Tate just smiled at him and shrugged. "She's clever, skip. She's one diabolical dyke, that one."

The skipper wasn't sure but he was hopeful. "But, maybe? Maybe soon?"

Ray Tate had enshrouded himself in the safe cloud of non sequitur and had taken to talking about birds. "You ever notice, skip, that there's a lot of fucking Canada geese in town? All those homeless people starving and there's a fucking shitload of geese, waiting to be cooked up? How come nobody ever put the equation together? We got skinny folks starving in the streets and we got, like, a million fat fucking geese strutting around like they pay taxes."

"Ray, Ray."

When the call came from Pious Chan, via the dep, the skipper was in his office with his feet up, thinking idly about Gloria the receptionist and the .45s. He'd seen Djuna Brown and Gloria in deep chitchat a couple of times and wondered if the dyke had lured her over to the other team. The concept destroyed his dozing dreams. Something was different with the dyke. She made effort to keep her unruly white hair in some kind of shaped 'do. The exhaustion that had slumped her bones inside her body had evaporated, as though she'd had some kind of marrow work done on her skeleton. Djuna

Brown still looked at him with her bitter eyes spitting hate, but when he wasn't noticeably around she seemed to bustle with efficiency. She and Ray Tate laughed a lot.

The dep called, his voice jocular, "Gordo, you douchebag. Where you been? I call and I call and you're never home. Don't you love me anymore?"

"Hey, hey, dep." The skipper knew he'd been swinging on a hook in the wind since the Feds had set up their own task force with the Staties. He played it low. "I been busy. Sorry I haven't got back to you."

"No matter. I know you guys been busy." The dep said it without laughing. "What'd you get last night? Thousand pills?"

"Well, eight hundred." The skipper had been disappointed. The tip from the local sector had suggested hundreds of thousands, based on the anxious rap of a strung out speeder.

"Wow, great. A little here and a little there, eh, Gordo? Chip away at the criminal infrastructure, it'll collapse."

"How's the Fed task force working out, dep?" The skipper didn't laugh but he took his shot. "They knocking down the double Chucks yet, got Captain Cook in the chain gang?"

"Well, Gordo, my boy, that's why I'm calling you."

The month for Ray Tate and Djuna Brown had been a cycle of rote. Raids on cookers had been amusing for a while but the media lost interest in minor takedowns and didn't show up for the photo op. Ray Tate noticed that Wally the boozer and Djuna Brown were first through the doors. There were some scuffles but none of the speeders or cookers had much muscle tone or firepower. Wally Brodski took an elbow in the face while subduing an inside keeper and got two weeks off. Djuna Brown got into a tussle with a landlord who thought it was a home invasion and Wally stood watching her get her shit handed to her until Ray Tate climbed over him and put the chains on the guy. Djuna restrained him from going after Wally.

Afterwards, alone at the satellite, Ray Tate took Wally aside. "Don't let them do this to you, Wally. We go into a place, we're all one gang. You fucking know that."

"She's a fucking dyke, Ray. C'mon."

"Right now she's my partner. My dyke partner, sure, but she's got the yellow letters on her back same as you, same as me, and the rest of us. What happens in here, that's one thing. Out there, that's another." Ray Tate laid on some bullshit. "My father-in-law told me you were a good cop, you'd never watch another cop get his shit shuffled. Don't you fucking do this, man."

"Ah, fuck you, Ray." But he had to listen: Ray Tate had the authority of dead bodies. Wally took the next door ahead of Djuna Brown and got his nose broken.

Djuna Brown somehow heard about it. "Don't do that to me, Ray, okay?"

"It isn't about you, Djun'," he told her. "Wally forgot something, that's all. I reminded him. I don't care if it's the fucking skipper on the floor: if he goes under them and you stand by and let them do it, well, we won't be partnering at all, you and me. The tribe comes first."

In the evenings they sometimes had drinks at out of the way bars on the river unless there was a door kick on the go. No one else wanted to socialize with them. Ray Tate wouldn't let his partner be excluded. She didn't offer to wrestle him and he didn't offer to paint her. They talked endlessly. They drove to Chicago to listen to a bunch of white college kids do imitation Junior Wells tunes. One night in the cold they sat by the river beyond the lights of Gastown and she came to know about his dreams of becoming a painter, of his girlfriend's father luring him into the cops, of his wife booting him. He came to know about her father, a taxi driver down in the capital, who finally accepted that she was going to be a miniature cop and signed her up for jiu-jitsu lessons. Ray Tate never spoke about the dead black guys and she never spoke about her dyke jacket.

The skipper avoided her when he could and button-holed Ray Tate about the progress of the conspiracy to spike her into the ground. Ray Tate pulled on a shroud and wrapped himself in bird life and blank stares.

One morning, the skipper bounded out of his office. "Okay, Ray, we're back in business."

Chapter 15

The day after Phil Harvey's pal had cruised his black F-250 pickup through the parking lot and spotted the beatnik and the black cop in the red Intrepid in the handicap spot, Connie Cook gave Phil Harvey a stack of money and they both vanished in different directions.

Phil Harvey never said where he was going. The Captain took his wife on a cruise through the Pacific Islands. When he returned, fatter and tanned, he swung into the cultural whirl of autumn parties, handing out donations to all manner of culture and art. He kept his eyes and antennae out for someone who could be the recipient of his peculiar true love. But no one set off his twisted tripwire and he brooded and ate copiously. He grew lonely. He missed Agatha and her blood and flesh, and he missed Harv and their collegial banter.

The labs had shut down. The water farms rusted. Thieves and boosters wandered the streets with their bottles of pills, looking for a buyer. The double Chucks dried up. They'd become notorious death pills and even the Chinamen weren't copying them anymore.

When Phil Harvey turned up he had no tan but he seemed relaxed when the Captain met him for hamburgers at a beer joint in the southern industrial section of town. They sat in the window and watched autumn snow outside, falling in a glittering sunshine.

"The ship was pretty good," the Captain said. "Buffet, all you can eat." He laughed. "When they saw me coming in for the buffet they just said, fuck it, called the head office in Atlanta and adjusted the bottom line." He chewed slowly. "No grilled hamburgers, though. What is it with cruise lines? You can get anything but a grilled fucking hamburger. Fuck, Harv, I missed this, buddy. What you been doing? You go away?" He looked closely at Harvey. There was something different but he couldn't put his finger on it. "You get laid a lot?"

"Naw. I hung out. Stayed away from the condo. Went out of town a little, hooked up with a pal. A lot of people are missing us, Cookie. A lot of people aren't making much dough. Anyway, I got bored and I went up to the farm and just hid out. You know there's a lake up there, way in on our property? Not a big thing, but I came across it out walking. Saw a fish jump in the air. There was a bear on the other side."

"Yeah? Yeah, really? Fish? No shit. A bear. But no mischief-making up there? You didn't pull out the recipe book, start baking little pink cakes in the barn?"

"Naw. No, Cookie. There's nothing up there to cook with. I decided: Fuck it, take it easy. Just me and the fishes and the beasts."

Phil Harvey was amazed that it could snow while the sun was shining. Things like that were sometimes coming to him, unbidden. In the north the mornings had been crusted with frosted dew and he'd sat for hours wrapped in his sleeping bag in the kitchen, watching through the window the crack and refreeze, watching the little footprints of small foragers melt. Shadows seemed blacker up in Indian country, edges sharper. The sky at night was vast and undiluted by ambient city light. He'd had an original thought, he believed, that the stars were holes poked into the sky, letting another light from another planet peek through. The only times before that he'd had that feeling were in the minutes after being released from prison: a rebirthing that suggested that the world was full of new smells and new possibilities. And although he'd returned to his old bad ways as quickly as he could, this time he thought might be different.

When he'd remotely picked up messages on his home phone that the Captain was back in town he'd felt a lot of disappointment and a bit of dread, the ebbing of the possibility of change for himself.

"So, we got no product to move, Harv?"

"Nope. I'll get cooking once you give me the word to go get some stuff. We'll have to use another stamp. Those double Cs are too notorious right now." He smiled at the Captain. "The heat didn't slow the Chinamen down, though. That Chinatown bunch are cooking with stuff they brought down from Canada. Making a fucking killing."

The Captain realized the difference about Harvey: he'd had left his curtain of hair tied back, indifferently exposing the scar tissue. And he didn't hide his angry, blurred hands. Connie pirated Harv's fries. "You seeing anything going on? Those cops in the red car? Any of that stuff?"

"Nope. Nothing. I haven't gone back to the condo since my guy saw them there in the parking lot. I haven't gone near Ag's old trap. The Camaro's under tarps up north and I'm driving rentals. I think it might have just been a blip, Cookie. They thought they had something, then when nothing happened they fucked off to frame some other innocent guys."

"You'd think with those fucking kids overdosing there'd be something."

"Well, there's been people around. When they grabbed up somebody with double Charlies they put them through pretty good, but nobody knows nothing. Then the Charlies ran out and headlines died down and things have been back to normal." Harv grabbed a fry before the Captain could.

"Well, then, back to business, Harv. Can you sniff around Willy Wong, see what his guys are up to? He's got that import firm, that's how he gets his precursors in from over the border. Labels the drums cleaning solvent or something, trucks them down. If they get grabbed, he goes Holy Fuck there's a crook in my importing business and somebody goes to jail, but not him." Captain Cook shook his head. "Fucking guy. Anyway, you want to put some guys together, maybe on standby. And I'll need you to do something else, Harv. Soon. For me."

"Something heavy?" Harvey had resolved to not bring the Captain out on any more missions. Lack of restraint was never a good thing. You could feel a thrill at mayhem but you shouldn't lose yourself in it. Mayhem was a tool, not part of a healthy lifestyle.

"Well, I'm lonely. I need a friend. Since Ag ran away and I been on this fucking trip with my wife, I'm not getting any." He stared out the window. "I think that's why I busted the buffet on the boat. I don't get any, so I eat. I eat, so I get fatter. I get fatter and who the fuck's gonna want to fuck a blimp on purpose? I need a pal, Harv. Long-term relationship." He smiled. "I got my eye out for something sweet, I'll let you know."

"C'mon, Cookie. There's hookers, do whatever you want, however you like it. There's peelers at the club, be glad to make acquaintance. There's no problem. This, grabbing up another chick, this is trouble. This is not a good time, start fucking around with kidnapping. We got to rebuild the business first."

"Harv, Harv. I thought you understood me. Anybody can fuck a peeler or a hooker. I tried with the ones you got me, before, those two tire biters. I really tried. But there's no love there — just money. Like buying a meal. But I want to create love, Harv. I want the ingredients for a loving relationship. I want what everybody wants but very, very few actually get. Once I find her, we'll use the same tricks as last time, okay?"

The Captain's appetite hadn't been sated by Phil's initial offerings. Predatory peelers had agreed to spend some time with him and were taken up to the farm. After a week, they were gone. Harv asked what happened to them and the Captain said they weren't satisfactory, that he'd given them each a wad of cash and dropped them back into their pathetic lives, none the worse for wear.

From his bedroom window the Captain had seen where the Burns family hid the emergency key to their home, under a planter on the rear deck. He'd invited the old couple over for drinks and dinner and sent Harv in while Agatha was out banging her boyfriend. Harv had gone in and filled suitcases with Ag's clothing and personal effects, then headed over to the boyfriend's place in a van and waited for her to come out. She was wrapped in duct tape, bundled into a sleeping bag, and on her way north before her parents got home.

"I need this, Harv." The Captain looked out the window. "Unless my Ag comes back. You think she's going to come back to me?"

"I don't think so, Cookie." Harv looked sad. "Really, I really don't."

Harv saw that the Captain had made a sad face but he couldn't help licking his smiling lips. "Cool, Harv. Get some gear together for my thing, and in the meantime we'll get up and at it on our thing. Use those wreckers from before, the day of the Chinese roundup. Those were good guys. Did they like me, Harv?"

Ray Tate and Djuna Brown were in the skipper's glassed office. Ray Tate was staring out the window as if studying the air currents, divining the invisible paths of birds. Djuna Brown affected boredom. She'd fluffed out her bleached hair into a wild 'do. The skipper wondered if Ray Tate was winding up for an avian lecture. This bird facet was new and the skipper had calls in to see how much documentation was needed for a psych write-out.

"Okay. Okay, you guys. We're back in business. Orders from headquarters. We're taking out this Captain Cook guy. We're taking down the super lab."

Djuna Brown said, "Cool."

Ray Tate said, "Wow."

The skipper glanced at Ray Tate, who now seemed to be documenting how many species of birds flew past the window. Djuna Brown had her eyes on his, a cat smile waiting to pounce. He thought he could smell peroxide in the air and suddenly wanted her out of his office. He was amazed at his enduring hatred of everything about her. He'd heard stories that she'd been a good cop, even though she'd been working up the woods amongst the bears and the wolves, that she'd made some good pinches. But there were other stories and it was those stories that scared him and his fear made his hatred deeper.

The skipper looked at Ray Tate as he spoke. "Yep. Back in business. The *Federale* brainiacs have got nowhere on Captain Cook, whoever he is, and his bubbling cauldron of evil, wherever that is. The double Chucks dried up after the two kids went tits up. The task force is hanging around headquarters doing a whole lot of nothing. So they come back to us. After all, we started the fucking thing. So how do you want to do it?"

Djuna Brown looked at Ray Tate and realized he wasn't going to speak. He looked more likely to start snapping his fingers and reciting free-form poetry. She looked at the skipper and widened her smile. "Ray's having a moment, skip. Thinking big thoughts. So, what do you want us to do? We're pretty much fucked from coast to fucking coast on this thing. Every twenty minutes the guys down the hall wander in and say, 'Hey we got a tip there's a major stash out in the east end, go get it.' 'There's a guy from Amsterdam coming in at the airport with a ton of blues, round him up.' So we do. The major stash is three stoner kids sharing a half a brain and two dozen bad-quality ovals. The guy at the airport doesn't show. The *Federales* ride their fancy cars around town with the cool radios under the dash and talk like cops. They kick down doors. They torture the speeders. Just like us real cops, except they couldn't find their dicks with both hands. And when they can't, now they come back and say, 'Hey, how about a hand, help us find our dick?'"

The skipper heard the lulling islands in her voice and seemed entranced by her Chinese eyes. He looked over at Ray Tate. "Ray? What do you think?"

Ray Tate's lips moved but he didn't say anything. He took a worn Audubon Guide from his pocket and fingered the tattered edges. His fingernails were chewed back and there were flakes of black and purple paint on his cuticles. "I think there is," he finally said, "a vast array of bird life in this city. You know that, skip? A preponderance of sparrows, a lot of pigeons, and prolific flocks of seagulls. The seagulls come inland for food because the lake is so polluted and there's nothing down there to eat. So they come up to east Chinatown and go nuts on the garbage, attack picnickers in the parks. Don't know why there's so many pigeons. But they shit an awful lot." He turned his eyes back to the window. "But sometimes you see swallows or robins, even sometimes a falcon or two. But an awful lot of pigeons, no question."

Djuna Brown gazed at him for a few moments, a fond smile playing on her lips. The skip wondered if Ray Tate was armed.

She nodded, leaned towards Ray Tate, and said brightly: "Yeah, Ray, a lot of pigeon shit, no question. I read that pigeon shit is so toxic that it can dissolve a statue in, like, no time, like ten or fifteen years. I suspect it has something to do with their diet. I also heard that the city spends hundreds of thousands of dollars blasting statues and monuments to get the stuff off. It runs in the drains and pops up in our water. Did you know that, skip? Hundreds of thousands in tax dollars, so we can drink liquid pigeon shit. Believe me, that can't be good for you." She stretched again and rotated her neck. She wore one of her endless array of ugly suburban pantsuits. Her bra was black where it peeked through the buttons of her stretched blouse. "Now, crows. Let me tell you about crows. Crows is no joke, don't get me started on crows —"

"Okay, focus, people." The skipper sat forward and steepled his hands. "The *Federales* can't do the job. The dep thinks we can. Can we?"

Djuna Brown started to speak again but Ray Tate overrode her. "Sure we can. But what's in it for us? At the end of this thing, they're going to fuck us all anyway. As soon as we get close, they're going to race in with the lights flashing and grab up everyfuckingthing we find. You go back to Intelligence Analysis, Djuna goes back sucking a whistle at holiday traffic up the Interstate, and I go back … Well, there's likely mushrooms involved and it's going to stink an awful lot like shit."

The skipper took all this sitting back in his chair, unable to look away from the unblinking eyes staring at Ray Tate in a friendly, expectant manner over the unruly beard. He was right and it wouldn't matter downtown that the skipper failed because all they'd given him were zombies, a dyke who burned her hair, and a gunman who wanted to play Officer Friendly in the cool uniform and the red lights over his head. "Well, we're going to do it anyway, right? It's all pensionable time so we may as well go down in a blaze of glory. Thing is, Ray, can we do it?"

"Sure, skip. No question. We can put the hat on these fuckers in, oh, I bet two weeks. Maybe ten days."

"Bullshit, Ray. The *Federales* have had a month and unlimited resources. They don't got dick."

"Yeah, skip, but they aren't ace investigators."

Djuna Brown smiled at Ray Tate. "And they maybe don't have everything there is to have, eh, Ray? Maybe they don't have …" She cut her eyes towards the door as though imparting a secret. "Maybe they don't have … the mystery clue."

The skipper couldn't avoid speaking to her directly. "What mystery clue?"

She ignored him

Ray Tate continued, "The question is: do we want to do it? Are we going to get the tools? We're going to need bodies, we're gonna need cars." Tate stretched and his joints cracked audibly. "Phil Harvey is our way in. He's the only one we've got a hook on, him and Agatha Burns." The skipper looked confused. "Agatha Burns, skip, the girl who went for a drive with Harvey and never returned?"

"Oh, her. She left the note on the fridge, right?"

"This case isn't wires and tires. We've got no phones to wire and we've got no one to drive behind. We need two approaches: one to set up some teams around town and put a fix on Harv. The other to backtrack Burns, try to figure who she is and where she hooked up with these mutts."

"Give me an action plan, Ray. How do you want to do it?"

"Someone on Phil Harvey's place in the Beach. Someone else on Agatha Burns's old place. Couple of guys out there, cruising mutts' hangouts, ready to move if something breaks out. We've got to freshen up the statewide hit on Harv. Me and Djuna are going to shape out Agatha."

"Two weeks?"

"Yep. Two weeks we'll back up a shitload of pills to your door, bring in Captain Cook in chains."

Wally Brodski stuck his head in the door and looked at each of them as though he suspected he was the target of a conspiracy. He had brightly coloured feathered fishing flies hooked into his shirtfront. His tie was a long silkscreened trout. "Skip? I'm taking a medical off. My ulcer's on fire. I can't do the night trick."

Djuna Brown took some hours to rest up for her sudden night shift. Ray Tate asked Gloria to scan the photo of Phil Harvey into her computer and make a half-dozen prints. When they were ready he checked out a Taurus and ran through the spots, his rover dialed to the local police grids, hoping for a call he could legitimately respond to. He got a quick crush on a dispatcher, loved her cool litany. She made gunshot sound like a sex act.

He drove with his elbow out. The autumn air had a sharp wintry chill and the brief snow had stopped. On the edge of Stonetown he came across two chargers tussling with a large Native panhandler on the sidewalk. He jammed the Taurus and got half out, but the chargers had the guy under control. The both looked about fifteen years old and he'd bet they didn't have five years on the job between them. But they were out and about and learning their trade. One of them looked up and somehow recognized the drab Taurus and a cop through the facial hair. He gave Tate a thumbs-up then ran his hand horizontally as though smoothing water: Hey, everything's okay. Ray Tate continued to cruise, taking the long way around up to his first stop, Phil Harvey's condo.

Bernie Gross sat in a pickup truck behind the building, sprawled across the seat, his rover off and his head crammed at an awkward angle against the passenger door. His feet stuck out the window and the floor was covered with food wrappings, beer cans, and fishing magazines. There was a mom-and-pop shop around the corner and Ray Tate went on foot and brought back two coffees.

"Bernie, Bernie. Wake-up time. C'mon, man. Fuck, look at this mess."

Bernie came around slowly. "Ray. Ray Tate, the last policeman. How we doing? We arresting anybody yet?" He straightened up and reached for the coffee.

Ray Tate stepped back with the cups. "Come out, Bernie. You come out to drink it. Stand up, man." He felt a huge sadness. There was almost nothing left on the job between the fifteen-year-old uniformed kids wrestling bums and this great fat slob, once a good cop, counting the minutes until he hit the big pension. There was stuff in Bernie's head and his heart that could fashion great cops of green kids, could create a lineage for generations to come. But Bernie had made a wrong move someplace and he gave up. His career was now a cycle of the brown jobs: court wagons, couriering, counting paper clips.

Bernie got his huge body out of the pickup. His upper face sat on an inverted pyramid of jowl. His eyes were shot red with dull, general hatred. "Okay, gimme."

"Any action?"

"There's no fucking target. They told me to sit on this place, so I'm sitting. Dunno who to watch for. What the fuck is this? If this is the new American policing, I missed the memo." The coffee cup lid wasn't secure and Bernie spilled coffee down the front of his fat shirt. He ignored it. "Wasn't supposed to be like this, you know? This job used to be a religion for the guys, most of them anyway. Now, well, look at you. Two good shoots, two mutts go toes up — two less to bust later. And instead of giving you a medal they're out to hack your ass with that dyke twat. Why you hanging in? Fuck them and their community outreach. You got the twenty-five in. Come fishing with me and Wally. We got a guy buying us a fishing camp up in Canada."

Ray Tate took an envelope of prints from the Taurus and handed Bernie the photograph of Phil Harvey. "Black Camaro. This guy with the burns on his face. Or a big fat guy with a branding iron, going 'Giddy-up.'"

Bernie took the photo without looking at it and sailed it into the pickup. "This is fucked, you know, Ray? They're just lining us up and the skip is gonna knock us down. But," Bernie made a wise face, "but two more weeks, Ray, and I got my time in. I'm fucking gone so fucking fast my fucking shadow'll still be on the fucking wall for a fucking week and those cocksuckers can kiss my ass. You like bass fishing? This place we're buying in Ontario, oh you gotta see this place."

"You'll make it, Bernie. No problem." He took his coffee and left Bernie leaning against his pickup, slurping and thinking about angling some bass.

Bernie terrified him.

He wondered if that's how it happened: you pretend to not give a shit and go on long bird rambles and nobody notices. Before you know it you're sleeping in a pickup truck covered in candy wrappers, counting the days to a very long fishing season and not giving the shit you used to pretend not to give.

At Agatha Burns's stash apartment in the Hauser South projects, Tate could find no signs of surveillance set up. He voiced out on the air and got nothing back. He went to the ground floor patio where the money man worked. The glass doors showed the place had been cleaned out but the former resident had left several lumps of dog shit scattered around and a bag of clothes pegs. The lock on the side fire door was still jammed and he stood in the stairwell and listened, sipping his coffee. No sounds. Climbing the stairways he kept his gun in his hand, craning out to look up where the keeper with the scattergun had been. At Agatha Burns's apartment the signs of the forensic collection were long gone. The door was locked and no one answered when he thumped. He trudged down the stairs.

Outside, the boneless black guy was sniffing around the Taurus. He recognized Tate's hair and beard with the wave of a can of beer. His gold chain hung down to his waist. Plastic bags appeared from the bottom of his baggy pant cuffs and slipped onto the pavement.

Ray Tate nodded in a friendly manner. "Hey, player, who's around?"

"They all gone. Just us folks here, now. Took that ugly ass fucking dog with them. Where your ho go?"

"Where'd they go? They set up someplace else around here?" Ray Tate waited. "You dropped something."

"Me? No, not me. I'll clean 'em up for you, you want."

"Do that, would you? I'd hate for some kid to find them, get curious. Where'd they go? The guys from here?"

The man put his big running shoe over the plastic bags. He shrugged. "Big pickup truck took 'em away a couple of weeks ago. After you was here. Where that ho? She got a man? She need a player?"

"Tell me about the pickup." Ray Tate realized the guy was mentally ill, that his cool jerks were the result of medication fouled by alcohol, not some inner hip hop. A puppet for the local traffickers, a feeble goof they stood up to attract the heat. Ray Tate doubted the plastic bags contained anything but talc. The clunky gold chain was chipping, he could see, showing dull lead underneath. "What did it look like? Who was driving it?"

"Black thing. Lots of silver. White guy with blond girlie hair came."

"Not the guy with the bacon face?"

"Him, no. He come here, he stay here, you know? You be taking his fried chicken ass out of this project with a spoon." The man started to get angry. "I'd shove that silver bad boy right up his skinny hippie ass, he bring that cooked mutton motherfucker face in front of this player." He calmed himself with a swallow of beer and nodded. "They took the ugly dog in the back of the truck, the ugly motorcycle mother-fucker with the scatter."

"You see the scatter?"

"He had it under his coat. Cut down the pipes real short so the shells stick out. Whoo, tough white boy. Fuck. You ho, where's that girl of yours at with that old lady hair on her pretty head?"

Ray Tate unlocked the Taurus. "You want to pick that stuff up, okay?" He saw the man was getting jittery, moving the beer from hand to hand. "You throw that at me when I drive away, next time I see you I'm going to run the car over you."

"I hear. I hear." His head bobbed, the whites of his eyes were orbed out, and when he smiled the long thin cords of his neck stretched painfully. "Peace out, peace out."

As Ray Tate left the parking lot he heard a yell and the beer can cracked off his back window. He laughed. "Oh, you fucking douchebag."

He headed out to the west end and cruised his wife's house. It wasn't quite dark outside but there were upstairs lights that he recognized as lamps he'd strategically positioned to make the place look occupied. The garage door was closed and he couldn't tell if his wife's Neon was inside. Someone had left a package of cigarettes in the Taurus and he fumbled at the lighter. Before things had turned he hadn't smoked more than two dozen cigarettes in two years, and most of those were while he and his lawyer were pacing out the results of the shooting team.

The house looked like somewhere he'd lived once, maybe, when he was another person. With some chargers from the Accident Reconstruction Unit he'd re-shingled the roof, with some firefighters he'd put in a new front porch and a deck in the back. The brother-in-law of a duty sergeant had sodded the lawn with something he said was Kentucky Blue. Twenty years in the house and Tate knew every piece of trim and moldings, every hidden flaw he'd covered with careful manipulation of plaster and paint, where every seam in the drywall was poorly sanded, where every edge of tile didn't quite fit and was disguised under base-boards. It was a trade you learned by doing, just like policing. You were as careful as your experience let you be and you had to make mistakes. You covered them up as best you could and swore to never make them again. And you made less and less as time went on. Just like being a cop. The house was a place of hidden but educational flaws and he'd been proud of all of them. He'd been a doorstep baby of the State and had lived in many houses, but never as more than a guest, cheap labour, or a sufferance.

It was good work, being a cop. At first it was just a job. But then it became something else, something that overtook him, something that he was good at, could be perfect at. In a drunken evening at the kitchen table once, after he'd been punched out in a bar fight and was recuperating, one of the visiting old-timers had called it a religion and used the words Faith and Duty.

"If you weren't a copper, young Ray," the old-timer had said, "what would you have been?"

Drunken Ray Tate had fallen for the sympathetic eyes of the old interrogator and said, "A painter."

But the oldster misunderstood. He'd nodded and said, "A good living. People always need their houses painted, you can make a good dough if you hustle, build up a client base."

He watched, smoking, as a firefighter two houses down carried an old armchair to the curb then went back and brought out a set of end tables and a box with magazines poking out the top. The firefighter put out a cardboard sign: Free. He'd been among the neighbours questioned by Internal Affairs after the second shooting. The buff firefighter had told the shoo fly to get off his property. You fat fucking slob, he'd said, you should be ashamed of yourself, going out in public like that, on the taxpayers' dime.

The whole enclave was men in uniforms: city cops, firefighters, emergency crews, a few Staties, two *Federales* who did consular security over in Chicago and commuted home for three-day weekends.

Ray Tate went to get out of the Taurus to say hello to the firefighter when the dash radio went off.

"Any Chem Squad bodies out there?" Djuna Brown waited out a few seconds of silence. Her voice was of islands and sand and she put even the honeyed dispatcher to shame. "Anybody? We got a good live sighting for Phil Harvey downtown."

Ray Tate double-clicked the handset and headed for the highway downtown. He called Djuna Brown on the mobile. She sounded excited. "Bernie spotted him. You fucking believe that? Bernie."

"Where at?"

She began laughing. "Well, old Bernie's at that discount sporting goods place on Huron Street and he's lined up to buy some hooks or something and two aisles over at the cash is Phil Harvey, checking some stuff out. Bernie gets outside first and out comes Harvey. Gets into a rental, grey G6, and he's away, southbound. Haven't heard from Bernie since."

"Nobody on the air?"

"Nope. Me and ye, Bobby McGee."

"Fuck that." Ray Tate scooped up the handset. "Chem Squad, anybody? C'mon."

A reluctant voice dragged up. "Yeah?"

"Wally? Ray. Where you at?"

"I'm off. Left the rover on by accident."

"But what's your twenty, Wally?"

"Ah. Ah, east Chinatown."

"We got Phil Harvey heading down Huron Street in your direction. Can you scope him?"

"Who the fuck's Phil Harvey?"

"Fire face. Guy on the wall in the office. Long, black hair, he's got a grey G6 under him."

"Ah, Ray, c'mon man. I'm off. I got issues."

"Just get over to Huron and see if he rolls by, okay?"

"Who's authorizing the overtime? I'm off, Ray, I can't work for nothing. The union."

Djuna Brown came on. "I'll authorize it."

Silence.

Ray Tate put the rover down, activated his dash

flasher, and found some shoulder. He voiced out: "I'll authorize it, Wally. You're golden, man."

"Yeah, Ray. But are you authorized to authorize?" But he was moving. The gambling club Wally favoured was a long block from Huron Street. Wally was puffing. "You gotta ... you gotta sign my notebook ... Ray ... Before shift ends ..." But he didn't make it. "Nah, nah ... No fucking way, Ray ... I gotta stop ... Fuck, my legs ..." He sounded like he was in tears. "Oh, fucking Christ. My lungs. Man."

Djuna Brown came over. Her voice had a different timbre and Ray Tate knew she'd abandoned the office and was in play with a rover. "Chem Six B rolling. Ray, where you at?"

"Ramping off at River. You head to the fishing shop, find the clerk, see what he bought. I'll come in to Huron."

"Hey, Ray." Bernie came on. "He got fishing rods, some line, some hooks and lures, weights. Duct tape. Rubber gloves. He's one of those guys thinks you need a six-pound test to catch a six-pound fish. He also bought a sleeping bag." He laughed. "He's a cooker, maybe, but this mutt's no fisherman."

Wally came on, his breathing under control. "Bern, you get the lures? The ones on sale? Mepps, right? It said Mepps in the ad. Any left?"

"Yep. Cleaned 'em out. Spinners, spooners, everything. We're in business, Wall. Dumb fucks."

"Beautiful."

Djuna Brown came over. "I'm heading downtown, Ray. I'm in a blue 500."

Ray Tate dialed the skipper's mobile. "Skip, we got Phil Harvey on the move downtown. We need more bodies."

"What's he doing? Where is he?"

"Someplace in the core, I think. We need some bodies."

"Where are the slobs? The fisherfuckingmen?"

Ray Tate told him Bernie eyeballed Harvey. He lied. "I got Bernie and Wally on perimeters. We need some cars to go into the core, flush it out." There was silence. A television set spoke in the background over a laugh track. "You want to roll the *Federales*?"

"No, no. Fuck, no. This could be our breakout. Let me see if I can scare up someone from the downtown sector."

Ray Tate gave the coordinates for the box. "He might've turned out of here anyplace, skip. But if he's in, we got him. Grey rental G6. No plate known."

"Think he's running with a trunkful of my pills, Ray? Tell me that and I'll tie up the wife and come out myself."

Ray Tate turned onto Huron Street, guessing north. Southbound a grey rental G6 slowed and Phil Harvey stared out into the Taurus with a faint grin on his face.

By the time Ray Tate cut a jerky U-turn the G6 was lost in the galaxy of red tail lights.

Chapter 16

Phil Harvey found a parking lot to dump the rental in and walked away juggling his bags of fishing gear, the sleeping bag in its sack hanging from his shoulder. From the shadows on the edge of the lot he watched cars pass. A white head in a square Ford cruised by and he recognized the black hooker who was a cop peering at parked cars. A few minutes later some ghost cars began crawling into the side streets, shooting spots into the rows of cars. He spent a few minutes scrubbing his back by walking like a crazy person in circles, with spins and dodges and weaves. He was on the Metro Transit bus. He was off and onto another. He was through a hotel lobby, through one set of revolving doors and out another. He took a taxi four blocks in one direction then told the driver another location the opposite way.

Connie Cook was sitting in a banquette in Gratelli's in Stonetown, impatiently looking at his watch when

Harv hustled his bags through the entrance. The hostess took a look at his marred, sweaty face, the billowing black leather coat, and the clutch of bags and started to shake her head. He said he was meeting someone and not to fuck with him, he'd had a day she wouldn't believe. Don't ask.

"Fuck, Harv, now I gotta get you a watch?" The Captain looked pointedly at his own wrist. "I said eight."

"Had to wipe my ass. Heat all over. I think those cops are up on us again." He kicked the bags under the table and slung the sleeping bag sack into the corner of the banquette. He sat back in shadow. When the waiter came by, Harv said he'd make it simple: "Take all the rum you got in the place and pour it into the biggest fucking ice bucket you got. Throw in some ice, then strap it to the front of my fucking head like a horse's pail."

Connie Cook laughed. The waiter asked if Harv wanted cola on the side and before Harv could rip into the guy's throat Connie Cook told him, "It's okay, Michael. Bring him a good triple dark rum and have one for yourself." When the waiter retreated, Connie Cook smiled. "Tell me. But first, did you get the stuff? For my sweetie-to-be, whoever the lucky girl is?"

Harv nodded, looking around. "Got it all. Got myself some fishing stuff, too. It was on sale. But I think, Connie, we might want to lay back on everything until we figure what the fuck's going on." He stopped talking when the waiter put a water glass of ice and another of rum in front of him. He poured rum onto the ice. "I was at the sporting goods place getting the stuff and there's a cop in there. Like he was shopping. He went out and when I went out, he's out there, standing around. He scoped out my rental. I see him grab up a radio or something and he's watching me fuck off. Then a little while later that guy I saw in the red Intrepid, remember, up at Ag's old place last month? The hairy guy with the black chick? Well, I'm going south and he's going north in I think a Taurus or some such piece of shit. When I pass, he does a U-boat in my mirror but I'm so fucking gone. I dumped the car and then I see that black chick that was with the hairy guy. She's in a Ford something. Then a bunch of ghosters with spotlights come through. That's what I saw. What I didn't see, I don't know. I washed myself, I'm pretty sure, but who knows what the fuck else?"

"Take a deep breath, Harv." Connie Cook waved at the waiter across the room. "Drink some of that stuff. You want something to eat? I had a dinner when you didn't show up, but I think I'm ready for a snack. Go for some oysters? Say, two dozen, half shell?"

"Ah, pass on that." Oysters made Harv think of lugers. Gratelli's was an upscale seafood place. He noticed some diners glancing toward their banquette at the rough sound of his voice. He struggled out of his coat and smoothed his hair back behind his ears. The waiter appeared with his little palm pad. "Steak. Well done." Harv had seen some shit and didn't find bleeding meat on a white plate appetizing. It reminded him of blood pooling on a tiled shower floor. "Baked potato. Whatever veggies are fresh."

Connie Cook went for the two dozen oysters anyway and at the last minute added a bowl of mussels and a deck of bread.

They sat watching the late evening crowd. Several people waved at the Captain but none came to their banquette. The waiter delivered plates of food and Connie Cook stuffed his linen napkin into his shirt collar and, with a bottle of hot sauce in one hand, lifted and slurped off the oysters with the other. With the oysters gone, he seamlessly began dispatching the mussels, sopping with bread.

Phil Harvey ate like a convict. His head was down over his plate and he kept it close to his edge of the table, looking up and around periodically as though someone might want to steal his steak. His wood handled serrated knife stayed in his fist, pointing straight up while he chewed.

Connie Cook studied Harvey's defensive dining posture. Fondly, he decided that no matter what, Harv wouldn't ever go back into the joint. If he had to, he nodded to himself, he'd spend every dime he had on lawyers and bribes. Harv had brought him into a new life and had become a genuine friend. "So, Harv. Willy Wong. What's up with him?"

"He's got a bunch of chems out at the import place in Gastown, big fucking drums full of the stuff. It sits there for a while until he's sure there's no heat on it, then he has some guys pick it up, split it up among his cookers. If the cops come around, Willy's got a stooge working who'll take the fall. Willy's a prominent businessman. Community leader kind of guy. Pals with the mayor. Rogue employee. Who knew?"

"So. How much has he got in there?"

"Not sure. A lot, though. I got a guy who told me there's a loading dock in the back with a camera over it. There's a bunch of tough guys hanging around. I figure we go in at night, take all the shit we can lift. We can get six forty-five gallon drums into a pickup truck and be out of there in minutes."

"Nice. Tonight?"

"Yep. Later on. I got my three guys that you met and I got another guy coming down from up north, he's got a big bastard F-250. We'll load 'er up and head up to Indian country, take it to the lab."

"Not the guy whose truck it is, though, right? Only two guys know where the lab is. Let's keep it that way."

"Sure. We'll do the rip on Willy Wong and I'll drop my guy at his place, about halfway up. I'll take the drums up and stow them then head back down to his place. He'll drive me down here someplace, drop me, and you can pick me up."

"A master of logistics, you are, Harv. A fucking master." Connie Cook beamed upon Harvey. One appetite sated, he made a subtle burp and announced proudly: "Phil? Phil? I think I got us one."

Harvey looked up. The Captain's face was wreathed with smiles like a sick boy in some kind of love.

Ray Tate had the skipper leave the alert out in the down-town core but gave up on catching up with Phil Harvey.

The G6 was located by a ghoster running the lots. The skipper said he'd contact the rental company in the morning, but for now there was nothing. Djuna Brown returned to the satellite, voiced out that she was nested, but no one replied. The slobs evaporated into the dreamland of fishing camps and trolling motors. Ray Tate took the Taurus home and painted until he was startled that the early indirect morning light filled the windows.

Chapter 17

The skipper arrived early so he could leave a 7:00 a.m. voicemail for the dep, bringing him up-to-date on the forward motion of the task force. He'd set his alarm for 2:00 a.m., got up from bed, staggered into the kitchen, and left a message on the dep's voicemail. He chugged a few and passed out again and before leaving home at 6:00 a.m., left another message. He hoped it would look like he'd been up all night directing his troops, going without sleep while they did a dragnet through the city's underworld. They noticed that kind of thing at headquarters, he believed. He wore the same clothing he'd worn in to work the day before and didn't shave.

The dyke was asleep on the leather couch in his office. Her ghastly pantsuit was wrinkled and stained with coffee. Much of her black bra was exposed. She slept with her mouth open and he saw she had perfect, little white rodent's teeth. The explosion of white frizz on her head was matted and some of it had stuck to her cheek where she'd drooled in her sleep.

He thought of kicking her to death but something stopped him. He had a moment that rocked him. Back in the days when he'd been a young policeman, a real policeman, he'd been part of a search team looking for a missing eleven-year-old. He'd been the one to find her, folded into a frozen curve under a tarpaulin, in a garage two blocks from a halfway house for degenerate losers. That girl had been blond and she too had stuff dribbling out of her dead mouth. Her clothing had also been in disarray. The effect on him had been profound: he spoke to the corpse and apologized to her for not finding her in time. He decided only sick bastards would want to look at that kind of stuff endlessly, and that very day he set himself on a career arc that would lift him from the streets, fast and far, no matter what it took.

Djuna Brown looked the same size as the eleven-year-old. A glimmer of realization sparked in the skipper's mind but he smothered it. He kicked the edge of the couch. She stirred and opened her eyes slowly, in a way he momentarily found sleepy and seductive, as though she'd awakened under the eyes of a lover. When she focused on him, first he saw fear, that widening of shock. Then she grabbed at her open blouse and when she looked up again he experienced her pure hatred. Wordless, he stepped back and away. She got up and hurried out the door in her slippers, wiping slick from the corner of her mouth, muttering.

As she crossed the office in the direction of the ladies' room, Ray Tate came through the door juggling paper cups of coffee with newspapers crammed under his arm. He looked bedraggled, as though his clothes had gone through a wash cycle while he was still wearing them. There were heavy streaks of black, dark blue, and blood red paint on his shirtsleeves and on the tail of the denim shirt hanging under his jacket.

"Ray, when your buddy there gets back from her tampon break, c'mon in. Conference time."

Inside the skipper's office Ray Tate, Djuna Brown, and the reclining skipper were kicking the shit. Djuna Brown had taken water to the coffee stains on her clothes and there were patches of wet on her pants. She'd clearly made efforts to smooth out the wrinkles. Her face was grey and dark circles were pressed under her cat's eyes. The skipper had the feeling he'd somehow insulted her by finding her crashed on his couch, having seen her defenceless in sleep.

"Okay," he said to Ray Tate, "run down for me this stuff from last night."

Ray Tate shrugged. "Djuna ran it. I was just a road rat."

She surprised him by lying for the team. "Bernie and Wally were set up downtown and Bernie spotted Phil Harvey. He voiced it out. We put together a moving box and went down there. He got away, left the rental jammed in a lot, and *phhhhht,* gonzo, Alonzo. The sector guys, a ghost car, found the G6 dumped. That's it."

"So, Ray, what've we got that we didn't have yesterday? How are we closer to getting my pills?"

"Well, skip, we know the boys are back in town. We know Phil Harvey's got something going someplace, probably in the woods, in Indian country, or in the badlands. That's maybe where the lab's set up. Isolated. No worry about neighbours complaining about the smell. He bought fishing gear and a sleeping bag so we can assume he's bunking in for a while, cooking something for Captain Cook. We know he's got to be heated up, the way he dumped out the rental and evaded our box."

Djuna Brown studied him. The office smelled of artist's chemicals and paints. She wondered about his night. It couldn't have been worse, she thought, than waking up with your boobs hanging out and seeing the fat, red Irish mug leering at them.

The skipper sat and gazed out the window. He wasn't looking for avian life. He was exhibiting the deep posture of a master investigator, determining where next to deploy his troops. Djuna Brown googled her eyes at Ray Tate. She held her nose and looked him over. He shrugged and mimed painting. She gave him a wide, sad smile and shook her head. She said, "Beatnik." Her anger and fear were gone. Her partner was here and she began to comprehend partners.

The skipper missed all this. The telephone rang and in relief he scooped it up and made notes as he listened. "Okay, our guys are on it. Who's running things over there? Tell them my guys are on the way." He hung up and forgot Djuna Brown was a dyke and

Ray Tate was a gunner. "Okay, kids. Showtime. We got some Chinamen down over in Gastown. Two are minor gun whips but it looks like the third one's been shot up pretty good and he's going for the egg roll special. The hammers are standing by. We're working."

"What's up with it? Why do we care?" Ray Tate looked at the skipper's grinning face and waited.

"Well, Ray, my boy, the shootout was at a chemical importing company. Owned by Willy Wong."

"I heard of that guy. The mayor's pal." Ray Tate stood up. "The Wrong Wong. The mayor of Chinatown. Mr. Presto!"

"Yep. And preliminaries from the scene say four or five white guys were rolling drums onto a big black pickup truck. They bailed out there. One of them looked like a big ugly woman."

"Phil Harvey."

"Sounds like."

"Any fat cowpokes dashing about, branding the citizens?"

"Nope. Just fast white guys." The skipper made a genuine rare smile. "Go get 'em, kids. Get me my super lab."

Willy Wong's warehouse was on the outer northern edge of Gastown, where the muddy sky was held up by tilting chimneys and squat fuel tanks. Willy Wong operated from a row of units with roll-up metal doors at the rear of an industrial strip. A pair of chargers were at the front of the place drinking coffee. One saw the red ball on the dash of the Intrepid as it rolled into the parking area and he waved and hooked his thumb around the back. Djuna Brown piloted the car carefully through a half dozen police cars and parked where she wouldn't get blocked in.

On the drive across the highway Ray Tate had flipped through his notebooks until he found the licence number for the black F-250 pickup that had rolled into their surveillance on Phil Harvey's condo. Using the rover he dialed to the Chem Squad channel and asked Gloria to put the plate through. He asked her to have the city run the owner, as well as Agatha Burns, with various spellings, aged in her twenties.

Djuna Brown swooped around a transit bus. "Housekeeping, Ray?"

"Just stuff we would've done a month ago if we'd been left on the case. This black F-250 is everyfucking-place. It was at Harvey's place, it went to Burns's old place in the projects, it might've at the Wrong Wong's warehouse shooting last night. Maybe we can put it under Phil Harvey."

Djuna Brown wasn't into talking about work. "Ray, let me ask you one, no prejudice, no nothing. Straight, okay?"

"Sure."

"Gloria? On the reception?"

Ray Tate dragged it out, "Yeeaaaah?"

"What do you think? You think she's okay?"

He shrugged. "I guess. I don't know. I barely notice her. Why, you and her ...?" He laughed.

"Another Chicago deep-dish of disappointment for the skipper."

"No, no. Jeez, Ray." She smoothly braked at a backlog and put the gumball on the dash and found the siren switch. She swooped onto the shoulder. Ray Tate grabbed the dash with one hand and the overhead grip with the other. "No, she was asking stuff."

"Stuff?"

"Yeah. What're you like. Are you married? That kind of thing."

Ray Tate was pleased. Even at speed her fingers curled around the steering wheel. He liked the look of her fingers and noticed the nails weren't chewed back. "No shit? Fuck. Good-looking woman, that Gloria. If you like non-dyke, white *Federale* chicks with guns."

"Not you, though, right?"

"Nope. My heart belongs to my art."

She gave him a feral smile of pointy teeth. "Beatnik." She looked happy. "She, Gloria, gave me a business card. For a place I should go to." She stared through the windshield. The block-up had dissolved but she left the light and siren on and steered over into the hot lane. "You know what she asked me? She asked if I was cutting on myself yet. She said she was born-again. If you can't find Jesus yet, she said, find a good hairdresser and wait until He comes along. Can we go there, after?"

He looked at the white frizzy hair. It was brushed and had a barrette over the right ear but it was still weird. He wanted to paint her, he decided. "Sure."

They rode in silence. He warned her that the exit ramp was coming up and she smoothly drifted to the right. On the ramp she shut down the light and noise.

"Djuna, let me ask you one, okay?"

"Sure. Fire away."

"This dyke thing." He hesitated. "Ah, look, how committed to that are you?"

"Who told you I was a dyke, Ray? Not me, Bongo."

They walked around the units and found a vast crime scene taped off. Numbered cones covered shell casing, chalk marked bloodstains on the ground, and bullet holes on the back of the building. The roll-up door was half-way up and it was peppered with rough perforations. A crowd of reporters was grouped outside the yellow tape.

"You're not? Really?"

"Imagine, huh?" She gave him a mysterious smile and wiggled her eyebrows.

A young charger watched them approach then waved them off. "You'll have to go around."

Ray Tate slipped his badge out of his jacket. "Chem Squad. Who's the duty?"

"Topper." The young guy went to a cluster of cops near the roll-up doors and spoke to a striper.

The striper looked up and made a big smile. "Ray Tate. Cockfuckingsucker, I thought they'd have you in jail by now."

Ray Tate shook his hand. "I told you, Topper, they'll never take me alive."

"Good man. Fuck them all."

Tate introduced Djuna Brown. Her name didn't register with the striper and he stared at her and shook her hand with a laugh. "Jeez, I thought you had to be twelve years old and four feet tall to be a cop."

She gave him a pretty smile. "An Irish guy, looked a lot like you, did the sign-up physical. I stood on a hundred dollar bill to get the extra four inches."

"Good girl." The striper looked around. "I can guess why you Chem guys are here. The short version is: four or five guys pull up, they lay a beating on a watchman, a bunch of mutts come out of the place, and it's Chinese New Year. Year of the Mutt, I guess. I dunno, I'm still writing Year of the Pig on my cheques ..." He waited for them to laugh. "So, anyways, we got two with pistol whips at St. Frankie, one with a gunshot at Mercy Med. First two victims are minor; basic attitude adjustment. The third guy's sniffing the incense. Our bandits roll out in a black pickup with drums of chemicals according to a cabbie who saw them loading up. The victims say nothing was taken, it was an attempted break-in, the cabbie saw the drums go out. Chinamen say black guys, the cabbie says white guys. Chinamen say they didn't see a vehicle, the cabbie says a black F-250."

Djuna Brown was writing it down. Ray Tate stood so the media cameras wouldn't pick up his face. "Anybody see a white guy, big fat fucker?"

"Nope. Just mutts. Steroid guys. And a guy looked like an ugly woman. Coulda been my wife from the sounds of it," Topper looked at the punctures in the overhead door. "Shot the shit out of the place. Chinamen won't say what was in the drums. The drums they didn't take in the truck that wasn't here, I mean." He stared at Djuna Brown. "You a city guy, honey? Where you stationed before this mess?"

"I'm Statie."

Boxcars locked into a train in Topper's head. "Oh. Oh, yeah. From up north."

Djuna Brown stared at him. "You got a problem, there, Top?"

"Dearie, take it easy. If you're with Ray, you're in the right gang. Me, I got nothin' against dykes." He looked around and whispered: "I think my wife? She's a dyke." He widened his smile. "She fucks like a dyke, anyway. Meaning: not with me."

Djuna Brown smiled into his charm. "You ever heard, Top, of a mustache ride?"

He shook his head. "She asked me once. I said: honey, if it ain't deep fried, I don't eat it. C'mon in the kitchen. She passed."

Djuna Brown laughed. Topper turned away and listened to his shoulder microphone.

"Nothing for us here, Djun'," Ray Tate said. "Let's see what they've got back on the F-250."

Topper called something out to a group of chargers and they carefully started stepping out of the scene. "Hey, Ray, the guy that got shot? He cracked the blank fortune cookie. Hammers are on the way."

"Okay, Topper, we're outta here. We didn't enter the scene, right? So no need to mention us, that we came around."

"No problem. Hey, tell your partner here how I got the name." He started laughing. "*Oy vey.*"

Chapter 18

The three wreckers were up and bouncing in the after-glow. They were gregarious and there were handshakes and hugs. It was far from the morose finale to the Captain's crazy branding frenzy in east Chinatown. There'd been no weirdness, just maybe a little chaos that comes with all sudden action. But none of them had been seriously hurt, no one had dropped his fudge. When the Chinamen at Willy Wong's warehouse had reacted, Harvey and the blond kid and the wreckers had gone to work and finished their mission. One wrecker had taken a metal bar across the shoulders but had shaken it off. Harvey had taken a whack in the upper arm from the same guy before Frankie Chase, the blond kid from up north, pulled his gun and opened up.

Dawn was rimming the sign of the truck stop north of the city, already casting everybody a long shadow. The five men had crammed themselves into the double

cab of the F-250. The forty-five gallon drums of precursors were in the back, covered with a tarpaulin
chained to the bed.

The wrecker who owned the gym was almost
dancing, juggling his paper coffee cup. "Fuck, Harv.
Fuck. Just like the old days." His breath showed in
the chill morning air. He wore a thin, unlined leather
jacket over a T-shirt but the temperature didn't seem
to have an effect on him. Harvey wondered if the guy's
nose ring ever got cold enough to ache in the winter.

"Nice, nice one, Barry. You fucking guys. Well, that
was beautiful." He screened his body and handed a wad
of cash to him. "A little noisy there at the end. You and
your guys might want to take a vacation, until it sorts
itself out. I think one of those guys was hurt bad."

"Fucking pussy cocksucker Chinamen." Barry
laughed, threw away his coffee and indifferently ran
his thumb over the stack of money. "Ooohh, nice." He
stared into the morning sun. "Like being a kid again,
Harv. If I didn't need the coin, I'd be doing this shit for
nothing. How's your arm?"

"Ah, fuck it. It'll hurt later. Right now a bit of
a throb."

"Good thing it was your left arm, Harv. Because I
know you jerk off with the right."

The blond kid was with the other two wreckers a
few feet away, smoking cigarettes. The kid chain-smoked
and sucked nervously at his coffee and periodically
glanced over at Harv. The two wreckers were laughing
haw-haw-haw biker laughs. They both slapped the kid's
back, calling him Shooter.

A red, chromed Cadillac Escalade crawled into the parking lot, crunching gravel, and stopped twenty yards away. Harvey could hear the radio playing, heavy on bass. A blond woman with long ringlet extensions sat inside, her hand draped over the steering wheel.

"There's our ride, Harv. You guys good from here? The kid there looks a little shaky, you know? He's gonna stand up? That guy he shot, he didn't look good."

"Yeah, he's cool." Harvey shook hands with the wrecker. "I'll keep an eye on him."

He had to keep his left arm up on the window ledge of the truck to ease the pain, but Phil Harvey wouldn't let the jumpy kid drive. As they passed up the highway he kept a tight ear on the kid's responses, listened for him swallowing too hard, licking his lips. He watched to see if he tapped his feet or drummed his fingers on the dash. He liked the kid and didn't relish leaving him in a hole in the ground in Indian country. He figured the kid had saved him from a wicked beating by the Chinamen.

They were just pulling into Widow's Corners when the news of the shooting hit the radio. The kid rushed forward to turn it up. No one was declared dead, although one of the victims, the perky woman's voice said, was in grave condition with gunshot wounds and a murder team was on standby. Two others were at hospital with minor head lacerations.

"Fuck, that was my guy, Harv. The shot guy. Fuck."

Phil Harvey knew the kid was about to step over a line. He'd seen the Chinaman get hit and go down, he'd seen the kid lean in like a matador to finish him, he'd seen the Chinaman's head jerk at the last minute. There were things that happened in the middle of things and people let themselves slip a little. It wasn't great, but it wasn't the end of the world either, usually. Not like Connie Cook, who'd obviously planned his revenge by having a branding iron made, had planned clearly to use it on the guys counterfeiting his product. The Captain had been looking to go crazy long before he got to the rooming house.

For the most part, on the long drive north the kid had been okay. Nervous and excited, but not drawing in on himself, shutting Harv out. He was even laughing and reliving the look on the Chinamen's faces when they came out of the warehouse.

But the kid had the power to put four other guys in jail, to completely change the path of their lives. It was a knowledge, Harvey knew, not many guys could handle when things got tightened up around their nuts. He wasn't worried about the wreckers: they were older guys and recognized that doing some time was just an interlude in the lives they'd chosen. Harvey had responsibilities to those guys.

At Widow's Corners he drove the F-250 into a restaurant lot beside a motel and told the kid they'd have breakfast. That he had to make some calls. They sat at the same seat he'd sat at on his way out after stashing the Camaro at the farm, where he'd waited for the kid to come pick him up. He thought he should have told the old guy up at the lab to turn the engine over on the Camaro and run it every couple of days. He thought briefly about Agatha Burns.

Harvey ordered some eggs and toast. The kid had an appetite and went for the truckers' all-in special, and that was, Harv thought, good. While they waited for the breakfast, he went to a pay phone and called the Captain.

"Hey, Cookie. How's it?"

"You been busy, Harv. Wisht I'd'a been there. Was it bad?"

"Naw. One of the … ah … other guys, might, you know … go?"

"I heard. Slow news days I guess. The radio's all over it. But you're okay, right? You got what you went shopping for? All the guys are okay? They miss me?"

"Oh, yeah. I took a whack, that's all. One guy asked about you, said where's that guy, came out with us last time. We coulda used him. I told him you were fucking up somebody else. Next time, he says."

"Perfect. Next time for sure. Good guys, those guys. Say hi to them for me." The Captain sounded pleased. "So, we got, what?"

"Six forty-fives."

"That's two hundred and seventy gallons. We can do a lot of good work with that much. What're you doing now?"

"Hang on." Harvey watched the kid leave the restaurant and go to the F-250. He slid his ass in and left the door open and sat sideways while he turned the key and fiddled with the radio. Harv saw his mouth move. He shook his head and then he got out and looked around, shut the door, and came back inside. He trudged with cement feet and waved c'mere at Harvey. "Ah, I got a couple of things to do up here, Cap, let me get back to you."

"Okay. Keep me posted." The Captain paused. In the background a loudspeaker announced a horserace. "Harv? My other thing. What about that? You ready?"

Harv felt heavy dread and couldn't source it: the kid who'd crossed a line, or the girl the Captain wanted grabbed. "Let's talk later. I'll be back tomorrow."

"You staying over?"

"Might have a bit of work still to do, I dunno." The kid sat with his coffee, staring off into space. "Maybe it'll take a couple of days to get back down. I'll let you know."

Connie Cook watched his horse being rubbed down in the stables. The jockey, a little girl with the face of a man and the ass of a midget, was polite to him but he knew it was because he was buying the oats.

"She's running well, Mr. Cook," the jockey said. "She's got this half-step we can make work for us. It'll take some time, but she's a good runner. We can make that half-step work for us."

"Okay, Mary," he said, appreciating that her freakishness was as part of her as his was of him, as Harv's was of Harv. He felt they all shared the kinship of outsiders, of the differences. "I'll come out one morning and watch her do her thing. You need anything?"

"Naw, no, Mr. Cook. Come out in the morning, sir, see her run. She's going to need some time, she's gonna spend some money. I hope you know that, going in." The jockey studied him looking for confirmation of something. "There's muscle and there's speed and feed, you know, but there's also heart. She's got the heart."

Captain Cook liked the jockey. If the horse ran backwards, he thought, he'd still give her a soft landing. She loved the horses like he loved the cheerleaders: with passion, with need. "Mary, go do it. Whatever it is, you go do it, okay?" He gave her a lifting of his jowls. "I'll talk to that trainer, that Paki. You take her out today and no matter what, I promise you, we're in business." He sparkled his eyes. "Unless I come back later tonight and she's still running to the finish. That's not good."

She laughed and for a second there became pretty. "We're going today in the fourth. If she's still running it at Christmastime we can come down together and throw oats at her."

"Atta girl."

Connie Cook's wife didn't like horses, didn't like their smells, didn't like their shit, and didn't like the denizens of the backtrack with their shy shuffles and slang. She liked the Cup races when the Canadian horses came down, when the trailers brought the runners up from Kentucky. She liked the dips and sips in the clubhouse. She liked dressing up and making gentle fun of her husband's extravagance. Connie Cook's wife stayed well away from the stables and sat in their box in her pillbox hat and scarf, talking with her cronies.

Connie Cook walked across the front of the stands and looked up at his wife. She was talking across the aisle between the boxes with Gabriella Harris-Hopkins, of the Harris Clothing Company and the Hopkins boutique brokerage. Gabriella Harris-Hopkins was forty-five years younger than her husband, Irving Hopkins, putting her at a tasty twenty-five. Not exactly in the ballpark of Connie Cook's tastes, but not too far out of it either. Connie Cook thought of her as a crass whore. Irv Hopkins was her third husband and he didn't blush when she announced she'd had her breasts enhanced as an anniversary present to him. Connie Cook especially hated Irv Hopkins's granddaughter, Tiffany, who was not much younger than her step-grandmother and still maintained her own boobs. He'd decided to maybe have Harv grab Tiffany, but now he wavered and thought about maybe grabbing them both. It would be a coup but fraught with problems unless he and Harv pulled in someone to help control them. It could be a disaster instead of true love. In any event, he decided, the lucky girl would be kept up at the farm for keeps and wouldn't make it back to the city. This meant a lot of driving. Connie Cook was looking into a sedan that would be comfortable on long rides. He didn't mind the long rides with the mounting anticipation, the teasing of himself when he stopped for coffee or gas. But he liked a lot of leg room; the new Beemer 7, maybe.

Idly he thought of having Harv get some disposable workers up there to build an underground bridal suite for his future loves, something with running water, lights, some furnishings, and maybe a video hookup. It wouldn't be necessary to saddle them with bad habits at all. He could just grind away on them, leave them healthy on the outside, keep them until they naturally advanced to their expiry date.

The mayor and an aide, followed by some news teams, came along the rail, the mayor stepping carefully in his suede Hush Puppies. He wore a blue tie decorated with horses, and waved up into the stands although nobody waved back. Someone booed, calling him a Commie cocksucker. People laughed but no one threw anything. The aide posed the mayor and several luminaries with the state flag and the Stars and Bars in the background. The mayor spoke about the city as a growing international sporting centre. He said the racetrack was a perfect example of equestrian sport, a pastime available to all the citizens of the city.

The aide spotted Connie Cook and waved him over.

"Mr. Mayor, you know Cornelius Cook? He was a great supporter in the campaign and is a patron of the arts community in the city."

The Mayor shook hands with Connie Cook. The aide nudged them together until the photographers got their shot. The aide spelled Connie Cook's name out for them.

Connie Cook heard the aide say, "Cook, he gives the limit."

He heard the mayor say something that sounded like, "That whale should get to vote twice."

The Captain's wife beckoned him. He laboriously climbed the stairs to the box.

"Connie, Gabby is involved in the most delightful project. She wants to build a gallery for homeless art. I said we'd be glad to support it."

"If art doesn't have a home, it should go to a free gallery."

Cora Cook told him to shush and affectionately pushed his arm. "Art by homeless people, Connie. Don't be such a wiseacre. Some of those people have talents they'll never get to develop."

"Connie," Gabriella Harris-Hopkins said, moving to interact her breast and his bicep, "I think if four of us start with a modest amount of seed money we'll be able to find donors without too much difficulty. Then we'll go to the city for matching funds. What do you think?" She was in the garb of racetrack patron: stylish tailored jodhpurs, sleek boots, and short, brown leather jacket over a knit sweater. Opera glasses hung from a beaded chain around her neck.

"Gabby," Cora Cook said, "your breasts may be perfect but don't flirt with my man."

He noted the effect jodhpurs and boots had on Gabriella's ass and then and there he decided a strong maybe. "Define: modest, Gab. Define: amount."

"Connie …" His wife looked horrified. "Don't be in a mood, Connie."

Gabriella Harris-Hopkins shook her head. "You're such a kidder, Connie." She gave him the smile she'd hooked her old husband with.

"I'll need a pack."

"What, sorry? Connie?"

"I'll need a plan, I said. Something that I can work from to determine my involvement. Just something for the bean-counters."

"Oh, a plan. Well, let me have something put together for you. I knew you'd be onside." She gave him an arch look. "If this gets going, we're going to have to spend some ... quality time together."

"Soon, though, with something written down, okay, Gabby? How's your week looking? My year-end, you know?"

"Well, Irv's off to the Bahamas tonight. I'm staying at the apartment in Stonetown while we have the alterations on the house done. Let me work on it, all right? I'll put something together and call you."

"Perfect." He made his decision and made a wide smile. "Perfect. We can do great things for those with great needs."

"Oh, Connie," she said, shaking her head. "You're such a kidder."

"That's what they say, Gabby."

Chapter 19

Ray Tate wanted to explore Djuna Brown's faux lesbianism. He found he was excited. As she piloted the red Intrepid away from Willy Wong's warehouse and headed back towards the Interstate to swing downtown, he said, "So, you, like, ah, do guys, huh?"

"Not white guys, no." She shook her head gravely. "So, anyway, how'd Topper get the name? He's a funny fuck."

"How about artists? Artists aren't black or white. We're just, ah, I dunno ... artsy." He inflated his chest. "We're all colours. We are, Djun', men of the people. Of all people."

"I never saw myself as an artist's moll. Do I, like, sit on a stool and get painted or sketched or something? Spend my evenings in cafés and rundown bars? Sorry, Morrie, no can do, buckaroo." She didn't look at him and he could see by the edge of her cat smile she was having a good time. She bumpered up and beeped a car out of her way. "So, Topper?"

"You don't have a husband or something, tucked away?"

"I bet it's because old Topper tops everybody. They tell a joke, he tells a better one. They got a story, he tops them with a better one."

Ray Tate thought about it. The rover called out to him and he was directed to call in on a hard line. He gave a ten-four.

"Topper. Topper was a uniformed sergeant downtown. He was assigned to an anti-Nazi demo and it was cold so he had a nip or two, deployed his guys around, daydreamed about retirement. A reporter from Chicago came up to him and asked for a crowd estimate. Topper said, I dunno, a thousand or something, who cared? The reporter said numbers were important and he pointed at a sign that said, Six Million Dead. Never Again. Topper says, Nah, four million, tops. The reporter is miked and Topper ends up on the news."

"Pretty funny guy, Topper."

"Well, there's a disciplinary hearing at the Swamp and as he's coming out, docked two weeks' pay, another reporter asks if he's anti-Semitic. He says, No way, hey my wife's a fucking Hebe."

She laughed. "I can see that. I liked him. Nice guy. That's what you want to be, isn't it, Ray? A Topper."

* * *

While Djuna Brown was undergoing a complex, odif-
erous treatment at a Stonetown hair spa, Ray Tate
used the reception desk console and called the Chem
office. Gloria came on and said the F-250 came back
to an address in a town up towards Indian country,
registered to Franklin Chase. Frankie Chase came back
as twenty-four years old, biker associate, convictions
for possession, possession, intent to traffic, possession,
extortion, assault, possession, and several traffic viola-
tions. "They're sending his mug over."

"Sounds like a bad boy, our boy, Gloria. Thanks."

Behind him a hair dryer was activated. "Where are
you? What's that?"

"Ah, hair dryer. Djuna's getting some work done."

"She went already? Good." She was quiet a
moment. "The other name you gave me, Agatha Burns,
with a U? I put it through and I got a call from Homicide
asking why I was asking about a missing." She paused
and said Goodbye to someone in the background. "I
didn't know Homicide handled missing persons."

"Yep. So, what'd you tell them?"

"I said I'd have to have the skipper call them."

"She came back from the system, though, right?"

"She's a missing person from last year. I looked
around. Her old man was a politician, lived up on the
lake. He came home one night and she'd gone, clothing
and some personal effects. He's got tons of dough and
he thought she'd been kidnapped but no ransom call
ever came in. There was some media stuff, a reward
offered, but nothing ever turned up. Because the
clothes and stuff was missing with her, it looked like

she'd taken off. I asked the missing person guy for a picture but he said not until they're in the loop. So I'm getting one from Public Affairs. It'll be here in an hour. Oh, and that guy, the Chinese man shot last night? He passed away." She sounded sad.

"Thanks." He didn't hang up. Djuna Brown was having something massaged into her hair. "Ah, this thing. For Djuna. The hair place ..."

"It's okay. She needed it."

He sat in a wood and leather armchair, gazing out onto the street of boutiques, dozing his way through pristine copies of hip magazines from the cosmopolitan cosmos. He wondered if people actually lived that way or if it was just magazine life. There was an article on lofts in Paris, vast spaces populated by narrow men and women in black clothing who seemed to do nothing all day except sit by vast windows and contemplate the meaning of art. To Ray Tate, whose original life inclination had been towards paints and pots and brushes, Paris was a resurrected dream from childhood. He was thinking if things went into the toilet with the job he could grab a reduced pension and jump onto a plane. How hard could it be?

He was calculating the cost of living in the daydream of Paris and examining his pleasure that Djuna Brown had outed herself as a hetero when a young woman came over and told him his friend would be quite a while.

"She's getting the full treatment," the woman said. "You know, while you wait, we could clean you up a little bit. A little less ... sixties?"

Afterwards he drove the Intrepid because she thought her nails might still be tacky. The car smelled of perfumed hair products and emollients. Ray Tate tried not to stare over at her. The bleached hair was gone, replaced by a helmet of spiky-looking jet black. Exhaustion was painted from her face. She'd been plucked and buffed. She'd somehow lost the mean pierce of her green eyes and they seemed wider and longer, more sly and Asian than he recalled. Her nails were still very short, but they were shiny and the traces of the chewing butchery gone. She looked cool and fun, as though some real person locked away inside her had been freed and given air.

She caught him looking. "Nice, eh, Ray? You don't clean up too bad, either."

His hair was still longish but neatly trimmed and swept back from his face. The beard was gone. She saw he had a strong jaw line and actual hollows under his cheekbones. The paint stains had been removed from his fingertips and fingernails. She kept glancing over to make sure it was him and not some Paris hipster.

He kept his eyes on the road. "Anyway. Anyway, two things: our F-250 from last month at Phil Harvey's condo comes back to a guy named Frank Chase, up north. He's a biker type, runs the badlands, doper. The usual. Agatha Burns, your pal, though, she's pretty interesting. She's a missing person. Took off from her family last year, hasn't been seen since. Gloria's getting pictures of both of them."

He slipped the car into a reserved parking spot at the Chem Squad offices. He went to get out but saw she was smiling.

"Djun'? What?"

"No."

"No, what?"

"No, I don't have anyone hidden away. No hubby. No boy toy."

He made a wide smile.

"We're gonna do something, aren't we, Ray?"

"I think. I don't know, but I think maybe, yeah. We be maybe gonna."

"You ever make it with a black chick, Ray?"

"No," he said, "but I never shot one, either."

Gloria had the photos ready at the reception desk. She smiled at them but didn't comment on their new personae. Ray Tate noticed she wore a subtle silver crucifix.

Djuna Brown looked at the missing persons photo and said the Agatha Burns in the flyer was her Agatha Burns. The mug of Frankie Chase was, Ray Tate was pretty sure, the same blond guy who drove the black F-250 into Phil Harvey's parking lot. Gloria said an inspector from the Homicide Squad was in with the skipper and a dep from the Swamp.

When they made their way to their desks the skipper called out and waved them into his office.

"The fuck's going on, here, Ray? You had Gloria put through some missing person?"

"Yep. Agatha Burns. You remember her, skip. She left the note on the fridge at the stash house, up in the projects. The girl Djuna was working back into Captain Cook."

The skipper skipped his eyes around. "Her. Ah ..." He'd let the mystery of the girl go by the board. "Refresh me."

Djuna Brown said to the dep, "We were going to work her, but you guys at headquarters took the case back, gave it to the *Federales*. Before we could do dick we had to shut 'er down, send everything down to those smart guys." She shrugged. "Skipper had us all over her, but ... *phhhitt,* the Feds bigfooted us before we could do anything."

The skipper looked relieved. He stared at her.

The dep said, "But you sent it over, right? In the investigative files? They fucked it up, right? They had it and they fucked it."

"Oh, yeah, everything went. Including the report about the burned female body the Staties found up north in Indian country about the same time. I guess they didn't think it was important." She smiled and shrugged. "Feds, what're you gonna do?"

The dep stood up. "Okay, it's back to us now. This Burns's old man is out of state politics now, but he's still a big shooter with the Democrats. What's her status, far as you know?"

Ray Tate shrugged "Well, like Djuna said, we think she's dead. That that might've been her in the lab truck fire up north. She was in with some cookers, this Captain Cook guy and a guy named Phil Harvey. Maybe they knew Djuna was scoping her out, buddying her up. We got a wit saw her leaving her pad with Phil Harvey about a month ago. We go in and there's a note on the fridge that if she disappears, ask Phil."

"You got that and you don't call us?" The dep shook his head. "What the fuck are you doing here, Gord? You got a half a fucking homicide and you, what? Hit the bars? A month old crime scene, that'll be just fucking pristine right about now."

Ray Tate patted the air in front of his chest. "Whoa. We got a team in, we did a forensic just in case. Like Djuna said, before we could move you told us to fuck off, so we fucked off."

The dep took it but didn't like it. He turned his guns on Tate. "And how's it going for you, Ray? You still in counselling, Ray? Getting the twitch taken out of your finger? I hear your wife kicked you out. Gee, I hope things are okay otherwise, buddy."

Tate gave him an even stare. "Well, I'm working on it, dep." He turned to the hammer from Homicide. "This might be your lucky day, Sam."

The hammer was bored. "How's that?"

"You might solve a homicide, right about now, before the body hits the floor."

The skipper said, "Ray ..."

"Cool-ee-oh," Djuna Brown said gaily. "I'm wet. City guys are so butch."

* * *

The dep kicked everyone out of the office and went at the skipper. The Homicide guy stood talking with Ray Tate and Djuna Brown. Through the glass it looked like the dep was fist fighting bumblebees. His mouth ratcheted. He pointed out the window towards the lake, he pointed up to heaven, he jammed his thumb down.

"Nice shot there, Ray, pardon the expression. Your partner here's got some fucking mouth." But the Homicide guy was smiling. "Where's the forensics on the apartment the chick went missing from? Who's the wit?"

"The *Federales* got the file, I guess. I don't know. We just did the work and got it in the ass. The wit is a dopey guy shuffling bags in front of the building Burns was staying at."

"We're going to take the Burns case. The old man's a good member of the big machine and he's always treated us okay before that fucking mayor got elected. We'll get the old guy some closure. What have you got on this Harvey guy?"

"Not much." Ray Tate gave him the address of the Beach condo, a précis of Phil Harvey's pedigree, and the description of the black Camaro. "I had him in a box the other night, but he evaded. He was pushing a rental. He's our lead to a guy named Captain Cook, some big fat fuck who runs a chemistry set. Your guys are doing that Chinaman murder out at Willy Wong's place? We think Phil was out there leading the charge."

"Okay, we'll take the Burns case. We gotta. When we look for Harvey we'll pass on any bits to you, especially if we see a fat guy. That sound cool?"

"I don't give a shit, Sam. The way this is going we're going to wind up with nothing anyway, the way it looks in there."

Inside the office the dep had his hand on the doorknob. He let go of it and rounded again on the skipper. When he left he slammed the door behind him and boiled out without looking at anyone.

The Homicide hammer left after him and the skipper waved Ray Tate and Djuna Brown in. He was pale and had sweat on his forehead. His hands shook. "Those fucking cocksuckers, oh, fuck." He sat down and shivered the vibrations of a boozer too far from a bottle. He looked at his desk drawer.

"We'll be back in a couple of minutes, skip. Do what you got to do." Ray Tate led Djuna Brown out of the office and down to reception. Gloria had fresh coffee going and Tate poured three cups. He added two inches of sugar to one and they went back in.

The skipper had some colour back and he looked embarrassed. Ray Tate could smell Canadian rye in the air. He passed around coffees and he and Djuna Brown sat.

"So, Ray, what's with this new look on you guys. You look like a horny college prof and she looks almost ... Anyway." He shook his head.

"You get two new guys this way, skip. The bad guys are used to a beatnik and a bleached dyke. Instead ... the new improved Chem Squad."

Djuna Brown nodded, "Ace detectives, masters of disguise."

"Okay, the deal is this, you guys. We leave off the Burns thing, give anything we turn up to the hammers. On Captain Cook, we gotta get out there, root him out. That's the way it looks, anyway. The only thing that'll save any of us is we stack up a mountain of pills for a press conference and pin this Captain Cook to the wall. Tie him to the overdoses, the brandings in Chinatown, then whip him through the streets for the chief. We got a week then we're all fucked." He looked at Djuna Brown and seemed about to say something but didn't. "So, Ray, what next?"

"Well ... we got a lead. Nothing we want to tell the Swamp about, but we maybe got a guy into Phil Harvey. The F-250 from the Willy Wong thing last night comes back to a guy we think is hooked to Harvey. He's from up north, so we're going to head up there, strap him to the truth machine."

Djuna Brown wrinkled her brow. "That up north thing. It seems a lot of stuff is up north. Harvey gets a speeding ticket, he's heading up. The F-250 is from up there. The camper fire that we think was Agatha Burns is up there. This super lab's gotta be out in the boondocks: it stinks and if anyone else was around, there might be complaints." She nodded to herself. "Indian country or the badlands."

Ray Tate nodded. "Yeah. This fishing gear Phil was buying, the sleeping bag, points north."

"Okay, go to it. Keep track of your overtime and I'll get it for you later, somehow. You need anything else?"

"Just a good fucking leaving alone."

"Done."

Djuna Brown looked up from her coffee. "There's got to be something between Agatha Burns and Phil Harvey. Like, how'd they meet? How'd this fat Captain get his hands on her? How come she stayed in the stash house and when she could get out, she didn't go home or call the cops?"

"We're not going to worry about that, Djuna." The skipper was startled that he'd used her first name. "Don't even fucking go there. Focus on Phil Harvey, focus on the Captain motherfucker, and my mountain of pills."

They went to leave. The skipper said, "Ray, stay a minute, okay?"

Through the glass they could see Djuna Brown working the phones.

"What's with this makeover madness, Ray? She looks almost fuckable and you look ... Well, Gloria better look out. For the both of you."

"New faces for old places. We're going to need a new car. The Intrepid's burned off. And not some fucking Taurus either."

But the skipper wasn't listening. "Why'd she do that? When the dep reamed me? She could've put me in the deep shit, letting the Burns thing go by. What's her game?"

Ray Tate shrugged. "We're just working the case, skip. It's our case. Right now, we're all in the same gang.

Your problem with her? Her with you? That's something else."

"Fucking weird." The skipper glanced out the window and fished his bottle from the drawer. He topped an inch into his coffee. "Let me talk a minute, okay?" He held up the bottle and raised his eyebrows.

Ray Tate put his palm over his cup and shook his head.

"Back before I got on the rocket I was part of a search party, looking for a missing little girl. She —"

"Sheila Battersby." Ray Tate shook his head. "Don't go there, skip. I know the story. Everybody knows the story. Let it go." He nodded at the skipper's cup. "You could let that go, too."

"It's hard. You know it's hard. This fucking job."

"This is the best fucking job in the world, skipper. You know why? Because you're never alone. You need help you don't even got to ask."

The skipper drained his cup anyway. "Yeah." He looked embarrassed and smiled. "So, the dyke, Ray. How's that going? You going to spike her in the ground for me?"

"Oh yeah, skip. Head first, so hard you'll see maybe just the bottom of her tiny little slippers."

"Good man."

Chapter 20

Frankie Chase leaned against the door of his F-250 as Phil Harvey headed north. Harvey's arm was starting to throb and he let his left hand rest on his lap. The radio news went through several half-hour cycles, each leading off with the murder at Willy Wong's. On the sixth cycle, Willy Wong gave a brief interview, describing himself as shocked at the events. He said it was getting too dangerous to do business in the city. He wanted a meeting with his friend the mayor to get police to root out the bad elements terrorizing Chinatown. A police spokesman came on and gave various descriptions of the bandits. Black or white. A black pickup or a dark car.

Frankie Chase turned off the radio. "Fuck. Black pickup."

Phil Harvey kept to sixty miles an hour. "Lots of black pickups. We'll put this one on ice for a while." He laughed. "You'll have to get something else. If this shit keeps up my place up north is going to look like a used car lot."

"Fuckin' guy died. Unbelievable. That one I gave him in the head? He jerked. I thought his timing was okay and I just took his ear off and was going to give him another one." He giggled. "I thought he'd cranked you in the fucking head. I thought you were gone, man."

Harvey became concerned. "Frankie. Listen to me, okay?" He took a deep breath. If the kid didn't absorb this stuff right he was going to have to go. Six weeks ago there'd've been no question; the kid would already be in the ground. But things were different now. Phil Harvey had a plan, maybe an actual future. "We're not going to talk about this again. You aren't going to reminisce. I'm not going to ask you anything, ever. If you ask me, Hey how's the arm? I'm gonna say I don't have any fucking arms, you got me confused with some other Harv. If the guys that were with us call up and even hint at talking about it, you go: What the fuck are you talking about? Never mind not talking on the phone. Don't talk at all. It didn't happen. Only five guys know what happened. That's a lot, but they're solid guys." He looked at Frankie Chase. "Four of them, anyway. Even if they all talk to the cops about it and you get hooked, well that's okay. There's no evidence. Only your own mouth can put you in for this, that or evidence." He had a sudden thought. "Frankie, where's the piece?"

"I got it. I almost forgot it, but I got it."

"Fuck, that's what I mean. Jesus, we're riding heavy already with the drums back there, now there's a fucking murder weapon in the truck." Harvey laughed but he made the hard decision. There was just too much to think about, too much to worry about. He had an exit plan from his life and he didn't want to trip over a murder charge for himself or Barry's guys on his way out.

He saw an exit ahead and changed to the right hand lane. He rolled off the state highway and drove until he saw a sideroad. He stopped the F-250. "Give me the piece. It's gotta go."

Frankie Chase rummaged under his seat. He took out a black automatic and wiped it down with the bottom of his T-shirt.

"Hey, no. Stop." Harvey stared at the gun. "Listen now, Frankie. There's things you've got to know. You wipe the piece with your shirt, you put your DNA on the piece. So now you're going to lose the T-shirt and the gun, both." He laughed. "You keep this up you'll be walking out of here naked, all the Indians jumping your white ass." He kept his eyes on the gun but didn't reach for it. "Okay, okay, let's just relax. Let's go slow, here. Pop the clip, clear the chamber."

Frankie Chase dropped the clip onto his lap. He cleared the sleeve and the round in the chamber bounced up onto the dash. He recovered it. There were four unspent shells in the clip.

"Now take off the shirt and spread it on your lap. Take out the shells from the clip. Wipe each one down and drop 'em on the floor. Wipe the piece down too. And the clip. The shirt's fucked now." He watched Frankie Chase closely as he removed his T-shirt. There were spider tattoos on both shoulders, a panther on his bicep. "Now, without touching anything with your fingers, make a little bundle of everything."

He took the keys from the ignition and got painfully out of the truck. Frankie Chase went to get out.

"You wait here. I'm going to go for a walk and lose this stuff. If we both go, that means two guys know what nobody should know. The gun won't walk into the bush by itself. So, you go or I go. I think I'd rather be the guy that knows, okay? Nothing personal."

"Sure, Harv."

"Put your jacket on, it's fucking cold. I'll be a little while. Stay with the truck, don't look where I go." He took the bundle carefully.

"Phil, Phil, I never thought of all this stuff. Fuck, I'm stupid."

"You're in the bigs now, Frankie," Phil Harvey said. "You'll learn. It takes time."

He went up the sideroad a ways and picked a tall tree as a landmark. Up at the farm he'd gone for long thinking walks and got slightly lost. It was the smoke from the farmhouse that saved him. If he hadn't left a fire going that morning, he'd still be out there walking behind himself. He picked a tall pine, glanced back where the kid was leaning on the F-250 facing the other way, then walked into woods. Two hundred yards in he used a branch to clear some autumn leaves. He scraped a hole in the ground, one handed. He put the T-shirt in, unwrapped the gun, filled the hole over the shirt, and scuffed it down with his boot.

He awkwardly reloaded the four rounds into the clip, tucking the gun under his left armpit, and then he cranked one into the chamber. He put the gun into the top of his boot and settled his pant cuffs. He realized he'd known what he was going to do the moment he didn't just leave the kid at the restaurant to wait while he took the drums at the farm. But he knew, once Frankie Chase knew where the farm was he was dead. He wondered why he pretended to himself that he had a choice; that the kid might not have to go. No way he'd be able to get the drums off the truck and into the lab by himself anyway.

A new future didn't just drop out of the sky, he thought. You didn't wake up one day and go, Oh okay, a new life for me, and just walk away whistling. You had to clean up after yourself. There was housekeeping to do: money to collect, debts to settle, plans to make, tracks to cover. Another few days, Phil Harvey thought, a couple of hard things to do, and ... Well, who knew? A haircut, that was for sure. And he'd looked into skin grafts, slowly reading his way through a book at the library. It was painful, taking skin from other parts of his body, but what wasn't painful?

The pine was off to his left and he headed diagonally so he'd pop out on the road from the other side of the F-250. He wished he'd brought the fishing gear up, that he could try to figure out how to put on a hook or a lure, how to fix a weight, how to cast his offering out into the lake. The library had had instructional books but he wasn't sure; he'd also read how to clean a fish and cook it and how to tell them apart from each other.

There were mountains out west, another book had told him, places where you could reinvent yourself and never see anybody if you didn't want to.

The rivers were silver and clean and land was cheap if you didn't mind hauling water, living by lamplight.

Back at the truck he told Frankie to forget everything about the gun, about the shooting. "After right now, before I get in the truck, you want to say anything? Because once I'm in there, if you ever mention it again you're going into a hole in the ground in the woods, right, Frankie?"

"Never happened, Harv. I'm okay, I'm cool."

A few miles before the turnoff to the dirt road that led to the farm, Phil Harvey told him to put his head on the dash, to put his coat over his head. "This is a place I don't want anyone to know about, Frankie. We leave here, same thing. You cover up."

"If we're leaving my truck, how are we getting out?" He struggled out of his coat.

"There's a crazy old guy up here, he'll drive us down to Widow's after we off-load the barrels and stash the truck. We'll get someone to pick us up, drop you at home and me in the city."

The kid nodded. "What a fucking day." He turned in the seat. "Look, I appreciate this. I just want you to know. You ever, I mean ever, need anything, Harv, you call me. I'll be there."

Harvey was wavering. He liked the kid. The kid had done the shooting, but no one would ever find the gun if Harv hid it. Without the gun, the T-shirt was just a T-shirt. Maybe some of Frankie Chase's DNA on it, a hair or two, and some burnt gunpowder. But without the actual gun that did the Chinaman, it was just a rag.

"No problem, Frankie. You go out on a thing, who the fuck knows how it's gonna turn out?" He shrugged. "That's the life, that's the game."

The kid hid his head under the jacket and Harv turned onto the sideroad. It was a huge responsibility, not just for himself but for Barry and the boys, but he decided to re-evaluate the kid's future, to keep an eye on him for a while, see what was what. If you killed every guy on his way up who'd done some heavy lifting, no one would get into the game. There'd be no one to do the work except morons.

A couple of hundred yards up he saw the main farmhouse and far beyond that, the old reprobate's pickup truck parked beside a tumbledown shack. The day had stayed as cold as the morning and a flag of smoke rose from the chimney of the farmhouse.

Harvey told the kid he could uncover his head. The kid did and looked around.

The door of the house opened and a face leaned out.

"Who the fuck is that?" Frankie Chase leaned forward to peer through the windshield.

Phil Harvey realized he was going to have trouble getting the drums off the truck after all. He had the black automatic out of his boot and very quickly he fired the remaining four bullets into the left side of Frankie Chase's head.

He felt very sad.

Chapter 21

Ray Tate and Djuna Brown decided to take advantage of the leeway the case had given them. They checked out a black Xterra and headed first to her place so she could pack a bag. He sat outside her leafy duplex and watched her go by the window, the inside lamps making a slim, flitting shadow. He felt like a schoolboy. When she came down she was wearing a bright *khanga* hat, a short, brown leather jacket, blue jeans, and had dumped her slippers for ankle boots and zany leggings. When she leaned to sling her bag into the back seat he made a show of checking out her butt. He saw the exposed tip of the barrel of her little automatic in its clamshell holster and her handcuff case.

In the four-by-four he drove the few blocks to his place. He told her she was looking like a hot beatnik chick and she gave him a smile.

"You don't know what you're doing, do you, Ray? I bet you didn't get laid a lot when you were younger. Right? This is all free-form jazz."

"Free-form jazz?"

"Yep. You're just hitting the notes and hoping you find a riff that makes sense. Smokehouse romance." She put her hand on his leg. "I can tell you this: you maybe got a shot, Bongo, okay? Don't work so hard."

He sat back, pleased, and pulled into the driveway of his apartment building. Upstairs he realized all he had was his uniform in plastic and piles of bum clothing. He quickly tried on a pair of blue jeans but it had been months since he'd been exiled into the wilderness and stress and bugs had eroded him; the jeans sagged and gaped and he bound them with the second last hole on his belt. He found the union sweatshirts and windbreaker they'd given him at the sector and a threadbare sweater, and some socks and underwear and stuck them into a gym bag; he added the bottle of gin from under the sink. At the door he looked around at his pathetic pad. Since the second shooting his life, he realized, had been about free-form jazz. Unplanned. Undirected. Without discernable melody.

Before leaving he went into the washroom and found a package of condoms his freckly policewoman had left behind.

When he came out in his sagging Levis, Djuna Brown was behind the wheel, laughing. "Jesus, Ray, you look like a prisoner of war."

She slid her handcuff case around onto her hip and slipped her clamshell holster off her spine and put it in the console. She belted up and made sure he did too.

Just north of the city she pulled into a huge Wal-Mart and Ray Tate went in to buy some pants and a jacket. She prowled through the glove compartment and when he came out of the Wally's she held up a plastic card.

"Bingo, Bongo. An all-in credit card. This must be one of the Fed's vehicles." She wiggled her eyebrows. "With this, man, we can head all the way west, set up on the coast, and live the beatnik life. By the time the bills come in and they catch on, this fucker'll be buffed flat."

"First, Djun', we have to torture Frankie, then take down Phil Harvey, the Captain, and the lab. Back up a shitload of pills into the skipper's office. Then we have to make sure we didn't make any mistakes. Then we either get fired or we get buried." He stretched and yawned. "Except for all that, we're on our way."

She drove back onto the Interstate and made a bubble around herself, flicking her eyes to the rear- and side-view mirrors every minute or so. He dialed in a Chicago radio station and locked it in, then went looking for a Canadian lite-rock program he liked to listen to at night. He went back to the Chi-town station and caught some sweet Butterfield: *"Baby I'm just driftin' and driftin', like a ship out on the sea …"*

She eased over onto an exit ramp and left the Interstate. She seemed to know where she was going. There were little wooden signs pointing ahead, naming half a dozen towns. He saw Porterville had been defaced to read Por Ville.

"This your old turf, Djun'?"

"No. A little further north. Indian country. It gets very weird up there very fast, once you go couple of hours on. Lots of work, especially Saturday nights. But, you know, sometimes ..."

"What?"

"Sometimes ..." She clamped her mouth and wouldn't let herself speak. Then she simply said, "Sometimes ... not." She thought of limp bodies hanging from trees like summer pods, of children huffing gasoline and dying with their faces crusted with vomit, of vicious domestic disputes fuelled by alcohol, and dead husbands and wives and lovers gutted like autumn deer.

But there were mornings, too, rumbling out of the mini-barracks in her huge Ford into a new sunrise, of doing walk-arounds and coming back to the truck to discover blanketed elders blowing smoke into the truck's grill because they knew she was as different as they were from the white cops who patrolled their community like they were troops stationed in a foreign war of pacification. The smoke was for safety, someone said, a blessing. She thought about young men coming into the barracks office after making sure she was alone on shift and bringing haunches of venison and careful instructions for preparing it. Of massive trout wrapped in moss and newspapers, already gutted but with the head still attached. She taught the giggling girls about their periods, the shy boys about condoms. She had her dad put together a shipment of books and paints and sewing supplies and send them up.

She wanted to tell Ray Tate about all that and more. She wanted to tell him about how she got the dyke jacket and why she wore it. She said: "We're here."

Frank Chase lived in a leaning single-storey house just outside Porterville. A cannibalized old Harley was in pieces on the lawn. There were two fridges with the doors removed, laying flat on the patchy grass and a stove by the side of the house, behind them a stack of old wood and curly tails of barbed wire fencing. A sign with the silhouette of a revolver on it warned of dogs but suggested dealing with the dog was preferable to running into the owner. There was a Confederate flag tacked over the living room window.

"No F-250," Ray Tate said. "Maybe nobody home."

Djuna Brown rounded the street near the house. Through the rear window they could see a woman in a cloud of steam at a stove, the window cranked open in spite of the cold late afternoon. The woman had long, straight, jet-black hair and looked Native. She wore a plaid shirt and was beautiful, even at twenty yards. She seemed to be singing or speaking with someone. Periodically she reached out of sight and pinched up a thick joint, taking massive inhales.

They drove back around the front. Mindful of the dog warning, Ray Tate took his gun from his boot and put it into his jacket pocket. Djuna Brown removed hers from the console and clipped it behind her back.

They weaved their way through the junk on the walk and the lawn onto the porch.

"How we going to do this, Ray? Cops or mutts?"

"Well, Djun', how about free-form jazz?" He pounded on the door. "We'll play it off her face." ·

She was nervous. "Cool-ee-oh."

To ease her, he said, "But if the dog answers the door, it's every dyke for themself."

She was smiling but stopped when the door opened. She saw the Native woman was a girl, seventeen maybe, and absolutely beautiful. She had bare, bruised legs beneath the plaid shirt that exposed hickies on her neck, and she had high cheekbones and placid features but her eyes were stoned and panicked. "Yes? What?" She looked at each of them. "What do you want?"

She looked like a victim. Ray Tate took his role. "Where's that motherfucker?"

"Who? Hey, who are you?" She looked over their shoulders to see what they'd come in. "What do you want?"

"Frankie Frankie Frankie. Where the fuck's Frankie?"

"He's out someplace. I don't know."

"He was supposed to be someplace and he didn't show up. So, where's he? He in there?" Ray Tate called past her. "Frankie, you fuck, come out here, you fucking dootchbag."

"Show up? He left yesterday. Down to the city, right? To do something with you guys?"

"With Harv. Harv's pissed. If Harv has to come up here ..."

Djuna Brown said, "You don't want Harv making that trip."

"Hey, no. Frankie left, said he was meeting Harv to do something. He was going to be back today but he's not back yet."

"If I have to fucking come in there ..."

Djuna Brown told Ray Tate to calm down. "Take it easy, man. She doesn't know. Guy's fucked off and left her in his shit." She asked the girl her name. "We have to find him, Sherry. We have to find him or Harv's going on the warpath. Did Frankie take off in the truck? That beauty F-250, double cab?"

The girl nodded.

"Did he take his piece?"

She nodded. "I think so. He just said there was something heavy he had to do down in the city for Harv and some guys. That him and Harv would come back and drop Frankie off, then Harv was going to keep the truck to go up north. Harv was gonna return it tonight and me and Frankie were going down to the city to drop Harv off and Harv was going to stand us a night out."

"North? Where north?"

She shrugged. "I dunno. Someplace, I guess."

"Sherry, if we don't find him, Harv's gonna ask you where to find him instead." Djuna Brown shook her head. "We don't want that. We can get with Frankie and straighten it out, cool things with Harv. But we gotta find him, find Frankie. Where do you think this place is, north?"

"I dunno." She thought. "A while ago, like last month, he had to go pick Harv up, up at Widow's

Corners, he said, take him down to the city. Harv needed a ride."

Ray Tate said, "Widow's what?"

"I know where it is," Djuna Brown said. "Indian country."

There was a Motel High halfway up to Widow's Corners. Djuna Brown knew it. "Clean enough. No satellite, though. No pool. They'll take the government card."

"Yeah. We should stop and get a couple of rooms." Ray Tate hoped the innocence on his face didn't look too phony. "Rest up and poke around tomorrow."

She smiled. "Sounds okay, Ray. There's a bar attached to the place. I might go get myself some dinner and company for the night."

"Yeah. Good idea. Me too."

She stretched her arms up against the headliner of the four-by-four and groaned. "I need me a good old skinny white boy." She put her hand on his leg. "I hope they still got the vibrating beds at the High."

They put it off until after they'd had hamburgers and beer in the diner attached to the Motel High. She caught him giving her long looks then snickering as he looked away. She felt her own magic and amused herself when he was discussing tracking down Phil Harvey by making little movements of her mouth or lifting her eyebrows and breaking his chain of thought. It had been a long time since she'd played with anyone, since anyone had played with her.

For his part Ray Tate had butterflies. He'd forgotten how to introduce the idea of condoms on the first date but was glad he'd brought them. Like a lot of cops, when he was younger he'd talked a good game. But except for his wife and a couple of young women before her and one freckled policewoman afterwards, he found making a move had become antique to him. There were a few cops he knew who were hard-hearted motherfuckers, but most of them had soul, had a weird kind of romanticism that was always being thwarted.

The diner was ramshackle and neon bright and there was a constant ping of microwave ovens going off through the serving window to the kitchen. The hamburgers were shaped too perfectly to be handmade, the buns were steamed from frozen, the French fries were uniform and limp. Behind the counter a short-order cook knew every driver and customer who came in. He'd stared at Djuna Brown in her *khanga* hat but before he could say anything, Ray Tate had badged him and taken him aside to show him the photo of Phil Harvey.

"This guy, you seen him?"

"What kind of cops are you guys?"

"Not Staties or Feds, so don't worry about it."

The man studied the picture. "Yeah. Scarred up guy, right. It don't show in this picture as bad as it is, but yeah he's been in a couple times."

"You know where he hangs out?"

The cook shook his head. "Nope. Wears a big fucking black leather coat. Came in, I guess, a month or so ago, first time I noticed him. Guy came and got him and they left."

"The other times?"

"Well, you ain't far behind him. Him and a blond guy came in today. Had a meal, like at noon, and left."

"You see what they left in?"

"Nope. They was here, they was gone. Just like all of us, eh?"

"I guess. What about the other time, a month ago. You see what he left in?"

"Don't recall. Dropped off first by an old geezer in a old, rusted beater. A pickup, I think. Grey?"

"You know the geezer?"

The cook looked around. "Well ..."

"Hey, look. I don't care about you or the geezer, whatever he is to you. I just want to catch up to this guy, see who's who in the zoo." He waited. "This is city work not state work, okay?"

"Geezer's name is Paul. He's got a problem, you know?" The cook touched the inside of his elbow. "He babysits a place up north a ways. Dunno where. There's a lot of these old guys, old poachers, dudes from the city give 'em work." The cook looked around. "Maybe something to do with drugs?"

"You think?" Ray Tate put a business card on the counter. "You see him again you call this number, okay? Maybe, if you get into the shit, you get a pass."

He sat with Djuna Brown and told her what the cook had said.

A group of Indians came to the door and the short-order cook intercepted them with a baseball bat. He glanced at Ray Tate and Djuna Brown. The Indians looked. They stood outside shouting at the diner but eventually trudged off toward town in their thin denim jackets and construction boots. It was cold with a slow but steady wind down from Canada, feeling towards early winter, and they huddled closely together as they vanished in the darkness. Ray Tate thought they looked like a lost tribe and decided probably they were.

Djuna Brown watched them through the window. "Somebody's got a lot to answer for in places like this, Ray. From here on up there's nothing but this shit, these greed-head fucking Christians. Pray on Sunday, sell moonshine to the Indians the rest of the time." She poured some beer into their glasses from the pitcher. "When I first came up, after training, they thought I'd last a week, maybe a month. Then they'd pour me out of the Spout. But the longer I stayed the more I liked it. I came to love it, like you love your little pieces of the city."

He didn't want to wait any longer before heading to their room. He didn't want her to be in a sad place, a place that might thwart what he had in mind for them. But he realized he didn't know much about her and hoped there were things he'd come to know, things she'd come to know about him. He realized he was thinking about his future, hers too, and that gave him the weightlessness of a revelation. She was only talking because he hadn't asked. He'd talk about his dead black men but never if she asked him.

Djuna Brown heard herself, heard the tone of her voice. "Fuck it, Ray. This is our first date, right? You don't want to know."

"Sure," he lied. "Sure I do."

"Ray, lemme ask you one. All things being equal, which of course they're not, what would you rather do? Go to the room and jam our brains out, or sit here and listen to me mope."

"Well, Djun'," he said. "Both."

"But first?"

"I'll get the cheque."

At the beginning, when he started to make his way down her body, she said, "Ray, you don't have to do that, you know. I told you I'm not a dyke, right?"

He stopped, looked up, and spoke with careful and serious enunciation. "Well, I believe you said you didn't say you were. Not the same thing. I can check my notebook if you want me to give sworn testimony."

He listened to her laughing and carried on. Inside he felt huge and complete and artistic, and full of laughter and something else. He thought of his wife, after the second shooting, after she found demonstrators in front of their split. Ray? Ray? You're not a racist, are you? She was a cop's daughter and her dad had never unholstered his gun, except for cleaning and duty inspection. He thought of the skipper and his hatred of Djuna Brown but realized it was simply a connection to the worst part of his life, a dead child in a garage. Djuna Brown had unknowingly revealed the moment when the skipper's soul exposed itself and he was embarrassed by it. Ray Tate thought of the story

Djuna Brown hadn't talked about but everyone had heard: after she beat the teeth out of her moronic partner she'd been ambushed by the roadside and found naked by a passing motorist. The legs of her uniform pants tied at the ankles and a bratwurst sausage glued into her freshly shaven crotch. Someone brought the battery-operated razor, someone brought the glue, someone brought the sausage. Who else but cops? The very best people in the world and the very worst. She should have shied away from ever wanting to be one of them but she hadn't and now she was here under his face.

She made a sound. He thought of a joke he'd once heard: how to do know when you've gone to bed with a lesbian? When you wake up in the morning you've still got a hard-on and your face is glazed like a doughnut.

He lifted his face to tell her that one. She grunted in urgent frustration and forced him down. His head was in a muscular vice of the cinnamon and the salty and he realized he was happy, felt that until now he'd walked a journey planned in advance for him from foster homes to high school to police college to uniform to plainclothes and back to uniform where he ended up with his Glock in his hand, standing over freshly dead black men. No one said: mix paints and slap them on canvas, dream about Paris, go down on a black chick, and when you've done all that you'll be … What?

She began shuddering and whooping and then went boneless and he realized she'd been as without as he had. She patted his head like a boy when she was done. "Ray Tate, the king of swing. Jazzy Ray."

"Well," he said modestly, moving back up her body. "It has been said I blow a cool axe."

After midnight, when she was in the shower, he took the gin from his bag and realized he'd forgotten to get mix. Wrapped in a towel he went barefoot out onto the icy motel landing and looked for a dispenser machine or at least an ice bucket. The machine was wrecked, there was no ice. He saw a group of Indians clutching bottles leaving from the back of the diner, the cook counting a wad of money.

He made gin and taps in plastic cups and carried them to the sagging bed. She came out of the washroom wrapped in a towel. They stretched out. She sprawled on top of him, weightless, he thought.

She began talking, her voice sometimes muffled, facing away from his face, her head on his chest.

She'd been one of only four minorities at the academy. The others were a dour heavy black woman and two Native ladies who looked almost identical. She was the smallest of them all and took some pretty good beatings on the self-defence mat. Often she found herself paired against the largest man, then the largest woman, the black one, then both of them together. There was a sexual aspect to the grappling, particularly with the black woman who loved to get her into a body scissors while overpowering her head with her breasts.

Throughout her training she ached and nursed bruises; she had twisted fingers from small Japanese come-alongs and shooting pains in her elbows and shoulders from the takedowns. She had hickeys on her neck from the sport of the larger men who could apply them thoroughly in the ten seconds it took to legally pin her down. But none of it bothered her; she deflected the interest of the woman and the men with humour.

"I knew it was going to be rough," she told Ray Tate, entwining their legs. "My dad drove a taxi nights in the capital and he saw cops all the time taking people down. When I told him I was going to apply he said I was too small. He wanted me to be a secretary like my sister or a nurse like my mum. When I told him I was giving it a try anyway he sent me to a self-defence school, twice a week for a year while I waited to get evaluated. Mostly what I learned was that you get up fast, afterwards, even if you lose. You look around for somebody else to get into it with. Even if you lose, my dad always said, make sure you're not the only one going to Emergency.

"Anyway, the physical stuff wasn't the problem. The problem wasn't even the guys, at first. There was one guy who just wanted me. He was a nice young guy, farm boy from up Stanton way; he just locked onto me. Hangdog stuff. Little notes in my textbooks, helping me up after we grappled on the mat, invites out for drinks. I wasn't too attentive to how I handled him. So one night when he asked me out for beers, near the end there, on a weekend, I said I couldn't, that I had a date. He was okay. You know, oh shit, sorry, I didn't know, sorry, sorry, sorry.

"So that night we all went into town on a bus. Everybody goes off to do their thing and I headed out in a taxi for a little restaurant, a little out of town. After dinner I go into the bar to have a couple of pops before heading back to get the bus. The other black trainee, Bernice, was off in a corner of the bar. She comes over and sits down. Nice to have a night away from the boys, she said, let's have a girls' night out. I right away told her her scene wasn't my scene. Okay, she said, and we had a couple of drinks and chatted. Just chitchat about this part of the course, that instructor, where we wanted to work when we graduated. It was okay. She had some funny stories about living down south — she was from near Knoxville — and we laughed a lot.

"So we get a taxi and we head back to the bus. We're walking up the road and there's the farm boy waiting to board. He sees us and he looks at me funny. I said to Bernie: Oh, shit, he asked me out. I told him I had a hot date tonight. And bang, just like that she's got her arm around me and twists my face around, plants a big fucking wet one on me. I thought I was going to choke on her tongue. She had a very long tongue. 'Stuck up cunt,' she said, 'see how you like being a dyke.' All night she'd hated me. All night she just laid back in the weeds and waited for a shot.

"After that I was a dyke. No way to undo it. Don't even try. All the guys I'd been friendly with, gentle with when they asked me out or flirted, you could see their faces, that Bernice was the honest one — she didn't hide her flavour. But I'd betrayed them, trying to pass as straight and leading them on. You can hop into bed with a hundred guys after that and it doesn't matter. Word got around. Boy, did word ever get around. They put me as far away from civilization as they could, way up north where they don't like blacks particularly, even if they're Christian blacks. Bar fights, domestics, kids killing themselves huffing gasoline in bags, kids killing each other because ... Well, who even knew? Frozen babies, burned babies, beaten babies, chewed babies. Jack-lighters and bear gallbladder poachers and guys who operate moonshine rigs. Laid-off workers hanging themselves from trees like empty pods."

She lay there a few moments thinking: I'm giving him all the bad stuff. She wondered if she should talk about sudden rivers of fish, kind old men coming by the bright wooden detachment with creels of trout and presenting them in respectful silence, the sickening but soulful smoky smells of sweat lodges, of the open-faced youngest children who came by with beaded god necklaces. Her pre-dawn rounds when she couldn't sleep, driving the big old cranky four-by-four through the Indian country, through the white trash Christian towns full of churches, wishing she could hate it all but loving it more and more.

"Anyway," she said, "they call it the Spout up here. If they don't want you, you go to the Spout and they pour you out." She turned her head and looked up to see if he was still awake. "Well, they poured me out."

He had to say something. "And you landed in my cup of love."

"Oh, Bongo." She shook with laughter. "Oh, oh, gag."

Chapter 22

Phil Harvey drove down towards the barn. Frankie Chase flopped in his seat but was secured by the seatbelt. His head lolled and dripped. One of the rounds had passed through and spidered the glass. Blood ran in an intricate pattern in the cracks. Bits of bone and grey matter adhered to the window. Harvey spun the F-250 around and backed the bed up to the barn doors. His arm and shoulder ached. He opened the doors one-handed then walked up to the old guy's shack.

"Hey, hey, old-timer."

The old man was snaggle-toothed when he creaked open the door. "Sonny, you got any?" His weak blue eyes scanned Harvey from head to toe, looking for bulges that might be packages of crank.

"First we work, then you can play, okay?" Harvey realized the old man was younger than he

was. Crank burned away youth and loaded you up
with years you hadn't lived yet. Harvey never really
liked making crank, although the profits were good.
Crank took you out into the badlands for customers
and you learned more about motorcycles than you
needed to know. He preferred ecstasy, the magic X
that took you to the cities, to the clubs. Done right,
X was a boost to good nature. "I got four oh-zees
for you. White as snow. First, though, work. Oh, and
bring that little groundhog gun you got. I saw some
ferrets in the barn."

The old man was rangy and had narrow shoulders
under a long tank top. The cold had no effect on him.
He went inside and came out with an automatic target
pistol. He shuffled barefoot beside Harvey, babbling
about chicks and crank and the jagged edges on the
sky that simply pissed him off. Several times he nodded
to himself and said, "What goes round comes round."

"You stayed out of the house, right? You didn't go
poking around up there?"

"I got my place. I got my own place and I stay to
my own self." He saw the drums on the back of the
F-250. "You cooking, boy? You mixing?" He studied
the drums. "Oh, that stuff. You're making the kid's
stuff. That stuff takes you the wrong way. Stuff." He
began a soliloquy that *stuff* was the perfect word, it
could mean anything. Stuff your nose, stuff your arm.
The couch in the kitchen of his shack had stuffing coming out. "Stuff. You can stuff a turkey." He cackled.
"But you better not stuff it up your ass, heh?" He wiped
something from his laughing mouth.

"I'll be cooking the crank soon. We'll get you right, get you through the winter. Right now, we got to get these drums off and inside. My arm's fucked up."

"Four oh-zees you said you got for me?" He unlaced the canvas and stood with his hands on his hips as though examining a global-sized problem. He nodded. "I'll drop 'em off, you roll 'em in with your foot. Then I'll stand 'em up inside where you want them."

"Okay, perfect. Gimme the gun, I want to kill some of those little fuckers."

The forty-five-gallon drums landed with a thump as the old guy edged them onto their bottom rims and rolled them off the bed. He counted each one as he did it. Together they rolled the drums into the barn. The old man repeated, "Day's work, day's pay," over and over again.

When the drums were inside and close to the worktable the old man leaned against one of the electric stoves and fingered the tracks on his arm. "That fat guy coming 'round? Haven't seen him in a while. How'd you get to be that fat? On purpose, you think? Those girls sure seem to like him. When he came up they'd get all excited like and when he took them back to the city he said they were tired and needed a holiday." The old guy began a run: "I didn't mind having them around they never come out he treated 'em good I think there must be somebody for everybody like they say do you think and those four oh-zees I guess you outta get up to the house there and maybe —"

Harvey had seen guys shot in the chest and stay standing while you experienced heart-stopping confusion, thinking that maybe you'd missed, waiting for blood on their shirts to appear and thinking that maybe it wouldn't.

He shot the old guy through the left eye and kept squeezing the trigger, tracking that gnarly cap of thin, dead hair as it fell. The sounds of the firing were sudden and like sharp hand claps but he still heard his brass tinkling on the wooden floor of the barn and birds fleeing the rafters as the room seemed to fill with gun smoke.

It was for love, he thought, it was for positive change. He reviewed his mistakes of the day. He had two dead bodies and only one arm that worked. He had a truck to make disappear. He had two guns to lose. Shell casings to gather from the F-250 and from the barn floor. He had a marathon of X production ahead of him. He had to somehow get back to the city to move the X to the Chinamen and to deal with Captain Cook's romantic desires for the last time. He had to decide whether to square the logs on the house he'd build in the mountains out west, or to leave them rough-hewn. Water would be a problem, maybe, and when he chose his plot of land he'd have to keep a mind to streams and rivers as well as the depth of the water table. It was love that made him ambitious and it was love that could make him careless.

He stared at the old man, blood running freely from his wounds, and wondered if this had been the old man's dream: to live in the woods with endless crank. And now look at how he'd ended up.

Twice in one day he'd done the hard thing. He still had some winter in his heart. But it wasn't like the other times. Frankie Chase and the old guy hadn't died because of money or greed or stupidity or weakness. They'd died for love, he believed, for a greater good.

He felt tired and sore but, overall, pretty okay. The old man's truck had pushed the F-250 easily into the lake. The lake was deep and the truck, with the windows rolled down, had burbled and swayed and finally, after a very long time, it had just disappeared in a whirlpool of its own making. The bodies were securely fastened inside by the seatbelts. The guns were buried far apart from each other and he wasn't sure he could find them if he tried. The brass was scattered. The old man's truck had become mired in the muck at the lake's edge, but with fast one-handed juggling of the steering wheel and the manual stick, Harvey had backed it up, turned it, and parked it beside the barn.

He stood in the sunshine looking at the farmhouse with a smile on his face. He could see where the setting sun was igniting the endless trees as they dripped in the autumn changes.

An original thought flitted through his mind. He was a season. He was going to change in increments. The light would shine on him and, given the chance, he too would ignite, he too would glow and change like foliage. Soon he'd be gone like the sun but he'd leave behind a piece of good.

He went into the barn and scattered wood shavings over the old guy's blood. The ants were already out and feasting. He tied his hair back and began assembling tubing and pails. He turned on two of the stoves, went back outside and tested the wind's direction.

Chapter 23

They drove north in the morning after a bacon and eggs breakfast at the diner. The same cook was on and he stared at them with deep suspicion. Through the plate glass window onto the parking lot Ray Tate watched drivers unearth themselves from their rigs. They stretched and blew visible clouds of breath. One did some vaguely Asian-looking slow motion movements then lit a cigarette. A middle-aged Native woman slowly climbed down from his rig, straightening her clothing and pulling her inky hair back into a ponytail. The pair talked like pals in the rising sunshine and the trucker gave her a cigarette and lit it. With a curiously tender movement the trucker touched the woman on the arm and she smiled up at him before heading up the edge of the highway, the backwash from southbound traffic whipping at her long baggy coat.

Ray Tate nodded through the window. "Romance."

Djuna Brown gave him a sweet smile. "Someone for everyone, right, Ray? Even killer beatniks and black dykes."

They finished their breakfast and while Djuna Brown paid, Tate went to the pay phone on the wall.

"Skip."

"Ray, where the fuck are you? We've been trying to raise you."

"Up in Indian country. Out of range, I guess. No service. No radio."

"You got my pills and you're heading back, right?"

"Soon, skip. We got a lead on Phil Harvey. I think he's up here, a little ahead of us. He went through here yesterday. We've linked him to a bush rat who babysits properties for the bad folks. I think maybe the lab's up here."

"Hang on, something else for you." The skipper rattled papers. "That camper truck fire? With the double Chucks and the dead broad?"

"Yeah, Agatha Burns."

"Nope. The examination showed a woman a lot older who's had multiple births. The Federal brainiacs have had the initial post mortem for weeks but it didn't mean anything to them. Now the hammers down the hall are getting DNA from Burns's parents for comparison to positively rule her out. I don't know what to tell you. Maybe the truck fire wasn't related."

"Except for those double Chucks scattered around the truck." He watched Djuna Brown standing in the sunshine outside the restaurant. Several truckers making their way in paused to look her over. In her leather jacket, leggings, and *khanga* hat she looked like a cool chick. Ray Tate had never actually had a cool chick, nor, he thought, had a cool chick ever had him. "Fuck it, skip. It doesn't matter. Maybe there's no homicide to put on Harvey, but we need him anyway, to get back to Captain Cook."

The skipper mulled this. "Okay. Fuck, I dunno. You're the guy on the scene. Play it the way you want. I can tell the dep you're on the trail. Did you check-in with the locals? Let them know you're playing in their pond?"

"We'll give them a heads-up. This is Djuna's old turf."

He hung up and went outside. They climbed aboard the Xterra and she meticulously adjusted the seat and mirrors. She did a fast left out of the parking lot and immediately got bumpered up behind a transport truck heading north to the Canadian border. She drifted in and out peeking for an opportunity to pass. The Native woman from the trucker's rig sat huddled in her big coat on a lump of rock on the sunny side of the road.

Ray Tate told Djuna Brown what the skipper had said.

"So, she's alive? Agatha?"

"Dunno that. She could be dead, someplace else. The truck fire might not have anything to do with Phil Harvey or the Captain. It stands the same: she left with Harvey, he had a gun, she left a note that Harvey was going to do her in, she hasn't been seen since."

She saw an opportunity and swung out past the transport. The driver sounded a long plaintive horn that faded behind them like a train whistle. "Last night, Ray, that, ah ..." She glanced at him. "I'm not like that, all that grim stuff. This place can give you the blues."

He touched her shoulder. "Indian country. Home of the blues."

The Spout was an hour north of the diner. It was a cluster of two gas stations, one opened and doing business with a single pickup truck gassing up, the other closed and abandoned, a variety store set up in a trailer with chicken screen across the windows, a bar that didn't open until after 8 p.m., a car dealership with four clunkers parked nose out, each with a cracked windshield and no hubcaps, and an Indian souvenir store with carved wooden beavers looking out the window. Two flags sat lank at the end of flagpoles above the Spout office and two four-by-four Ford Explorers were backed in, jammed close to the front door where a piece of plywood covered a busted window that looked like it had been blasted by shotgun fire.

"Nice. This fucking place is an hour away by telephone," Ray Tate said. "We should check-in with the guys."

"Fuck the guys," Djuna Brown said, slowing only momentarily to look at the detachment. "The guys can go roll it. I've met the guys, Ray, and I have to tell you: I found the guys wanting."

"We might need 'em, Djun', if Harvey's up there with a battalion of heavily-armed speed freaks. Pull it over. I'll go in."

But she didn't stop. She went past the detachment and rolled into the open gas station almost touching the bumper of the pickup truck. "Let's look around a little, first," she said. "We'll scope it out, see what's what."

She tapped at the horn to move the pickup truck forward. A brown Aboriginal face partially obscured by a curtain of black hair came out the driver's side window and glared. She tapped again and hung the guy the finger. He exploded, burly and pumped, out of the cab with a black tire iron in his fist.

"Djuna, Jesus Christ, we're working here."

"Chill, Ray. These guys are pussy. You can kick his red ass." She leaned out of her window. "My man here will kick your red ass, buddy, you don't move that fucking beater."

The man had a big stomach but was massive through the chest and he held the tire iron loose at his side and seemed to be timing his steps into a windup. He bobbed his head sideways around the driver's window at the driver. "Da June Ah, my girl."

"Buck, I told you, move it, right?"

He grabbed his crotch. "Move this world, girl, cause it's moving for you." He was laughing and came up on the driver's side. He looked insanely happy. "You back? You going to bring law and order to Dodge? Run the bad guys out of town?"

"Absolutely, Buck."

He shook her hand through the window and seemed reluctant to let go of it. "You back, really, you going to come back?"

Djuna Brown was radiant. She introduced Ray Tate to Buck, calling him the last honest man. "Just here on a job, Buck. Looking around a little. We're looking for some guy. Anything going on?"

Buck shook his head. "Nope. Been pretty quiet. Some city folk in their fancy cars, that's all. Some of them go in the woods for a while, then come out and head home."

Djuna Brown nodded. "Nature lovers."

"Maybe some of them. The others?" He gave Ray Tate an empty face. "Heap bad medicine."

"You see a big black double-cab Ford? Lots of chrome?"

Buck shook his head.

She asked, "A guy, face all burned up with scars?"

"I didn't see nothing, Da June." He studied the sky for a few seconds then looked at her. "Didn't hear nothing." He seemed to be waiting for something. He said, again, with emphasis, "I didn't see nothing, I didn't hear nothing." He looked at her expectantly and rubbed his nose.

She listened twice to what he was saying. "Smell, Buck. You smell anything?"

"Well, the smell. Maybe up by Passive there's a smell. Like old eggs. Used to be we'd go in there and hunt and fish, but now there's signs and an old white devil with a gun. Some fences." He gave Ray Tate a gapped smile and spoke sonorously, "The ancestors moan. The earth

mother, she weeps. You shouldn't fence in your mother."
He winked.

Ray Tate met his eyes. "I'm hip."

Djuna Brown nodded. "Passive. Up past or down
before?"

"Up past. The smell is bad especially when the
grandfather wind blows from the west."

Ray Tate asked if he knew a bush rat named Paul.
"Drives an old pickup."

"You already been up there, seen that old devil with
his gun? So you know." He turned to Djuna Brown.
"You should come back up here, Da June, you're closer
to us than to them white devils down there." He smiled
again at Ray Tate. "No offence to your man, there."

"He's a beatnik, Buck." She gave him a business
card. "My man's a man of peace to all people."

With a solemn nod, Buck said to Ray Tate, "Good
luck to you with that, sir."

"Call, Buck, if you need me." She put her hand on
his on the doorframe. "I miss the mornings."

"The morning says she misses you." He stepped
back, got into his truck, and left the gas station in a rush
of engine. Djuna Brown put the Xterra into gear, waved
a complex finger sign at Buck's departing truck, and
rolled forward. She gassed it up herself, went inside with
the credit card, and came out with an armload of treats.

She seemed in deep thought as she drove and Ray Tate
watched their passage through the cut rock on both

sides of the road. There were small stacks of stones on top of the rock cuts, Indian-looking designs. He saw a small shrine at a crossroads with trinkets and some cracked pots arranged in a design around them. There was an abandoned trailer that had undergone scorching fire. Four children, two of them dark brown with black hair and the other two dark but blond, ran down a hillside chasing wobbly tires.

As though talking to herself, Djuna Brown said, "They didn't care that I was a dyke, even if I wasn't. They said the mother was a woman, so how bad could it be, to love the mother of the earth? When I did the dawn patrols, after I took the teeth out of my partner, they'd come out in front of their trailers and wave me down, blow smoke onto the truck for my safety. Very mystical stuff, very loving. They'd invite me out on Fridays and Saturdays so the guys from the detachment wouldn't go too far. All the bad stuff, all the dead children, the dead old folks, the head-ons on the blind curves, none of that moved me like how they accepted me. When I left here, I cried. It was the worst thing they could do to me, transferring me out of the worst place."

Ray Tate watched the sadness on her face. He felt a thumping in his chest, out of all proportion to any investment he had in her, in her life. He realized he loved everything: her voice, her skin, her cinnamon, her wit. Her sadness and her heart.

She handled the increasingly sharp turns in the road with the four fingers of each hand on each side of the steering wheel, sliding close to the rock face when she went in blind, coming out a little wide, the Xterra holding the road like glue.

"When this thing's down, Ray, we should take a holiday, see what's what with us."

"Well, Djun', all I can offer you is gin and taps and mad Parisian beatnik love."

"Cool-ee-oh, Bongo. Tonight let's —" Her head whipped. "What did the cook tell you? About that old bush rat's vehicle?"

"Rusted out old pickup. Grey."

"Just went southbound, looked like a woman or a guy with long, black hair behind the wheel." She spun into a U-turn.

Through the window of the diner they saw Phil Harvey on the phone. He looked exhausted, his forehead leaning against the wall as he spoke, his hair hanging loose. Inside his black leather bat coat he sagged. The short-order cook watched him. When Harvey hung up, the short-order cook waved him over and they started talking. Harvey took some money from his pocket and gave it to the cook. Outside he looked at each vehicle in the parking lot, missing the Xterra backed in among a half dozen rigs. Harvey went inside and came out with a coffee. Favouring his left arm, he boarded the pickup and headed south.

Chapter 24

Cornelius Cook was impatient. Gabriella Harris-Hopkins's ass haunted him. He dwelled on the boots and the jodhpurs. If she wasn't wearing them when Harv did his deed, Connie Cook would have to locate a pair of each.

In his bedroom he snacked away on frozen malted chocolate bars and flipped through the newspapers. There was an array of photographs taken the day before at the racetrack. His wife and Gabriella Harris-Hopkins posed with a short Colombian jockey. She looked snobby and resistant and perfect. The step-granddaughter was there but for Connie Cook she didn't hold the heat Gabrielle boiled up in him. There was the mayor with a wardman, the mayor with a pair of predatory builders who smiled like rats. No mayor with Connie Cook. Whale, he thought. Should get to vote twice, he's so fucking fat.

When Harv called, Connie Cook was getting anxious. Figuring the time it would take to get the drums of precursors up to the lab, even allowing for notoriously bad Interstate traffic, he figured Harv would have contacted him by now.

"Where you been, Harv. Fuck, what's going on? Where you been all night?"

"I'm still up here. I couldn't get away. There were ... ah ... you know?"

Connie Cook didn't know. He loved the obscure gangster talk, the paranoia that every phone was bugged. He didn't care, anyway. "So," he said, mimicking Harv, "so, ah, you're, ah, gonna come ... home? You delivered the ..." His mind groped. Through his bathroom door he saw a bottle of mouthwash on the sink. "You delivered the mouthwash?" He smiled proudly to himself.

"Yeah, yeah, yeah, no problem. I had a problem with ... some people I hadda straighten out."

Cops or crooks? Connie Cook said, "Their guys or our guys?"

"Our guys. It's okay now. I'm on the way. But I'm gonna need a ride at some point, get the rest of the way in. I'm driving a wreck and if ... those ... other guys spot me driving it, they're gonna pull me over and take the fucking plates off. You want to ... ah, meet me?"

"Sure. Where?"

Harvey said, "Let me think." After a minute he said, "Ribs. Remember the ribs, that time we were heading up? With the sauce you liked?"

"Ah, I think. Ah, yeah."

"Motorcycles out front. You said you'd need two of them, one under each cheek of your ass, to —"

"Yeah, yeah, I got it." Connie Cook laughed. "Yeah, but when? What time? Because I need you Thursday night, Harv, to, ah, pick up that thing for me, that thing I really need, you know?"

"Okay. You know how many … treats you've had? Up there? Don't say the number, but you know, right?"

"Sure. Every one of them." Three girls had been brought up for Connie. Agatha Burns was the third. The first two had been cheap and tawdry and had misread his needs, making sounds of pleasure at the worst possible time. Ooo, they said, taking to the crank nicely, ahhh. Two that would never be missed. Scrags, Harv called them. "Yeah, I know the count."

"Well, add two to that. Then, wait an hour after you get there. Take a cellphone just in case, but don't use it unless I call you, okay? So, that place, that time. Wait an hour."

"Perfect. And Harv. The other thing I need. Thursday night? Right? I got it —"

"Let's talk when I see you, man, okay? I promise you, you're going to get what you need. We're back in business."

Connie Cook's wife was in the front living room lifting stacks of books from a cardboard box when he came down the stairs. He'd be expected to absent himself while a dozen of her cronies, including Gabriella Harris-Hopkins, sat around and imagined symbolism and subplot in the latest literary bestseller. His wife often invited the writer to attend.

"Book night, Thursday, Connie, okay? No fooling around, sending us pizzas." She gave him a stern smile. "No male strippers at the door with candygrams. I mean it."

"Promise. I'm heading up north sometime Thursday to a mine site for a couple of days."

"Do they ever find gold in those things, Connie? Except for the money you pour in?" When he didn't answer, she said, "Are you going to help Gabby out, that donation she needs? She'll be asking me about it."

"Yeah. I think. Tell her she's got to get something on paper, okay, or we're all going to be homeless artists." He looked at his watch. "I gotta go."

Halfway back to the city Harv left the state highway and began working through a grid of county roads. He kept an eye on his rear-view, especially when he crossed unpaved back roads, looking for a telltale cloud of rising dust behind him. The pickup was a shimmering mess. It ran like a dog with a broken back. South of Apple Grove he backed the truck over some ruts into a country driveway where he'd have a view of anything following him.

The big Taiwanese stamping machine had turned out forty thousand pills by dawn. They were wrapped in tubes of foil and fitted through a rip in the passenger seat of the pickup with his silver fluted revolver. Any bent Chinaman in the east Chinatown would pay a buck each, easy. That was half the going rate for bulk but for Harvey it was all profit. Another mad bout of chemistry and magic and he could get to a hundred thousand. They all had lightning bolts on them. They were all a bright pink. He'd have to be careful the Chinamen didn't rip him but there were fallbacks and ways to prevent any Chinatown gambit.

He'd do the grab for Connie Cook Thursday night, move the victim up to the farmhouse to await Connie's arrival. The transit would be done in a rental van. While he was waiting for Connie he'd be the crazy cartoon chemist. When Connie arrived to claim his prize, Harv would give him the bad news: goodbye. He'd disable whatever vehicle Connie came up in and would leave in the van. He'd become really fond of the fat pervert and planned to send someone up to the farm to rescue him.

An old farm wagon pulled by a tractor came rattling down the road. Harv had a minor thunderbolt: what if I was him and he was me?

For a moment there was a cloud of snow across the fields then it was gone. It meant something and he reached for it but it eluded him. Maybe we're all snowflakes and life is when a wind blows us alive, briefly, until our season ends? Far off clouds edged down over the lake from Canada.

Christ, he thought, I'm tired. The click and hum of the tablet-pressing machine was still in his body rhythm. His shoulder ached.

An Xterra came down the road and passed, a clean-cut guy in the passenger seat consulting a map. Harv couldn't see who was driving. But it passed and didn't pause.

Agatha Burns had been mortified that she'd sucked his burned fingers, licked his glistening cheek. He'd never met a real victim before in his life. Everyone asked for it in some way. Being too young and born beautiful, where was the crime in that?

I'm sorry, Harv, for what he made me do. I just want you to know that.

He closed his eyes for a minute and recalled the exact moment, the exact sound of her voice.

He opened his eyes, smiling.

The Xterra was full across the front of the pickup. A black woman in a stupid hat was leaning on the passenger side door, smiling tensely back at him with her hand under her leather jacket and a pistol half-drawn. A clean-cut guy with a gun in his hand, pointing it at Harv's windshield, stood a couple of feet off his front fender.

The woman called, "Don't move."

At the same time the man called, "Put your hands on the wheel."

Harvey didn't know what to do.

He heard the man call, "Oh, fuck. Hang on, Harv. Djuna, you do it."

"Okay." She called, "Hands on the wheel, Harv."

Harvey heard them laugh.

The clean-cut guy said, "Well, that was professional."

The woman laughed and said something that sounded like, "*Rongobongo.*"

Harvey tentatively put his hands at the top of the steering wheel, expecting to absorb a bullet.

The black woman with her gun fully out came up alongside the passenger side, not crossing the white guy's field of fire. She jerked the passenger door open. "Sorry about that, Harv. We don't arrest a lot of people. Conflicting directions can lead to tragedy. They taught us that. Is that right, Ray? Clarity is your friend?"

The white guy had come up the driver's side while she was talking. He was smiling. "Yep, otherwise: heap bad medicine." He had the driver's door open and Harvey by the back of the collar of his leather coat and on the ground even as Harvey mentally put bleached blond hair on her head and a dripping beard down the white guy's face.

"Lawyer." His shoulder ached from the impact and as he waited for the handcuffs he flexed his wrists so there'd be some slack when they were secured, even if they were tightened up. The man patted him down and Harv heard the depressing clank of cuffs. The woman said something and after a moment the guy didn't handcuff him.

"Fucking lawyer."

The woman rounded the front of the pickup. "Harv, Harv. Don't be like that. You can trust us, man, we're not like all the others." She seemed positively gay to meet him.

"Lawyer."

The white guy said, "Maybe later. Right now I could really use a coffee. It's been a long day. You up for a coffee, Harv?"

"Law-*fucking*-yer."

"Okay, if you're sure. But we haven't arrested you

or anything. We're just saying: let's get a coffee. You don't have to talk. You haven't done anything wrong, right? We'll talk, you just listen."

"If I'm not busted, then I'm walking."

The white cop shrugged. "Then we'll arrest you and that means no coffee for you. Whatever."

Harvey climbed to his feet. "I'm not talking."

The black woman said, "Cool-ee-oh. Most people in your position, in my experience, they just fucking talk themselves into trouble. Right, Ray? Blah blah blah and the next thing you know they're behind the pipes, going, *Fuuuuck*, how *stupid* am I?" She ran her hand lightly over his pockets. "You ever notice, Harv, how there's not many mute people doing time? Think about that, buddy."

The white cop nodded. "Tell you what, Harv, let's go for a cup of coffee. We'll leave the pickup here. When we're done, we'll fuck off and go about our business, you can go about yours."

Harvey looked from one to the other. "What's this about?"

"Well," Ray Tate said, "at first we thought it was about murder. But it turns out maybe you didn't put Agatha Burns in the ground after all. Maybe. Now it's about a great fat fucking master criminal and pills with double Cs on them."

"You talk, I walk? That's it?"

"Unless you confess to something outrageous and we have to arrest you for it."

Djuna Brown said, "My advice, Harv? Listen first and then if you really want to, maybe you can say something. Maybe. But I have to tell you, I'd be really fucking careful." She leaned towards him and whispered: "This guy? This partner o'mine? I think he's a rope smoker, high all the time, looking to just get laid and watch a parade." She snickered. "I think we both better be careful of this guy, you and me, pal."

Ray Tate kept his gun in his jacket pocket and his hand on the gun. He didn't belt himself into the Xterra and sat slightly sideways, facing Djuna Brown as she drove, but keeping an eye on Harv sitting in the middle of the back seat. The intelligence file on Phil Harvey put him as a suspect in at least two homicides. The cop in him wished he'd chained Harvey up but he recognized Djuna Brown was developing a nice style of her own and she'd at least made Harv smile.

They found a coffee shop in a little hamlet where the state road ran under the Interstate. There were baskets of new potatoes, autumn melon, and herbs near the cash register. A man reading a Minneapolis newspaper looked surprised to see them. He stared at Phil Harvey in his bat coat. The place was empty and he told them to sit anywhere. They sat at the farthest table from the entrance and said nothing until after they'd been served mugs of coffee. Harvey sat with his back to the door, Djuna Brown and Ray Tate facing him.

Djuna Brown took off her *khanga* hat and ran her fingers through her spiky hair. She stirred her coffee. "I gotta ask you one, Harv, nothing to do with why we're following you around the countryside. That, there, on your face. That's gotta hurt, right?"

Phil Harvey looked at her closely and raised his eyebrows slightly but said nothing.

"No, Harv. That came out wrong. What I mean is, I mean, I knew it hadda hurt when it happened, but now? Do you ever forget it's there?"

He tilted his head and sipped his coffee.

She shook her head. "Sorry, not my business." She gave him a small smile and stared directly at the mass of scar tissue. "The only reason I ask is that a friend of mine's kid was playing in the garage, lit himself up with some solvent. Horrible, wicked mess of his ear, neck, and shoulder. Not as bad as what you got going on there, but it ain't a mild dose of acne either. Long story short: the little guy says it still hurts, that when he dreams about it, he gets the pain all over again, like it's happening right then. I babysat him a while ago and when he woke up screaming I told him that'll go away. But really, I don't know. He wants to stay in and never go outside." Her face became sad. "He calls himself a circus freak."

Phil Harvey seemed to have forgotten Ray Tate was there with a gun in his pocket. He couldn't take his eyes off hers. They sat in silence for several seconds.

She lightly clapped her hands together, "Okay, sorry. So: why we're here. You know who we are, right? We're the Chemical Squad. I'm Trooper Brown with the Staties. This beatnik here is Ray Tate with the city. You've heard of the Chem Squad, right?"

Phil Harvey made a single blink.

"Good. Anyway, we're pretty much fucked from coast to coast on this thing we're doing. Probably we're going to lose our jobs after we fuck this up a little more. So, what we're doing, Harv, is we're looking to seize some pills. Double Cs on them. Save our jobs. For a while, anyway." She glanced at Ray Tate. "Right?"

"Killer pills." Ray Tate nodded and forced a yawn, "Bummer."

"Yep, Harv, those ones. Captain Cooks."

There was a flicker in Harvey's eyes.

"Oh, we know about the Captain, Harv," she said. "We've been on this a long time. We know about Agatha Burns's stash house up in the south projects. But you know that because you seen us up there. We know she moved a bunch of boxes out of there and put them in the back of your cool Camaro and you guys drove off together. Her and you and a silver gun. She hasn't been seen since. At first we thought, Whoa, neat, we got a homicide, find Harv and link him up, promotions all around. See, she left a note behind, said if I vanish, whip Phil Harvey with bicycle chains until he tells you where my body is. Then … Ah, what else, Ray?"

Ray Tate was content to sit back and watch her work. It was pure free-form jazz. It was hard, he knew, sometimes, in an interview to shut the fuck up and let the one doing the work, work. Everybody wanted to get their oar in the water, pull for the winning team. Always a mistake. When she wanted him, when she sensed her voice might be taking up too much space, she'd toss him a softball. He said, "Then there was a camper truck blew-up up north, dead body inside.

Turns out it wasn't Agatha like we thought, it was some old broad."

"Right, Ray. Then, Harv, there's an incident in Chinatown, bunch of kids get branded with double Cs. This is where the trouble really began for you guys. The kids were students being looked after by Willy Wong, a pal of the mayor. Now, we know this mayor's a fucking dipshit, but c'mon, putting a branding iron to people's flesh? He's pissed off and he's right for once. There's things you do and there's things you don't do and branding girls on the tits, that's too weird, even for Chinatown."

Phil Harvey seemed dazed. His head started to shake but he caught himself.

She gave him a few seconds then continued: "Then those two other kids died of an overdose — Double Cs. In the mayor's ward. Well, that's that. The leashes come off and away we go. Get that fucker Harv, they said. Noose him up with barbed wire, put him so far back in a cell he'll get sunlight by U.S. Post. Melt the key. My God: stop the madness."

Ray Tate was impressed. It was a perfect interview even though it was borne of free-form jazz. It had a *Bitch's Brew* quality that somehow, impossibly, came together and you could find something warped in there to snap your fingers to. She had facts but she presented them slightly wrong. She didn't mention the Chinaman getting the blank fortune cookie at Willy Wong's warehouse, but she got Willy's name in there. She didn't look at him so he didn't speak. He waited for her to change gears, let up pressure on one place, apply it in another.

She did. "Not for no reason, Harv, but let me ask you: you went through something there on your face, right? And it hadda hurt, it hadda hurt like nothing else hurts that you could imagine. And it had to stink something awful, I guess. So how come you'd put that fucking iron on a girl's tits? What the fuck is that all about? I interviewed that poor little girl and I gotta tell you, if you'd been in firing range at that moment I'd've just shot your fucking nuts off. Fuck — ah, shit, you fucking cocksucker." She rubbed her face and got up unsteadily. She had tears in her eyes. "Never mind. Ray, I'm gonna buy a melon. Anyone want one?"

Phil Harvey turned to watch her walk to the front of the shop.

"She's not much of a cop, Harv. You've met a lot of cops in your time, I know you have. You ever seen one like that? Laughs and cries. Buys melons. Probably not much of cook, either."

Harv twisted again to look at Djuna Brown paying out the melons. He murmured: "How old's the kid? In the garage?"

Ray Tate had found his role and he shrugged. "This is her interview. You know how it works. We don't do good cop bad cop. We do strange cop weird cop and she's both of them. But there's rules in my job, there's rules in yours. Me? I don't give a shit. People get fucked up if they're not careful. You fool around in a garage and there's stuff in there that'll burn you, well, hello? You can't be surprised that you get burned. Same thing, you don't watch the temperature when you're cooking, whether it's making fried potatoes for dinner or cooking something else for profit. But hey, you know that too, right? Me, I don't mind a good crispy French fry once in a while."

Harv stared at him.

"I know, Harv, I know. I'm an asshole." He wanted to give her time to get back into her bag with Harv. He needed Phil Harvey to like her more than him. He prattled. "But like they say: If you want sympathy, it's in the dictionary between shit and syphilis. I have to tell you, I'm putting in my papers so I don't give much of a shit about Double Cs or how you burned the girl's boobs. Fuck her, right? I'm moving to Paris. That's in France. I don't speak French but that just means I won't have to listen to mutts lie to me in English all fucking day."

Harv looked at him in absolute neutral. Ray Tate felt a chill.

Djuna Brown sat down and put a bag of melons under her chair.

Ray Tate said, "Harv spoke, Djun'. He wants to know how old the kid is, got burned in the garage."

"He's eleven, Harv." She turned to Ray Tate. "Sorry about that, guys. I kinda lost it. If you had boobs you'd understand."

Phil Harvey looked at her, then looked away, then looked back, "There's a vitamin E cream he should use. It don't work very much but he'll feel he's helping himself, got some control. He'll see it working even if nobody else does. He should fuck everybody and go out. Be who he is. If the family's got dough, graffs."

"*Graffs?*"

Harv nodded. "They take skin off your ass or something, graff it on your face. Sixteen grand and get in line. Or get some bum ID and go over the border to Canada, maybe get it for free." He stopped talking and clamped his mouth.

"Sixteen grand. Jesus." Djuna Brown took out her notebook and made some marks. "How come you haven't had it done, Harv? You're a high-miler so I'm not gonna bullshit you and tell you you'd be a good-looking guy again, but how come not?"

He got an innocent look on his face. "Sixteen grand. Where'd I get that kind of dough?"

Ray Tate waited for Djuna Brown to laugh then he did too. He said, "Nice one, Harv."

"Guys," Harvey said, "I gotta go now."

"Hey, if you gotta, you gotta." Djuna Brown drained her coffee. "We're heading down towards the city in a few minutes. Get yourself a coffee for the road. We'll give you a lift. That old beater you're driving won't make it, man. Anyway, at least have a melon."

Ray Tate watched Harvey thinking about getting up. He waited for her to shift gears again.

She put her cup down and made a face. "You know, the other night we were hanging out, me and my buddy here, and we had nothing to drink except gins and waters. Gins and tap waters, who the fuck drinks that? Alkies, that's who."

Ray Tate said, "And beatniks. The cool folk in the nighttime." He leaned confidentially to Phil Harvey. "It's the big thing right now, Harv, in Paris. I read it in a magazine."

"Them folks, gin-and-tappers, them's us." Djuna Brown shook her head solemnly. "I never thought of myself that way. When I was in high school, think about this, Harv, when I was in high school do you think I could ever imagine a series of events that would take me from my homeroom class to a grimy pad in the middle of the night, fighting off a beatnik pervert? That I'd become a gins and taps kind of girl? Me neither. But there I was, getting stupid at three in the morning with this here hipster. Then again, Harv, I bet the last time you were in the bucket waiting for parole you never thought of a possible series of events that would have you shooting the shit with some cops, buying melons in the countryside, right? Sitting with guys trying to help you out from the mess you've got yourself in. Life. It's a winding road. So, look, I know you're worried. But we don't want you."

"I'm going now. I'm not putting anybody in. Under no circumstances does that happen."

"Hey, Harv? We're the Chemical Squad. We don't lock people up, we handcuff pills. We investigate a bit then we swoop in and suck up all the chemicals, leaving the host body drained, to wander the underworld and tell the tale, instill fear and confusion. We're like vampires. 'Hey,' we hear guys go afterwards on the wiretaps, 'Hey, where the *fuck* did those *fucking* guys swoop down outta? Yikes. They're everywhere.'" She looked at Ray Tate, pleased with herself. "Them's us, them guys."

"So that's it?" Phil Harvey made a reluctant laugh and shook his head. He looked like he'd enjoyed Djuna Brown's riff. "You just fucking want pills? No people?"

She shrugged and looked at Ray Tate.

"That's the game," he said. "We just want chemicals and this week we want Double C pills. Pills, Harv." He wanted to put her back in the game: "We don't get no points for bodies, right Djun'?"

"Bodies, no." She tilted her head as though weighing in with a complex thought. "Pills is good, bodies is trouble. Bodies need warrants and reading those confusing Constitutional rights and handcuffs and stuff. Pesky shit. Then you got to get sobered up enough to go to court and make sure you didn't make any mistakes, depriving liberty of some poor citizen. So, no, we don't do that, Harv. You ever heard of us taking in a serious body?" When he didn't speak she continued. "Or how about this one: you ever see a cop giving evidence against a guy, getting in the box and in the middle of telling his lies to the jury he just starts puking up gins and taps on the prosecutor? Juries think it's fucking funny when it happens but it can tank the case when they get in the deliberation room. 'That cop puking on the lawyers?' they say. 'Seemed a little sketchy to me, that guy.'" She shook her head. "Me? I'd rather not say nothing under oath to nobody." She felt she'd said enough and sat back.

Ray Tate said, "You know we're on you. We're an inch from that place you got up near ... Passion?"

Djuna Brown said, "Passive. The stinky place off the highway there. A day or two, we swoop, Harv."

Phil Harvey was startled. "Ah, fuck ..."

"Yeah," Ray Tate said, "we know about that. We know there's that fat prick in all this someplace, causing no end of misery. If we're going to pile on anybody and wire him up to the pain machine it's him. We're going to take that guy. We like you, Phil, but we don't want you, short of murder. Give us the pills, give us the fat guy, take a hike, get your face fixed."

Phil Harvey shook his head. "No bodies. I don't tip nobody over." He was silent for a long time then looked from one to the other and said to Ray Tate, "I think your car alarm's going off."

Ray Tate immediately stood up and left the shop.

He was dozing in the passenger seat of the running Xterra when Djuna Brown came out of the shop with Phil Harvey. They stood a moment on the little parking area, close enough that their visible breaths mingled. He noticed how little she seemed, swinging her bag of melons, her chin lifted towards Harvey, massive in the sinister leather coat. His hair was tied back in a ratty ponytail. He'd found some sunglasses somewhere and in spite of the gathering darkness he'd put them on.

Phil Harvey looked away and said something.

She nodded and tilted her head.

He said something else and pointed across a field opposite the shop.

She turned and looked and made a beautiful smile.

Harvey handed her something and she put it into her pocket.

Ray Tate twisted to see what they were looking at. But there was just a lone tree with clouds roiled above it.

For some reason Djuna Brown touched Phil Harvey's arm as she walked over to the Xterra.

She dropped her melons behind the seat and started up as Phil Harvey stood watching them. Ray Tate looked over his shoulder as she drove off onto the road and headed to the Interstate. Phil Harvey didn't move. He stared at the tree in the field.

Djuna Brown checked Tate's seatbelt as though he was a child. Just before they reached the highway back to the city she pointed at another lone tree on a hilltop.

"See that tree, Ray? You know there's more of that tree under the ground than on top — a lot more than we see? Harv was talking about that."

"Wow." Ray Tate nodded. "Heavy."

"No wonder he thinks you're an asshole." But she laid her hand on his thigh.

Chapter 25

Connie Cook was into his third plate of ribs, paper napkins tucked into his shirt collar, a crumpled field of them stained red across the table. He felt pretty good. The waitress was a pal. When he'd asked for a hot red sauce she'd said, How hot? He'd said, Honey, you don't got a sauce hot enough that I can't eat. She had a wicked smile and said, Oh, yeah? She came out of the kitchen with an unmarked bottle and held it over his platter. Say when. She began soaking down the meat.

The ribs were fiery and he sweated immediately. His nose ran, his scalp tingled. He enjoyed himself immensely, sitting in a country place with his jacket off, bullshitting with a waitress, sucking meat from bones, stacking them into a log house on the side plate. Fat he was, sure, but he had the impression the hot red sauce was melting the blubber. His bland skin was taking on a healthy pink glow. When he looked up he saw the waitress pulling on a ski jacket over her apron and handing her tickets to another woman, he called her over.

"You off?"

She nodded. "Those are pretty good, huh?" She lifted an eyebrow. "And the sauce? I didn't bring you the real hot stuff. I took pity."

He laughed and reached into his pocket. "I feel like I just blew a fireman."

"Been there, done that." She laughed, a pretty middle-aged woman his wife's age who, he thought, might have missed the boat at some point and had accepted the fact. There was poorly covered grey in her hair and she had clear, direct eyes. He put a twenty on the table.

"That's okay, mister, we split here, it all goes in the pot." She zipped her jacket. "Good to see a man that knows how to enjoy a meal."

"Look," Connie Cook said, "there's gonna be a good tip on the bill. The twenty ... Well, I needed this, okay. I'm in the middle of a hard couple of days and this ... Well, I want you to have it. Humour me."

"Sure. Thanks. Come again, huh?" She took the twenty and on the way out he saw her stuff it into a big glass jar full of bills and change. As she passed through the door Phil Harvey came in in his bat coat, a canvas sack over his shoulder.

Connie Cook felt sad. His life had been a litany of girls and women who rejected him. Connie the Whale. Cookie No-Nookie. A translucent lump in the lives of people who saw him as a melting iceberg of blubber. Sharpies. Predators. As he watched Harv locate him at the back of the dining room he thought, once I get all this bad shit out of my system I'm gonna come back up here, have another plate of ribs, see a little about the waitress. His wife could have it all, the house and the cars and the country place and the stocks. He had enough stacked cash from his dealings with old Harv to get himself away, get into shape, get that grey in the waitress's hair fixed up. They'd sit on a porch someplace and joke about hot red sauces.

"*Fuck* am I starving and I'm fucking frozen." Harv dropped into the seat opposite, put his knapsack beside him, and grabbed up some ribs. His hair was back behind his ears, straggling out of a ponytail. "This fucking life." He gnawed at the meat and threw the bone away onto the table. He double swallowed. "Jesus fuck, Connie." He reached for Connie Cook's beer. He felt his lips were blistering. "Cocksucker. Are you fucking nuts?"

"Hard day, Harv? Should I have ordered the hot ones?" Connie Cook waved over at the replacement waitress and pointed at his beer and at the plate and held up two fingers. "Have some more ribs. I know you like 'em hot but they didn't have any really hot sauce." Connie Cook felt pleased. He realized he never got to joke with anyone except Harv. Harv was a buddy and genuine, a real guy, a real pal.

"Man, Connie, I don't know how you eat this stuff. My asshole's going to have heartburn in the morning."

The waitress put down two beers. Harv drank his off with one hand and pointed at the glass with the other and made a circle above the table. The waitress nodded.

Connie Cook sat back, satisfied. "So, Harv, tell me. How was the day in the criminal underworld?"

"Let me give it to you all at once, Connie. Here goes: We got the drums up to the place, got them unloaded. I hadda bring the kid up with me, account of my arm seizing up from one of the guys at the warehouse, had a tire iron or something. I blindfolded the kid. We did the heavy lifting and had to stash his truck because it was all over the news. Then I blinded him again and drove him in the old fuck's rattletrap down to the restaurant and he called down for a ride. So when I go to take the pickup back up to the place, the old fucker's gone. Don't know how he did it because I had his truck. But he's gone. No sign. No nothing. I got the place ready to start work then headed down here. The pickup died and I left it by the side of the road, gave a kid in a van twenty bucks to drop me near here. And here I am." He kept his face frozen. No mention of the Chemical Squad, no mention of giving the guy who owned the shop a hundred to drive him back to the swaybacked pickup so he could retrieve the forty thousand pills and the gun from inside the passenger seat, pretending to be lost and running the guy ragged, just in case the Chemical Squad had guys on him. The pills and the gun were in his knapsack.

"Just as well the old guy's gone, with what we're going to be bringing up there soon, huh?" He looked at Harv carefully. He didn't care much, right then, about cranking out the X. "You know what I mean, right? Thursday night?"

Harv nodded. "Yeah. I'm going to need everything

you can give me, Connie. I don't want to get the wrong thing, you know? When I go shopping."

"I got it all. The time, the place she'll be at. How do you want to do it?"

Harv thought. He scraped at a rib with his knife. The waitress put down two more beers and Harv took them both to his side of the table. "Ah, can I get inside? To get the … thing?"

"Not this time. This time she'll be coming out. It'll be late at night, the street's dark, not much traffic." Connie Cook gave him a big smile. "In fact, Harv, you're doing the grab at my place."

"Not your wife, I hope? She finally got you nuts?"

"No. A pal of hers. She'll be in there most of the evening Thursday, then she'll be coming out. They're having their book club night. It usually goes to maybe ten, ten-thirty. Get there a little early, scope things out. The one I want is Gabby. Five-ten. She's got this shiny blond hair, slim chick. Drives a new Lexus, really dark blue, it'll look black. Personalized plate, something to do with her name. You'll know it, when you see it."

"What if she doesn't come out alone. What then?"

"Get creative. But if this doesn't work I'm not gonna like it but we'll do something else. She's got this kid sometimes around her, a little younger, same looks. She might do for now." He thought dreamily for a moment that the step-granddaughter might attend, although he knew she wouldn't, and Harv could grab them both up. Stuff them in the sleeping bag, in the back of a vehicle, and after that it would be Connie's party. Quality time, the bitch had called it. It could be a long winter, if she survived it. The farmhouse would be snowed in. How he'd get in there for visits, he didn't know. Snowshoes? He laughed at the thought. Snowmobile, that was more like it. Roar up to the place slow so she could hear the engine and begin panicking. Oh, no, it's Connie the Oak. Help. Yikes. "Maybe follow her? She's staying down in Stonetown, that big old stone building a couple of blocks up from the river. Condos. Maybe, there?"

"And crank? You going to shuffle her up."

Connie Cook was pleased. "Nope. This time I'm going to win her over with my love, Harv. It might take a little while longer, but I'm a persuasive guy." He sat back to let the waitress put down the platters and some more beer. He caught her looking at him. When she went back by the serving window she commented to the cook, something he thought was nasty. "Anyway, once you've got … Once you've picked up the groceries then head on up there. Set her up in the main house, call me on my mobile, and I'll come up. I'm gonna need the house, Harv, okay? You'll have to put something in the barn, keep you warm while you sleep."

Harv thought about sleeping in a drafty barn with the smell of chemicals in the dust. But he nodded. "Sure. I'll get a tent, pitch it in there. But what if things don't work out. The … groceries don't get delivered, one reason or another?"

"Needless to say, I'll be disappointed. We'll have to come up with another plan. But you go back up anyway and I'll probably come up. If we're both up there, we might as well do some … baking? You know? Get back in the game." He shook his head. "I hope you don't break my heart, Harv."

"No worries, Connie." Harv sucked some meat off some bones. "A jacking. I'll make it look somebody tried to jack her car, maybe whacked her, and took the body away with him."

"Nice. Good thinking." He'd made a tall box out of interlocked rib bones, fashioned into a log cabin.

Harv stared at it, mesmerized.

"I got a lot of love in me, Harv. A whole lot of love."

Djuna Brown made her security bubble and cruised along inside it. Not many cars passed the Xterra. She seemed to know when to change lanes and when to idle along in the slow lane. Ray Tate found some cigarettes and they both smoked, the windows cracked, the SUV swooshing along. Late season cottagers clogged the slow lane, their backseats and roof racks stacked with all manner of lost summer fun. Trailers pulled boats of all kinds; canoes seemed balanced on car roofs. The white lines zipped by. In the light of oncoming traffic her face was perfect and mysterious. Policing was a learning curve, he thought, a discovery about the without and the within. She wasn't the same deadbeat, slipper-wearing, morose, feral creature he'd first encountered at the elevator at the Chem Squad. But it wasn't just one way. He'd come to understand that loving was in the small things, in the hints of possibility, of change. It was in the laughter, the sadness, the surprises. Now he couldn't imagine a life without her in it. Even his day-dreams of Paris were populated with her nimble fingers, her sly eyes, the on-again, off-again Caribbean breeze in her accent. He'd learned as much as he'd taught and he'd learned about balance, that he didn't have to play out the cards he'd been dealt. There were more cards in more decks and you just played a hand as far as you could then folded and got a new round.

He hadn't told her there was probably surveillance around. The dep's horrid little minions, he assumed, looking to knife a buyout into his back. He'd seen the same car in the city near his apartment a couple of times, clocked it a few times in his rear-view mirror. But he was used to it. Catching him drunk on the streets with a loaded gun on his ankle would do the trick. But he'd been careful now because he'd had a mission since he met her.

She didn't know it but she was an agent of change. She'd brought the skipper face to face with his hatred of her. It was about a dead child who froze in a fetal posture with goo stuck to her face. Ray Tate had no doubt the skipper would put her down if he had to, but no longer would he take as much pleasure in it. Ray Tate assumed the skipper knew about the little headquarters' squirrels who were tracking him. He was sure the skip would tip him off when it was time. The skipper, as much as Djuna Brown, was a cop and no amount of booze or nasty business would take every drop of that out of him.

"Ray? Talk to me, man. Keep me awake."

He offered to take the wheel but she said city guys couldn't drive worth shit. "You like me, don't you,

Ray? I gotcha."

"You do. Got, be I."

"I haven't had a guy in a long time. I mean ..." She gave him a sideways look. "I mean I've had to bang a few for personal maintenance, put the nightstick to a few others, but none of that was, like, romance."

He smiled. "Tell me about Harv. What's up with him? That shit with the tree under the ground?"

She straightened out her arms and put her head back against the headrest. Her eyes flicked across her mirrors as she spoke. "Harv. Harv's deep. I was surprised that he wanted to talk to me at all. I don't think he likes you, Ray. You must've said something while I was getting the melons."

"I did. I told him your friend's kid deserved to get French-fried for being an idiot, playing with solvents. Harv didn't like that, much." He slipped his cigarette butt out the window. The air outside was fully cold with an ice edge. "The kid? How'd you make that up, like that on the fly?"

"No, Ray. True story. Maybe the burns aren't quite as bad as I made out, but for sure the kid is scarred up." She was silent a few minutes. "He didn't say much, old Harv. He did say he didn't kill Agatha Burns. Funny that. We know it wasn't him on the branding iron in Chinatown, but we said it was and he didn't deny it. He didn't seem to mind we thought that. But he didn't like it when I said we thought he did Agatha in. He said he didn't kill nobody, ever, which we know is a lie. But he specifically said, Nope, he didn't do her. What do you think?"

"Fuck if I know. I don't actually care, at this point. The hammers from Homicide can figure it out. What did he say about the Captain, about the lab?"

"He didn't talk about the Captain at all. He said if all we wanted was pills, how many would it take? To make me happy, make us go away? I said couple of hundred thousand, but what would really make me happy is getting the lab. Bodies? Sure, I said, if we have to. But the lab, the pressing machine, the precursors they're using? Hog heaven for the poor little black girl working with the heartless beatnik." She glanced over at him and reached a hand onto his thigh. "I know you got a heart, Ray-o. I seen it."

"So, how'd you leave it? With Harv? I think we should've either chained him up for being ugly or stayed on him, see where he went."

"He's gonna call. He has some thinking to do, some stuff to weigh in his mind, and he says then he'll call. If he does, he does. If he don't, he don't. There's issues old Harv has to work out." She indicated a lane change, slipped out, and indicated her way back in front of a sports car having trouble in the gathering wind. They were closer to the lake. A few streamers of snow came off a field to the west. The Canada Express. "Harv's been a crook for, like, forty years. He's careful. He thinks a lot, but he doesn't think like we think, you and me. He thinks about ... I think he thinks that ratting someone in would mean he wasted forty years of his life, toiling in the fertile fields of crime. I think he's thinking about a way to give us what we need, keep us off his back, and not have someone do time for it, especially him."

Ray Tate didn't like it much, but it was her play. Free-form jazz wasn't without some flat notes, some riffs that didn't go anywhere. And, he thought, what's the worst that could happen? The dep put him down, the dep put her down. Worst case: they go to Paris and eat snails on a wide boulevard of shady trees. "Okay, so we wait for him to call."

"He'll call, Ray." She was quiet a few minutes. "All that stuff him and me talked about? I don't think it mattered. I think what he really wanted to say, for some reason, was that, about the trees. To share it. About there being more tree under the ground than on top of it. He seemed dazed, thinking about it."

"Weird." He didn't care, actually, he thought. He wanted her to push the Xterra as fast as it would go, to activate the lights and noise, and speed to her place or his place.

"Yeah, weird. I said to him, Maybe people are like that too, Harv. Maybe what we see in people is only what there is to see. That there's more of the person underground and out of sight than there is walking the earth."

"What'd he say?"

"Nothing. But he nodded as though I'd received some message he'd been trying to send."

They were quiet until they reached to top edge of the city. She said, "Ray, sixteen grand. That's not much for a dope dealer like Harv. How come you think he didn't just go and get his face fixed?"

"What did he say? Be who you are?"

PART THREE

Chapter 26

They spent the night at Djuna Brown's duplex because they needed mix and Ray Tate knew he had none. They didn't get around to the refreshments for several hours. She'd laughed when his hands were on her on the stairs, hushing him but laughing.

"Jesus, Ray." In bed she ran her hand up his back. "You could hang a knitting needle around your neck, use it as a bullet proof vest. Who's been feeding you, boy?"

They were hungry and they sat at the kitchen table. She wore his sweater and looked in the fridge and found some prepared salad. There was mix in the fridge door but she swore out loud and said she was out. She mixed gin and taps at the sink, her reflection in the window smiling at him.

They poked at the salad and sipped at the gin and taps. Twice she caught him staring at her, about to speak.

She was concerned, but she waited. It might be a time for revealing moments: afterglow blues or the emergence of a hitherto unexhibited facet of his character. If, she decided, he asked her to do anything, to get him a drink or turn on the radio, anything at all, she'd decline.

But he simply nodded to himself and got up and went into the other room. When he came back he had his shirt and jacket on and he sat down opposite her with his elbows on the table.

Then he wouldn't look at her at all. He began speaking.

Devon Johnson was first: twenty-one, six-four, Jamaican black, father of four, and husband of none. He had three baby-mothers, young welfare women in the projects, and by all accounts a nice guy, a stickman with the ladies, part-time dent puller in a body shop. His mother's grief, afterwards, was genuine and palpable.

"At the inquest she called him My Boy," Ray Tate told Djuna Brown staring and remembering in the middle ground. "Almost never by his name. My Boy was a good boy. My Boy had had some trouble, but never with guns. My Boy smoked a little reefer but no crack." Ray Tate rattled the ice in his gin and taps. "She bore me no ill will, she said. She said she didn't like cops, but she wanted to be truthful. I remember she looked at me with pity at what I'd done."

In the middle of a blistering afternoon Devon Johnson and three other fellows came out of a mom-and-pop on

Clinton Street. One guy had the money, one guy balanced a stack of cartoned cigarettes as he waddled comically across the sidewalk like a dizzy circus clown, one was stuffing the lottery tickets into his jacket, and Devon Johnson had nothing in his hands but the gun and was halfway to the car when Ray Tate, then a charger in a one-man ghost car, swung into the one-way street the wrong way, bailed out with his gun in his hand, and said clearly in an incredibly calm voice: "Don't move or I'll shoot you."

Devon Johnson fired cowboy-style, his pistol swung to bear vaguely on the sound of Ray Tate's voice. He fired a shot that broke the front passenger window of the ghost car, skipped off the steering wheel, exited the open front driver's window, and splintered off a piece of wooden telephone pole across the street. Ray Tate felt his heart beat twice, then very quickly he shot Devon Johnson dead, emptying his gun into the centre of Devon Johnson's considerable body mass, making a hit ring you could cover with a coffee mug. Ray Tate thought he'd missed completely with every shot — there was no discernible or immediate effect on Devon Johnson, except for a slight rippling of his black Free Mumia sweatshirt as he died on his feet. Watching the dead man standing in front of him, Ray Tate held his breath and gathered his stones, and reached for another clip: Can I do this again? Fall, you motherfucker.

After Devon Johnson fell, Ray Tate held his empty gun on the other suspects until the troops arrived. Witnesses told investigators Devon Johnson had pointed the pistol directly at Ray Tate and was firing when he was killed. It was a heavily Italian neighbour-hood and witnesses referred to the main players as "the officer" and "the eggaplanta." Ray Tate detailed the shooting close enough to the witness statements. He was made a sergeant by the end of the summer, was named Policeman of the Month, and got a three day weekend down in the capital.

"So," he said, "that's Devon Johnson. Stickman. Gunman. My Boy."

"You don't have to tell me, Ray. I know."

"Let's get 'er out of the way, Djuna. I'll talk now, here, tonight, but I won't do it again, okay? You got questions, ask them anytime." His glass was empty, the ice melted. She went to the sink and mixed a couple more.

He didn't wait until she sat back down.

"Mkumba Masi was a schizophrenic," he said to her reflection in the window above the sink. "He didn't take his medication. There'd been a snowstorm down from over the border and he was trapped in his rooming house. He couldn't get out to fill his script and for four days he looked out the third-floor window at the snow building up, coming to smother him. There'd been a suicide in another rooming house up the block and I was heading there on foot, through the snow-drifts, to sign notebooks for my guys, and he just came howling through the snow."

Mkumba Masi, screaming at the gods in the sky to make it stop snowing, came out of nowhere. Ray Tate, calm and focused to the point of super reality, saw every detail of the tribal scars carved into the pores of Mkumba Masi's cheeks, saw the frayed neck of his denim shirt, even smelled on his breath the boiled goat of the rancid putari stew he'd eaten earlier in the day.

"I thought he was calling for help, I couldn't see the machete he had down the back of his belt. When I did, well, it was out and he was too close for me to pull my gun. We went down in the snow. He wasn't that big, but he was wiry. That strength, you know? They get from someplace when they really need it?"

The two men engaged in the middle of the street and went down into the snow. Ray Tate remembered going you-asshole-you-asshole-you-asshole at himself, holy fuck where's the machete? Where's his right hand? When he got control and got his gun out he fired blind. The rounds went through Mkumba Masi's denim shirt, through the left-hand pocket, the Virginia Slims package within, through the thin body, and out the back, all three being later found lodged in a parked car. One of us, Ray Tate thought, is on fire: flames from his gun had ignited both their clothing.

"There was trouble afterwards," he told Djuna Brown in her kitchen in the middle of the night. "All those folks who never gave a shit about Mkumba Masi when he was alive, all of a sudden he's their cause. A little rioting, a lot of editorializing. Those buttons came out, you saw them? My photograph with a red line through it. Killer Kop. Ray Gun. Tate Equals Hate. No promotion this time for old Ray. We'd got a new mayor by then and it was goodbye Charlie. A month off and then into the weeds, looking for a guy that was poisoning dogs. Then this."

"Silver lining, right?" She came around the table. "You got the girl."

"Jeez," he said, "I sure fucking hope so." He bit his lip. "You know, the first one? Devon? That never bothered me. He had a gun, I had a gun. Fair fight. But Mkumba Masi? I was a bigger guy then, I lost a lot of weight since. But I was bigger than him by about forty pounds and a good six inches. I should've been able to control him, crazy strength or not." He took a deep breath. "That's what we do. We're cops. We control. But ..."

She wrapped him up and put her face next to his. She felt his body make a small convulsion but it might have been a silent hiccup.

At the office while they waited for the skipper to go through his morning messages they checked their phone mailboxes. Ray Tate had one from a man named Carl who said the guy with the scars on his face had come in the day before, driving an old grey pickup truck. You know, the guy said, Carl, at the restaurant up Widow's Corners way, and is there a reward? Ray Tate deleted it with a laugh.

Djuna Brown had one from Buck, who talked slowly and endlessly about her coming back up north, bringing justice to Dodge, and he had a new venison recipe she'd love. He warned her that if she had to ever prepare bear she should cut every single trace of fat from the meat; it went rancid very quickly. What else, what else? Oh, yeah, by the way, that place up Passive way? Ten clicks north of the town, driveway to the left with a white gate at the entry. Watch out, he said, for the old, snaggly dude, he was heap bad medicine. Djuna Brown laughed too.

The skipper hung up his phone and waved them into his office. He looked pale and drawn but his eyes were clear. A bottle of anti-nausea tablets and a black coffee stood on his desk. Ray Tate recognized the signs: the skipper was taking a cure and his body wasn't liking it much. He'd lost the aggressive look he habitually wore. He looked shaky and weak. He didn't look at Djuna Brown as if she was a celestial. He gave Ray Tate a friendly nod.

"So, where we at, after you guys disappear up in Indian country?"

Djuna Brown said, "A quarter million."

"Dollars?"

"Nope. The evil X. With double Chucks on each of them."

"Where? When? Should I call public affairs?" He looked at her as though without the blond madness on her head she was another person, a cop almost. "Set up a press conference?"

Ray Tate briefed him on their day up north without actually saying anything. "We got a lead. There's gonna be a quarter million double Chucks, at least, in a place we don't know yet. We're waiting for the call."

"Quarter million. Beautiful. At twenty-five bucks a pop that's ..." The alcohol cells screaming in his brain left him confused. "Fuck, that's a lot."

"Six million, street value. In real terms, just between us," Djuna Brown said, "fuck all, really. But they're killer pills and we're going to get them. Nice double Cs stamped in 'em."

"Strange that they'd bring back the Cs after those kids died."

"I thought so, too," she said. "I figure they figure the logo is so well-known folks'll go for it, just to be cool." She shrugged. "Get high and cheat death."

"What about the lab, Ray? Can we get the lab? The super lab?"

Ray Tate nodded. "Yeah, I think so. Separately, from another source, we might have a fix on where their smoky cauldron is. Not likely we're going to get bodies to go with it. Maybe an old fucker who guards the place."

"This Captain guy? Phil Harvey? Anybody?"

Djuna Brown shook her head. "Not Harvey, anyway, unless the hammers figure out he killed Agatha Burns and where he put her body. We got nothing on the Cook guy. Maybe the old fuck at the lab will give us something we can chase down, lead us back to the players. But right now? At least a couple of hundred thousand double Chucks for probably maybe, the super lab for a maybe maybe."

"Nice. Decent. Fuck, guys, I didn't think you could do it."

Ray Tate shook his head. "What the fuck, skip? You thought we were, what, riding around the countryside looking at property to buy? Ace investigators you called us."

Skipper held up his hands. "Yeah, yeah, yeah. Okay, I knew you could do it. But how tight is it? Can I call the Swamp, put them on alert? What's the next move?"

"We wait. We're gonna get a call, probably later today, maybe tomorrow. Then we move in."

Djuna Brown said, "We're going to need to move fast, once we get the word. Tactical guys in case there's a cadre of speed demons on the site. Some Haz-Mat guys in bunny suits to take the lab apart. The place where we think it is is about four hours north of here in Indian country, so a helicopter wouldn't hurt. My people are going to want a piece of it. It's their turf. We gotta keep the Staties happy, right?"

"I got it, I got it. An example of what can be done when all levels of policing work together, target organized crime groups where they live … yak yak yak." He clapped his hands together then squinted in pain at the noise. "All right. Do me a continuation report and an action plan. Best case, worst case. I'll start things moving with the dep." He was smiling. Djuna Brown had never seen it before. "Ray, stay a second, okay?"

After Djuna Brown had left the office, he said, "You've got somebody, right? Inside? Someone feeding us this stuff?"

"Djuna's got a guy, skip. You can't do this without a guy."

"Do I want to know his name?"

"Believe me, skipper, you don't."

"But the organization's been penetrated, right? I can say that?"

"Sure. We're burrowed to the very heart of the

murderous double-Chuck conspiracy."

"Beautiful. And the guy, he's a working guy, though, right? A guy in the know? Will he testify? You didn't promise him anything?"

"This guy is Djuna's guy. She worked him, she turned him. I just held her coat. But, I think, no way does he come out into the light. We're not taking down bodies, anyway, so no need for nobody to testify to nobody about nothing."

The skipper looked through the glass at Djuna Brown on the telephone. "What's up with that other thing? Anything going on, there?"

"Not yet. I'll drop her soon, skip." He had no inflection at all in his voice. "She'll go down."

"Bullshit. You fucking guys are partners. I can't fucking believe it. The gunner and the dyke. Sounds like a fucking fairytale for test-tube babies."

"Tell you what, skip. You go two weeks with the coffee and the airline pills then we'll talk, okay? I've been there. In two weeks it'll all look different and, if you don't mind I say so, you'll shake your head and go, Fuck what an asshole I was back in those days." He got up. "And you can pull those fucking mutts off, that's following us around. I think I'm putting my papers, after this, so it'll be win-win for you."

The skipper shook his head. "Not me, Ray. I got nobody behind you. Must be the dep. The dep don't like you, man. If you guys don't tank, I'm going to be holding my nuts. One in each pocket."

Ray Tate laughed. "Great. You'll feel like a copper again."

* * *

While they waited for word from Phil Harvey they each went home. Djuna Brown thought she scoped a car down the block, backed into a driveway. She didn't care. The dep or the skip, she didn't give a shit. She and Ray Tate were on their way to making the case and after that, well, Tate had been talking about Paris. She'd heard they dug blacks in Paris, thought they were cool, and she felt she kind of was.

In her duplex she cleaned up the mess from the night before, smiling. With her cellphone beside her ear, she stretched out on the couch, thinking about Ray Tate and slept.

Ray Tate went home. The apartment was musty and he opened the windows to let the cold air in. It smelled like snow. He took a long shower then sprawled out on the futon but couldn't sleep. He got up and mixed colours. The yellows and oranges and bright reds meant nothing concrete to him, yet, but he had an inkling. He put the pallet aside and with a number six charcoal stick and a fluid hand he sketched Djuna Brown from the back, standing at a sink, her reflection in the window in front of her, looking at him. He used his knuckle to fudge the lines of everything except her face.

Chapter 27

Phil Harvey had Cornelius Cook drop him off at a city bus. He slung his knapsack over his shoulder and said he'd call once he had something set up to pick up the groceries. All the way down from the rib place Connie Cook had talked about getting a backhoe into the farm and making an underground cavern. Like a pantry, he said. For when the hunger really comes over me. Phil Harvey, who had a good strong imagination, shuddered but laughed and made suggestions for piping in air, for soundproofing, for waste disposal. If they built it close to the lake, he said, they could have water. A generator could heat up several dozen gallons, and the place would be pretty homey, he said.

He stood in his bat coat, leaning on the Mercedes. "I'll call you, Connie, we'll work out the moves."

"Perfect, Harv. Once we get the fun stuff out of the way, though, we'll be wanting to get to work. You okay for money right now?"

"I'm okay, Connie." He saw the look of pleasure on the Captain's face. Connie Cook always looked for signs that friendship wasn't based on his wealth, that he was loved for who he was. "I'm in good shape."

Phil Harvey went to the back of the bus and sprawled out. He felt crawly. He'd spent time with degenerates but that was inside when that kind of thing was squeezed to your surface by the weight of time and the repetitious madness of cellblocks and footsteps. Anyone could slip a little and could come back from it unless they were serving time for so long their souls warped for keeps, and after that really there was no point. He watched people boarding. Most spotted him and stayed toward the front, near the driver.

There was no way, he thought, he was putting anyone in. Not even the crazy fat fuck. It wasn't done, although it had been done to him. Phil Harvey didn't have much, but what he had he kept. If he had to lift the weight then he'd lift it. Just because he was leaving the life didn't mean he had to leave wreckage and bad feelings behind him.

He rode the bus to the end of the line, part of his mind daydreaming out how to notch logs together to make a stable house. Flitting through his thoughts was the black chick, the cop with the soft voice and her sudden anger that he'd branded the girl in Chinatown. He'd wanted to tell her it wasn't him, but that meant it was someone else and even that, Harv felt, was too close to ratting. The Chem Squad could have all the double-Cs he could make, but no way anyone — even that loony, fat bastard — was going to do time because of anything Harv did.

At the end of the line the driver called to him. He disembarked and waited until the driver turned to retrace his route. Then he boarded the next bus and rode it to a convention hotel where he squirreled himself away in a pay phone kiosk.

The gym guy, Barry, was leery about going back into east Chinatown. "We've raised some havoc, there, Harv. There's a bounty on us." He paused. Harv heard the rhythmic clinking of weights. "Ah, that other thing? You know? Is that solid?"

"Yeah, the guy'll be okay. He took off. I can guarantee he won't talk, you know?"

"Whoo. Okay." The gym guy grunted for a few seconds. "Okay. This thing, can you get them to come out? Out of Chinatown? Maybe downtown someplace? Where we got some control."

"Sure, I'll ask him. I just need you for some stand arounds, you know? Nothing heavy."

"I'll get the same guys as last time. Ah, Harv? They were a little ... concerned with that guy. The blond guy. My guys are solid, but for sure he won't come back and talk?"

Harv made bubbling noises. He hung up and walked down the station to another pay phone. He called the manager of a restaurant on California Street. "I've got forty at two."

The man jabbered. "No, no, this is a restaurant, not for dirty business."

"Forty at two, tonight."

"You call some other place, eh? Call a friend. You need crazy help, mister." The man hung up. Harv waited a minute then redialed.

Another man, with a deeper, less accented voice, answered. He recognized Harv's voice. "Come down and have dinner. Tonight there's crab. Good stuff, not the stuff in the tanks."

"Naw, I need takeout. You deliver downtown?"

The man laughed. "Come to Chinatown, Mr. Harvey. See the exotic sights. Meet old friends. Learn a new culture. Bring a fat friend. Bring a blond friend."

Harv laughed. "Yeah, yeah that was bad, I admit. But I straightened it out for you. One for one."

"You've driven the market down. Say, forty egg rolls for a dollar twenty-five?"

Harv didn't care. The man knew he couldn't go to Willy Wong; Willy Wong was of a sensitive type, who view brandings and rip-offs and shootings as an encroachment. Harv wanted to get as much cash together as he could, as quickly as he could. The mountain cabin of his imagination was a constant image in the front of his mind. Once he was escaped from the life he'd need little to live on. But there might be suspicion if he caved. "One and seventy-five. And the next delivery at one and fifty."

"When, this other takeout? How many egg rolls?"

"Day after tomorrow," Harv said. "At least this many, again."

The man clicked his teeth. "One and fifty for this one, and one and seventy-five for the next, depending how crispy are the egg rolls, how much meat inside."

"Done." Speaking in circular terms, Harv arranged a meeting at an upscale steakhouse just on the edge of Stonetown. "I'm bringing some friends."

"Friends," the man said. "Friends are good to have at any time of life."

Barry the gym owner said he'd bring his little crew to a coffee shop near the steakhouse a half hour before the transfer. He asked how heavy Harv wanted them to be. Harv said it was a Chinatown deal and probably it wouldn't hurt to bring some drills.

Harv sat in the coffee shop and ran through his moves. He didn't allow himself to think of chinking the logs in his new log house on the edge of a western river. Whether he'd square the logs or leave them naturally rounded wasn't a concern he needed to deal with, yet. A fireplace or a wood stove could be determined later. More than anything he looked forward to original thoughts, even though he doubted he'd ever had one. The roots of a tree underground had been Agatha's. The slim little black cop had responded cannily, confirming Harv's own tentative theory that people were indeed like that. He tried to determine when to call her, to let her know where her double-Cs were without giving up the super lab. The cops might be able to unravel the Captain's complex paper trail and find him hiding in the ownerships. And there were dead people around the property. As much as he had mixed feelings about the fat fuck, Harv recognized it was the luxury of not having to chase a buck every day that made the leisure of thought available to him. He owed Connie Cook something for that.

Barry slid into the booth opposite. "Deep thoughts, Harv? You look like one of the stone philosopher guys down in front of the museum, sitting here. State of the world, daydreaming?"

"Nah. Just figuring how to get out of there with the money, without the hounds of Chinatown chewing on my ass."

"Well, no fear, Harv," Barry said. "That's what we're here for. The guys'll be along in a sec."

They sat a moment. Barry went and got a coffee and a refill for Harv. He sat heavily, all steroid neck and shaved head with a long pigtail left at the back. "That guy? What's up with him?"

"My blond guy?"

"No. You say he's square, he's square. The other guy. The fat guy."

"Well, he's around, we're doing some stuff. He's a little odd, but a lot of people earn off him."

"A little odd." Barry looked uncomfortable, but determined. He had something to say. "You and me, we've done time, right? We've done some tough stuff. We've come up the old way, before the Chinks and the blacks and who all knows who all. We may not be friends, but we're pals. Am I right?"

Harv nodded.

"And if I was doing something with someone and you knew that someone was wrong, say, a rat or a cop, you'd tell me?"

Harv nodded.

"Because you know how things are, right? Don't matter to you, at the end of the day, if I get pinched. That's the life. But if you knew, before, and if you could, you'd give me a heads-up, no sweat off your ass? Barry, you'd say, that guy, he's a rat or a cop, walk away, man. And because we've pulled time and we've done tough stuff, I wouldn't say a fucking thing. I'd drop whatever it was I was into and I'd go home and pack and go down to Antigua for a month. It's like that, am I right, us?"

"Barry, you're right. What are you thinking? I can tell you, the fat fuck's no cop. He's no rat." He saw for the first time that Barry was intelligent, that he had a human component that, although it didn't get as much exercise as his muscles, it was there. Tree underground, he thought.

"No, I don't think he's a rat or a cop." Barry leaned forward. "He's worse, Harv. He isn't of our life. He isn't of anybody's life. He's a fucking spaceman. I've done stuff and for a while afterwards I've said to myself, Fuck but that was bad. I'll never forget how that guy looked. I'm gonna have nightmares about that poor prick. That's okay, that's normal. Because after a while you do forget, you go, Fuck it, that's the life. But this guy …" He kept his eyes on Harv's. "I've seen stuff happen to guys inside and outside, it was worse inside where guys got no real control over themselves sometimes. I seen guys where a message had to be sent, a message that was serious and had to be done to make things work. But your guy there? Last night I'm going to sleep beside my woman still thinking about him and his fucking branding iron, that girl's tits. That smell. I can still fucking smell it."

"I know, Bar', he went a little far. I'll talk to him."

Barry saw he wasn't getting it. "Let me try again, I'm fucking this up, must be the 'roids." He looked out the window where his guys pulled up in an Escalade. He held up his palm to the window and turned back to Harv. "I like you, I've always respected you. Everybody does. When you had no dough, well, you didn't whine, you went out and made some. When you had some, it was party time on Harv. You're of an older generation than us guys, you took the beatings and you stood up, and when the judge said three years or four years or five years, you pulled your time. But this guy, this fat fuck? Me and my guys're going to do this thing with the Chinamen tonight for you. If it flies right, we'll make some dough off you. If it goes sideways, well, we've got the equipment and those fuckers won't have to click their heels to find out they're not in Chinatown anymore, but they're gonna think it's Chinese New Year anyway. But after this? After tonight? No. Not if he's anywhere near it."

"Fuck, Barry, c'mon. It's the life, man."

Barry shook his head. "It isn't, Harv. I don't give a fuck what a guy does to make some dough at his end. But think about it: where was the end there, in the basement? We already had what we went for, right?

Pills, dough. If you can tell me what the fuck that was about, where the end was in what he did, well, I'll listen. Maybe you can convince me, but I doubt it." He waved his guys in. "We do man's work you once told me, when I was young and I needed a talking to because I missed something for some guys and those guys sent you over to explain things to me." He grinned fondly. "A painful lesson, it was, Harv, that much I remember. But it stuck. You know that in the basement with the girl, that wasn't man's work. That's some other kind of creature and I don't want me or my guys around it."

"Jesus, Bar', you all feel like this?"

"Yeah, Harv. We talked and this is where we're all at. We see him around, we're going to take him out. No profit in it, no end for us. That's okay." Barry smiled. "He's a rabid fucking dog, Harv, and he's had his one free bite. Community service, think of it as."

There was nothing to do in his rental van speeding north except think and crunch little pills to keep his eyes open and the car on the road.

The Chinamen and Barry's crew had been well-behaved. One of the Chinamen glared at Harv throughout the entire transaction, relentless as the bags were moved across the restaurant, as the steaks were ignored on their bloody wooden platters. There was a shuffling of personnel as each side took their bag to the basement washroom and came out nodding. A Chinaman flashed a gun on his lap. Barry, who had a shopping bag on the top of his table, saw it and poked the end of a sawed-off at the Chinaman and smiled as though he'd like nothing better than some gunfire with his tenderloin.

Harv, in the basement, checked the wads of money, mixed up hundreds and twenties, trying to determine if any was fake. He couldn't tell. No one could. The Chinese were in with some Koreans and the Koreans ran print shops across the city, turning out currency so perfect that even if you got bogus you could still run it through a teller at a bank.

When Harv came up out of the basement he made a sign. One of the Chinamen walked past Barry's table and smoothly picked up the knapsack. He went to the basement. When he came out he made his own sign to his people. Protocol called for one guy on each side to leave the restaurant and call on a cellphone to the next guy on his team, who would wait until one of the other side left. The Chinamen didn't bother. They got up and swaggered out as a gang. Harv and Barry discussed possible problems when they hit the street. Finally, Barry said, Fuck it, and, with his scatter in the bag, went outside. He stood pumped and prowling by the door until Harv and the rest of his crew came out and headed for their vehicles. After Harv paid him off, Barry made a point of shaking hands and saying Goodbye, Harv, while the others shuffled their feet near the Escalade. They wouldn't look at him.

He didn't stop at the restaurant south of Widow's Corners. The place was poisoned. He had bags of groceries in the back of the rental and a pound of coffee to float him through the night. For a while, on a stretch of dark road with no traffic going either way, he allowed himself to think he'd already left the life and was driving to his cabin on a mountainside in the far west, returning perhaps from a dinner out in a nearby mining town, maybe with a woman beside him for company, someone who saw through the scars on his face and hands, who believed it was from fucked-up work on an oil rig. The idea of Alaska came to him. He knew guys who'd lammed out and headed north. Half the state was guys named Smith and Jones who said they came from a general direction instead of a town or city. People accepted that. You could reinvent yourself, he thought, although not in that exact term, and he wondered if you had to hate yourself to do it or if you just had to have had enough of yourself in general.

He decided he'd do the work to satisfy the funny little black girl cop. He'd genuinely liked her, although her partner was just a cop like every other cop he'd ever met. A thug with no heart, a guy chasing his pension and fuck everybody else. But the little cop had been funny and sad and angry, all in one package. He'd bet living in her life wasn't easy. She'd said she'd pull back the legions of Chem Squad detectives and give him two days to come up with a stash of double Charlies.

"Me and him, out there in the truck," she'd said, "we're the two you see, Harv. It's the guys you don't see that are gonna give you problems. I just want to put this case down, get promoted, and get away from all those white city fuckers. He's okay most of the time, but really, at the end of it, he just wants his pension, dump his wife and kids, and go to Paris to fuck all day and drink all night. Nice guy, but limited."

"And you can get me free for a couple of days? What'll you tell him, or your bosses?"

"Fuck them, Harv. I'd tell you about my life as a cop but believe me, you wouldn't believe me. You can get vitamin E cream, go for skin grafts. Doesn't work like that for black folks." She'd looked over his shoulder at Ray Tate in the truck. "You know who he is, eh? Who they fucking partnered me with? He's the guy shot those black guys, down in the city."

He decided he'd put the double Charlie head on the pill presser and make her the two-hundred-thousand pills. He'd switch heads and crank out lightning bolts until the sound drove him crazy. Then he'd return to the city and do the final grab-up job for the Captain. The deal with the Chinamen to dump the next batch of lightnings would require careful thought and planning: he'd have no backup, with Barry and his crew waiting in the weeds to whack the fat Captain. Then he'd gather up his dough and take a train west to the ocean and work his way back east a while and north into the foothills.

As he peered into the darkness for the turnoff to the farm he thought about Barry and the crew. He couldn't have any part in Barry's plans for the Captain. Betraying a partner was as bad as ratting him out. But if the next twenty-four hours went smoothly it probably wouldn't matter anyway. Connie would find his entire life changed. Harv had a plan for his pal.

In front of the farmhouse he sat and thought about looking at the moon a while.

There was a light on in the front window.

He went into the barn and turned on the lights, pulled the drop cloth from the pressing machine, and turned on some space heaters. A half hour, he decided, until the place was warmed up enough to work in. Then he'd have to kill the heaters: they were an ignition source and when he was mixing the fumes would fill the place so gradually he wouldn't notice their thickness through his mask.

He went to the rental, gathered his groceries and clumped up the steps to the farmhouse, pretending it was his western refuge. "Jesus fuck," he said, "home at last."

Chapter 28

Ray Tate and Djuna Brown met for breakfast at a coffee shop near the satellite. While he went to the counter to order food, she called Gloria at the office and said they were in the area and would be in in an hour. Gloria said the skipper hadn't made it in yet and there were calls stacking up from the chief's office, from the dep, from the *Federales*, and from the hammers of Homicide. Djuna Brown said to give her a call if he showed up before they got back. She folded the phone and watched Ray Tate bullshitting with the girl behind the counter. She could tell the counter girl liked him, was flirting. He looked fit and slim and nothing like a killer beatnik cop in a short, brown leather jacket, blue sweater, blue jeans, and hiking boots. He looked like an old perpetual student or a cool, young professor. The girl at the counter laughed and he laughed with her. Djuna Brown had trouble believing he was the same bent guy she'd seen that first morning, standing with the skipper outside the elevator, looking at her appraisingly through red eyes above a grey beard. Of course, she wasn't the same shuffling depressive wearing embroidered slippers, either.

When Ray Tate brought down coffee and a plate of breakfast buns she asked about his night. She saw the black dust in his fingernails, the charcoal in the creases in his knuckles. "You could've come over, you know? I got gin and the water was on."

"I wanted to. I got to … I did some drawing and before I knew it the sun was coming up. I grabbed an hour or two. This thing I think is going to break soon. Unless Harvey conned you."

"Nope." She was positive. "He'll call. We'll get the pills, be a hero to our kind. One thing I'd like, though, and if you overrule it that's okay. We're pretty sure we know where the super lab is, right? We could go up there right now and grab up Harv in action and probably a shitload of pills. But me? I'd rather wait. Let Harv do his thing and when we get our stuff and he gets clear, we take the lab."

"You like our Harv, don't you?"

She dug into her jacket and brought out her fist. Ray Tate stared at it. When she opened it there was a wrinkled half tube of vitamin E cream. "He gave it to me at the coffee place. So I wouldn't get the wrong stuff for the kid. Yeah, I like Harv. He's a bandit and probably, they say, a killer." She made a sad smile. "But nobody's perfect, right?"

"Not me, that's for sure."

They sat chewing on scones and sipping their coffee. A crowd of cattlemen with exaggerated bowed legs moved up the sidewalk outside like a posse, in their ten-gallon hats and western-style suits. They wore convention ID cards around their necks.

"So, what's our plan?"

He shrugged. "Wait for Harv to call, I guess, if you don't want to nail down the lab right off."

"We'll give Harv a couple of hours. If nothing, then we'll get the skipper to put together a raiding party." She made a cat smile. "So, what'd you draw? All night?"

He looked out the window. "Ah, you know. Jugs of water, flowers in pots. Student stuff."

"I'm sure."

He made a small smile. "When this is over? We should talk."

She touched his hand on the table. "When this is over, Ray, we should talk French in Paris. I got lots of lieu time. And the way you live I figure you've got some dough put aside. You can keep me in the style I've become accustomed to. Beatnik glory."

"Cool."

Her phone buzzed. "Oh, please, let it be my buddy, Harv." She answered with her last name, nodded at Ray Tate, and listened. "No, I can talk. I'm sitting with my buddy, Bongo ... Yeah, him ... How many? ... When? ... Where? ... Any chance you want to help us out with the other guy? The Captain? ..." She laughed. "I know you're not, but I hadda ask ... You know, I know you don't know, but if you did know, it'd be nice to give some closure to Agatha Burns's family ... Like I said, Harv, I hadda ask ... I'm cool with that ..." She nodded as though Phil Harvey could see her and held up the tube of vitamin E. "I got it right here. After we do our thing today I'm gonna take it over to him ... You know, you didn't have to do that, right? ... I know ... I know ... I know ... Tommy's his name ..." She got a very sad look on her face. "Harv ... Harv, I know you don't want to hear this from a cop, but maybe you should look at yourself, I think there's probably some roots under there, a little different than the tree up top, you know? ... Harv? Hello? ..."

"Gone?"

"Yeah. I think I mighta fucked it there, at the end. I just wanted him to know ... you know?"

"Sure. So, what'd he say?"

"Today. Today's the day. He'll call in a couple of hours, let us know where to pick them up. We're not going to see him at all. We won't see him again, he said."

"Okay, Djun'. First we get the pills, then we're going to the lab, raise a ruckus, lay waste in Indian country."

She nodded. "I hope he doesn't get caught in this thing."

"Djun'? He's still a mutt, you know, old Harv."

"I know," she said sadly.

The skipper had fallen. His eyes looked like angry red orbs, veins like purple tortured worms writhed in his forehead. He was sitting with his feet up, listening to someone rag him out, massaging his temple with his free hand.

From the doorway Ray Tate could hear the voice and the tone of the voice on the phone but not the words. He held his thumb up.

"Hang on, hang fucking on," the skipper said into the phone, palming the receiver. "Tell me, Ray, oh please, Jesus."

"Today's the day, skip. Waiting on the coordinates. We get the pills then, I think, we're going for the super lab."

"You know where the lab is?"

"Yep, probably. First the pills, then the lab. Has to be in that order. Clean sweep, unless you want bodies in chains. Bodies, we don't got."

"The *Federales* want back in. They want all you got." The skipper held up the receiver. "The Big Chan's cut a deal with the Feds, I don't know why, the fucking mayor's gonna go nuts, this gets away from us. But I made a deal for us with the dep. We take down the double Chucks, they get the lab."

Ray Tate stared at him.

"C'mon, Ray."

"Skip, you drunken fucking cocksucker," he said, "I'm booking medical-off. My ulcer's acting up."

"Ray."

"Fuck off."

* * *

They left the building without speaking. They didn't take a company car. Instead they walked up the hill, huddling arm in arm against a north wind. Lake effect snow had blown in sometime and stopped and the headstones in the cemetery were edged in pure white relief. He steered her past the local station and up the street towards his apartment.

"My place, Ray. I got a fireplace. I got mix. I even got bedding we can shred."

She tugged him off course and they went through the streets to her duplex. At the foot of the steps something caught her eye along the block. "They never fucking give up."

He looked and saw a grey car with the engine idling at the corner. "Let's give 'em something to report in their dailies," he said and wrapped her up in his arms.

Laughing, she flipped the finger at the surveillance car and slapped his ass as they went up the steps.

The flames in the fireplace came from Union Gas. They took bedding from the bedroom and made a nest on the floor. She mixed drinks and put on a Cesaria Evora CD.

"They got you, Ray, you know that? Dereliction. Insubordination. Beatnik goofiness." She sipped and sparkled her eyes at him. "Weird. You don't do the job and they get you. You do do the job and they get you anyway."

"Paris. I got the early pension already. I got some dough put aside."

"Cool. How do you say Cool-ee-oh in French?"

They played around. He had his hand trapped inside her bra. "What do you think? Paris?"

"Sure, whatever. Right now," she said, "let's do sixty-eight. I really like that, Bongo."

He laughed. "Sixty-nine, you mean."

She made a wicked smile. "Nope. Sixty-eight: you do me now and I'll owe you one later."

He laughed again. He felt a strange freedom. "So, what do you think? You up for it, for Paris? Bohemian frolics."

"Me and you? Well, I guess, okay, maybe. No weird stuff, though, okay? No berets, none of those scarf things you wear around your neck like some fruit." She giggled. "Especially no moustache I'll have to wax."

Her mobile rang and she sprang up to get it from her jacket. She answered with her name, listened without saying anything for a few moments, then hung up. "Harv. Our stuff is ready for pickup. What are we going to do about it?"

"Fuck it," he said. "Call it in to Crime Watch."

She sat beside him and ran her hand over his face. "I got a better idea, if you're up for it. Didn't you say you got a good pal in the Staties?"

Chapter 29

It was colder north of the city. A stiff wind was starting up and the faintest traces of snow gathered then vanished in clouds. The treeline swayed like dancers. An audience of identical grim crows sat in a row on the hydro wires. Ray Tate's pal on the Statie gun team backed his truck up to their rental car so they could talk door-to-door. The Statie stared across at Djuna Brown. "You clean up good," he said, making a smile. He was a lean man with wide shoulders and a right eye that had a sniper's mean squint under a long-billed, blue baseball cap with a crossed rifles logo on the front.

Djuna Brown gave him a minimal smile. Staties weren't her favourite people.

"So, Ray, bring me up-to-date. What the fuck are we doing here?"

Ray Tate gave him a brief rundown on the double Charlie pill pickup and the possibility of a super lab in

Indian country. "There might be a tie-in to a woman who died in a truck fire, a lab that exploded just over a month ago. Maybe murder."

"These pills, they the ones that killed the kids in the city?"

"Yep. Double Chucks. Death on the tip of your tongue."

The Statie nodded. "Hmmm. They any good?" He sat and thought, sighting distances to trees, parsing the wind and its effect on a travelling bullet. He stared at the line of crows, appraising regret. "So I get this straight: you guys have a stash being dumped for you. You might have a monster lab. You might have a hook into a fatality that might or might not be a homicide. All this, right? So how come you don't go pick up the pills, set up on the lab, solve the case, be a hero to your people?"

"City politics. You don't want to know. We can just call Crime Watch and pick up five hundred bucks under my wife's name if you don't want it."

The Statie shrugged. "Sure. Yeah. I think so. I should touch base with my brother. He's a major at headquarters. What do you guys want out of it?"

"Dick."

"Hang on." The Statie reversed and creeped his truck back up the road a little. Through the windshield they could see him talking into a mobile.

"What do you think, Ray?" Djuna Brown made little fists and stretched.

Ray Tate shook his head. "Dunno. They want it. I mean, who wouldn't? There's going to be a lot of press, drinks all around. I can see him being suspicious simply because it's a gimme." He watched her dig in her pockets and take out a cigarette. "Someone hands you something for no reason you can think of, when they could keep it themselves, they go, Whoa, what's wrong with this?"

"This is the guy you called, right? About me, back at the beginning? The guy who figured I'd been in the shit before they put me in the shit?" She lit the cigarette with a match and waved out the flame. He could see she was nervous.

"Yeah. Good guy. He's got some funny stories about Indian country."

"Here he comes."

The black truck rolled forward down the sideroad and stopped, driver to driver. "He wants to know about bodies. The guy dropping the stash? Can we get him?"

Djuna Brown leaned forward. "Nope. The dump's already been done. The stuff's just sitting there. Waiting. Nobody around."

"Can we track him?"

"Nope. He's our guy. I think he's already long gone." She handed Ray Tate the cigarette. "Maybe, maybe when you hit the lab, maybe there's some guys hanging around there. I dunno."

"And you've got good coordinates on the lab?"

She nodded. "I haven't been there, but I think I can find it."

The Statie tapped his mobile on the top of the steering wheel. "A warrant would be nice, for the lab. What about that?"

Ray Tate shrugged. "Sure. But we don't have tight

coordinates, we don't have a talking co-operator to put into the warrant. What we have is someone who told us about a bad smell in the air, chemical stuff. It'll be: you go where your nose takes you."

Djuna Brown leaned to speak across Ray Tate. "And there'll probably be no major kingpin guys in there, anyway. No trial, no lawyers, so who gives a shit?"

"You guys write anything down in your books? About this meeting or anything else?"

Ray Tate shook his head. "We're someplace else right now, entirely."

She said, "Yeah, we're someplace, getting it on, doing sixty-eights."

The Statie smiled. "Who owes who?" He backed up his truck and went back on the phone. They watched him nod. When he came back he nodded. "Okay. He says first things first. We get the stash and we keep it quiet, if there is a stash. Then we set up on the lab tonight if we can find it and go in, first light."

Ray Tate said, "Who we? We who?"

The Statie nodded at Djuna Brown. "Her. She can find the place. No offence, Ray, but there might be some guys in there with guns, and … Well, you know? Besides, we want to keep this Statie, right? Rub shit into the city's head and make 'em bleed?"

"Naw, naw. That isn't right. We're partners. You just want her as a hostage to wear the hat in case it all goes sideways."

"Ray," Djuna Brown said, "it's okay. I'll take it."

Ray Tate thought about it. He'd just wanted to give the whole steaming pile of shit to someone else and take her back to one of their places for the night, to get up the next day and start his paperwork to dump out of the job. Book airline tickets and learn from a book how to buy condoms in French.

She said, "C'mon. Think of the skipper's face, the dep, when this hits the press while they're still pulling their pricks." She gave him a deep look. "Then it's bohemian Paris for me and you, Picasso."

"Yeah, okay." He looked at the Statie and said, "Hang on a sec. Back it up." When the truck rolled back, he got his door open, climbed out of the rental and into the passenger side of the truck.

The Statie said, "Is this beyond partners, Ray? This is something else, right?"

"Maybe. Maybe. I dunno. But I'll tell you this: I like you. We had some good times on the training courses. But if she doesn't come out of this in the same condition she went in, I'm coming looking, okay? You can think what you want, her and me, and you might be right and you might be wrong."

The Statie looked at Djuna Brown through the two windshields. "She's a good-looking woman, Ray. With all the stories, I expected a fucking big behemoth. She's cool, right?"

"She's beyond cool."

"No heavy lifting, I promise you. If this works out, maybe a little something for her, I don't know. We'll take it slow. We'll get the stash and if it's there, then we'll set up on the lab." He stared at Ray Tate for a moment. "Look, you're not in the city now. We don't do those things to our own, in spite of what happened to her up north. That's a fucked place, Ray, that's Indian country. She'll be okay with me, man."

Ray Tate got out of the truck and into the rental.

"Okay, he's taking you. I'll head back to town, see if Harv or anybody shows their faces. If I'm lucky, I'll spot him and follow him up to the lab. We'll be having bacon and eggs ready when you guys roll in."

"Over medium, crispy bacon, don't forget." He could see she was shaky as she opened her door and climbed out. But she said, "Don't worry, Ray, okay?"

"I mean this, Djun': don't think of Paris, don't think of gin and taps, okay? Just go hard. Listen to that guy, he's square."

She gave him a small grin, biting her lip. She leaned over and gave him the softest of kisses. "Cool-ee-oh, Bongo."

Alone, Ray Tate headed the rental back to the city. When he got in range his rover picked up the skipper on the base station, voicing out for him. The skipper voiced out to the mutts, Wally and Bernie, but they had no time for him. He shut off his rover and headed for home, resisting the urge to turn around. But he didn't know where Phil Harvey had made the drop. He wasn't even sure where the super lab was. Just at some stinky place north of Widow's Corners.

At his apartment he couldn't paint. He'd been up for two days and he stretched out on the futon. He got up. He stood by the window and watched trees shedding their leaves. He saw the back half of a grey sedan parked on the street, a wisp of exhaust coming from the tailpipe. He wanted to go down and pull the fuckers out of the car through the grill, but there'd be other cars around, headhunters from the Swamp looking for a bump and a serving of fruit salad on their shoulder boards. They were vermin and they worked away like chisels on the best blue job in the world. He made a gin and tap and sat watching nothing on television. He found some old stale cigarettes, lit one and choked on it, and called his daughter. His wife answered and when she recognized his voice, put the phone down and called Alexis.

"Dad. What's wrong?"

"Nothing. Just having a drink, here, wondering how you're doing."

"Mom says they partnered you with a black lesbian." She made a little laugh. "She said she beats cops up."

"Well, she's a tough biscuit, all right."

"You used to call me that. A tough biscuit. But she's okay, though? You're safe with her?"

"Ax, she's fine. She's a little odd, but you'll like her."

"Cool-ee-oh."

Ray Tate laughed. "Funny you should say that. She says that."

Alexis was silent for a few seconds. "You want me to drop by? Or you want to come out here? We can go out for dinner."

"Naw, we're in the middle of a case. It'll be done in a day or two, then ..."

"Then? Then what?"

"Well, I'm thinking of quitting." He cleared his throat. "Moving, maybe, to Paris." He waited and cleared his throat again. "Ah, ah, with ... her?"

"A black lesbian? I didn't know you were so cool, you know? Very subterranean."

"Tell me about it."

They spoke for a few more minutes about her plans for a photo trip to Asia and made plans for dinner later in the week. For the first time that day he told someone he loved her.

He took his drink to the window. The grey car was gone. The phone rang and the display showed the skipper's home number. He ignored it. A few seconds later it rang again. He ignored it. When it rang a third time he saw Djuna Brown's mobile number displayed.

"Ray? We got them. Just like Harv said. There must be close to a half-million of them, all with double Chucks on them. Bags of the fuckers. Beautiful."

"You're okay, right?"

"Yeah. Yeah, this guy is okay, this pal of yours, old pal 'o mine. We're setting up up north of Widow's Corners. Gonna take the lab in the morning."

"Cool-ee-oh," he said. He told her about talk to his daughter, what he'd said about moving to Paris with a black dyke.

"What'd she say?"

"She said —"

There was a knock at the door.

"I got someone knocking. You okay? Stay close to that guy, okay? He's a good guy."

"Okay. I'll call you in the morning when we're

going. Tomorrow night, gin and taps on me. We can take French language courses, mon ami."

The knocking on the door was louder. A cop's knock. The skipper. He went to hang up. "Hey, Djuna? Wait a sec."

The knocking on the door became louder, more insistent.

"What, Ray?"

"I, ah …"

She laughed. "You're crazy about me, ain't you, Ray? I gotcha, Bongo." She was gone, whooping.

Ray Tate hung up the phone. It was close enough to telling her. He smiled as he cracked the door.

The first bullet took the lobe of his right ear off. He reeled sideways, ducking away.

The second missed him completely but he felt it buzz, hot.

The third went in low, above his belt buckle on the left-hand side, and then he was lying on the floor, crabbing for cover and scrabbling for the gun in his ankle holster and going in his mind: Fuck fuck fuck.

There were more shots fired that might or might not have missed him.

Then he felt a burning punch in his left shoulder and thought, Oh, cocksucker, cocksucker, you got me that time.

He had his gun out and began rolling to triangulate on the open door and the shape filling it.

The shape standing there was enveloped like a magician in a cloud of blue smoke. Yellow flame reached into the room, looking for him.

He heard screaming although he hadn't fired a shot.

He thought: Is that me?

Then he thought: I hope this isn't another black guy.

He said to himself, Fuck him if he is.

Then he unloaded his gun into the crowded doorway until he passed out with a mouth full of copper pennies.

Phil Harvey didn't wait for anyone to pick up the pills. He'd left them where he told the little black cop they'd be, behind the fourth tree on the north side of the county road running east, exactly 4.2 miles south of Widow's Corners. He'd done what he could. Hopefully the pills would take the heat off him and the crazy Captain and the rest of the crew. Harv didn't care, really, but he couldn't live calmly on his mountain with the thought of someone going behind the pipes for something he'd done.

He had a couple of things to do that night and then he'd be done with it all. The life would be gone and another one would begin. Harv knew he was a season and in change. Cured logs, he thought. Fresh raw logs would dry out and contract for months after he built his house then the window frames would have gaps around them. He'd read that, slowly tracing his finger across the page of a book. He'd have to buy weathered logs that wouldn't shrink.

Heading south to the city with his bag of lightnings in the back of a rental van, he debated with himself

about whether to get one of the new enamel-looking
wood stoves or shoot a wad on a fireplace and chimney.
A different life, where a gun was long and not cut down
to fit under a coat or in a bag. A life where a gun was a
tool not a weapon. The gases, he'd read in a book left
in the shelves of the farmhouse, the gases of sunset were
caused by pollutants irradiated by the setting sun. What
was that all about? He'd have to think on that one.

Passing the town where Frankie had lived he
thought of pulling off the highway and visiting the
girlfriend. Frankie died in the life, he'd tell her, and
maybe he'd invite her to a better life. He'd need
someone, he thought, to talk it out with, to reveal
his ideas and insights. He didn't want to become a
wandering muttering fool traipsing the hills and valleys, talking to himself. He could, he thought, try to
write them down but he'd been writing some letters
backwards all his life, back in the days when it was
called stupid instead of dyslexia. He wished he could
talk some more to the little black cop. She'd instantly
understood the roots of the tree and the tree itself.
He believed her when she said she had the tube of
vitamin E cream in her hand when he spoke to her
on the phone. Tommy, she'd said the boy's name was.
Her partner, Harvey thought, that was one bad old-
time copper. There was something between them,
he'd intuited immediately. The old-time copper was
going to Paris. Was that his mountains and valleys?
He reminded Harv of all the good-time old coppers
who'd battered him, thinking they could change a
soul. A bullet in the face, Harv thought, that would

put the copper in his place, show him in a sunrise flash of gunsmoke how things were.

He continued through. Frankie's town was gone after a trio of defaced off-ramp signs.

He swung into the city inside a blaze of roaring trucks and complex designs of tail lights that looked like little red galaxies ahead of him. City traffic was light. Harv made it into east Chinatown quickly. He had no backup and there was no point in bringing the buyer's thugs out into the city: they wouldn't let him walk away twice. He drove directly to the restaurant and parked illegally in front. There were young guys inside the place, visible though the wide front window with Chinese characters painted onto it. With the heavy bag of lightnings in one hand and his ribbed .44 inside a sweater in the other, Harv went inside and up to the doddering old fool sitting on a stool at the cash.

"Fifty thousand for one seventy-five."

The old fool looked at him. "You the crazy guy. Out with your dirty business." But he smiled and reached for a mobile phone under the counter.

Harv grinned tightly back at him and went through the restaurant, past blue-haired toughs sitting at a round table and sat at the back. He put the bag on the floor beside him and the sweater on the table, easing back the cloth to reveal the long ribbed barrel. He felt a little insane and asked a waiter for tea.

He'd come to like tea over the past month. Coffee wasn't something that fit into his life anymore, although Agatha Burns had begged for it, begged for anything that would give her a boost. He'd given her tea as she screamed and worked her way through the cellular adjustment she'd had to make to get out from behind the crazy Captain's imposed habit. At times she said he should have killed her. At times, in pity, he wished he had.

She'd said, Harv, I was beautiful once.

He'd said, Ag, you're beautiful now.

She'd said, What about Connie? Does Connie know you didn't off me?

He'd said, Don't worry about Connie.

She'd seemed obsessed when she said, What he made me do, that night in the hotel, I'm ashamed, Harv. I never …

He'd said, I'll be back to get you. I'll take you home to your parents, you'll be okay.

She'd said, Can I go with you, Harv?

Of course she couldn't go with him. He felt something for her. That's why the old broad at the camper truck had to be incinerated. Agatha and Connie Cook would be left behind like the old black leather bat coat he'd come to hate. He'd read that trees and flowers grew subtly in the direction of the heat and light of the sun. He'd find himself a new sun out in the mountains, a sun that would —

The old man behind the counter walked over to the table of blue-haired young guys and muttered. One of the blue-haired guys nodded, punched a key on his cellphone, and carried it over to Harv, handed it to him without comment and returned to his table.

"Mr. Harvey? Mr. Harvey?"

"I've got fifty thousand at one and three quarters."

"Sure. No problem. I'll send someone. But at one, for fifty."

"One fifty is a very good price. These egg rolls are like the others."

"We would pay more, say, even two for fifty, in return for a favour."

"What favour?"

"The big fat one, the one who burned the children? Who sent you to steal the drums? A favour for six fingers, you know who I mean?"

Six fingers, three on each hand, straight up: WW. Willy Wong. One of his faces was as the protector of Chinatown, shepherd of students from Canada, of Triad fugitives. Everyone would know that Willy Wong had been robbed, that the students had been tortured. Everyone would watch to see how strongly he reacted. Chinatown would require an extravagant public corpse.

"Six fingers would like to spend some Chinatown time with this fat man. If you arrange it, we will send two for fifty."

Harv watched the blue-haired guy watching him. A hundred thousand. With what he had set aside, he could live in mountain mists forever on that kind of dough. He could burn it in the fireplace or stove to keep warm when he was too tired to go out for kindling. He thought of Barry the gym owner and his crew, of their look of distaste in the basement in east Chinatown. He thought of Agatha Burns being made to lick his face, suck his fingers. And tonight's target for the sick prick, whoever she was, would just feed the cycle of the crazy Captain's escalating appetites. It would be easier to just let him die at the hands of Willy Wong. But Harv believed there was a way to stop his madness without putting the Captain in the ground or behind the pipes. He had to get away clean, at peace with himself, with no prisoners or bodies left behind.

"Done." He nodded into the phone and said, "Done. But cash, and tonight."

"Perfect, Mr. Harvey. Give the phone back to that fellow who gave it to you. He'll go and get your money then you take him to where this fat man is. After this, you shouldn't come anymore into Chinatown, okay?"

Harv put the phone on the table and pointed at it. The blue-haired guy got up and took it back to his table. He listened and gave Harv an A-OK sign. The guy beside him laughed. Harv, though, knew that in their world the A-OK finger sign meant You're worth nothing. Zero. The blue-haired guy made a smiling show of getting up and shrugging into his leather jacket. He drank off his teacup and with his car keys jangling in his hand, walked towards the kitchen exit, winking at Harv. Harv knew the blue hair was dust sprayed on. It was technique. If the guy had to do something and run, he could shake his head hard as he made his escape, shaking out the blue, looking like one of a thousand other young guys loitering on California Street.

When the blue-haired guy came close to the table Harv stood up and shot him through the middle of his face. The guy went straight down, a haze of blue dust and red mist rose like a rainbow in the air where his head had been.

For a moment everyone was frozen except Harv.

Inside that moment he wheeled like a dancer and shot another blue-haired Viet in the middle of his chest. He pegged a round at another guy but knew he'd missed even though the guy hit the floor yelling in pain.

Harv left the bag of pills and the sweater on the table and headed for the door, the gun dangling in his hand. People scattered, rocking the tables, dumping the chairs, and diving to the floor. The room was full of blue smoke and, he thought, the noise was impossibly loud and endless.

The old man at the cash stood up and said, his voice very faint to Harv's hollow ears, "Oh, you crazy guy," leaving his mouth open.

"When you see him, tell him I'm no rat." He fired into the open mouth and the wall behind the man became textured with bits of bone, a splash of blood, and grey matter.

He was early to do the pickup for the crazy, lovestruck Captain. There were several SUVs in front of the house and some sleek sedans parked on the curb. He backed the van up to the Lexus with the personalized plate, the rear doors a few feet from the sedan's trunk. On a quick walk-past he looked through trees and Connie Cook's stone gates, saw the large, bright picture windows, the shapes of people moving around with drinks in their hands. He wanted to creep close, to hear what they were saying. What did rich people talk about?

What was so fucking interesting? A book club, Cookie had said, where people talked about reading. What the fuck was that all about? Harv had read a lot of books in the joint, read them slowly, knowing his lips were moving but keeping his hand over his mouth so no one would see. But he'd never had the urge to discuss a book with anyone.

Back when he'd snaffled up Agatha Burns for the crazy fat fuck he'd wandered the curving streets and cul-de-sacs, figuring out the best place to grab her, the best route out onto a busy street that would lead to the Interstate that led north. The Captain hadn't told Harv then about the purpose of the kidnapping. No worries, Harv, I'll have the parents over to dinner. Get the girl. Take her north. Wait for me. Harv had thought maybe it was a kidnapping for ransom and by the time the Captain had started turning Agatha into what he wanted her to be, it was too late. Harv had done shit but he'd never wished he hadn't done any of it, never wanted to roll back the clock as if anyone could. But with the Agatha Burns snaffling, he found himself trying to unwind his life.

For this, tonight, there was no excuse. There was no end in it, no payoff. The road of the day to this place in the night had been full of sudden twists and turns. Leaving a bag of double Chucks for the cops to pick up, committing a minor massacre in Chinatown. All to protect the Captain, all to allow himself to find a piece of quiet in a mountain he could only imagine, to sit on his mountain and know that no one was losing a chunk of their life because of him.

The door of Captain Cook's house opened. Women stood in the doorway. They sounded drunk. Kisses all around.

Harv thought about shooting all of them.

Harv thought about not doing the grab. Just walking away and going up north, bringing Agatha back to the city then making his way west. But the Captain had a hard jones: someone else would be recruited, more Agathas would be made to vanish and deteriorate. The Captain would continue his crazy spiral until he went too far, made too many mistakes. Tonight's gift for the crazy fucker had to be one that would make him stop.

Phil Harvey eased back into some bushes between the front of his van and the gates to the Captain's house.

He thought of Barry and his crew and their looks. He thought of Barry and the boys having their eye out for the Captain, doing a public service by whacking him.

Cars started and crept away.

Harv thought of the three Chinamen he'd just shot. Of blue dust and blood in the air.

Two women, drunkenly arm in arm, came along the sidewalk. The other cars were gone.

One woman said, "— up north at some gold mine that needs his money."

The other woman laughed. "He'd just waste it on food. Connie's getting a little … portly?"

Harvey leaned back quietly, letting the women go by. He smelled booze and perfume. The women stopped and chatted.

"Don't worry about Connie," one woman said. "He's a pussycat."

"Well, he'd better be," the other woman said. "He's a really, really, really big pussycat."

They laughed. They parted with air kisses and promises to call. One woman passed closely by him, the other dug for her keys in her purse, tilting it to the streetlight.

In his black leather bat coat Harv felt like a creature of the night, a piece of the night, swooping.

Connie Cook waited in angst by his cellphone. He pulled his Mercedes into a takeout Mickey Dee's near the Interstate and ordered three family specials. The drone in the window stared at him and shrugged and spoke the order into his headset.

Connie Cook checked the clock on the Benz. If Harv had made his move when the book club broke up, he should be on the way, if he'd grabbed up the treat. The phone should be ringing and the crazy Captain should be on the road, blistering his way north, to love. But the phone didn't ring. He took his orders of burgers and fries and drove around the food outlet to the front parking lot. He checked that the cell was charged and operating and began working on the food. In front of the joint a young couple, the girl looking like his lost Agatha and the boy looking like some needy jerk, felt each other and laughed. If Harv didn't call, Cornelius Cook thought, maybe he could entice the girl into the car, do his own shopping, show Harv how it was done. A snack, to get his juices flowing.

When the phone buzzed he grabbed it up. It was past midnight.

"Harv, Harv?"

"Jesus, Cookie. This one's a fighter. I got her okay, she's in the bag, but I'm running way late. I think one of the other broads saw it go down. I got to dump this van and get something else."

"But you got her, right? You closed the deal?"

"Oh, yeah. I had to give her a couple of shots, but she's in the back." Harv yelled, Shut the fuck up. "This one, fuck Connie, you got taste. This one is class."

"Yep. I got the eye, Harv." The Captain reached under his stomach into his growing crotch. "So, what now? When can I begin the honeymoon?" He was exuberant. "Fuck, Harv, I fucking love you. You did it. Jesus."

"Well, the way it's going, I'm figuring with changing vehicles and getting back on the road, I won't get up there much before dawn. You want to get up there any time around then. If I get there first, I'll have it ready for you."

"Yeah yeah yeah yeah. I'm on the way. If I get there first, I'll get things ready. You did it? Fuck, Harv. You fucking did it."

"But this one has to last you, Cookie. I can't do this every couple of months. The other broad saw what was going down, I think, so I'm gonna be hot."

"No problem. We'll get this thing straightened out. You cook while I introduce my new pal to the new reality of romance. We'll move the … groceries, right? The groceries, collect the money and you … Well, a bonus, you keep it all from this cooking. Wherever you want to go, you go. You go on me. A vacation." He realized he was babbling and simply said, "Fuck, Harv. I'm on my way."

Harv was just a few kilometres from the super lab, keeping the van in the single lane at a steady sixty miles an hour, a good nighttime driving speed, wary of big horned mammals that might jump into the roadway. His gaming with the fat fuck would give him a night of freedom to cook and package. To plan and scheme.

This was the dangerous part: if you got hooked, how do you explain a sleeping bag in the back seat with a duct-taped woman in it? It was just past midnight and he could cook up a harvest of pills before the fat fucker arrived in the dawn to claim his prize. Harv planned to leave the Captain and his new true love abandoned at the lab after he disabled one of the cars, the Mercedes or the van, and tried for a quick deal with someone, maybe the Greeks that came down from Canada every week, or the Italians at Stateline. If the pills didn't move right away he'd just dump them someplace for Barry and his crew to pick up, and head for the bumpy mountains of the unimaginable west.

At the turn into the driveway he didn't see the cammie clad figure with night scope huddled down off the side of the road, his face smeared with goop to absorb the light of the moon.

But Harv did see the moon. It rode in the sky as placid as he hoped to become.

He decided to learn more about the moon, about the doings of the lunar.

Ray Tate knew he'd done something right. The form in the doorway stopped screaming and stopped shooting him, which is all he wanted. He saw a vague lump slouched against the other side of the hall, legs splayed, the soles of hiking boots facing him at opposite forty-five degree angles, blood running away from the body. The face was mostly gone. He couldn't tell who it was.

He said to himself, Good shooting, Ray, you still got your chops. But he knew it had been luck: he'd just aimed his gun into the doorway and unleashed some free-form jazz; no aiming, no breath control, no real melody in there. He laughed on his floor and leaked, staring up at the ceiling, amazed he never realized how ugly it was.

The super, old Mr. Lilly, crept in his slippers to the edge of the doorway and peeked around the jam. He said, Holy fuck, and crossed himself.

As he started to become very cold, for a scant moment Ray Tate saw Devon Brown and Mkumbi Masa beckoning him like old pals, their lips moving incessantly.

He saw a freckled uniformed copper wearing men's underwear and sagging socks, arising, yawning, from his futon, her blond hair a-tangle, opening her mouth to speak and speak and speak at him.

He saw his daughter whispering at him from behind her camera: "Keep very still, dad."

And Djuna Brown singing and a chorus of old, crusty duty sergeants telling endless war stories and wry jokes. He heard the island voice telling him she had no mix. He smelled cinnamon and felt very cold. All the voices, the duty sergeants and the women and dead men, grew in volume until it was a loud racket in his ears and dying became a reasonable warm alternative.

Chapter 30

Two hours before dawn the Statie sniper tapped softly on the door of the nightroom and sang, "Wakey wakey. Briefings and worms for the early birds."

Djuna Brown opened the door immediately. She wore a pair of fatigue pants rolled up at the cuffs, a sweatshirt that came down almost to her knees, and had bare feet. "I'm up, I'm up." Her hair was brushed and still wet. The cot behind her had been made up, complete with hospital corners, the way she'd found it when they assigned her the room. She looked at the false smile on his face. "What?"

He lied and she knew it. "Nothing. Pre-op stress. Sixteen or seventeen more cups of coffee and I'll be riding up there sitting on top of the helicopter. You don't get airsick, do you, dearie? Our pilot was out drinking last night and he's in a foul mood."

She gave him a smile but she knew he was talking

too much, wasn't telling her everything. She wondered if the skipper had somehow tracked her down, had put the kibosh on the morning operation. Maybe, she thought, it was some huge Statie joke: the briefing room would be full of Irish fuckheads and knuckle draggers from Widow's Corners, waiting to maul her. It would be a legendary and complicated scam that would be told for years to come, how the dyke was sucked into thinking she was doing cop work but when she got there found herself being hooted at by old pals.

The Statie waited while she got her things together, then led her down the long quiet hallway to a flight of metal stairs and they rattled down. "We clocked a van going in after midnight. The guy on the night scope said it looked like a guy with very long hair. Couldn't tell if he was alone or not. Could be a dozen bandits in the back, armed to the teeth."

She felt a little sad. She'd hoped Phil Harvey had done whatever he had to do and gone away to get his skin *graffs*. "We have to talk about that guy, if he's in play."

He nodded. "Do it once, at the briefing, okay? I don't want our guys going in there if there's something they should know, and don't." He opened a door and led her to a silent cafeteria. A man in tactical garb was loading a coffee filter into a drip machine. His camouflage pants were puttied into his black boots and he wore a T-shirt. He nodded at them sleepily. They grabbed coffees. The Statie sniper said there were buns and other good stuff in the briefing room. He asked how she slept. He asked her if she'd ever gone tactical before.

She made appropriate responses and wondered what was going on off-stage, what she didn't know about, what he wasn't telling her. She said: "You heard from Ray? What's he up to?"

"Ah," he said, pushing open a pneumatic door and ushering her through. "I tried to give him a call a while ago but his phone went to message. You guys are, hmmm, doing stuff?" He walked faster, not waiting for her to respond. He nattered. "That reminds me. I'm gonna have to take your cellphone off you. We're operational, okay? Loose lips sink ships."

"Lemmee give him a quick call." She took the cell from her jacket.

He took it from her hand. "You can call after."

The briefing room had a weird fluorescent hyper-reality: everything was sharp edged and detailed. After the silence of the corridors the lights made an almost invisible hum. Outside the row of windows the world was deeply black with the ending of night. There were two dozen people in clusters in the room, all but one a male, none of them sitting in the arc of chairs in front of a chalkboard. The lone woman was tall and energetic and dressed for office work in a tweedy two-piece suit, medium heels, and nylons.

Everyone turned to look at Djuna Brown carefully as the Statie sniper led her in. From the corner of her eye she thought she saw her sniper shake his head briefly. The men in the room looked away. Some nodded. The woman continued staring at her, then waved her over and led the way to the chalkboard. Her heels clacked briskly on the tile floor. Passing between the men, most in various stages of camouflage, all of them big and buff, all of them suddenly silent, Djuna Brown felt tiny and was glad she hadn't worn her lucky slippers. As she passed through, a couple of the men gently touched her shoulder and she became afraid. Standing beside the woman she felt grimy and urchin-like.

"Okay, grab seats," the woman said, picking up a piece of yellow chalk and bouncing it on her palm. She looked, Djuna Brown thought, like a strict schoolteacher settling down unruly students. "This is Djuna Brown, she's one of us. She's been detached to a task force, chemicals, in the city." The woman smiled easily. "But she's come home now. Back to pleasure her own kind."

The men laughed. Djuna Brown thought she was going to instruct them to welcome her to a new school. She noticed some of the men still looked at her sadly. Her Statie sniper stood behind the last row of seats, his arms folded, his mouth grim.

"Okay, kids, here's the deal," the woman said. "This morning we're taking down a drug lab up near Passive. We don't have a lot of intell. We've got people up there, off the property, keeping an eye. A vehicle went in there early this morning, one person aboard, either a woman or a man with long hair. It was a van so we don't know who might have been in the back. So: we assume the place is populated with heavily armed nogoodniks. There's a main house and several outbuildings scattered around, if one of the local detachment guys is to believed. There's been a bush rat working in there. He's been seen with a varmint gun. The road in is about a half mile long. Again, according to the local guy. In an hour we're choppering in. The chopper'll drop us on a concession road about four miles east of the target property entrance. We don't want to wake anybody up in there, nice to catch 'em napping. The local guys'll RV with us there and drive us to the site. We walk in." She looked at the window. "Nice morning for a hike."

"Us?" one of the guys said. "You coming in, inspector?"

Another laughed. "Yeah, it's about those shoes. Manolos?"

"Ferragamos." She smiled gently. "Now, about the guys running this. What should we know?" She stepped back. "Djuna?"

Djuna Brown didn't feel so little. She sipped her coffee. She felt like she was in a room full of Ray Tates, of cops. "The guy with the long hair, going in, is, I think, a city thug named Phil Harvey. He's got a sheet longer than his hair. He's done a lot of time. We got a witness in the city says he goes armed. Intell says he's put at least two people down. Then there's the bush rat. An old snaggle-toothed guy we're told has a gun of some kind, something, roaming the place. The other guy that's come up is this great fat fellow we haven't seen yet, but we're told he's the guy behind the lab. He's psycho: he used a branding iron on some ecstasy cookers down in the city. There's a blond guy that's been around. Biker wannabe. He might be in there. Who else? Don't know. Vehicles? Harvey's been seen driving rentals, he's got a black Camaro under him but we haven't seen it in a while. The blond guy drives a buff black F-250 pickup, double cab. The old guy had a busted-back old grey pickup, he might still have it. Phil Harvey was driving it in the back roads, last time I saw him."

A radio squawked and the inspector stepped away from the group to respond. She listened, the unit held quiet and close to her ear, and said, Ten-four, and came back.

Djuna Brown continued: "By background: there was a chemical task force set up with the city and the Feds and us. Everybody sent down their best ace investigators." She waited for the laugh and when it came she smiled prettily. "We were getting whipped by these guys turning out pills with double C markings. Some kids died on them. There was torture and mayhem. We tracked the lab to up here and here we are."

One man said, "And the city guys? And the Feds? What time to do they arrive?"

Djuna Brown shrugged her shoulders and glanced at the windows. "I think they're gonna miss it. They'll be pretty pissed off. Mad as Chinamen with no thumbs."

They all laughed but nobody asked.

"We doing a warrant?" a tactical guy asked. "We all have to read the warrant before we go in. Have we got a warrant?"

"Let me just," the inspector said to Djuna Brown, stepping up. "The wind's changed up there. One of the scouts said there's a strong smell of chemicals coming from the west. I'll call a prosecutor, but I think he's going to say there's a public hazard, we have to act."

A tac guy said, "Terrorism, maybe?"

"Yeah, good thinking," the inspector said. "Maybe Osama bin Cookin'.'"

They all laughed. A little too hard, Djuna Brown thought, noting their careful looks at her.

Djuna Brown wore a set of cammies and a woollen watch cap. The inspector wore a dashing looking trench coat belted over her suit and a blue silk scarf tucked in around her throat. They were in the middle of a convoy of three four-bys, racing from headquarters to a nearby airfield. Djuna Brown thought the inspector smelled gorgeous and glamorous. She was lightly perfumed, her hair was scented with shampoo, and dry cleaning chemicals were noticeable on her clothing. She held a rover on her lap. A dash radio muttered. The driver leaned to adjust it. The inspector made small talk. "So, how was it, down in the city? On the task force?"

"It was okay." She felt guarded for no reason she could imagine. If this was a Spout trick, it was elaborate. But, she thought, something else seemed to be going on.

When she didn't say more, the inspector laughed softly. "But you missed us up here, right? Widow's Corners. Those fuckers." She turned her head and looked at Djuna Brown. "I know all that. Everybody knows all that. But the guys up there, they weren't assigned up there because of their charm and tact. Those guys in the briefing room? My guys. If I was up there and what happened to you happened to me, they'd jump in their jackboots into the place and lay fucking waste." She turned on an interior sidelight and picked up Djuna Brown's hand, tilting her nails to the light. "This is nice. You get these done down there?"

Djuna Brown let her hold her fingers a moment. She had the impression the inspector wanted to talk about anything except something. "Yeah. In the city." She eased her fingers free. "My guy took me for a treat. He's a city guy, my guy."

The inspector laughed very loudly and called to the driver. "Mack? Hey Mack, she thinks I'm gay, hitting on her. Am I gay, Mack?"

The driver laughed. "No question, inspector. Queer as Harry's hatband. You've served more tongue than a deli sandwich maker. Your husband told me, the night you dropped the fourth frog."

"Four kids," the inspector said to Djuna Brown. "Four kids, I fucked one guy in fifteen years and I still got this fucking job."

Mack said, "Heads up, inspector," and reached to turn up the dash radio. A voice said a vehicle had just turned into the driveway. One white male on board. A Mercedes, dark blue or black.

The helicopter contained Djuna Brown and six members of a tactical team. The pilot came in low from the east and aimed at a dim crossroads lit by cones of headlights where three marked SUVs were parked on the shoulder. As the helicopter drifted to a stop in the air and slowly kissed down onto the road, Djuna Brown saw familiar faces from her old barracks. In the breaking dawn they looked like refugees with upturned desperate faces, waiting for rescue.

The pilot waited until the prop stopped twirling. Djuna Brown's Statie sniper said, "Okay, we're tactical the minute your boots hit the ground. We're the boys with the toys and you stay by me." He pulled a vest from the floor near his feet and held it out to her.

She shook her head. "I'll be okay. I'll stay behind you."

He said, "You don't dress up, you don't go to the ball."

He helped her fit herself into its intimate heaviness. "You got some room in there for me, I think. If the shit hits the fan, just pull your head in, pull your arms and legs in, and lay on the ground. The defensive turtle position. Unflattering, but effective. We'll come get you later, find you a good home."

The pilot had a handlebar moustache. He waited until the team was off-boarded and called to her, "Hey? You free later? We can get some beers, take 'er up, snap off the lights, goof on the citizenry."

"Love to," she said, "but I got to get down to the city, hook up with a partner o'mine. He's a city guy, but he's okay."

He gave her a teasing smile. Then he frowned. "Oh, fuck. I'm sorry, man. How is he?"

She thought he was playing with her. She stumbled. "How he who?"

"Your partner. The city guy, Tate, right? I heard it on the radio."

She shook her head as her foot hit the ground. "What?"

He said something she couldn't hear over the backwash of the rotors.

Her Statie had her by the back of the vest. "C'mon, let's go."

"What happened to Ray?" It made sense: the quiet looks, the sympathetic turning away, barring her from using her cell to call out, the constant babble and chitchat. "What's he talking about?"

"Look, we don't know. A shooting, anyway, down in the city. He was hit, we don't know how bad. They got him to hospital."

"Who shot him?"

He shook his head. "We don't know. He put down the shooter, we know that: no suspects outstanding." He saw her eyes were huge. "Maybe, you should hang back? We can get the chopper to take you down to headquarters, get you down to the city."

She looked into his sympathetic eyes. "No. I'm going with you guys."

The team leader called out and she walked across the road like she was on stilts. The team leader waved the local detachment guys over. They came up the road a ways, then looked at Djuna Brown and unsubtly turned their backs, muttering. The team leader saw their curled lips and looked at Djuna Brown and raised his eyebrows.

She shrugged. "I used to work up here." She looked around for the Statie sniper. He was off to the side on his cellphone. He looked at her and shrugged and shook his head.

The team leader asked, "You have some chick stuff going with them? I don't need any surprises up there, friendly fire problems."

"If there's gonna be a surprise," she said, "it won't be for you."

He stared at her a moment, weighing, then he walked over to the guys from the Spout and assigned them to guard the trucks and the trees. With a circular hand signal he called his team over. "We're going in on foot, but they don't get to play. They're dudes with 'tudes. Djuna's going to come up behind." He nodded to her sniper. "Mark, you hang back with her."

He laid out a point man and the team started in, well-spaced, in their tin hats.

Chapter 31

Connie Cook wasn't stupid enough to think he was normal. In the middle of his debaucheries he sometimes focused briefly on something, a strand of hair, a rivulet of blood, a sound of despair, and went to himself, Fuck, what am I doing? But the sheer pleasure of abandon and revenge welled up and overcame and he felt a rising in his chest that felt like he imagined love to feel. There were moments in there when he felt his power was the only power that could stop the fear and pain. His mind usually effectively blocked the knowledge that he was the one orchestrating it. The knowledge of some inner goodness was enhanced when he thought of his fondness for Agatha Burns. The strippers, he knew, were disposable people before he ever met them. He was merely a step in the path of their lives, a force of nature. And a final step and a crucial step in the stages of his own metamorphosis. But

Agatha. He couldn't dispose of her himself, it would demean and negate all the love he'd felt for her over the months they'd spent together. My love has grown, he thought. I have grown. Letting Harv end his relationship with Ag had been necessary. But now it was time to move on, don't dwell.

This, he thought, this'll be the last one. My life of crime is over. Harv can take over everything, we can just get together once in a while, talk about old times, about my buddy the gym owner and his crew, about the fun in the Chinese basement. We'll have a history based on the mutual understanding of colleagues, unlike those Chicago Mercantile sharpies, those donation hustlers who peck at my body like wild birds. Me and Harv can talk in a language no one understands. A subtext that'll make us grin while everyone else goes, What?

Connie Cook slowed to watch for the turnoff into the farm. He didn't see the cammie guy in the bushes aim his night scope at him. It was clear in the sky with some thick, barely visible clouds that billowed and crisped up with the light of dawn before it made itself known to the earthbound. There was a fortuitous moon riding in them. He thought of an old poem they'd learned at school. "The moon was a ghostly galleon, tossed upon cloudy seas …"

After this one, after Gabby, I'll settle it all down a bit. Love will be what comes to me, not what I pursue, capture. I'll get my good nature back. I must have had one, once, I know I did. Cora loved me and loves me in spite of this globe of flesh I carry around. When I crush an opponent I'll do it with wit and humour. Hatred will become my enemy. But it'll be hard. My father was hated and feared. He thought he was respected, but his oppression and ruthlessness made the Cook name a notorious legend. You've been Cooked, jocular people told a crushed victim and now you'll get Eaton, the name of one of old Cook's business cronies. I'll get it all out, leak out all the poison from this huge body, then I'll become a smiling fool, a donating dunce, a benevolent Buddha. I'll be who I am, what I was meant to be.

He rounded the curve to the farmhouse. The window was a yellow square. He crept the Mercedes into the clearing close to the steps.

A figure moved by the window.

Harvey came out of the barn. He waved and called, Cookie, welcome.

The air smelled of phosphorous and chemicals.

Connie Cook happily hailed, "Harv, hey, Harv."

He realized if Harv was coming out of the barn, then who was walking past the window in the main house? He climbed from the Benz. "What the fuck, Harv? Who's that up there? In the window? You put her loose? Fuck, man, I wanted to unwrap her, see the look on her face."

Agatha Burns heard the Mercedes purr outside. She heard voices, Harv welcoming in his bass voice, the Captain querulous. She looked at the sleeping bag struggling in the corner of the main room.

The woman called out.

Agatha said it would be all right, just relax.

The woman said she was suffocating, bleeding.

Agatha said, Control your breathing.

The woman said, Who are you?

Agatha said, I was beautiful, once.

The Agatha Burns waiting for her future to begin over was glowing. Her hair was shampooed and blond again, and parted on the side, neatly, as it had been when she was kicking up her legs and cheering the team to victory. Her teeth remained greyish but that, she knew, could be fixed, if she wanted to. She had muscle tone. Harv had chained her to the stove for the first month, giving her enough freedom to work out. In the evenings they'd had tea together, pored through the shelves of books about camping and house building and irrigating. At first she'd loved Harv for not killing her then she came to love him for his questions, his observations, his excited alerts of bears outside the window. For the shyly covered lips that moved when he read. His scars disappeared from her vision. She saw him as he'd been as a beaten boy with broken teeth. His hands, neither the scarred messy one nor the other less damaged one, hadn't touched her except to hold her hair back while she vomited. But she saw in his eyes his own rehabilitation, his determination to undo what had been done to her.

"We'll get you straight, Ag," he'd said, that first dawn as her body began a molecular revolt, leaching of the crank, her cells wondering what happened to that good stuff that entered her blood through her veins, off her tongue, up her ass. She heard them demanding:

Where's that good stuff? We're gonna get noisy, we don't get it. And for weeks they went crazy under her skin, acrobatic in her brain, fogging her eyes, and forcing her teeth to gnaw at the inside of her mouth.

Harv made endless tea. She screamed. Harv brought cellophane-wrapped cakes full of cloying cream. She moaned and rolled on the board floors of the farmhouse. Harv talked and she puked. Evenings Harv rocked in an old creaky chair and told stories of the brutality of his life. She froze and sweated and squeezed her balled fists between her thighs, under her armpits. No self-pity for old Harv. He laughed with no regrets of the boisterous life in the streets and cages.

When Harv was gone on his trips to the city to, as he put it, wrap up his old life, she was free to roam the length of the chain handcuffed to her ankle. Sometimes when she was loud she heard an old voice singing outside the door, Kick it, you kick it good, girl. Cackles, laughter. She tried to entice the old fool in but he never touched the doorknob. She ate at the food Harv left within reach: cakes and bags of prepared salads and cellophane bags of apples and mixtures of nuts and raisins and dried fruits. She drank water from the sink, became accustomed to the raw lake taste of it. A porcelain bowl was left for her use, rough toilet paper and napkins from roadside diners. She made tea from little bags, she walked and walked her convict circle, and one day she awoke clean. It was like a sudden impossible sunrise, a daybreak.

One night after the frustrated rebellious cells had fled the streams and ponds of her body, her long-absent period returned with a vengeance. She surprised herself when she was too embarrassed to ask Harv to bring up tampons the next time he went to the city. Instead she wrapped used tea bags in wads of toilet paper. This, rather than the absence of chemical and addiction in her body, told her she'd kicked. She'd found her character and identity and experienced shame.

One night, conversationally, she asked Harv, "How'd you let that happen to me? With Connie. The crank?"

And he said, "I forgot. I forgot who I was."

In front of the house, Harv calmed the crazy Captain. "Relax, Cookie. C'mon in." When the fat fucker began hyperventilating and looking for an exit route, Harv took a silver revolver from behind his back. Ambient light from the sky and the window winkled in the flutes of the long barrel. "Inside, Cookie. C'mon."

"Who is it? Who's in there? What are you doing, Harv? You setting me up? Cops? Chinamen?"

Harv was disappointed. "Cookie, if you knew what I done the last couple of days for you, you wouldn't talk this shit. I'd never give you up to cops or Chinamen, you fucking know that." Harv shook his head. "Fuck, Cookie, fuck." He indicated the Captain should go up the steps. "No pal of mine dies or does time because of me."

"What's going to happen, Harv? Tell me."

"I'm leaving. You're staying with your sweetie, here. I'll send someone up to get you once I get clear."

"We made a lot of money, Harv. A lot of fucking money. And now what?" He glanced at the barn. "You're ripping me?"

"I thought it was about the money, Cookie, at first. But it wasn't." He wanted to put his hand on the Captain's shoulder, to commiserate, to explain. "You're weird, Connie. Fuck, man, I'm weird. But you hurt people when you don't have to. You've got no restraint. You've got all the money in the world, and you ... Well, you act like an asshole."

Connie Cook dreaded going up the steps. "What's in there, Harv?" He stared at Harv and Harv thought he looked like a big, disappointed baby. "My guys, my security guys'll find you, Harv. They'll get you."

"Go on in, Connie. You get a last treat, you do what you want with her, but you better have your shit straight when the guy I send up here to get you gets here."

"You're gonna kill me. I know it, Harv. Harv?" He stared at the house.

"I could've done you by now, I was going to. Right, Cookie? I could've done you in the city, anytime."

"Do it, Harv. If you're going to fucking do it, fucking do it. I'm not going in there." He turned and tried to shuffle away. "It's the Chinamen."

Harv took him by the collar of his jacket. "No, Cookie. Never. I fucking love you, man." He pulled him towards the steps. At the top the door opened.

Connie Cook saw a backlit figure he couldn't make out but he heard Agatha Burns's voice, strong and friendly, "Connie, welcome."

* * *

The gun team moved quickly but slowed as the smell of chemicals and wood smoke became sharper. There were dark shadows off to the side of the track. Inside them, Djuna Brown stretched her hand out and put it lightly on the utility belt of her Statie sniper. She kept pace, keeping her eye on his right hand. When it went up from the elbow, she stopped. When the fingers snapped forward, she moved.

The air was grey light when they reached the clearing. The team leader muttered into his mouthpiece. Two of the team members slipped away, one to the left and one to the right. The team leader tilted his head, listening to his headset.

"There's several buildings, there's lights in a farmhouse. There's people moving past the windows. The Mercedes and the van are parked to the left-hand side, empty."

Djuna Brown watched a shadow imperceptibly ease up the side of the house, stopping under a window. Another shadow went the other way, around back and out of her view.

The team leader listened and repeated in a whisper: "Long-haired male inside with a gun to the left of the entrance ... He's got a fucked-up face ... Silver revolver ... Fat male standing over a sleeping bag, far wall ... Female standing by the stove to the right of the fat guy ..." He stopped repeating what he was hearing, then picked his litany again. "Ten-four ... Barn clear

... Shack down the road, clear ..." He spoke, "Four and five, secure the vehicles ... Two, get some high ground and set up on that window..."

Djuna Brown took her nifty little pistol from the clamshell holster.

Her Statie sniper put his hand on her shoulder. "No, dearie. When we go to work we're the only fools with tools." He watched her holster it.

She thought about Ray Tate. The only case he was involved in was this one. It could have been Harv for some twisted reason. It could have been Captain Cook, whoever he was. It could have been any number of speeders or cookers in that milieu. Chinamen, bikers. A lot of people could know they were close to breaking things up.

Agatha Burns didn't think the crazy Captain looked like much anymore. Just the sad, fat, old pervert who'd watched the cheerleader routines from his window, doing who knows what with himself. She'd thought throughout her kicking, chained to the stove, of torturous things to do to him. Give him a habit, the fat bastard, she thought. Stick things way up his ass, drink his blood, chew his copious flesh, watch him die by the mouthful.

Harv had asked if she wanted him offed. She surprised them both and shook her head. He'd looked relieved as though she'd confirmed some deep belief he harboured.

But watching Connie Cook standing over the moving sleeping bag she feared for the woman inside. She looked at Harv. He was smiling. She decided that, no matter what, even if she had to find a way to kill both Connie and Harv, there was no way she was leaving the woman behind.

"Who is it? What's happening? Is the lady there?" The woman's voice was muffled and high-pitched. "Hey, hello? Miss?"

"That's her, Cookie, your new sweetie," Harv said. "Knock yourself out."

"Don't do this, Harv, c'mon, man." But the crazy fat fuck couldn't keep his eyes off the struggling sleeping bag. "Let's all just walk away. You need dough?"

"How could you do that to me, Connie?" Agatha Burns said.

"Open 'er up, Cookie."

"I don't want it, I don't want it. Let's just get out of here." But his eyes were glued to the rippling sleeping bag. "C'mon, Harv. Man."

Agatha Burns said, "I never did anything to you. I was just … there."

"No, Cookie." Harv raised the gun and pointed it at the shivering Captain. "There's guys who want to put you down like a fucking dog, Connie. There's Chinamen who've got a kitchen set up just for you, stew you in a pot. There's cops who want you in a cage. I told them all: no. I don't rat. I don't give up my partners for the bucket or the ground."

* * *

Djuna Brown didn't have to touch her Statie sniper to orient herself. The dawn grey had cleared and she could see him and the team members ahead of her. The smell of wood smoke made her think of her early morning patrols in the Spout.

Quietly she slipped her little automatic out of her holster and kept it in her pocket, just like Ray Tate had.

She heard the team leader repeat, "... Guy with the face has his piece on the fat guy ... Partial view ... No clear view ... Tommy, when you get the shot ..."

Connie Cook looked into the deep black hole in the fluted silver barrel.

He bent awkwardly and pulled hesitantly at the zipper on the sleeping bag.

His fat fingers trembled with fear or excitement.

This would be his last packing for love. After this he'd have to deprive himself and dispose of her before the minion Harv sent up arrived. If Harv really did send someone. He'd have to let go of his pursuit of love. Sculpture, maybe, he could take up sculpture and daydream while he did it. Turn something into something else, a chisel and a hammer and whatever implements lent themselves to honest talent that must lurk inside his fat hands.

Phil Harvey wanted to go to his secret mountain. He'd decided on a wood stove, made of cast iron, identical to the one in the room. The wood smoke was fragrant. The stove, with the iron door shut, contained the heat and there'd be no fear of flash fires. Logs crackled. He said, "Ag? I decided. Cast iron stove. That's it." He became impatient and stepped into the Captain to poke him with the gun. "Open her up, Cookie."

First the blond hair then the eyes. Connie Cook inhaled mightily and pulled the zipper the rest of the way.

His wife looked at him and said: "Connie?"

Connie Cook turned away, losing his balance and falling.

Harv aimed the gun down at his face.

The team leader listened and said, "Okay, green light, Tommy ... You're green ..."

Djuna Brown heard a single cracking shot. Then a scream from inside the house.

A second later the team leader said, "Ten-four ... He's down ... The fat guy's moving ... The girl's moving ...Ten-four ... Where's the gun? ... Bob tee up, you're the second man ... Everybody, have eyes for the gun ..."

Agatha Burns saw it all backwards. First Harv was on the floor. Then he fell. Then there was a fist-sized piece of skull, the cap, sliding slowly down the wall and a mess behind Harv's shredded head. Then the window cracked with a ping and then there was a sound outside of a gunshot.

Harv fell straight down. It was magic, as if some conjurer had spirited the bones right up out of his body.

Agatha Burns crouched over Harv, looking for his head with her fingers, as if she was blind or in a dark room and it was a prize.

Connie Cook had no idea what had happened. For some reason he thought of internal combustion — death gathered perhaps from within. That Harv's wicked life had exploded at the top of his spine and had just had enough.

He felt incredibly sad. He'd lost a pal, lost his best friend who, Connie Cook knew, only had his best interests at heart.

"Harv. Oh, Harv." The gun was on the floor, there, free, and he picked it up, unknowingly saving himself by moving out of the sniper's view.

Agatha Burns moved on her knees away from the destroyed Harv. She said, "Harv?"

Cora said, "Connie?"

Captain Cook said, "Cora." He brought the gun to bear on the sleeping bag. Then on Agatha, then his own head, then back at Cora.

Agatha Burns moved to block his view of Cora, one hand reaching behind her onto her face. "No, Connie."

Connie Cook believed death had come from within the room. He had to get outside. His body lumbered to its feet but inside he felt he was moving as if he were two hundred pounds lighter, twenty years younger.

It was over. He felt exposed and naked. All things were haunting. Dead strippers he'd left with shovels of dirt on their mouths, on their glassy eyes. Agatha's screams as she disappeared under the power of Connie and his purple oak dick. The breasts of the Chinese girl in the basement. This death of his best friend, Harv. But also of the waitress with the hot red sauce and the smart mouth, of Harv's face when he gave him the vitamin E cream, of them eating hamburgers and Connie snatching Harv's fries. His sense of loss was overpowering. How, in such love I have, have I such hatred?

Death had come somehow from within the room, from within Harv. He had to get out. At the door he clutched the knob and turned a moment, entertaining the thought of just killing everyone in the room and himself. If there was no one with a memory of him, none of it had happened.

His wife looked at him around Agatha. She'd seen him fat and naked in their home, at the cottage, at the lake. He'd always looked for the twist of disgust but had never found it no matter how hard he looked and that, he knew, meant she hid it well or he just wasn't observant. Who could look at this globus thing and not twist their lips, avert their eyes? He was shamed and finally knew that she'd loved him as he could never love himself.

On the porch he suddenly understood the meaning of the crack and penetration of the window, of Harv's head just going away in a puff of sudden pink, of the crockery clatter of fractured skull bone, of that faint booming that followed.

Looking towards the roadway he saw a tall, athletic man wearing camouflage clothing and a tin pot hat rise from a crouch and start moving towards him with a machine gun up to his shoulder.

The man yelled, "Police." Then he fell down.

Behind the man was a smudged black face under a watch cap, an impossibly tiny woman, standing straight up. He heard her call, "Hey, asshole."

Djuna Brown heard her Statie sniper say, What the fuck? as she shouldered herself into him. He sprawled. She moved around him to get clear in case he tried to grab her legs. She felt herself smiling and thought she might have murmured: That fucker's gonna wear his ass for a hat.

The team leader shouted: "He's out he's out. Police. Don'tfuckingmove, asshole."

Captain Cook was facing Djuna Brown from thirty feet. He seemed to forget the gun in his hand. Seemingly of its own volition it aimed where his head and body focused.

Djuna Brown took two giant steps, the boots on her feet much heavier than her lucky embroidered slippers, but that was okay because she was, they said, only three feet tall and weighed fifty pounds. She needed the grounding. She set herself, the roots of a tree gnarling in the earth.

She didn't think so much about Ray Tate. Ray was a big boy. She thought of the Chinese girl at the

Emergency with her breasts branded with blistering double Chucks. And either this fat fuck had shot Ray or Harv had, and there was no collecting penance for that pal 'o mine from old Harv.

Connie Cook realized he had the gun in his hand. He had trouble disengaging his fat fingers. He shook it but it wouldn't leave his fingers. It went off from inadvertent pressure, bucking as the bullet hit the ground between his feet, but it gave Djuna Brown permission.

She thought the six rounds she fired sounded like someone enthusiastically but briefly applauding the final end of something. All the bullets, she believed, went into him, and he sat down and slumped over himself, his legs doing a jerky dance.

Agatha Burns, with blood and matter up her wrists, and a woman with her hands behind her back staggered out on the porch. Around the porch came a man in fatigues. He secured the women and rolled them from view of the door and off the porch. Both were screaming something but all Djuna Brown could hear was men's voices. Someone was yelling into a radio. The helicopter appeared in the sky, oscillating like a predatory bird as if to find fine focus. The props put up loose soil and whirling dead leaves. Djuna Brown's sleeves rippled. With her free hand she pulled off her hat as though welcoming a surprisingly cool breeze into her hot hair. Tac team members called to each other in anxiety. Someone bellowed, Fuck, I don't know, send all the medics you got, we've got people down down here, you dumb cocksucker.

Her Statie sniper was beside her, his hands running over her body, looking for leakage or holes, feeling under her vest, up in her spiky hair. He was saying, You're all right, you're all right, and Holy shit. "You had to do it, it was a good one, don't worry, don't talk to anybody. Nice, nice. You done good, you done good. Holy fuck. Very, very good."

She thought he looked suddenly young and confused and maybe afraid. He was looking at her differently, as though she'd just returned from a voyage to somewhere he'd never been. She wanted to ask him if he'd crossed over yet, if he was on her and Ray's side of the job. He was, she saw, a tough but pretty white boy with pinches of pale around his mouth. What are you doing in a place like this? You should be mowing a lawn, drinking a beer, and windsurfing. You should grow a daring moustache. I'm a hundred years older than you and I'm not of you anymore. I'm only meant for the killer beatniks. She went to tell him that, get a smile, but she felt like she was gargling.

He pried the gun from her hands. His subconscious had counted the rounds fired and knew the gun was still live and he was gentle and firm peeling off her fingers.

Djuna Brown looked at him, her eyes vacant, then looked at her hand as he held it. "I think," she said, her fingers maintaining the shape of the butt and the trigger, "I think I need a new manicure."

She looked at him as though she'd never seen him before.

"You know, my guy in the city, Ray? He took me out, got me a makeover. He's a cool one, my guy."

She laughed. "He's a beatnik, you know."

She sank her little white teeth into her lower lip. "We're moving to Paris."

She was crying. "That's in France."

Epilogue

The skipper was driving to work when he saw Ray Tate dodging and limping through traffic, north of the cemetery. Tate held his hand to his side and seemed deranged, shouting curses at the speeding motorists. He had a bundle of white gauze on his ear. The skipper pulled his company car to the curb, got half out, and called, "Ray, hey, Ray?"

Ray Tate stopped on the sidewalk by the tall picket fence. His hair was long and he had a full grey-streaked beard. He wore a hydro parka, blue jeans, and hiking boots. There was paint on his cheek. He favoured his left arm.

"C'mon, Ray. I'm headed downtown. Let's get a fix."

The skipper's car was warm and the radio played softly. There was no smell of booze or puke. The skipper's eyes were clear and his hands steady. Ray Tate carefully buckled himself in and looked askance at the skipper, unbelted, but he didn't say anything. They approached the midtown office building where the satellite office had been. A Space for Lease sign was erected on two-by-twos near the entrance. The skipper swung into the parking lot anyway and together they crossed to the coffee shop. The skipper held up two fingers to the cook and led the way to the booth at the back.

"You didn't put your papers in yet, Ray. What's that all about?"

"I'm thinking on it. Going to see how it works out, with the shooting."

"Nice piece of work, that. She nailed you pretty good, but you put her down."

Ray Tate waited until the cook put the coffees down. The skipper tore open a bag of sweetener. Ray Tate drank his black and said, "When they told me who she was, I went What the fuck? Who? Never fucking saw her before in my life. Still, right now, I couldn't pick her picture out of a photo array."

The skipper shrugged. "It was a dyke thing. She had a hard-on, or whatever, for your partner there. I heard when they searched her files at the Gay-Glo office there were surveillance pictures of you and Djuna, a clock on your movements, a copy of your personnel file." The skipper looked out the window. "Who'd'a figured that? A cop trying to do in another cop for doing a cop? Weird stuff. But you'll come out of it clean. She was a fucking loon."

"I guess. So, where'd you end up?"

"Headquarters. We're doing city corruption. The planners and the builders on the lake. Special task force." The skipper drank at his coffee. "You, if you hang around, I hear you're going to the Marine Unit. If you don't put in your papers, I mean. The slobs, Bernie and Wally, are down in Florida pissing off the marlins until they come back and open their fucking bait shop or whatever up in Canada. Your partner, there, she just jumped herself straight into the same shit she came out of."

"Hey, she's happy."

"Let me ask you one, Ray, okay? What's with her? I mean, you guys fucked me good but you fucked the fucking mayor better, with giving the case to the Staties. The fat fucker at City Hall went nuts. No way he gets elected dogcatcher after this. With what they were doing to the planning department, he'll be lucky if he doesn't end up pulling a pound in Craddock. The black community went nuts when we took down the Bik-Bigs. And that photo of the mayor hugging old psycho Captain Cook there, at the track? The Mayor and the Serial Killer. Fuck. But her? I know I was shit-faced through most of that stuff, but there, at the end, she coulda put me in the smelly brown stuff. But she didn't. What's that all about?"

"Dunno, skip."

Outside the window the snow began, running steady and heavy. Cars slowed down, pedestrians moved with caution. Winter coming down from Canada had been born late, coming at Christmas, but with the new year came snow that blew sideways. It was grey and banked and iced over. Ax had left for a trip to Asia and he regularly received handmade postcards of photographs of water buffalo, oxen, smiling Asian faces. He'd bought a home computer and learned to email, tapping messages with the fingers of his right hand. Only when she was overseas did Ax write to him about Djuna Brown setting up outside the family home, waiting for her to come out then taking her for coffee. Ax didn't say what they talked about but she said Djuna Brown wept that she wasn't there for her partner. She said, Ax wrote, you had to be who you are.

The skipper was still fascinated by Djuna Brown. "How come, Ray, she wore that dyke jacket when she didn't have to? I mean, you guys were jamming, right? That's what sparked off the Gay-Glo chick. How come she didn't just say, Hey, I'm no lesbo, so fuck off? She'd've had an easier ride, all things in."

"Dunno, skip. Chicks, what you gonna do?"

The skipper smelled turpentine from Ray Tate's hair. There was paint on his fingernails and on his shirt cuffs. His eyes were hollow black holes and he looked like he hadn't slept in a week. "I'm dry, Ray. Six weeks dry. Fucking hard go of it, I'll tell you. How about you? You sipping a little?"

"Nope. Just waiting for the shit to settle, then I guess I'll go down to the Marine Unit and laugh at the fucking snowmobilers after spring thaw."

They sat with little to say.

The skipper finished his coffee and put some singles on the table. "Sparrows, Ray. Outside my window in the morning, driving me nuts. How come so many sparrows?"

Ray Tate looked at him and made a small smile. "Sparrows. Fuck sparrows, skip. Should be a bounty on the downy little bastards."

"That's my boy," the skipper said with relief.

Bundled in his hydro parka, Ray Tate walked back north, up the slippery hill, and past the white cemetery. He veered off and walked past the local station but there were no freckled blond policewomen with men's underwear and sagging socks.

He thought of the last time he saw Djuna Brown, the new white slicks on her arm, the round Trooper hat held in both hands.

"You could have anything, Djun', you could get down here, if you want."

She'd sat on the edge of his futon. The hospital had given him a sack full of painkillers, bandages, and a colostomy bag until his innards were healed, but he was on his ass. A nurse came by every few days to bitch him out for standing at his easel. The futon was as lumpy as it had ever been. A crew led by his daughter while he was in hospital had painted the walls and ceiling.

"You looked good on TV," he said. She had. She was a poster girl. She was black and a little Chinese and a chick and, most believed, a dyke. The State Police commissioner had made a point of touching her often as he detailed her daring exploits: a serial killer caught and put down in a wild gunfight, a meth lab seized, a notorious bandit killed, a kidnapped girl returned to her family after more than a year, the wife of a prominent but insane businessman rescued. Four bodies and three muddy skulls had been found on the property. A sky-scan was ordered, looking for the glowing heat of decomposition.

She'd smiled and leaned to kiss him, careful of his bag. "I be the hero, Bongo. I be the chick o' the day."

The press had loved her, had loved her sly eyes and little rows of sadly smiling teeth, her modesty. There was talk of a book, a movie. No one put the dead Gay-Glo chick downtown together with Djuna Brown the northern hero. "You had the place done over, Ray. New paint and I spy a new set of bedding there. I bet if I look in the fridge I'll find mix, right?"

"Ax did it."

She saw a canvas, face in, and crossed to it in her sleek, black highway boots. She gently turned it. It was a slash of greys and blacks and the darkest blues: a smudge of a tiny woman in the corner of a box. An elevator, she realized. There was a slumping loss to her posture. She wore embroidered slippers. She had the wide hollow eyes of the saddest trapped creature in the saddest world.

When she turned she had tears in her eyes. "Fuck, Ray, you got me, man. You got who I was." She lay down beside him on the futon. "You ever think, Ray, of living up north?"

He felt grief. He'd found her and lost her. He felt like a kid who'd made a perfect snowman and had to stand there, himself frozen, watching it walk away. "You can have anyplace you want, Djuna. You could get posted down here. We could have … something."

"We have something now. It's portable, you know?" She stretched. "You should see the mornings up there, in my Spout, even the winter. There's a coldness so cold that it makes you realize you're a warm creature. There's a lot of blacks and whites, especially in winter, but there's colours, too, people to be captured down on canvas. They need stuff up there, they need police, they need a soft hand, they need artists."

"You're going?"

"I've gone. Trooper sergeant in the Spout. Boy, were they ever pissed off when I insisted." She hugged him. She was crying; he could feel it hot on his neck. "Come with me, Ray, take some leave and give it a month. Like a holiday. And there's lots and lots of birds, all the time up there."

He thought about it. Fishing, which he'd never done. Hunting, which he'd never done. There would, of course, be birds. There were birds everyfucking-place, although he didn't actually care about birds at all. The way she described the dancing smoke of dawn, the silver skin of morning dew, he could find use for the oranges and yellows smeared on his pallet with the thumbhole in it.

But he knew that for him it wasn't the time of the artist and might never be. It was still the time of the cop. "I can't. There's people down here that need police. There's kiddy cops that are about fourteen years old and there's no one to grow them into real cops.

Some of them are going to die, some are going to fuck up and somebody else is going to die."

"Like me, eh, Ray? Father Ray. Fix the busted, find the cop inside and bring her out."

She put her round hat on the floor and sat to tug off her boots. She took off her uniform. She was careful of his tubing and bag, of the wadding covering his shoulder. Out of the uniform she was tiny. They snuggled down under the duvet. Her toes found the buttery calluses on his cop feet. They couldn't do much but they did what they could.

Afterwards she said, "It's only a four or five hour drive to up there. Maybe eight, the way you city guys drive."

He said: "Let's just play it loose, Djun'."

"Free-form jazz, right, Ray?"

He smelled her hair. "Cool-ee-oh."

In Djuna Brown's rented house on the far northern edge of Widow's Corners the telephone rang. She took it on the first ring. She listened and said she was rolling, looking at the clock beside the bed, and said: "Okay, I'm notified at oh-four-nineteen. ETA: thirty minutes. Black, no sugar. Major crime scene requested."

She rubbed her face vigorously with both palms to warm it. Her own hands on her own face reminded her of being a little girl, trying to rub the colour off. She brushed her hair, blind, and clipped it back. She pulled on woollens and her uniform and her parka and her mukluks. She glanced out the window where the marked four-by-four, backed in beside the house, was covered by the night's snowfall, and tucked her uniform trousers into the boots. The room was cold and she thought she could see her pewter breath. She took a moment to shake out her Arctic sleeping bag and dress the single bed with it.

She went to sleep at night thinking of Ray Tate, hoping to entice him into her dreams. But she always woke up with her impulse to shove her Statie sniper down, out of her way, so she'd have a clear shot at the fat fuck. She mourned Harv in a detached cop way. She mourned the lost possibility of what Harv might have become if he'd explored the roots kept hidden underground. When Agatha Burns told her how Harv hadn't killed her, but instead made her kick and had talked about lives missed, ideas and concepts, and home building and codes of behaviour, Djuna Brown mourned his opportunities, untested.

She'd never given the wrinkled tube of vitamin E cream to Tommy. It sat by her bedside. One day, she thought, I'll snare a man and bring him back here.

And after I've fucked him stupid, he'll go, What's with that tube of stuff?

I'll go: persistent crabs, I can't kick 'em. So he wouldn't be there in the morning when Ray, she dreamed, would show up with his easel over his shoulder, released somehow from his duty that kept him on the city streets.

Ray would like it up here, she thought. It was a place of real policing, of gin and taps beside the potbellied stove, of whispers of beatnik dreams of Paris, and paints and pots. There was life here, she believed, there was love, even if it was a sad love that manifested itself in peculiar and savage ways. Things got crazy with the cabin shut-ins, the alcoholic depressions and tremens, the beaten children and the domestic bloodbaths. Crazy but not insane. You could find a reason, you could find a cause for it all. There were answers and you could learn from it. It was crazy, maybe, but it wasn't madness. It had a gospel.

Me and Ray, that beatnik pal o' mine. We've both been there, we've both crossed over. Maybe to careless murder, maybe not. We both found whatever it is we're good for. We were summoned and we weren't found wanting. We stood and delivered it up. We did what we had to do. I believe I know this. I wonder if Ray, my city guy, does.

Outside she unplugged the block heater, started the truck, fired the heater, and climbed out. As her dad had taught her she brushed every bit of snow off the body and glass. She boarded the big four-by-four and rolled it down the driveway, the heater blasting still cold and the window open a bit so she could hear the exquisite pain of the tires crunching the snow's reluctant crust. She went on the air as she drove out, pushing her headlights ahead of her, out into an undulating, white, new world she felt she had ownership of and responsibility for. She voiced out: "Trooper Sergeant Brown en route ..." she looked at her watch, "four forty-four a.m."

The dispatcher came back with a synopsis. Five children had lived in the trailer she'd been directed to and now there would be none living. There would be two grandparents hanging like winter pods from rotting rafters. There would be a man, once both a father to five and a son to two, now neither to any living, in the snow in front of the trailer, his shotgun between his knees and his head innards on the trailer door.

It's a heartbreak place, all of it, this white world, she thought, flicking on the overhead rack lights but leaving the siren silent so the living could sleep.

And the real benefit to the heartbreak was it told you had a heart.

As if in revenge for her contentment, it began to snow heavily.

"Snow away," Djuna Brown laughed, a girl again, Ray's bohemian girl, once and maybe again, or maybe not. "It's all just free-form jazz."

More Great Castle Street Mysteries from Dundurn

Sucker Punch
Marc Strange
978-1-55002-702-0
$11.99

Joe Grundy is an ex-heavyweight boxer whose main claim to fame was that he got knocked out by champ Evander Holyfield. Now he's chief of security for a posh old hotel, the Lord Douglas, in downtown Vancouver, and life is pretty good. But then a young neo-hippie inherits more than half a billion dollars and decides to give it all away. As soon as the kid checks into the Lord Douglas with the intention of holding a press conference to announce the scheme, Joe knows big trouble is headed his way, especially when the kid winds up dead.

Grundy sets out to discover who murdered the would-be philanthropist only to collide with suspects and sucker punches around every corner. Joe had some pretty tough battles during his days in the ring, but this time the stakes are higher, the opponents are lethal, and the final count could be fatal.

Innocent Murderer
Suzanne F. Kingsmill
978-1-55488-426-1
$11.99

When zoology professor Cordi O'Callaghan reluctantly accepts an invitation to be a lecturer aboard the *Susanna Moodie*, a vessel ferrying tourists through Canada's Arctic, she figures it will be a breeze. Seasickness aside, Cordi becomes entangled in the deaths of two of her fellow passengers, both members of a close-knit fiction-writing group. The fatalities are ruled accidental, but Cordi suspects they're anything but. However, she lacks evidence and credibility, according to Martha Bathgate and Duncan McPherson, her sometimes reluctant sidekicks who try to keep her grounded.

After Cordi returns to her home in the Ottawa Valley, she hits the trail and stirs up a hornets' nest of lies, intrigue, jealousy, and greed as she grills potential murderers, one of whom takes offence and stalks her. Getting marooned on pack ice, a harrowing trip in an airplane and a hot air balloon, and a mysterious fire all add to the menace that threatens Cordi as she attempts to nail down a killer.

Blood and Groom
Jill Edmondson
978-1-55488-430-8
$11.99

Someone in Toronto has murdered nearly bankrupt art dealer Christine Arvisais's groom-to-be. Former rock band singer and neophyte private investigator Sasha Jackson lands the case because she's all Christine can afford. The high society gal was jilted at the altar and she's the prime suspect, not to mention Sasha's first major client.

In order to trap the murderer, Sasha enlists her ex-boyfriend and former band mate to pose as her fiancé, but will her ruse make her ex the next victim on the hit list and lead to her own untimely demise?

Available at your favourite bookseller.

DUNDURN PRESS
www.dundurn.com

What did you think of this book?
Visit *www.dundurn.com*
for reviews, videos, updates, and more!